The Poor Relation

By Susanna Bavin

The Deserter's Daughter

A Respectable Woman

The Sewing Room Girl

The Poor Relation

a&b

The Poor Relation

SUSANNA BAVIN

Allison & Busby Limited
11 Wardour Mews
London W1F 8AN
allisonandbusby.com

First published in Great Britain by Allison & Busby in 2019.
This paperback edition published by Allison & Busby in 2019.

Copyright © 2019 by Susanna Bavin

The moral right of the author is hereby asserted in accordance with
the Copyright, Designs and Patents Act 1988.

All characters and events in this publication,
other than those clearly in the public domain,
are fictitious and any resemblance to actual persons,
living or dead, is purely coincidental.

All rights reserved. No part of this publication may be reproduced,
stored in a retrieval system, or transmitted, in any form or by
any means without the prior written permission of the publisher,
nor be otherwise circulated in any form of binding or cover
other than that in which it is published and without a similar
condition being imposed on the subsequent buyer.

A CIP catalogue record for this book is available from
the British Library.

10 9 8 7 6 5 4 3 2 1

ISBN 978-0-7490-2378-2

Typeset in 10.5/15.5 pt Adobe Garamond Pro by
Allison & Busby Ltd.

The paper used for this Allison & Busby publication
has been produced from trees that have been legally sourced
from well-managed and credibly certified forests.

Printed and bound by
CPI Group (UK) Ltd, Croydon, CR0 4YY

To the memory of Freddie Shires
(née Winifred Joan Dorothy Bourke, 1924–2012)
In her first job, in the 1930s, Freddie was so adept at training new recruits to the office that her boss didn't want to promote her … which is how Mary's story starts in this book

And to Christina Banach, with love and admiration

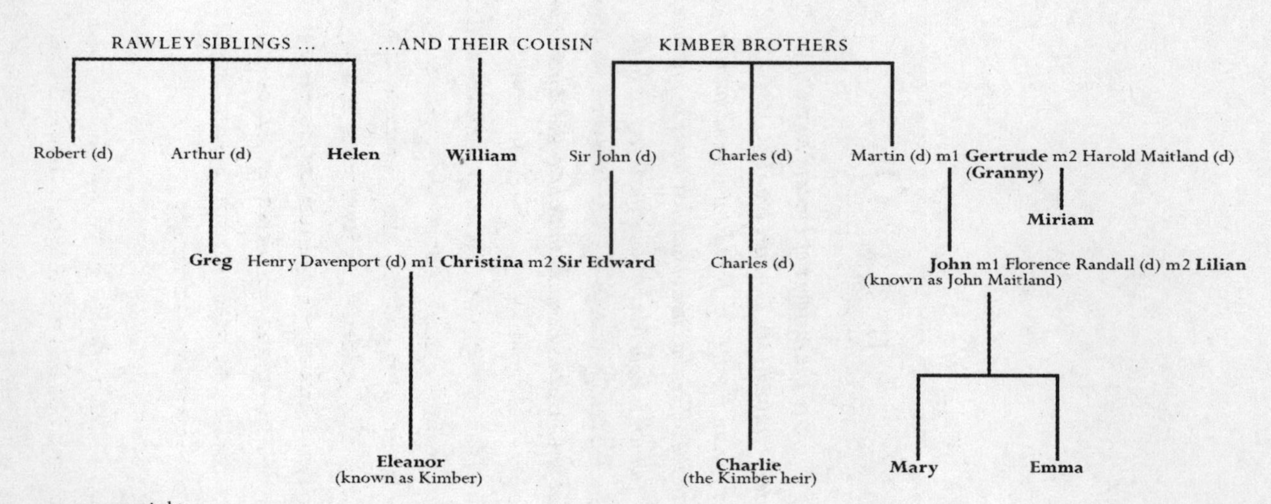
RAWLEY AND KIMBER FAMILY TREES
RAWLEY SIBLINGS ...
...AND THEIR COUSIN
KIMBER BROTHERS
Robert (d)
Arthur (d)
Helen
William
Sir John (d)
Charles (d)
Martin (d) m1 Gertrude m2 Harold Maitland (d)
(Granny)
Miriam
Greg
Henry Davenport (d) m1 Christina m2 Sir Edward
Charles (d)
John m1 Florence Randall (d) m2 Lilian
(known as John Maitland)
Eleanor
(known as Kimber)
Charlie
(the Kimber heir)
Mary
Emma
m = married to
d = deceased
bold = characters in the book

Chapter One

Town Hall, Manchester, May 1908

Annoyance rushed through Mary, followed by a twist of surprise. It wasn't like her to flare up, even if it was only on the inside. As Mr Treadgold left the office, she smoothed her skirt and touched the pen and pencils in the groove on her desk, as if they needed lining up. Bright sunshine poured through the windows. Earlier, this had felt like a promise of good things to come, but now golden darts lay strewn in a jagged pattern across the floor. Earlier, she had run her fingers over her desk, picturing the sit-up-and-beg desks in Accounts, imagining herself perched at one of those, writing in a ledger, imagining what she hoped would be her future.

More fool her.

Her hands clenched. She hadn't felt this way the first time, nor the second, but this was the sixth time – the sixth! – in five years, and dismay and disappointment had long since evaporated. Heaven help her, that first time she had questioned whether it was her own fault for trying too soon. She had even worried that Mr Treadgold might think her uppity. Huh!

'I say, Miss Maitland,' said Spotty Ronnie, the proud beam dropping from his face. 'Are you all right?'

No, she jolly well wasn't. Her skin felt tight. Rising, she shook hands. Spotty Ronnie's paw was moist; she held her smile in place. Mustn't look like a bad sport.

The beam reappeared. 'I thought for a moment you were about to be a sore loser, but then I thought, no, not our Miss Maitland. Far too sensible.'

Sensible. Oh yes, she was that, all right. Not one to make a fuss. A good girl. Hadn't she always been a good girl?

'You're a good girl,' Dadda had said after Mam died, when Mary was ten. 'It's your job to take care of baby Emma now.'

And 'You're a good girl,' he said, when he married again and she didn't kick up a fuss, unlike Granny, who had created an almighty stink.

Well, for once in her life Mary Margaret Maitland was going to kick up a fuss. Not in front of Spotty Ronnie, though.

'Congratulations, Mr Dearden.'

'Ta very much. The best man won, and all that.'

The best man? The only man. Not even that. A boy, a youth. Was she supposed not to mind losing out to a young shaver?

The town hall clock struck midday. How proud the sound had made her when she first worked here. The chimes had rung out to reinforce her position, first as office junior, then as a lady-clerk. She was twenty-three now and the chimes had marked ten years of her life.

The door opened to reveal the grinning face of one of Ronnie's cronies. Ronnie snatched his bowler and scarpered. Whoops of delight floated back to her. The thought of Spotty Ronnie sharing his triumph brought heat to her face.

The moment had come.

She could get carpeted. Mr Treadgold might puff his way up to the fourth floor and complain to Dadda, and then she would get carpeted at home too. But if she didn't speak out, she would wish she had. It was a question of self-respect.

She marched to Mr Treadgold's office, her shoes tap-tapping along the tiled corridor. The door stood open, just as Mr Treadgold liked it. He sat bent over his work, thinning hair glistening with oil. He finished writing and applied blotting paper.

Making sure her toes hadn't committed the cardinal sin of crossing the threshold uninvited, she knocked.

'Please may I have a word?'

'Can't it wait?'

Normally she would have withdrawn at that point. 'It's important.'

'Very well.' Mr Treadgold waved her into the chair opposite his own. He added the blotted sheet to a pile of papers, touching the sides to bring everything into alignment. 'What can I do for you, Miss Maitland?'

Folding her hands in her lap, she composed her features into a pleasant, if serious, expression. Kicking up a fuss was no reason not to be professional.

'I'd like to know why I didn't get the promotion.'

Mr Treadgold blinked slowly, as if, by the time he opened his eyes, she would have withdrawn the question.

'I've always understood you found my work satisfactory.'

'More than, more than.'

'Then why haven't I achieved promotion? I've applied . . . several times,' she fudged, ashamed to put a number to it.

'And jolly good applications they were, too.'

She was in no mood to be fobbed off with a compliment. 'Then why wasn't I successful? Was I considered less competent than other applicants?'

'Gracious me, no. Quite the contrary. You're an excellent member of staff.'

'But those lads who were given the posts . . .'

Lads. Yes, lads, a mere sixteen or seventeen years of age.

'You trained them perfectly. When young Mr Dearden takes up his position in Parks and Cemeteries, I'll receive a flood of compliments on the quality of his work. I know, because it's what happened when Mr Chatham went to Schools and Mr Dent went to Transport, and it happened with the others as well. You're a marvel, Miss Maitland. You have our working practices down to a tee.'

Her fingers tightened. 'But if I trained them effectively, surely that means I also am suitable for advancement.'

Mr Treadgold smiled complacently; his cheeks bunched under his eyes. 'My dear Miss Maitland, you could run the Lord Mayor's office with one hand tied behind your back.' He chuckled. 'But I could never part with you, as my colleagues are well aware.'

'You told them not to select me?'

'It's a great compliment, Miss Maitland. You're too valuable here.'

'Training up the youngsters.'

'Precisely. Such a weight off my shoulders.'

'So they then get promoted.'

'Of course. Young men have to get on.'

'And young women don't?'

'Not in the same way.' His tone dripped with kindness. Good grief, was he comforting her? 'A young man must one day support a wife and family, whereas a young lady who works is simply saving towards being married.'

'Suppose she doesn't get married?'

'There, there, my dear, you'll meet somebody.'

Humiliation chilled her. It was bad enough having Granny waving Aunt Miriam's single state under her nose, but to be pitied by Mr Treadgold was intolerable.

'I wasn't referring to myself. I was speaking in general terms. But I am talking about myself when I say it's unfair to keep me here while offering promotion to those spotty herberts simply because they're male.'

'Miss Maitland!'

She was into her stride now. 'Am I to understand I'll never be considered for advancement?'

'That's an impertinent question.'

'Because if it is the case, and if I'm valuable because I teach others the ropes, shouldn't I be paid more than they are in recognition of my expertise?'

'Miss Maitland, you forget yourself.'

'It seems a reasonable request.'

'Reasonable? To demand two wage rises in one go?'

Cold enveloped her. 'Two?'

'One to bring you up to the young men's salary, another to take you higher still.'

She stared. 'You mean – I earn less than they do? Less than Ronnie Dearden? Even though I'm over twenty-one, not to mention considerably more experienced?'

'The two of you do the same job, so of course he earns more. That's only right and natural.'

She hardly knew which objection to express first.

'Why was I interviewed for those other posts, if it was known you wanted to keep me here?'

'You're excellent in interviews and it's good for the young men to have competition. We can't have them thinking it's being handed to them on a plate, can we? I suggest you return to your desk. I'm surprised and disappointed by your remarks, which suggest an unexpected tendency to the hysterical, and not at all what I expect from such a good little worker. The process of application and interview has evidently taken its toll, so you'd do better not to put yourself forward again.' He awarded her another complacent smile. 'After all, you're well suited where you are.'

'She says not, but she's taken it pretty badly.'

Spotty Ronnie's words carried through the half-open door. In the corridor, Mary froze, clutching the box of papers to her chest.

'Poor old love, she's been sighing her heart out all afternoon.'

Poor old love? Her heart beat an indignant tattoo. She felt like walloping young Mr Dearden round the ear. And she hadn't been sighing – had she? Ah. Not sighs, but huffs of outrage. If only she could write her resignation and slap it on Mr Treadgold's desk, right under his patronising nose. But Dadda worked upstairs, and the thought that Mr Treadgold would fetch him to drum sense into her was too humiliating for words.

Balancing the box of papers with one arm, she thrust open the door and marched in. She wanted to stick her nose in the air and not so much as glance at Spotty Ronnie and whoever he was blabbing to, but that would be tantamount to wearing a sign round her neck proclaiming, *I was listening*. She smiled at Ronnie and at—oh, dear heaven, not Billy Arbuckle from the post room. That young blabbermouth would scatter news of her suffering all along his route as he collected letters for the evening post, blast him.

Dumping the box on her desk, she slipped her hand into the pocket of her navy serge skirt. There it was: the precious advertisement. In her dinner hour, she had purchased the early edition of the *Manchester Evening News* to search the job vacancies. She had no reason to scan the column headed AGENCY WORK – FEMALE, because that was for women in service, but a boxed advertisement halfway down had caught her eye. It was headed *Employment Agency for Educated Women*. Underneath, it stated the opening hours and an address on Wilbraham Road, not far from where her family lived near to the recreation ground in Chorlton: an opportunity practically on her doorstep. The mere thought made her heart bump.

Today was Tuesday. If she wrote a letter this evening and posted it first thing tomorrow, the agency would receive it tomorrow afternoon, so it was reasonable to request an appointment on Thursday evening, when, according to their advertisement, they stayed open until seven. Perfect.

No, it wasn't. Her parents would never agree. 'You're fine where you are,' would be their attitude, and 'What would the Kimbers say?' But she couldn't stay where she was just so as not to run the risk of being frowned upon by their grand relations.

There was nothing else for it. She would have to do this behind her parents' backs. They would be disappointed and upset, but this was something she had to do.

As six o'clock approached, she tidied up and changed into her outdoor shoes before sitting at her desk to wait for Mr Treadgold to walk through the row of offices over which he held sway. He appeared, bowler-hatted and carrying a rolled umbrella, bade them good evening in the manner of one conferring a blessing, touched his hat to her and went on his lordly way.

Spotty Ronnie made a dive for the hatstand, but it didn't matter how quick off the mark he was, he was obliged to do the gentlemanly thing by holding the door for her. Sometimes she made him wait, just to see the agony on his features, but not today. Today she could have flattened him in her eagerness.

As often happened, she met Dadda on the stairs and they walked together across Albert Square to the tram stop. He offered his arm and, as she took it, a couple of girls from Parks and Cemeteries passed them, chatting together. Her insides tightened with envy. Did they plan to meet up later? She always went straight home with Dadda. She loved and respected her parents and wanted to be a good daughter, she really did, but sometimes she felt . . . stifled.

Oh, that word. The first time it had flitted across her mind, guilt had thickened her throat, but now she recognised it as the simple truth. Now she dared wonder what it would be like not to be under the family thumb.

Was it possible to be a good daughter and also spread her wings?

'I didn't get the promotion.'

'I know.' Dadda didn't sound even the least bit upset. 'Mr Treadgold informed me yesterday.'

'Yesterday!' She bit her lip. Adopting a moderate tone, she asked, 'Did he tell you in advance those other times too?'

'Naturally. A courtesy to a colleague. He and I are both senior clerks.'

She felt a swell of vexation. 'You might have told me.'

'I beg your pardon?' It was said mildly enough, but that was Dadda for you. She had never heard him raise his voice, but that didn't mean he wasn't master in his own house.

'I'm sorry, Dadda. May I ask why you never told me?'

'By applying and being interviewed, you performed a service – and it's not as though you need advancement. It's my job to support you.'

There it was again, that question. Was it possible to be a good daughter and also spread her wings? Her pace quickened, then immediately slowed as she felt the pull against Dadda's arm.

Was it possible? She was about to find out.

Chapter Two

Blasted rain, drumming on the stained glass. Soon they would traipse outside and stand about in it while it dripped down their necks and the vicar droned his way through that ashes to ashes, dust to dust claptrap. Or did dust come first? And did he care? No, he ruddy well didn't. The sooner Uncle Robert was six feet under, the better.

Greg Rawley sighed and felt sympathetic glances coming his way. They must think him succumbing to a grief-stricken moment when all he felt was profound boredom. The old boy was dead: so what? His only sorrow was that it hadn't happened in time to save him from sinking up to his eyeballs in debt.

Debt. It was funny what you could get used to. He hadn't been brought up to live beyond his means. He had attended a good school before being shunted into a dreary office, doomed to a life of accountancy. Fortunately for him – yes, fortunately, though it hadn't seemed so at first – he had lost his parents before the commercial arithmetic, balance sheets and double entries could reduce his brain to soup. It had come as a dashed shock, losing them together in that train crash, but the pain was obliterated the instant he got his hands on his father's bank books.

The old bugger had been rich. Not rolling in it, but far better heeled than his moderate lifestyle had suggested. Mother had been just as bad. She had received an annuity from some long-dead relative, and what had she done with it? Enjoyed it? And if she hadn't wanted to spoil herself, had she treated her son? Not a bit of it. She had saved half and given away the rest – not to her son, mark you, not to her own flesh and blood – but part of it in charitable donations and the rest as a pension to the old biddy who had been her nursemaid donkey's years ago. And she had had the nerve to leave Greg a letter of wishes that was presented to him along with Father's will, in which she hoped he would continue assisting the old wretch. Not that there would be any annuity to help him do so, because that had died with her, but even if it hadn't, he wouldn't have dreamt of wasting any of it on a crone who should have made a better job of saving for her dotage.

As for the Poor Law brats, the wage-earning children and juvenile drinkers, let them sponge off someone else; and if they couldn't find a crackpot with masses of cash, let them go to the workhouse – or the colonies – or to the devil. Who gave a bugger? Not Greg Rawley.

He had more pressing matters to attend to, like discarding the tortoiseshell cigarette case that had been his parents' last birthday gift to him, in favour of one in solid silver. Then there was the open-face watch they had palmed him off with when he came of age, when they knew that what he wanted was a hunter with his initials engraved on the cover.

After that, it had simply been a matter of consigning his battered old canvas-covered trunk to the bonfire and indulging in a smart set of portmanteaux covered with solid leather before he embarked on his travels, like one of the nobs setting off on a Grand Tour. Entitled. That was how he had felt. Entitled. And a bloody good feeling it was, too.

It was time to follow the coffin outside and, yes, it was still pissing down. He glanced at Aunt Helen, looking like an old crow in her black. Correction: an old-fashioned crow. Puffy sleeves like that hadn't seen the light of day since the last century. Whatever old Robert had done with his cash, it obviously hadn't involved a magnificent dress allowance for Helen. Mean old basket.

Still, all the more for him. By Christ, he was going to enjoy this money. He could get his creditors off his back and still be quids in. That old house must be worth a pretty penny. He might flog it to some nouveau riche upstart – yes, and savour Helen's shock. It was high time he paid her back. The old bitch had scuppered his chances with the only girl he had ever loved.

Uncle Robert would have left her something, but there was no danger of its being substantial. He hadn't believed in putting money into women's hands.

'I inherited Helen,' he had been fond of saying. 'My father wrote it into his will that I was to be responsible for her welfare, should she remain unmarried. Of course, she's made herself useful, keeping house for me, and she doesn't eat much, so it's worked out well, one way and another.'

Presumably Aunt Helen would get a cottage and a modest sum, which would revert to the estate once she popped her clogs. Old Robert would want to pass on his estate intact to the nearest male heir. Greg allowed a smile to flicker across his face. Not long now. A few minutes in the rain, then sherry and ham, accompanied by the usual tommyrot about what a fine fellow the deceased was, after which the solicitor would do his bit – and it would all belong to him.

Nathaniel glanced around the Rawley morning room. He hadn't been in here before; the late Judge Rawley had preferred to talk business in his study. The room felt stuffy this afternoon with all these people, dampness clinging to their clothes. The old codgers: that had been Judge Rawley's name for his former colleagues. Their wives were with them, one or two with plummy voices and an air of grandeur, others with prettily crumbling skin and a soft tremor about the hands.

His eye fell on a startlingly pretty girl across the room. Eighteen or nineteen years old, slender and fair, how fragile she looked in her black.

'Lovely, isn't she?'

He turned to find the judge's sister, Helen Rawley.

'Eleanor Kimber,' said Miss Rawley.

'One of *the* Kimbers?'

'The very same. That's Sir Edward over there – eyebrows like caterpillars – and the lady with her back to us is Lady Kimber. She's the one Eleanor got her looks from, but don't waste your time waiting for her to turn round. She's pretty hard-faced these days.'

'You don't sound keen on her.'

Miss Rawley lifted one shoulder in a shrug. Starch crackled. Her gown was an extraordinary creation covered in ruffles and rosettes. 'Actually, I think you'll find it's the other way round. She isn't keen on me.'

The old girl seemed determined to be outspoken. He answered like with like. 'Why?'

'Something that happened a long time ago – and, for the record, she was the one at fault, though you'd never think it after the way she's cold-shouldered me all these years.'

'But she's come today, though perhaps she's here as Sir Edward's wife, and he's here for the legal connection. That is, I imagine he's a magistrate?'

'There's a family connection too.'

'The Rawleys are related to the Kimbers?' asked Nathaniel.

'Not to the Kimber family, but to Lady Kimber.'

'She was a Rawley before she married Sir Edward?'

'To be accurate,' said Miss Rawley, 'she was the widow of Henry Davenport before she married Sir Edward, but before that she was a Rawley. Henry Davenport was Eleanor's father, but he died when she was a baby. I think of Lady Kimber as a niece, or I used to when she was still speaking to me. She's my cousin's daughter.'

'So she's . . . what? Your second cousin? First cousin once-removed?'

'Distant cousin with bells on. It's difficult to think of someone from a younger generation as a cousin. Not natural.'

He had had enough of her carping. 'It's a decent turnout. It's good to know Judge Rawley was held in high regard after his retirement.'

Miss Rawley snorted. 'I wish they'd clear off, the lot of them. Just listen to them, full of what a sterling chap he was.'

'They're trying to comfort you.'

'They've made me hopping mad.' Miss Rawley's faded eyes were suddenly overbright. 'My brother didn't drop down dead, you know – of course you know. I had my doubts when Doctor Slater broke his leg and we had to have you instead, but my brother couldn't possibly have had better care. Mind you, after what he did to help you with that clinic of yours, it was the least you owed him.'

Charming. Nathaniel didn't know Miss Rawley well, couldn't say he wanted to, but he had heard her do this before, pay a compliment, then in the next breath knock your feet from under you. Did she really not know that his regard for the judge had been genuine?

'He was known for weeks to be on his way out,' said Miss Rawley. 'But these people singing his praises today, did they say to him, "Look here, old chap, you've been a good friend to me", or "I admired your handling of the So-and-So case", or some such? No, they didn't. But they're queuing up to say it to me and I feel like slapping the lot of them.' Her voice cracked and dropped to a fierce whisper. 'It would have given him such a boost. Such a boost.'

It was the first sign of vulnerability he had seen in her. Even during her brother's final days, she had never shirked her duty, assisting the nurse in everything from changing the sheets to emptying the bedpan, staying up around the clock, asking probing questions and not once flinching at his replies.

'Don't look now, but here comes Greg – my nephew. He's the last person I want to speak to. Have you noticed how he's been eyeing up the place?'

Sympathy vanished. 'Sounds as though you don't particularly care for him.'

'And whose fault is that?'

First Lady Kimber, now Greg Rawley. How many others had Miss Rawley fallen out with – without, of course, it ever being her fault?

'Excuse me if I slide away,' she murmured.

Nathaniel glanced at the nephew. Maybe ten years older than himself, early forties: handsome face and good build, but carrying a few extra pounds that suggested easy living. He exuded an air of confidence and cultivation, but Nathaniel sensed something else too, something shrewd. Exquisitely turned-out, from the discreet gleam of gold collar studs down to the patent-leather toecaps – and as for the suit, well, Rawley was carrying a lot of money on his back.

'Mr Rawley.' An older gentleman approached. 'You too, Doctor Brewer. I'm Harold Porter, solicitor to the deceased. It's time for the reading of the will.'

'You can't need me, surely?' said Nathaniel.

'You're Doctor Nathaniel Brewer, are you not? Then if you'd be so good . . .'

Perhaps Judge Rawley had made a bequest to the clinic. In his heart, Nathaniel gave thanks. He looked round for Alistair. 'Should I fetch Doctor Cottrell?'

'Ah yes, your partner at the clinic. No need, sir. It's just your presence that is required.'

Mr Porter led them into Robert Rawley's book-lined study. His rack of pipes still stood on the oak desk, but the air was empty of the sharp-sweet scent of tobacco. Three chairs, evidently from the dining room, stood before the desk. The household's two middle-aged servants were already present. They bobbed curtsies.

'If you'll excuse me, gentlemen,' said Mr Porter, 'I'll fetch Miss Rawley.'

Nathaniel approached the staff. He knew the thin one by sight because she had always answered the door to him. He felt sorry for her, a woman her age being required to wear that silly frilled cap with the ribbons tied under her chin.

'I know you've both worked here a long time. I'm sorry for your loss. I imagine Judge Rawley was a good master.'

The women gasped. He turned to see Greg Rawley had seated himself behind the desk.

'Get out of that chair!'

Helen Rawley stood frozen in the doorway, an age-spotted hand splayed across her chest.

'I think you'll find it's my chair, now, at my desk, in my study,' Rawley said, coolly.

'Not until the will has been read,' his aunt retorted, but Nathaniel caught the tremor in her voice. He wished himself anywhere but here. Other people's family squabbles weren't for him.

'It's customary on these occasions,' said Mr Porter, 'for the solicitor to sit behind the desk.'

With a shrug, Rawley got up. He rested his hand on the first of the three dining chairs. Nathaniel stood aside for Miss Rawley, expecting her to take the middle seat, but she rustled to the other end. Nathaniel hesitated. To sit in the centre felt presumptuous, but he had no choice.

Mr Porter opened a document, which crackled as he unfolded it. 'I have here the last will and testament of Robert Augustus Rawley. I'll begin by summarising its contents to ensure we all know where we stand. Firstly, there are bequests to Mrs Elizabeth Burley and Miss Edith Ames in recognition of their years of service.' He nodded dismissal at the women. 'I'll speak to you afterwards in the kitchen.'

With murmured thanks, they departed.

'Everything else, including all moneys and the property known as Jackson's House, goes to Judge Rawley's nephew, Gregory Arthur Rawley, with the judge's sister, Helen Amelia Rawley, retaining a life interest.'

'Retaining a – what did you say?' Greg Rawley demanded.

'A life interest. That is to say, while everything belongs to you, Mr Rawley, you cannot dispose of it, because your aunt is entitled to live in Jackson's House and have the use of the interest on all savings and investments, with which to run the household and supply her personal needs, though she may not touch the capital itself. Neither may you touch the capital, Mr Rawley.'

'That's preposterous!'

'These are your uncle's wishes. Judge Rawley's father committed Miss Rawley to his care and he was the sort to take his responsibilities seriously. It was your uncle's hope, Mr Rawley, that you would settle at Jackson's House. He was aware of the . . . ahem . . . coolness between yourself and your aunt and while he was ignorant as to its cause, he was prepared to put it down to Miss Rawley's sharpness—'

'Hang on,' Nathaniel interrupted. 'You shouldn't make personal remarks in front of me.'

'I merely seek to explain Judge Rawley's wishes. He wrote letters to the three of you, making this very point, among others, so I'm not speaking out of turn.'

'Letters?' Miss Rawley repeated. 'Holding me to blame?'

Nathaniel would have given her a sympathetic glance if he hadn't been so confoundedly uncomfortable.

'Shall we move on?' Mr Porter suggested.

'No!' The word exploded from Greg Rawley. 'I want to discuss this life interest twaddle. D'you mean to say that everything is mine—'

'Entirely and absolutely, Mr Rawley.'

'—but I can't have it yet?'

'You may live in Jackson's House, which is now yours, and the interest on the money will be more than sufficient to cover the household bills and keep you in comfort.'

'But I can't touch the capital.'

'Precisely so.'

'Can I sell the house?'

'Gracious me, no. It's your aunt's home for her lifetime.'

'What if she went elsewhere?'

'Come now, Mr Rawley, surely you aren't suggesting . . . ?'

'Answer the question, man.'

'Were Miss Rawley to move out,' Mr Porter replied, 'the terms of the will would still apply. After all, she might at any point choose to return.'

'So the house and the money are mine—'

'Entirely and absolutely.'

'—but I can't have them until—'

'Quite so,' Mr Porter cut in.

'I'll contest the will,' Rawley declared.

'Such an action would merely leave you out of pocket.'

Rawley surged to his feet, slamming his hands on the desk and leaning towards the solicitor as if about to blast him to hell and back. Instead, he flung himself away, marched out and slammed the door, sending a vibration humming through the room.

Mr Porter sighed but didn't appear perturbed. Were family brawls all in a day's work?

'Fear not, Miss Rawley. The will is watertight. About the letters . . .'

'Oh yes,' she exclaimed, 'the letters where my brother publicly blames me. It's insufferable. Good day.'

She bounced to her feet. Nathaniel hurried to open the door. She stalked out, head held high, but he caught the soft sound of a sniff. Oh hell.

'With the family members gone, there's no point in my remaining. I don't know why I was here in the first place.'

'You're here because you're named in the will, Doctor. Take a seat – please.'

Reluctantly, he complied. 'A bequest to the clinic, I imagine.'

'Judge Rawley mentioned your crusade to bring affordable medical provision to the slums of Moss Side.'

'He was good enough to lend his weight to the scheme – and if he was generous enough to leave a bequest, frankly, sir, I'd rather have been informed at the outset and despatched along with the servants, so as to avoid the family row.'

Mr Porter gave him a heavily patient look. 'There is no bequest. Judge Rawley chose you to oversee fair play, as it were, in the family situation he left behind. I'll take care of any legal complications that arise, though none should. Your role is that of impartial friend to the parties.'

'I have no intention of playing umpire between the Rawleys.' Good God – between those two? 'Couldn't you do it?'

'Judge Rawley chose you.'

'Ah.'

'Ah indeed, Doctor. You could, of course, refuse to act, but that would be unwise. You wouldn't wish to be known as the man who spurned the duty entrusted to him.'

'I'll consider it,' Nathaniel said, stiffly, but he knew his arm had been well and truly twisted.

Chapter Three

The only thing that could go wrong would be if Dadda took the aisle seat on the tram, trapping her beside the window. As they boarded, Mary headed for the front, then turned and indicated an empty seat she had passed. With other passengers behind him, Dadda had to swing in before her. Good.

As they arrived in Chorlton, she waited until the last moment.

'There's something I need to do. Will you ask Mother to keep my tea warm?'

Jumping off before he could ask questions, she hurried along, searching for door numbers, though the shops didn't appear to have them. At last she found it, over the road from the Lloyds Hotel: a door in between the grocer's and the tobacconist's. On the door frame, a small card said EMPLOYMENT AGENCY FOR EDUCATED WOMEN.

The door swung open. She jumped back as a girl appeared, wearing a long cardigan over a crisp blouse with a violet necktie knotted beneath a stiff collar. She had strawberry-blonde hair, on top of which was a colossal hat lavishly trimmed with silk forget-me-nots. As she stopped short, another girl cannoned into her from behind.

'Oh, I say! Were you on your way up to see us?' the first one asked in a plummy voice. Beneath the strawberry-blonde hair, her complexion was creamy, with freckles dotted roguishly across her nose.

'I thought you were open till seven.'

'We are, but there's not been so much as a dicky-bird all afternoon, so we thought we'd sneak off early. Come on, Kennett, back we go.'

Beyond the flowery cartwheel of a hat, Mary glimpsed brown feathers sticking up on a brimless hat. Kennett: what sort of name was that? And what about the appointment she had requested for today?

She followed them up a narrow flight of stairs to a square of landing, with a door on the right. She entered a huge room. Pleasure rushed through her and she was about to admire the spacious office when she realised the front half of the room was set up as a sitting room of sorts. There was no time to feel surprised: she was too busy trying to catch her heart before it could plummet into her shoes as she took in the state of the office area. The desks were untidy, the waste-paper basket overflowed and on top of the filing cabinet was a pile of papers that should undoubtedly be inside it.

Disappointment clenched in her stomach. She turned away, focusing on the sitting area, as if it was of consuming interest.

Large windows overlooked the wide street. Three battered sofas and an assortment of chairs made a rough square around a low table, which housed a stack of books and piles of pamphlets. Against one wall was a sideboard, the top of which did duty as a bookshelf. Why would they have an area like this in their office?

'Welcome to our domain,' said Kennett, removing a pearl-tipped hatpin. 'Take a pew. I'm Josephine Kennett and this is Angela Lever.'

Dark-haired Miss Kennett sat at one of the desks, so Mary took the chair in front, only to realise that Miss Lever was seated behind her at the other desk. Feeling like piggy-in-the-middle, she turned the chair so she was sideways to them both, trying not to be put off by their untidy desks.

'I wrote to you. I'm Mary Maitland.'

'And we wrote back,' said Miss Lever, 'inviting you to pop along tomorrow after work. We were going to stay late specially.'

'I haven't received anything.' She looked at Miss Lever.

'Come straight from the office, have you?' said Miss Kennett and Mary swung her head back again. 'You'll find the letter waiting when you get home.'

'That's why we felt free to slope off early tonight. Good thing you caught us.'

'Will you help me? I didn't go to high school, if that's what you mean by educated. My parents didn't put me in for the scholarship.'

Oh, the difficulties of being the poor relations! The Kimbers presumably wouldn't have minded her attending high school, but the neighbours might have thought the Maitlands were getting above themselves. You trod a fine line when you were related to the neighbourhood's most important family.

'You sat a town hall entrance exam, though, didn't you?' said Miss Kennett. 'Girls have to score eighty per cent to pass. The pass mark for boys is sixty-five.'

'We really must think of a better name for ourselves,' said Miss Lever. 'That word "educated" must deter a lot of women. But finding jobs for educated women is what we do.' She looked at Mary. 'Calling ourselves "for ladies" or "for gentlewomen" would draw in hordes of the impoverished well-bred wanting to be companions – and "for women" is too general. We don't want the factory fodder.'

'We're interested in girls like you,' said Miss Kennett. 'Good basic education, nicely spoken, neatly turned-out. Many girls automatically go in for shop work, never realising there are other possibilities.'

She felt an eager flutter. 'Does this mean you'll help me?'

'How would you like to be one of the first female librarians?' asked Miss Lever. 'There are several posts. We haven't been asked to put candidates forward, so you'll have to apply direct to the corporation. I'll write down the details. Let us know how you get on.'

Mary bit down on a smile so she couldn't grin like an idiot. She was about to strike off in a new direction, she really was – and she would make the most of whatever opportunities came her way.

Now she had to confess at home where she had been and try to talk her parents round. Dadda wouldn't be pleased. Neither would Lilian, not to start with, but if she could get Lilian on her side, that would go a long way towards smoothing things with Dadda.

That evening, she waited until Emma went to bed. She

washed up the cocoa mugs while Lilian was upstairs, kissing Emma goodnight, then she returned to the parlour. They lived in the back room, keeping the front room for best. They even had their drop-leaf dining table in the back room.

She settled in her usual chair. The basketwork chair was hers, and Dadda and Lilian had the armchairs.

'Dadda, Mother, I've got something to tell you.'

Lilian uttered a tiny gasp. Mary explained quickly before she could blurt out something hopeful about having met a young man.

'I don't like the sound of this,' Dadda declared. 'A women's employment agency, indeed!'

'It isn't for women in service.'

'Suppose it gets out that you've been to an agency – no one will question what kind. You realise you're in danger of bringing the Kimber name into disrepute? And why would you do such a thing? You're suited where you are.'

She said, in her most reasonable voice, 'Mr Treadgold won't let me move on.'

'You should be flattered. He's a splendid fellow. A female working at the town hall – that says something about you, Mary.'

'She knows that.' Lilian leant forward. 'From what you've said of him, John, I'm sure Mr Treadgold is a fine man, but Mary would rather be guided by you. What do you think, love? Is she capable of more?'

'No doubt she is.'

Mary watched in admiration as Lilian twinkled – there was no other word for it – at Dadda. 'Imagine our Mary as one of the first lady-librarians. She'd be a pioneer.'

'A pioneer! I don't want any daughter of mine setting tongues wagging.'

'I only meant it would be a responsibility. Not just being among the first, but working with dignity and quiet confidence. Who better than our Mary?'

'Aye, there is that. So long as she wouldn't lose respectability.'

He sounded gruff. Not vexed-gruff, but you've-talked-me-round gruff. Mary knew it was safe to laugh.

'Oh, Dadda! Can you think of anywhere more respectable than a library?'

'Let me see your application when you've written it,' said Dadda. 'I'll see if it's up to snuff.'

The words were mildly spoken, but that was how he issued his commands. As if she couldn't produce a decent letter unaided!

Mary planted a smile on her lips before entering the room. Three gentlemen were crowded behind a desk. They rose, inadvertently nudging one another. When she sat, they resumed their places, with more nudging. Swallowing a desire to laugh, she placed her bag at her feet and folded her hands in her lap. Demureness was important. No decent girl wanted to be dismissed as unrefined.

The questions were easy at first. They asked about her background, her reading habits and her present position, all questions for which she had prepared her answers. She handed over the sealed character reference Mr Treadgold had provided and watched as they passed it round. Something in their glances made a qualm twitch to life in her tummy.

'Mr Treadgold says he's shocked and disappointed by your wish to leave. He says he'd placed his trust in you to remain in his department. We don't want a fly-by-night.'

Beast! He had dropped her right in it.

'I'm hardly that, sir.' She forced her features to remain impassive. 'The town hall is the only place I've ever worked and I've been in Mr Treadgold's office for seven years.'

'Why have you applied for this post?'

'I'd like the challenge of being one of the first women to hold such a position.'

'Challenge, eh? Not very feminine.' He scribbled something.

'I'd like to work with the public. I believe . . .' She stopped, as three pairs of eyes widened.

'We shan't let our lady-librarians work with the public. It wouldn't be tolerated.'

'Fancy a female librarian asking a new gentleman member for his name and address. We couldn't sanction such boldness.'

'Of course, that isn't to say we'd never consider permitting women to work behind the counters . . . eventually . . . just to see the books in and out.'

'Then I'll have to prove myself, won't I?' She said it in a pleasant voice, so she didn't appear pushy. Being demure all the time could be a right nuisance.

'Thank you, Miss Maitland,' the man in the middle said, with what she took to be an insincere smile. 'You'll hear from us.'

It was unseasonably hot that Sunday as they trooped down Sandy Lane to have tea in Candle Cottage with Granny and Aunt Miriam. Candle Cottage was a pretty little house and going there ought to have been a pleasure, but Mary's toes had screwed up in embarrassment too many times whenever Granny told someone that it was her 'grace-and-favour residence, courtesy of my Kimber in-laws'. Honestly, didn't she have any shame? Well, no, frankly not. The rest of the Maitlands might spend their lives tiptoeing on social eggshells, but not Granny.

Mary drew an extra breath before stepping over the threshold, for all the good it would do. The atmosphere closed around them, thick as soup. Granny didn't believe in fresh air. She didn't have windows open and, with the sun beating down, she wouldn't open the curtains either, for fear of fading the carpet.

They all crammed into Granny's parlour for dainty sandwiches and cake.

'So, our Mary is going to be a lady-librarian,' said Granny.

Mary turned to Aunt Miriam, eager to share her success. 'Why don't you apply? You might prefer it to teaching piano.'

'You'll do nowt of the sort, our Miriam,' Granny snapped.

'You know I've never liked teaching the piano, Mother.'

'It's ladylike.'

'But if it's acceptable for Mary . . .'

'Aye, well, happen she's got a brain in her head. Not like you. If you apply, I'll write a letter meself and tell them library people that you're man-mad and hoping for a spot of slap and tickle behind the bookshelves, and I wouldn't be far wrong, would I? So you can stop thinking it right this minute, lady. I'm not having you doing owt but teaching piano, us with our Kimber connections.'

'Now then, Mother,' said Dadda. 'Related to the Kimbers we may be, but we have our livings to earn.'

'And whose fault is that? If you'd gone back to using the Kimber name when they wanted you to, who knows where we'd all be now?' Granny looked at Mary. 'I expect them library people wanted you because you're a Kimber.'

'They have no idea.'

'You never told them?'

'Of course not.'

'More fool you. You should write and tell them, our John, let them know what's what.'

'I'll do nothing of the kind.'

'Then more fool you, an' all. You do realise that if Sir Edward and that there Charlie-boy drop down dead, you'll be Sir John.'

'That's most unlikely, Mother.'

'You never know. Sir John Maitland: that's my dream, that is. You'd have to change your name back to Kimber. That's your real name, the name you were born to.'

'May I remind you, Mother, that you were the one who changed my name to Maitland after my father died and you remarried?'

Granny ignored that. 'Sir John Kimber, and we could all live at Ees House. Let Lady Snooty-Nose Kimber put that in her pipe and smoke it.'

Chapter Four

'Have you invited the Maitlands to Sunday lunch yet, my dear?' Sir Edward asked.

Lady Kimber dropped her gaze. No, she hadn't sent the dratted invitation yet, and if she had her way, it wouldn't go at all. It wouldn't be so bad, playing host to her husband's lower-class relations once a year, if it weren't for that frightful harpy of a grandmother, drooling over the Sheraton and asking impertinent questions.

She composed her features to meet her husband's dark eyes across the snowy linen and Rockingham china adorning the breakfast table.

'Not yet.'

'Maitland's a decent chap. I know his mother's a trial, but don't forget his father was a Kimber – my Uncle Martin.'

'Your Uncle Martin must have been the biggest fool ever to

walk the earth. Fancy being taken in by a common shop girl.'

'Poor fellow. I know he lived to rue the day.'

'At least he died young. That must have made it easier to ignore the widow he left.'

'But there was still his son, d'you see? John was a Kimber by blood – and by name in those days. He and I were lads when Martin died, and my father said we must do the right thing by John, so long as we kept the mother at bay, of course. Then she remarried and changed his name to Maitland to spite us. If she hadn't done that, he would have the family name to this day, and so would his daughters.'

Lady Kimber shuddered. Profound as her loathing was of Mrs Maitland senior, at least the old hag had, albeit in a fit of pique, removed the ancient name of Kimber from her descendants.

'At any rate, we must have them,' said Sir Edward. 'See to it, will you, my dear?'

She gave a tight smile. Lifting the tea-kettle off the stand beneath which the little heater burnt, she topped up her cup.

'More tea?'

She reached for his mug. The Kimber breakfast china was one of the joys of her life, but Sir Edward insisted upon a gaudy mug with *A Present from Colwyn Bay* painted on it. Men!

He glanced through the post. 'Here's one from Charlie.'

Dear Charlie. 'Does he say when he's coming?'

'Indeed, he does. He'll be here after midsummer.'

'After the Maitlands' visit, then. That's good. We wouldn't want Maitland skeletons clanking out of the family cupboard in front of visitors.'

'Charlie isn't a visitor. He's our nephew – well, he's my cousin's son, whatever that makes him.'

'Nephew.' Their marriage might not have been blessed, but Sir Edward had drawn children to him, claiming the closest possible connection to them. So Charlie was his nephew and Eleanor his beloved daughter.

'Charlie's father was the same relation to me that John Maitland is, except that Charlie's father married a suitable girl. Most important of all, Charlie's my heir. Why not invite your Aunt Helen while he's here? Bury the hatchet once and for all, eh? It'll be lonely for her without Judge Rawley. Or perhaps just call on her – that might be easier, less of an occasion. It's a pity Eleanor had that invitation to go away with the Rushworths. I'm sure she'd have liked to go with you to see Miss Rawley.'

Of course she would, which was precisely why Lady Kimber had sent her away. Taking Eleanor to the funeral had been a mistake. Not that she could have been left behind, not at her age. Naturally, she had been intrigued to see her unknown great-aunt. Lady Kimber had seen, too, the longing in Helen's face when she looked at Eleanor.

You needn't think you're getting your claws into her. Not after what you did to me.

The evening after the funeral, the Kimbers had dined with the Rushworths, who were about to set off for the Lakes. Lady Kimber had deftly wangled an invitation for Eleanor, to remove her just when she might want to see her great-aunt. When Eleanor returned, there would be another matter to occupy her.

'What are you smiling at, my dear?' Sir Edward asked.

'I was thinking of Eleanor.'

'I'll be glad to have her back. No one butters my toast as well as she does. I hope she doesn't meet anyone on this jaunt.'

'Goodness! What put that in your head?' Had he somehow picked up her thoughts?

'She's that sort of age. Call me a foolish old papa, but I'm not ready to part with her.'

How tempting to show her hand, but she hugged her hopes close. Yes, Eleanor was precisely that age. And Charlie, who hadn't seen her in two or three years and undoubtedly still thought of her as a timid little miss barely out of the schoolroom, was going to get his socks knocked off.

Nathaniel changed into his professional clobber as if he were dressing for battle. Damn Barnaby Clough. It had been yes sir, no sir, three bags full, sir, while Judge Rawley was alive, but now Clough wanted to drop the project like a hot potato. For two pins, Nathaniel would have returned the favour by dropping Clough, but he and Alistair needed Clough's godforsaken building in Moss Side.

'You won't get anything out of Clough without my help,' Judge Rawley had warned them. 'He doesn't give two hoots for the poor, but he'd sell his own mother to be an alderman. I shall, in one breath, discreetly give him to understand that I'll support him in his ambition and, in the next, remark upon my interest in your proposed clinic.'

Sure enough, when Nathaniel and Alistair had approached Clough, he had been only too willing to grant them free rein with his building. Furthermore, in his anxiety to fawn all over Judge Rawley, he had agreed to meet the cost of refurbishment.

But no sooner had Judge Rawley passed away than Clough changed his mind.

Nathaniel lifted his chin to attach his collar. Fresh starch chafed his neck as he slotted modest mother-of-pearl studs into place. Fastening his bow tie, he caught his expression in the mirror. His mouth, with no waxed moustache to soften it, was set in an uncompromising line. He ought to smooth his expression before meeting Clough, though it wouldn't be easy. The man was a toady and a social climber of the first water. Hence his doctor's garb today. Nathaniel was certain his professional regalia would create an impression. So, here he was in his frock coat with silk-faced lapels, grey-and-black striped trousers, waistcoat of white pique and black bow tie. His black silk topper was downstairs on the hallstand, though he drew the line at carrying a cane.

Downstairs, Imogen appeared, clothes brush at the ready. She kept his clothes in tip-top condition, so why she needed to brush his shoulders every time he was about to set foot outside, he didn't know, but he submitted without a murmur. She was a good little woman.

'I'm not sure how long this will take,' he said.

'Don't worry. I'm making a stew that will bubble away nicely.'

She presented her cheek for a kiss. He caught a whiff of the lavender water she always requested for her birthday.

Soon he was running up the front steps of Clough's house. A maid showed him into the sitting room. 'Overstuffed' was the word that sprang to mind – just like its owner. Plump upholstery was buttoned as if to stop horsehair bursting forth and the cushions were padded so thickly they looked ready to pop. Even the antimacassars were crocheted from something closer to wool than fine cotton.

Clough lumbered to his feet, thrusting out fingers like sausages. He was one of those buffoons who thought it manly to squeeze hard.

‘Good of you to see me,’ said Nathaniel.

‘Pleasure, m’dear fellow,’ said Clough: Nathaniel hadn’t been a dear fellow without his frock coat. ‘Take a seat.’

He placed his topper on a table beside an armchair, taking a malicious pleasure in flicking out the skirts of his frock coat as he sat down.

Clough sat opposite, flabby thighs squashing into the arms of his chair. He wore a colossal handlebar moustache, possibly to compensate for the scarcity of oiled strands plastered across his bald pate.

‘What can I do for you, Doctor Brewer?’ Clough chuckled. ‘As if I didn’t know.’

‘I’m here concerning the property in Moss Side. You assured Judge Rawley of your cooperation.’

‘But he has passed into the great hereafter and my circumstances have altered accordingly. One has to have one’s own interests at heart.’

‘What about the interests of the less fortunate?’

‘The poor are feckless and work-shy.’ Clough puffed out his paunch, increasing the strain on his waistcoat. ‘Well-known fact, sir, well-known fact.’

Oh, the temptation to say: You’re a pompous, self-serving idiot and I’d like to boot you up the backside.

He said, ‘I’ve no intention of wasting my time or yours. I know Judge Rawley was prepared to put in a word for you in the right places, but wouldn’t you rather earn your place in society?’ No, obviously not. ‘Look here, Clough, I can’t propose you for membership of a smart club and I don’t have the mayor’s ear, but I have access to certain charitable committees. What d’you suppose their reaction will be when they hear you’ve dropped out?’

'Are you threatening me, Brewer?'

'Not at all, but you'll put me in a dashed awkward corner if I have to explain your change of heart. Think of it this way. I'm in a position to sing your praises to the Lady Chairmen of half a dozen committees. You know the stratum of society these charitable ladies inhabit.'

He could practically see the cogs turning in Clough's head. The full lips pursed thoughtfully beneath the monstrous moustache.

'The day the clinic opens,' Nathaniel declared, 'I'll pin a ribbon across the doorway and Mrs Clough can cut it for the camera. How's that?'

'Yes . . . yes . . .' Clough murmured to himself and Nathaniel knew he had won. He ought to feel pleased, but he was sick of the sight of this complacent buffoon. He glanced about, noticing the glossy wax fruit beneath glass domes and the brown Lincrusta wallpaper that looked like panelling. Good grief. The room was as false as its owner.

He couldn't get out of there fast enough.

The Ees House visit was going to be on Sunday. Due to leave school soon, Emma had been included in the invitation for the first time. She couldn't stop talking about it.

'Word of warning,' Mary cautioned, as they took their shoes upstairs after Dadda had given them their evening polishing. 'Don't say too much downstairs or Dadda will think you're getting ideas above your station.'

Emma looked aghast and Mary's heart beat faster for her. She had promised Mam in her coffin to take care of her new sister. She was sure that was what Mam had wanted. Why else would she, in her dying moments, have named the baby Emma? That had always been Mary's pet-name – Emmie or Emms, because of her initials. Even after Dadda married Lilian, Mary kept a special eye on Emma, feeling she was fulfilling her promise to Mam.

'But you and I can talk about it,' she said. 'It's best to be prepared.'

She drew Emma into her bedroom and onto the bed. The mattress dipped, tipping them towards one another. Ozymandias, King of Kings appeared from nowhere and sprang between them. For a cat who wasn't allowed upstairs, he left an inordinate amount of marmalade fluff on their eiderdowns.

Emma scratched the back of his neck and his purr cranked into operation. 'Go on.' Her eyes sparkled.

'The Kimbers won't meet us at the door. The butler will let us in, only when a butler does it, it's called admitting you, and he'll show us to where they are. If it's like the other times, they'll be seated at the far end of a long room called the saloon and we'll have to walk all the way down it to reach them and you don't know when to start smiling.'

'Oh.' Emma's face fell.

'Don't worry. They'll be politeness itself. Manners maketh man and all that. It's only Granny we have to worry about. Everyone's on edge, dreading her saying something excruciating, and then you can see the Kimbers' faces freeze before they start being gracious again. Sir Edward thinks highly of Dadda; that's what you must remember.'

'It doesn't sound at all agreeable. Certainly not worth getting ragged for at school.'

'That used to happen to me. And if it wasn't ragging, it was being sucked up to.'

'Or being called stuck-up.'

'We've nothing to be stuck-up about. It isn't as though the Kimbers have anything to do with us beyond a card at Christmas and dinner once a year. We don't even rent one of their houses, because we don't want folk thinking we're taking advantage.'

'But it is special having grand relations, isn't it?' Emma said wistfully.

Mary gave her a hug and stroked her hair. It was smooth and dark, as unlike her own fair waves as it was possible to be.

'Do the family tree for me, like you used to when I was little,' Emma begged.

'Don't be daft. You know it inside out.'

'Please.'

Mary couldn't resist. She had always loved playing the big sister. She spaced the names across a sheet of paper: *John Kimber – Charles Kimber – Martin Kimber.*

'Martin was our grandfather. John and Charles were his brothers. John was the oldest, so that made him Sir John.'

Below the names, she wrote: *Edward Kimber – Charles Kimber – John Maitland.*

'They each had a son.' She drew lines, connecting them. 'Sir Edward is the son of Sir John. This is Uncle Charles, who was killed in the gales when you were little. He wasn't our real uncle, but it's polite to call him that. And this is Dadda. Grandfather Martin died when he was a baby and then Granny married Grandpa Maitland and changed Dadda's name.' She glanced at Emma, amused to see her concentrating. 'Here are Eleanor . . . Charlie . . . and you and me. Eleanor and Charlie are our second cousins, and one another's second cousins, because of our fathers being first cousins. Strictly speaking, Eleanor is a step-cousin, because she's from Lady Kimber's first marriage.'

'Do you ever wish Dadda was still called Kimber?' The reappearance of the wistful note didn't escape Mary.

'Don't forget he chose to be called Maitland. Granny changed his name to spite the Kimbers, but when Grandpa Maitland died, he could have changed back. Granny wanted him to, because she was afraid people would forget her grand connections, and the Kimbers said he could, but Dadda refused. He said John Maitland was who he was and who he always wanted to be. Mam told me that. Don't you think it's splendid? I do.'

'Do you think the Kimbers will mind that I'm going to work in a shop?'

'Sweetheart, has that been worrying you? It's not just any shop. It's part of a successful dressmaking business. They're more likely to question why I'm leaving the town hall. Dadda says I'm not allowed to say it's because of not getting promoted, in case it sounds as if I'm dissatisfied with my station. I'm to say he let me apply to be a lady-librarian because of my love of reading.'

She drew in a breath – and then remembered not to let it out on a sigh. But she felt like sighing. As the poor relations, they were required to be ultra-respectable, though they never got any thanks for it. It was part of their station in life.

Chapter Five

Nathaniel hummed 'Goodbye, Dolly Gray' as he arrived at the colonel's house in Withington for the meeting.

'I know what talking to yourself is the first sign of, but I'm not sure what singing to yourself means.'

He turned to find Alistair walking up the path behind him. They shook hands.

'In this case, it means Clough has been pulled back into line.'

'Thanks to your powers of persuasion,' said Alistair.

'With a little help from my frock coat. Why is the meeting being held at this time? I barely had time for anything to eat after morning surgery. Is the colonel's Saturday golf teeing off early?'

'Apparently, it's to accommodate a visitor Palmer is bringing with him.'

Colonel Fawcett's maid admitted them. Meetings were held around the colonel's dining table. The dining room – indeed, the whole house – was filled with the trophies and trinkets of a life spent in India and the old boy loved nothing more than to spin a yarn attached to one of his mementoes. Nathaniel had learnt not to look at the tiger-skin rug, the ornaments or the photographs of Europeans buttoned up to the back teeth. Hard-hearted perhaps, but it was the only way to get the business of the meeting attended to.

He nodded a greeting to a couple of local worthies and the PIP man, who represented Projects for the Ignorant Poor.

'Bloody patronising name,' he had commented to Alistair when he first heard it.

'Who cares, as long as they stump up the funds?'

As they had soon discovered, it was more than a name: it was an attitude. Nathaniel had to keep a tight rein on his tongue whenever the PIP man started bleating about having to do the poor's thinking for them.

Like now. The PIP man was comparing the poor to children – '. . . and you wouldn't expect children to make their own decisions, would you?' – and the meeting hadn't even opened.

'Afternoon, Palmer,' said Alistair as Mr Palmer, their chairman, walked in, followed by a stranger. 'Who have you brought along?'

'Name of Hobley,' the visitor replied, without waiting to be introduced. 'I'm from the Means Test Office and I'm here to stop you going ahead with these preposterous plans.'

All through dinner, Mary kept glancing at the official-looking letter on the mantelpiece. It must be to do with her new job. Her pulse quickened, but she couldn't open it until after dinner. If it had come by the first post, she could have read it before she went to work, and its contents would have made it easier to ignore Mr Treadgold's loaded remarks about nobody's being indispensable. Instead it had been waiting when she and Dadda arrived home. They worked until one on Saturdays. Lilian had met them at the front door to relieve Dadda of his outdoor things, placing his slippers in front of him and helping him into the tweed jacket he wore around the house.

Dinner was served immediately. Afterwards Dadda sat in his armchair with the newspaper, which had waited untouched for him. Mary was going to make a rotten wife one day: she could never last a whole morning without reading the paper. Perhaps she would read it secretly, then iron it smooth, ready for the man of the house.

When Lilian carried in the tea tray, Dadda folded the paper. Lilian took her place in the armchair opposite his. Mary sat in the basketwork chair and Emma occupied the rush-seated chair. Mary's heart burnt with the need to open her letter; but she must sip her tea and make light conversation while sitting in her appointed chair. Would there be rioting in the streets if they changed places for once? Would the mighty name of Kimber be besmirched?

Lilian got up to clear away. Finally! Plucking the letter from behind the clock, Mary slit the envelope. A single glance sent chills coursing through her, but she managed to say, 'I'll read it later. Sit down, Mother. I'll wash up.'

Outside the room, she snatched her breath in shock. The corporation had changed its mind about lady-librarians and her offer of a job had been rescinded. But no matter how upset she was, she must keep it to herself. If Dadda knew, he would ask Mr Treadgold to overturn her resignation.

Would she be able to find another post before her notice ended?

'. . . and you won't change my mind, no matter what arguments you employ,' said Mr Hobley. 'It's more than my job's worth to give an inch on this matter.'

Nathaniel clamped his teeth together. This was Hobley's answer to everything. It was more than his job was worth to let matters regarding the clinic proceed unchallenged. It was more than his job was worth to contemplate subsidised medical fees for the poor. It was more than his job was worth to climb off his blasted high horse and show a spark of compassion for wretches less fortunate than himself.

'If you're permitted to set up this clinic, you'll undermine everything the means test stands for. I believe it's your intention to educate these females in matters of hygiene?'

'Hygiene and its links to health,' said Alistair.

Mr Hobley turned a challenging eye on him. 'In other words, you propose to give these women ideas above their station.'

'Above their station?' Nathaniel couldn't keep silent a moment longer. 'Give me strength.'

'That's what I said, sir. It's at odds with the principle and purpose of the means test, which exists to provide support for the lowest kind of people. We don't want their heads filled with unseemly notions.'

'What's unseemly about knowledge of hygiene?'

'It would make them dissatisfied with their lot in life.'

'Whereas at the moment they are, of course, content.'

Mr Hobley bridled, his facial features shrinking in a display of self-defence and spite. 'If that's your attitude, there's nothing more to be said. I came here with an open mind—'

'Like hell you did,' Nathaniel muttered.

'—prepared to discuss this matter and reach a reasonable conclusion, but apparently that's beyond you, which merely reinforces the correctness of the Means Test Office's decision. I'll bid you good afternoon, gentlemen.'

The next moment he was gone.

'I'm sorry.' Nathaniel looked round the table. 'That was my fault.'

The PIP man shifted awkwardly. 'If the means test people are pulling out, Projects for the Ignorant Poor won't support you. We work closely with them.'

Gathering his papers, he left.

'What do we do now?' Nathaniel asked.

The colonel perked up. 'Reminds me of a dashed ticklish situation back in '94 – or was it '95? Now then . . .'

Mr Palmer took shameless advantage of the colonel's pause. 'As I see it, gentlemen, there's only one thing we can do. I know how determined Doctor Brewer and Doctor Cottrell have been from the outset not to approach any charitable committees, but under the circumstances . . .'

Nathaniel met Alistair's eyes across the table. The LBCs – the Lady Bountiful Committees. Oh no.

'We want this clinic to be part of the system,' he said, 'not subject to the whim of a committee that might withdraw support in a year or two with a change of lady chairman.'

'I'm sure these committees are better regulated than that,' said Palmer. 'I suggest the Deserving Poor Committee.'

Nathaniel bit back a snort. 'Who decides who is deserving?'

'Lady Kimber and her committee members.'

'Lady Kimber?'

'Yes,' said Palmer, 'wife of Sir Edward Kimber of Ees House.'

'She was related to Judge Rawley,' Nathaniel recalled.

'Who was a good friend to the clinic,' said Alistair.

'Whom Brewer looked after through his final illness,' added Palmer.

It took Nathaniel a moment to realise that all eyes were on him. He knew what was coming next.

Mary consciously relaxed her shoulders. They lived in the back room, but here they were in the front room, sitting quietly in their best clothes. Her hat and Lilian's were freshly trimmed with silk flowers – just a few; mustn't be showy – and Emma's boater sported a new ribbon. They were waiting for the carriage. When you were the poor relations, not only must you not keep your grand relations waiting, you mustn't keep their servants waiting either.

A carriage rolled up with the Kimber coat-of-arms on the doors. Mary came to her feet along with the others. Heat wrapped itself round her the instant she stepped outside. She placed a gently restraining hand on Emma's shoulder. Mustn't look too eager, not with the neighbours watching. It was an excruciatingly difficult moment. If you smiled at the watchers, you looked swanky, but if you didn't, you looked stuck-up.

It was sweltering in the carriage. The leather seats were soft as butter and smelt like new shoes. Dadda pulled down the windows and more heat plunged in.

They went via Sandy Lane to collect Granny and Aunt Miriam.

'You look peaky, Miriam,' said Lilian.

'She's got one of her heads,' said Granny. 'She's brought it on herself, same as always. I told her, Miriam, I said, I'm entitled to go to Ees House and where I go, so can you.'

'But, Mother,' protested Miriam, 'it's different for you. You were married to a Kimber and John was born a Kimber, but my father was plain Harold Maitland. I don't know why Lady Kimber invites me. I suppose she has to, since I live with you, but I'm sure I'm not meant to accept – or you're not supposed to accept on my behalf.'

'You see the kind of nonsense I have to put up with,' Granny snorted. 'You're a fool, Miriam.'

'Mrs Maitland, please,' said Lilian.

'What our Miriam has never understood is that, as my daughter, she's in a privileged position. I wish I'd changed my name to Kimber-Maitland when I were widowed second time round. It would have reminded everyone who I am and maybe it would have eased the bitter disappointment of John's stubbornness in remaining a Maitland. It grieves me to this day, our John, not that you care. And you could have been Kimber-Maitland too, Miriam, and perhaps I wouldn't have had to tolerate your stupidity about visiting the ancestral home.'

'I couldn't possibly use the Kimber name.'

'I don't see why not. If Eleanor Davenport can get away with calling herself Kimber, I see no reason for you to be shy about it.'

'You make Eleanor sound like an imposter,' said Lilian. 'Sir Edward changed her name when she was tiny.'

'What would you know about it? It's nobbut five minutes since you wed your way into the family.'

'Anyway,' said Miriam, 'Eleanor has a right to the name. I haven't.'

'Her "right", as you call it, is that her mother wed a Kimber and, in case you've forgot, our Miriam, that's what your mother did an' all.'

Mary looked through the window, distancing herself from the unpleasantness. They were alongside Chorlton Green, where the trees around the edge cast enticing pools of shade. She sat forward, hoping to catch some breeze, but Lilian plucked at her arm.

'Sit back, love. You don't want to be seen gazing out or it'll be all over Chorlton that you were lording it and I won't be able to hold my head up round the shops.'

Mary sank back, careful not to lean into the leather in case she stuck to it. There were times when she wished the ancient water meadows after which Ees House was named would rise up and flood the dratted place.

The family swayed as the carriage turned right, passing between lion-topped gateposts onto the long drive, presently drawing to a halt before the grandly protruding porch. For a Kimber, the coachman would have climbed down to open the door and pull out the step, but he wasn't about to do anything of the kind for mere Maitlands, and it was left to Dadda to assist his womenfolk. There was nothing quite so humiliating as being snubbed by your rich relations' servants.

Dadda rang the bell and they waited long enough to stop looking at the door and glance at one another.

'Should you ring again?' Emma suggested.

'No, love. It's a big house and the butler might be a long way away.'

'He should be looking out for us,' Granny snapped.

The door swung open and she stalked inside even before Mary saw the butler. Please don't let Granny make a show of them. Some hope. Then she heard Emma's gasp of delight and smiled to see her sister gazing at the grand staircase that boasted more carpet than the whole of their house. To one side of the hall was a vast fireplace, and in the middle stood a gleaming table, upon which was a bowl filled with yellow roses, their fragrance mingling with the honey-spicy scent of beeswax. Mary felt a moment's pride: her own home smelt of beeswax. It made them the same as the Kimbers. Or did it make them the same as their servants?

She tried hard not to see Granny running her finger along the underside of the table.

'Would you come this way,' the butler invited them as though conferring a great favour, 'if madam has finished inspecting the cleaning?'

After a lunch of succulent roast beef and Yorkshire puddings, served on elegant white china with a dainty maroon-and-gold pattern round the rim, Lady Kimber proposed a walk in the gardens. Granny insisted on stopping indoors, claiming her old bones weren't up to exercise in this heat. It was a blatant lie and Mary could see from the Kimbers' faces that they knew it, but they could hardly challenge her, so she was left behind.

The flower gardens glowed with colour, their generous borders spilling over and blurring the edges of the paths. Sir Edward took the lead, walking with Dadda, their heads bent together in conversation. Lady Kimber followed with Lilian.

'Look, Aunt Miriam is on her own,' said Emma. 'Coming here can't be easy for her. The rest of us are proper Kimber relations, but she isn't.'

'How grown up you sound.'

'I am grown up – nearly. You forget how old I am.'

Mary smiled at the note of telling-off. They caught up with Miriam. How pale she looked. Not that she ever had much colour, but her skin looked faded, her eyes strained.

'Perhaps you should have stopped indoors with Granny,' said Emma.

'She only wants to have a nose round and I'm not being a party to that, thank you.'

'Why don't you sit down?' Mary suggested. 'That rose arbour has a seat. You can join us when we go back in.'

Miriam allowed herself to be settled. Leaves rustled, accommodating her. Velvet petals drifted to the ground. Mary and Emma hurried to catch up with the others.

As teatime approached, they went indoors, Lady Kimber leading the way to the morning room, where Granny had been left. With the men letting the ladies precede them, and Lilian pausing to help Emma remove her boater and gloves, Mary found herself behind Lady Kimber. Her Ladyship froze in the doorway. Mary managed not to cannon into her, at the same moment catching the tail-end of a movement – she gasped in horror as Granny sprang clear of the sideboard.

For a bone-chilling moment, she was sure Lady Kimber would utter a remark that would carry to the whole party, but Her Ladyship merely shifted her elegant shoulders the tiniest amount inside her apple-green silk dress and glided into the room. Mary slunk in after her.

'Please sit down,' said Lady Kimber. 'I'll ring for tea.'

Lady Kimber positioned herself on a sofa long enough to accommodate the entire Maitland family, smiling an invitation at Eleanor to join her. Mary's gaze travelled from mother to daughter. Was this how Lady Kimber looked years ago? Had her eyes, now hardened to flint, once been that wonderful misty blue?

Then there was Sir Edward. With his dark eyes, broad forehead and thick dark hair shot through with iron-grey, he was a Kimber through and through. You only had to look at the family portraits to know that. Even though Dadda had the same amount of Kimber blood in his veins, he wasn't a Kimber to look at. He was a big sandy bear of a man. Mam had said that Dadda was the image of Granny's pa, who had been an ironmonger in Withington.

'What's your opinion of this Old Age Pensions Act?' Sir Edward asked him.

'It's sure to improve the lot of a great many old folk and their families. It'll ease hardship and confer some dignity and, goodness knows, if you live to seventy, you've earned those considerations.'

'Assuming you meet the criteria.'

Granny drew herself up: Mary went cold.

'Of course,' said Granny, 'having married into the Kimber family, such things are beneath me.'

There was a moment of silence, then Lilian said, 'It was kind of you to include Emma in the invitation.'

'She's leaving school soon, unless I'm mistaken.' Sir Edward looked at Emma. 'Have you a job?'

'Yes, sir,' Emma whispered. Lilian gave her a gentle nudge and she said, 'I'm going to work in a shop.'

'Emma isn't the sort for exams,' said Dadda, 'not like our Mary. We thought shop work would suit. In the right kind of shop, of course.'

Mary squirmed. Was he apologising?

'Perhaps you've heard of it,' said Lilian. '*Constance and Clara*.'

Lady Kimber's fine brows arched. 'They're dressmakers. Rather good ones.'

'They're opening their own drapery and haberdashery next door,' Lilian explained. 'That's where Emma will be. We're proud of her.'

'The shops in that row are Kimber properties,' Sir Edward remarked, 'so you'll be answerable to me, young lady, as well as Miss Constance and Miss Clara.'

He gave Emma a mock-stern glance and she looked ready to sink through the floor. Dadda and Lilian chuckled dutifully, but Mary didn't. She was relieved when Emma's embarrassment was broken by the arrival of plates of dainty sandwiches and cake-stands arrayed with brandy snaps and petticoat tails alongside plump slices of cherry cake.

'You're still at the town hall with your father, I take it?' Sir Edward asked her.

'As a matter of fact—' Dadda began.

Before Mary was obliged to spew out a stream of barefaced lies, Granny demanded, 'Where's our Miriam?'

Mary caught her breath. Poor Miriam, trapped in the arbour. Was she too overawed to return? 'She was tired and headachy, so she sat on a bench.'

'I'll send a footman,' said Lady Kimber.

'I'll go – if I may,' Mary offered. It would be a hundred times worse for Miriam, being fetched by a servant, not to mention her own desire to escape the conversation about her work.

'I wouldn't hear of it.'

'Quite right, too,' Granny declared. 'That's what servants are for, our Mary.'

Another of those frightful pauses; then the door opened and Miriam crept in, her face grey with embarrassment.

'I apologise. I fell asleep. The gardener found me.'

'One of the gardeners, you mean,' Granny corrected her. 'You don't think the Kimbers keep just one, do you?'

'Thank you. That'll be all,' said Lady Kimber and Mary noticed a young maid hovering in the doorway, no doubt memorising every juicy detail for the delight of the servants' hall.

'Please sit down, Miss Maitland,' said Sir Edward.

'I'm sure tea will revive you,' said Lady Kimber.

Their good manners were impeccable, but Mary fizzed with the certainty of what they would say when their visitors had gone.

Miriam sank onto a chair, pressing her fingers to her temple.

'Is your head still bad?' Lilian asked.

'You have a headache?' Sir Edward sounded concerned. 'And we dragged you out for a walk.'

'It's nothing,' Granny declared. 'She's fine.'

'No, she's not,' said Dadda. 'I think, if you don't mind, Your Ladyship, we'd best leave straight after tea.'

'There's no need for us all to go,' said Granny.

'We arrived together and we'll leave together.'

'Well, thank you very much, our Miriam.'

Chapter Six

Lady Kimber stood on the front steps at Jackson's House. Never mind the heat of midsummer, she wore a long stole with foxtails, because their reddish hue complemented the light brown of her costume, as did the pheasant feathers adorning her wide-brimmed hat. The ensemble was new and she looked her dignified, bosomy best. She had dressed to dazzle. What woman wouldn't, when meeting the love of her life, even if it had all been over and done with years ago? She didn't pretend otherwise. She had long since given over lying to herself. Years ago, she had told herself she could be content with Henry Davenport and that had been the most monumental lie in the history of the world.

She hadn't told herself the same lie when she married Sir Edward. The time for lies was long past. She had set her cap at him to gain his title, his land, everything that made him a

Kimber, not for her own advancement, but to secure the best background she could aspire to for Eleanor. Her heart had been broken for the second time by then – again by Greg; no one else had the power – and it was her daughter who gave her a reason to wake up in the morning. For Eleanor she would do anything – even, for the second time in her life, marry a man she couldn't love.

On the day she married Sir Edward, she had ceased to be Christina. She had become Lady Kimber, embracing the identity wholeheartedly. For Eleanor's sake.

Now she was back at Jackson's House. It was impossible not to be swamped by memories. She was here to see Greg, her Greg. Always her Greg. Always and for ever, in spite of everything.

The front door opened and her heart pounded as she set foot in the house that had seen her great love affair – and her heartbreak.

'Mr Rawley, please.'

'I'm sorry, m'lady, he's not here.'

'What Edith means is, he's away,' said a new voice and her bones froze as Aunt Helen descended the stairs.

'When will he return?'

'I couldn't say. Please stay. The morning room catches the sun at this time of day . . . as you may recall.'

Vexation warred with good breeding, though what she predominantly felt was outrage at being manoeuvred into socialising with this infernal creature who had brought her young life crashing about her ears. Oh, the temptation to turn on her elegant Louis heel and march out, but she had greater dignity than that. Besides, she needed to know when Greg would return. He wasn't here: a fist squeezed her heart.

She entered the morning room, her gaze flying across a blur of velvet and walnut to where Greg had once seduced her on the hearthrug. More than once, actually.

Sunshine streamed through the windows that overlooked the back garden. In the corner of the thick privet hedge was the old wooden door through which she and Greg had crept the night they eloped. He had carried a lantern, holding her elbow as they hastened down the years-worn path to the bridge. Jackson's Boat, it was called, Lancashire this side, Cheshire the other. Their footsteps had made a soft clatter on the wooden planks as they raced to freedom. Her heart had clattered too, just as it was clattering now.

But freedom had been short-lived. She had been dragged back by Helen, all the pleading and fury in the world counting for nothing. Helen had handed her back to her distraught parents. They had laid the blame squarely at Greg's door. But even more than him, they blamed Helen, who hadn't seen the love affair blossoming under her nose. They never forgave her. And they weren't the only ones.

Oh, the misery of the months that followed. Her parents had produced Henry Davenport and pushed and pushed until, hearing Greg had gone abroad, she had given in and married him, a bride at eighteen, the same age her beloved Eleanor was now, joined to a man her father's age – but that had held a certain appeal at the time, offering a suggestion of being protected and looked after. And after all, Greg had vanished.

Now he was master of Jackson's House. What did Helen make of that? That had been cruel of Uncle Robert. Or maybe he hadn't known. Certainly, Helen had bent over backwards to keep the failed elopement secret.

She looked at the old lady. She had been scrawny, badly dressed and energetic in those days. She was still scrawny and badly dressed, but Lady Kimber had no intention of underestimating her by imagining her too old to have energy.

Helen returned her gaze, eyes wary. Had she too been overtaken by a storm of memories?

'Won't you sit down?' said Helen. 'I was so pleased to see Eleanor at the funeral. Such a lovely girl, so pretty. I wish you'd brought her today.'

'I'm surprised you even suggest it.'

'Wasn't she curious about me?'

'It doesn't signify if she was. She's going to be kept busy from now on.'

'Ah yes, she's at that age, isn't she?'

'I'll be keeping a close eye on her.'

'Like I failed to keep on you?' Helen asked tartly. 'Perhaps I'll get in touch with her once she's married, then she can make up her own mind.'

'You'd like that, wouldn't you? But it won't happen.'

'How can you be sure? Once she's married—'

'She'll still have me at her side to guide and prepare her.'

'Prepare her?'

'Eleanor will be the next Lady Kimber. She's going to marry the heir. I'm in the enviable position of knowing my daughter will succeed to my title. How many women can say that?'

'And what do the young people think?'

'Eleanor has always looked up to Charlie. She used to follow him around when they were children and he made a pet of her.'

'It's a big step from that to marriage.'

'Not so big. They haven't seen one another while he was at

Cambridge, but he's staying with us now and let's just say that when Eleanor walked into the room, he looked twice.'

'I hope she's happy, that's all.'

'Really? That's an improvement on what you wished for me. When do you expect Greg back?'

'I-I couldn't say.' Helen stumbled over the change of subject. 'He's in London, I believe.'

'Closing up his rooms before he moves here permanently?'

'I couldn't say. I'm not sure he'll even come back.'

'Don't be ridiculous. All this belongs to him now.'

'Ah. You haven't heard about the will?'

She listened in increasing astonishment as Helen explained.

'I hope you aren't contemplating anything foolish,' said Helen. 'Coming here, looking for Greg . . .'

'Same old Aunt Helen. Never could leave well alone, could you?'

'I'd have been only too pleased to leave things alone, had they been well.'

She came to her feet. 'Goodbye.'

'Don't go – please. Please.'

She waited. Helen might have got in that veiled dig, but victory wasn't hers. No one with those anxious, pleading eyes could gain victory.

'Won't you please stay? Edith's fetching tea.'

Hope and fear grew in the old woman's eyes. Lady Kimber turned and left.

I have an appointment regarding my new job. Well, it was half true. Mary finished the note, signed it, slid it into an envelope, addressed it to *John Maitland Esq.* and dropped it in the post-tray. Dadda would read it at his desk around the same time that Lilian received the postcard she had sneaked into the pillar box in Albert Square that morning, saying she would be late home for tea. Would she have good news for them later? That half-truth was going to generate a flood of questions and she needed to be able to talk confidently about fresh prospects.

As six o'clock struck, she hung back, to Spotty Ronnie's evident frustration. She couldn't afford to bump into Dadda as he left the building.

At last she was on the tram, willing it to go faster. Alighting at Wilbraham Road, she hurried to the agency, throwing a prayer heavenwards as she hurried upstairs.

'Look who it is,' Miss Lever said. 'I say, are you all right? Have a seat.'

She poured out her troubles. 'So I need another post before my notice is up.' Catching a look passing between the two, she stopped. Would they have nothing for her?

Miss Kennett indicated a door in the corner. 'Be a duck and pop the kettle on, would you? I know it sounds a frightful cheek, but Lever and I need a private word.'

She found a minuscule kitchen with a sink, a gas ring and a couple of shelves bearing a surprising quantity of crockery. When she brought a tray through a few minutes later, she was greeted by smiles.

'That letter you wrote us was jolly good,' said Miss Kennett, 'better than most we receive, and your experience sounds just what we're after for a new post right here with us. We need an efficient body to run the office. Lever and I are fine at pointing women in the right direction, but we're not so hot on record-keeping and so forth.'

'We need someone to keep us in line.' Miss Lever leant forward coaxingly. 'Would you give it a go?'

'So,' Lilian sniffed, 'they want a dogsbody.'

'I'll be responsible for the clerical side of things,' Mary explained. 'First I'll get the office routines up to scratch—'

'Like I said: dogsbody. Two upper-class ladies playing at working and needing a skivvy.'

'It's not skivvying. It's responsible work – important, too, helping women find decent jobs.' Something stiffened inside her: defiance. She smoothed her expression.

She had never seen Dadda angry, but he had a way of looking serious that spoke of displeasure.

'I'm not happy about this: the job itself or the way you got it.'

'I thought you'd be pleased I sorted out the problem myself.' She wasn't, wasn't, wasn't going to apologise.

'It's not up to you to do that,' said Lilian. 'You should turn to your father.'

'I'm over twenty-one,' Mary cried. Dear heaven, what was the point of being called sensible all your life if you couldn't be trusted to cope in a sticky situation?

'Aye, and a decent girl, properly fetched up,' Lilian retorted, 'which makes it all the more surprising and disappointing you went behind our backs.'

'I would visit this agency and see what's what,' said Dadda, 'but she's already taken the job and can't back out without looking bad. We can't have a Maitland being unreliable.'

'Thank you, Dadda,' Mary murmured.

* * *

'Here he comes, the wealthy landowner. We weren't expecting to see you again, Rawley, now you've gone up in the world.'

Others glanced up from their cards and nodded at Greg through the cigar smoke. He nodded back. Wealthy landowner, indeed. If only they knew. Well, let them believe he was rolling in it.

'You know how it is,' he remarked. 'Mustn't forget the fellows I used to know way back when.'

'Before you struck it rich,' Bertie Maxwell quipped and there were one or two chuckles, but only one or two. Play was serious at this table, tucked away in a private room where the evening clobber was of the highest quality and the collar studs were twenty-two carats, and some of the stuff had even been paid for.

Greg waited while the hand finished, watching closely without appearing to. The atmosphere was tense, expectant, taut with concentration.

When he was dealt in, he felt an unexpected pang. He had gone to Manchester with hopes riding high, more than hopes, downright expectations, certain he had left this life behind, and that if he ever sat down at a card table again, it would be purely from choice. Yet here he was, back where he started, needing money, having just one way to get it, and surrounded by men who were as keen to take everything from him as he was to take it from them. Damn Uncle Robert.

The bitterness didn't linger. Nothing did, nothing could, once play started. You couldn't afford to let anything distract you. More drinks arrived discreetly, and empty glasses were whisked away by invisible hands.

He didn't do badly. He won some, he lost some, but he won more than he lost and that was what counted.

‘I’ll call it a night. Must leave something for those in greater need.’

There were a few good-natured jeers, though he took note of those who stayed silent and drew his own conclusions about their likely financial straits. Sliding his winnings into his Italian leather pocketbook, he let his gaze skim across the pleasing number of banknotes. Not a bad trawl for a few hours of effort, though nothing compared to what was needed to drag him out of the mire.

He shrugged himself into the edge-to-edge evening overcoat the manservant held for him, thrust his fingers into white kid gloves and clapped his black silk topper on before accepting his cane from the man and flipping him a half-crown. He believed in tipping. It made you look affluent and guaranteed you good service next time.

He tapped his cane on the step outside the club, feeling its rounded top fill his palm. The top gleamed like any ornamental cane top, but someone who picked it up – not that anyone ever did, aside from the occasional servant, he was careful about that – would have been surprised by its weight. A good, solid weight that could deliver a socking great blow. Just in case.

He took a cab to his rooms in Mount Street. Might as well enjoy the money while he had it.

He unlocked his door. The gas lamps were burning. That telltale stench smote him – and there, seated in his armchair, sat Mr Jonas, blowing smoke rings.

He couldn’t keep the edge out of his voice. ‘What are you doing here?’

‘You disappoint me, Mr Rawley. Is that any way to greet an old friend?’

'How did you get in?'

'Through the keyhole, down the chimney, or maybe I materialised in a puff of smoke.'

Mr Jonas took another drag of his foul-smelling Turkish cigarette, closing his heavy-lidded eyes as he breathed out a stream of smoke through his nostrils like a contented dragon.

'Come in, Mr Rawley, please do.' He waved his cigarette expansively. 'Make yourself at home. Oh, I was forgetting – it is your home, isn't it? An interesting point. I suppose it depends upon whose funds pay the rent.'

Growling beneath his breath, Greg removed his outdoor garb. He went to the sideboard and pulled the crystal stopper out of the Scotch decanter. He waved the decanter at Mr Jonas, who shook his head.

'Now then, Mr Rawley, I thought you knew my tastes better than that after our long acquaintance. Our long and profitable acquaintance.'

Bitterness twisted in his guts, but he said affably enough, holding up the port, 'Top you up?'

'I don't mind if I do.'

A lesser mortal would have held out his glass, but not Mr Jonas. Greg gritted his teeth as he filled the glass that stood on the small circular table beside the armchair. His armchair, and his table, where he placed his nightcap. He imagined smashing the decanter on Jonas's head. Or there was his cane. What satisfaction there would be in hammering that face to a pulp, in shattering the skull and exposing the brain, making all those dastardly calculations and percentages come spilling out all over the carpet so he could stamp on the little blighters, grinding them to powder beneath his heel.

'So, Mr Rawley, here I am enjoying your hospitality and feeling a mite surprised that you haven't sought me out, you and I enjoying such a long association, and you owing me what you owe.'

His jaw clenched. He was damned if he was going to crawl to this bastard. 'I knew you'd find your way here sooner or later, though I imagined you'd wait to be let in.'

'But such is my eagerness to congratulate the new landowner. I'm your greatest well-wisher, Mr Rawley. I flatter myself that I've anticipated the rise in your fortunes – and your fortune – no less eagerly than you have yourself. May I offer my heartiest congratulations on the demise of your relative?'

'You'll get your money.' Bloodsucker.

'But will I?'

'What the devil d'you mean? I've inherited, haven't I? Naturally it'll take time for everything to come through. Red tape, you know. That's always the way with these things.'

'Quite right too. I like to see my own affairs handled with that kind of care. Everything signed and sealed, as it were. The trouble is, Mr Rawley, when you say it'll take time, how much time might that be?'

'Well, you know how lawyers are,' he hedged with a hint of joviality.

'It wasn't the lawyers I had in mind, Mr Rawley. It's Miss Helen Rawley I'm thinking of, and how long she might live.'

Greg chucked back some Scotch. It burnt his throat. Jonas knew. Christ, Jonas knew.

'How the deuce did you find out?'

'Come now, Mr Rawley, you can't expect me to divulge professional secrets. Suffice it to say that I know and I extend my sincere sympathy.'

'You know I'm good for that loan.'

'I wasn't suggesting otherwise. We trust one another, don't we? You trust me to provide the readies when you're in need and I trust you to pay me back – plus a little consideration.'

'Plus a bloody great consideration.'

Mr Jonas spread his hands, evil-smelling cigarette in one, port in the other. 'I've always done my best to accommodate you, Mr Rawley, even to the extent of lending you a generous sum in anticipation of your inheritance.'

'You'll be the first I pay back. Can't say fairer than that.'

'No need to trouble yourself as to who gets what and when, my dear Mr Rawley.' Mr Jonas took a moment to blow a lazy smoke ring. 'I've bought up all your debts, so now you owe everything to me.'

Chapter Seven

Mary's last day at the town hall couldn't come quickly enough. Mr Treadgold bade her a disapproving farewell, which made her all the more glad to leave, and the next morning she walked to work, smiling to think that when Emma left school, they could walk together, as the agency was a few doors down from *Constance and Clara*.

Miss Kennett and Miss Lever made her welcome and left her to get on with it, which suited her perfectly, but when she called Josephine 'Miss Kennett', she was immediately told not to.

'Call me Miss Kennett in front of clients, but the rest of the time we're Angela and Josephine, and you're Mary.'

She had noticed that Angela and Josephine called one another by their surnames, which seemed very modern, but she was glad not to be Maitland. That would have been too rum.

She asked about the sofas and chairs at the other end of the room.

'Meetings,' explained Josephine. 'We have friends round, like-minded people, and they bring their friends, and occasionally we have a speaker. We discuss women's matters. Now that we know what a wizard you are on that infernal typewriting machine, we'll have you bashing out letters and leaflets, pages of facts and figures, too.'

'There's a meeting next Tuesday,' said Angela. 'You're welcome to come.'

Mary couldn't commit herself without permission.

'I don't want you embroiled in anything inappropriate,' Dadda warned her that evening.

'It'd be nice for her to go out,' said Lilian. 'I'd rather she put the world to rights in a respectable place than that she gave her time to a soup kitchen in the slums.'

'There is that. What's this meeting about, Mary?'

'To discuss putting working-class girls into service with middle-class families, so they learn better habits of behaviour and hygiene.'

'That smacks of socialism to me. There are good reasons for social differences.'

'It's so that when they have families of their own, their children will be cleaner and healthier.'

'That sounds reasonable. Mind, I'm not having you turning into a socialist.'

'No, Dadda.'

'Or one of these newfangled feminists.'

'No, Dadda.'

* * *

As far as Mary was concerned, there was just one disadvantage to her new job: she didn't earn as much, while the only decrease in her outgoings lay in no longer paying fares. She still had to fork out for housekeeping and the Hospital Saturday Fund, as well as her share of the burial insurance and the money for her bottom drawer that she had been handing over to Lilian ever since she opened her first wage packet.

When she suggested her keep might go down, she didn't get the words out before Lilian cut her off.

'That's your lookout. You chose to work there.'

They were folding sheets. Lilian increased the speed, a sure sign of vexation.

'You don't like my being there.'

'No, I don't. I don't like you working for those toffee-nosed females.'

'They aren't toffee-nosed.'

'They're posh, you can't deny that, and they're taking advantage of you – oh yes, they are. They could have helped you get a job with the same salary as before. They're taking advantage, paying you less, and now you're trying to fob me off with less keep. Well, I'm not having it, and you wouldn't either if you had the sense you were born with.'

'But I love my job. I don't mind earning less.'

'Fancy ideas don't buy much coal. You can't have it both ways, love. What about your future? You're twenty-three, not a young lass any more, and they're not exactly queuing up outside the front door, are they? What if it never happens to you? It doesn't to some. Look at Miriam. You're welcome to stop here with Dadda and me, but we won't last for ever, and what will you do then? Live with Emma? She'll get wed and no mistake, a softy like her, and there you'll be, spinster sister, spinster aunt, living under another woman's roof, and all because you didn't earn as much as you could when you had the chance to put it by for later.'

'If that's what you think, you'd better give me back my bottom drawer money and I'll put it in the savings bank.'

'Nay, I won't give that back. That's like saying you've no chance.'

'Now who wants it both ways?'

'A good mother believes her girls will marry, whatever her private worries. I've been a good mother to you and no one can say otherwise.' Lilian held the folded sheet to her, her expression changing from vexed to anxious. 'You do think I've been a good mother, don't you?'

Mary hugged her, the sheet between them. 'Of course I do.'

'That means the world to me, and after I've just had a go at you an' all.'

'I don't understand why you're so against the agency when you helped talk Dadda into letting me attend the meetings.'

'I want you to meet a young man, of course, one who'll appreciate a clever lass like you. I want you to be happy and by that I mean happily married, and that means meeting the right chap. A marriage of convenience is all very well, but I'd like you to marry for love.'

Dare she ask? 'Is that what you and Dadda have – a marriage of convenience?'

'Nowt wrong with that. I was a widow at the end of my savings and your dad needed a wife. Granny had her foot jammed in the door, and he wasn't best keen on that. It wouldn't have ended there, neither. Candle Cottage is a grace-and-favour house for Granny, but the Kimbers have no obligation to

Miriam, so goodness knows where she'd have ended up – some grotty little bed-sitting room. Dadda wouldn't have allowed that. He'd have brought her here. Can you imagine the whole lot of you squeezed in, and Granny ruling the roost? So he married the widow next door.'

Mary had never heard her speak so frankly. Did this mean Lilian saw her as a confidante and friend as well as a daughter?

'I'll tell you summat else. It gave me the chance to have children. Having daughters is a dream come true for me. It was easy enough with Emma, her being so young when it happened, but I reckon me and thee haven't done badly.' Her eyes were dark with worry.

'Not bad,' Mary agreed. 'Not bad at all.'

Lady Kimber received Doctor Brewer in her elegant morning room. She liked the look of him. She was a great believer in first impressions. He was good-looking in a lean, rather stern way, with the firm tread and unconscious grace of an athlete. His eyes should have been darker. They were hazel, but they bore an intensity that should have rendered them black: he was focused on his mission and she respected that. But there was something else about him – maybe it lay in that brief smile he had given upon introduction, something that suggested good humour beneath the serious facade, maybe even a sense of fun. She had been fun-loving herself once.

She was well disposed towards him – until he uttered the fatal name.

'If you imagine that your having been physician to the late Judge Rawley will further your cause, permit me to disabuse you at the outset.'

'It was not my intention to give offence.'

The words were courteously spoken, but he stopped short of apology. She would have dismissed him out of hand had he tried to lick her boots.

'What brings you here, Doctor?'

'I'm here about a new clinic for the poor in Moss Side, which I hope you will find warrants the support of the Deserving Poor Committee.'

'Tell me about it.'

'A colleague and I will donate regular hours and we'll employ nursing staff. There will be a baby clinic and a nit nurse. We have a building that requires attention – repairs, whitewashing, extermination of vermin, and so forth – but which will provide waiting and consulting rooms, offices, storerooms and a teaching room.'

'A teaching room?'

'We'll provide classes on nutrition and hygiene. If the women can be helped to make improvements in the home, the community will become healthier in body and mind. I trust that will make the community deserving of your support.'

He was correct, but she wouldn't be drawn. 'Matters are obviously in hand. Why have you waited so long to approach me?'

'We hoped not to require funding from a charity committee.'

'What changed your minds?'

'Unfortunately, funding from Projects for the Ignorant Poor was withdrawn.'

'For what reason?'

'The means test people object to our offering medical attention at a reduced cost.'

'And so you reluctantly find yourself here? Very well. The Deserving Poor Committee will consider your request.'

'Thank you, Your Ladyship. I have taken the liberty of bringing the relevant paperwork with me.'

No wonder he had wanted to be financed by the authorities. He didn't fancy being at the mercy of upper-class females, full of hot air and prejudice. Well, if he worked alongside the Deserving Poor Committee, he would soon learn that she didn't run her committees like that.

Goodness, but Charlie could do with a bit of Doctor Brewer's fire.

Mary's eager mind gobbled up the agency meetings; she felt modern and informed, grown-up, too, in a way she never had before. Living at home and working at the town hall had kept her under the family thumb, but now she was aware of her outlook developing.

'As an agency, we're here for the educated woman,' said Angela, 'but as campaigners, we have a duty to represent working-class females.'

She learnt about the lives of unremitting toil endured by those poor creatures in the sweated industries, who earned a pittance hemming or beading, sewing buttons onto cards or fringes onto shawls, even bending corset-steels or making coffin-tassels. Her own clothes were simple enough, but when she purchased a card of hooks and eyes, she looked at it with new and painful knowledge.

She had always known herself to be capable. Now she felt ready for independence. What would it be like to live as the others did? Angela and Josephine shared the upstairs of a house on Edge Lane, while others occasionally mentioned landladies or laundry arrangements. They talked about, what was called in Maitland parlance, their chars – only when they spoke of them, they called them their treasures. Mrs Bethell would laugh her head off if Mary called her a treasure.

In such company, she felt obscurely ashamed of living at home. When the front door closed behind her, she resumed the mantle of dutiful, unquestioning daughter, so could she truly say she had spread her wings?

She mustn't let that niggle spoil her new life. She attended every meeting she could, though there were times when she had to tell barefaced lies at home. Dadda would have hauled her over the coals had he known of the discussions about votes for women.

One evening, the talk turned to forcible feeding. Mouths slackened as everyone's credulity stretched to snapping point.

Josephine shivered. 'It's abominable if it's true. Fancy! One minute you're protesting and the next you're in prison, having food forced down your throat.'

'Hunger-striking has been a good strategy so far,' Ophelia Cardew observed. 'It put the frighteners on the authorities.'

'And now they're putting the frighteners on us with these rumours. It has to be rumour. This is England, for God's sake.'

Mary shivered. When the conversation moved on, no one attempted to steer it back, falling instead into the familiar subject of women in the sweated industries.

'Here – borrow this,' Angela said, handing her a copy of *The Sweating Debate*.

'Thanks.' She couldn't take it home for fear of provoking an untoward reaction, but she could read it in her dinner hours.

'Would you like this as well? It's *Three Weeks* by Elinor Glyn.'

'Thanks, but I've read it.'

'Really?' Josephine perked up. 'What's it like? I've heard it's rather saucy.'

Everyone looked at her. Did they expect her to condemn it as fine for uneducated girls, but beneath the likes of themselves?

'Well, when I say I read it, actually guzzled it would be nearer the mark.' She was rewarded by smiles and laughter. 'It took the town hall by storm.'

'Never!'

'In deadly secrecy, of course. The lady-clerks passed it round behind the men's backs.' She grinned. 'It fell open at all the best pages.'

This was greeted by more laughter. How wonderful to feel accepted.

She held up the volume. 'Who wants it first?'

Two or three girls made pretend lunges; Bobby Kennett yelled, 'Me first!' and made a grab. Mary laughed. If there hadn't been young men present, she might have shared the naughty poem that had done the rounds of the town hall, in which the author's name had been rhymed with 'sin' and 'tiger skin'. 'Undulate' had become the word of the moment, though she couldn't recall whether Miss Glyn had used it or it had been coined by one of her colleagues in a fervent moment at the stationery cupboard.

'Lucy's having it first,' said Angela.

'Shall I put that in the minutes?' Mary teased.

Minutes hadn't been kept before, but it was one of her skills. At the town hall, she had been one of only two lady-clerks entrusted with the duty – not that they had received any recognition, least of all financial.

'Your minutes are frightfully good,' said Angela. 'No one need worry about missing a meeting now.'

'They're readable, too,' said Josephine. 'You have a knack for writing. You'll have to rejig our dry-as-dust pamphlets.'

'Happy to,' she said and set to with a will, producing results that were admired at the next meeting.

'Ever considered getting published?' Ophelia asked.

Thinking it a joke, she smiled, then realised everyone was looking at her. Her heart gave a leap of pleasure. She felt drawn to the idea. But was she good enough?

'We wouldn't suggest it if we didn't believe in you,' said Angela.

It was on the tip of her tongue to say, 'Thanks. I'm flattered,' but that wasn't how she felt. Well, yes, she was flattered, of course, but mainly what she felt was . . . determined. Here was something fresh to strive for.

During her dinnertimes, she ensconced herself in the meeting area, studying the pamphlets and booklets. At home, she examined the *Manchester Evening News* and looked through recent copies of Lilian's *Vera's Voice*, which was principally a story paper but also ran articles, from how to soothe eczema to how to wash a sheepskin rug. Although most articles were of a domestic nature, one copy included a piece on the benefits of fresh air and another had one on working wives.

That gave her an idea.

Ophelia had told her about the Happy Evenings club she ran, which aimed to tempt poor children and youths off the streets before they fell into bad ways.

'That's what I'd like to write about,' she told Ophelia. She hesitated before asking, 'Lady Kimber isn't your patron, is she?'

'What an odd question.'

'I know she does charity work.' No one at the agency knew of her link to the Kimbers. Were this one of Lady Kimber's pet projects, she might be able to come clean at home. So far, she had kept quiet about her ambition to write, uncertain whether it would be regarded as a worthwhile activity or a horror to be forbidden lest she make a show of herself.

'Sad to say, no, she isn't,' said Ophelia. 'We could do with a benefactor to stump up cash.'

Mary skipped the meeting the following Tuesday, pretending at home it was on Thursday, which enabled her to go to Happy Evenings instead. She couldn't risk Dadda's forbidding it.

Ophelia and her cronies had the use of a church hall. When Mary arrived, a game of skittles was in progress, the onlookers' whoops and jeers suggesting things were hotting up. Younger children were seated at a table, playing pick-up-sticks or Happy Families; further down, girls clustered together, with slates and chalks. At the far end of the hall, older boys had commandeered the bagatelle board.

One of them noticed a couple of little lads watching. 'Yeah, come on, you two,' he said and the older ones made room.

'Join in,' Ophelia advised Mary. 'You'll find out more and the youngsters will enjoy it. They don't get much adult attention, or if they do, it's more likely to be a clip round the ear.'

Mary used a deck of cards to teach beggar-my-neighbour and clock patience, produced silly chalk drawings beside which the children's efforts looked like masterpieces and handed round lemonade and buns at half-time, but the crowning moment was leading a motley team to victory at skittles.

'It's been a good evening,' she told Ophelia as they locked up. 'The older ones take care of the young ones, don't they? And the young ones hero-worship them in return.'

She spent a few days writing and perfecting her article. When it was ready, she tried to give it to Ophelia to read before she submitted it to the *Manchester Evening News*.

'Heavens, don't do that or everyone you write about will be chopping and changing what you've put. I know you'll have done a good job. Good luck getting it in print.'

A problem remained.

'I can't use my own name. My family doesn't know I'm doing this. It could be tricky using our address too.'

'Use ours,' Angela offered.

'Sign the article with a pen name,' said Josephine, 'but put your own name on the covering letter. It might be a good idea to be M. Maitland rather than Mary.' She shrugged. 'Sad but true.'

Mary instantly knew her pen name: F. Randall. Mam had been Florence Randall.

As she dropped her article into the pillar box, her hopes soared.

The office door flew open and Josephine rushed in, a smile lighting her face. Mary had always thought of Angela as the pretty one, but now she saw how lovely Josephine could look. One hand clamped her straw hat to her head while the other brandished an envelope.

'Urgent delivery for *Mr* Maitland.'

Mary came to her feet. Angela tweaked the letter from Josephine's fingers and thrust it at her. She didn't know whether to be excited or frightened silly. She ripped open the envelope and pulled out a letter.

'*Dear Mr Maitland, Thank you . . .*' Her eyes rushed ahead. 'They've accepted it. It's going to be published on Saturday. *Please find enclosed a postal order . . .*' She stood staring. Seven and six!

'Your first earnings as a writer,' said Angela. 'Congrats.'

Josephine laughed. 'That's put a sparkle in your eyes.'

'This calls for cream buns,' said Angela. She settled her cartwheel-hat with its profusion of silk forget-me-nots, jabbed in a hatpin, snatched up her handbag and disappeared.

'Now you have to decide what to write next,' said Josephine.

'When I started work, my father sent me to night school to learn to use a typewriting machine. I could write about things women can learn that will help them get better jobs.'

At the next meeting, she glowed with joy as her friends made much of her.

Ophelia had another idea.

'Remember what you said to me at the end of the Happy Evenings? Did you mention it in this article? No? Then write another Happy Evenings piece concentrating on that. It might appeal to *Vera's Voice*.'

'Thanks. I will.'

'I've heard about a new clinic for the poor in Moss Side,' added Katharine Fordyce.

Mary felt bubbly inside, but there was another sensation too, like an itch under her skin. She had to come clean at home, but it wouldn't be easy. Dadda was bound to feel she should have sought permission – but what if he had said no? Besides, she hadn't wanted permission. She had wanted to act independently.

But that didn't mean she didn't want her parents to be proud of her.

She couldn't wait for the *Manchester Evening News* to drop

through the letter box that Saturday teatime. She snatched it from the mat, aching to find her article but knowing she must wait.

When at last her father set the paper aside, she couldn't stop herself reaching for it.

'May I? There's something I want to find.'

'Mother has it next.'

'Let her, love,' said Lilian. 'I'm busy with my sewing.'

She scanned the paper. There it was! She knew what it said, word for word, but she read it anyway, the newsprint causing her heart to pitter-patter. Folding the paper open, she held it out.

'Dadda, did you read this?' If only he would say what an excellent piece it was!

'Can't say I did.'

'Oh. Only I wish you would read it.'

'What for?'

Suddenly it felt grubby, trying to get him to read it first. 'Because I wrote it.'

'What d'you mean, you wrote it?' His gaze dropped to the paper. 'But this was—oh. I see.' His lips clamped shut and he inhaled through his nostrils. 'F. Randall.' A short silence, heavy with displeasure. 'F. Randall.'

'Who's F. Randall?' Emma piped up.

'Your mother.'

'Your real mother,' Lilian added softly when Emma looked at her in confusion.

'Leave the room, Emma,' Dadda ordered. 'This isn't for your ears.'

Mary had to drop her gaze to conceal her vexation. 'Really, Dadda,' she said in her mildest voice, 'you make it sound as if I've desecrated Mam's memory.'

'You knew you were doing wrong or you'd have used your own name.'

'I don't believe I've done wrong.' How unfair that she had to moderate her tone while he could be as brusque as he pleased. 'I didn't use my name because I thought you wouldn't wish it.'

He expelled a sound that was part exclamation and part laugh. 'You're right about that. Whatever possessed you?'

'I'm good at writing. I can write letters and minutes—'

'Which is a far cry from this.'

'It was suggested at work—'

'I might have known.'

'Please, Dadda, if you'll just listen. It was suggested at work, but it was my choice to do it and I think I've done it rather well. Certainly the *Evening News* thinks so.'

'Don't get clever with me, miss.'

'I'm not. I wish you'd read it, Dadda. The Happy Evenings movement is growing and if someone reads my article and decides to take an interest, then—'

'You'll have changed the world single-handed? Don't be an ass, Mary. And what do the Kimbers think of' – he made a point of searching the article, though she knew this was for show – 'Happy Evenings?'

'I don't know.'

'Suppose it's something they don't approve of and it gets back to them that a Maitland has endorsed it?'

'There's no reason they should ever know. They won't recognise Mam's maiden name.' Anyway, weren't the Maitlands entitled to their own opinions?

'That's beside the point. You should have asked my

permission. The only thing you can do now is promise not to act so inappropriately again.'

'If by that you mean—'

'I mean that you will not write anything else for publication.' He looked at her expectantly – and confidently. 'I require your promise on this, Mary.'

Chapter Eight

'A perfect afternoon – but you always pick a glorious day,' said Aline Rushworth. 'I don't know how you do it.'

Lady Kimber smiled. She was famous for garden parties soaked in sunshine. The rear of Ees House with its flower-bedecked terrace running the full width of the building formed a handsome backdrop to the sweep of lawn, where her guests mingled.

'How lovely our girls look. A delight to the eye.' And the most delightful was her own daughter. 'I always dress Eleanor in sweet-pea colours. So suitable for a young girl and perfect with her fair colouring. Sweet-pea for day and for evenings at home, and white for evenings out.'

'Who are those young people coming down the steps from the terrace?'

Lady Kimber, who never missed the smallest detail, affected to see them for the first time. 'Friends of Charlie – at least the fellow is. He's a Cambridge man: Bobby Kennett. His mother was a Chisleden. The girls are his sister and her friend, Miss Lever. They dabble in social reform. They have an agency that seeks out better jobs for women with some education.'

'Is Charlie interested in one of them?' asked Aline.

'Gracious, no. They're girls only in so far as they're unmarried and under thirty. To them, he's nothing more than the younger brother's friend.'

'You've met them before?'

'No, but when Charlie asked me to invite them, I found out everything I needed to know.'

'Background?'

'Good families, untitled, old money.'

'Votes for women?'

'They wear the jewellery and attend the rallies, and I believe Miss Kennett once knocked off a policeman's helmet, but they've never chained themselves to anything or set fire to pillar boxes.'

'I should hope not. They'd do better to find husbands.'

They wouldn't be half so interesting if they did. Lady Kimber watched as Charlie brought them to meet her. Bobby Kennett, dark-haired, lanky, cutting a dash in a cream linen suit and a jaunty boater with a striped band. The girls – stupid convention – the young women were several years older. One was tall and dark; she must be the sister. She and the Kennett boy shared the same good cheekbones and oval faces – a pair of thoroughbreds. The friend's face was heart-shaped and, beneath her flower-strewn hat, she had eye-catching hair, somewhere between fair and red.

When introductions had been performed, she questioned the young women about their work and wider interests. She had plans for them. Charlie lacked the advantage that applied to most heirs: he hadn't grown up on the estate he was to inherit. His father had died in the gales back in '01, which, tragic though it was, should have provided the ideal opportunity for Charlie and his mother to move into Ees House, but Dulcie had wanted to live near her own family. She had brought Charlie to Ees House for holidays, during which he was made much of, not just by the Kimbers but by their staff and tenants. It had afforded him masses of experience in the happy side of privilege without exposing him to the responsibility side and she feared he was . . . lightweight.

There. She had said it, though only to herself. He was a dear boy, honest and generous and a good sport, and he could charm the birds out of the trees, but the Kimber inheritance required more – and she wanted more for Eleanor.

Which was where Miss Kennett and Miss Lever came in. Their society would rapidly educate Charlie in the matter of social responsibility in a way he would readily embrace, as coming from a young, modern source that included the opportunity to make new friends.

It would be good for Eleanor too. Lady Kimber was drawing her into charitable works; but it was with the Miss Kennetts and Miss Levers of this world that the future lay. The women's movement, as long as it wasn't crushed to smithereens by public opposition to the radical element, was set to do good things – was already doing them – and Eleanor needed a voice in that, as well as on the age-old charity committees. She must bring together modern social reform and traditional good works.

And she deserved a worthwhile husband at her side when she did it.

'I'm sorry you got stuck with Colonel Fawcett,' Nathaniel told Imogen as they were returned home by cab. Had he been alone he would have marched home, letting the night air refresh his mind after an endless evening of enforced fraternisation with strangers. They had come from a function hosted by the colonel for local do-gooders with money burning holes in their pockets. The colonel had cornered Imogen and regaled her with tales of the Empire. 'You must have been bored silly.'

'No, I wasn't – well, maybe a little. I hope it didn't show. I'd hate to let you down.'

'You'd never do that.'

The evening had been a trial. He was happy to talk about rats pouring down the chimney and bugs spewing out of the walls, and rickets and ringworm, and any other complaints you cared to mention, but stick him in a room with a load of strangers who expected a bit of charm and he was lost. He never had been able to make conversation for its own sake. Small talk? Small minds, more like.

What he felt like now was a long run across the meadows to clear his head and tax his body. Well, it would have to wait until morning; he would run before breakfast. He enjoyed the sense of freedom and the challenge of pacing himself across a long distance. After a good run, he was too invigorated to feel tired.

The next morning, when he came home after his run, the first post had arrived.

'There's a postcard from Evie,' said Imogen.

A postcard from Evie.

He was thrown back in time to that other postcard. *In prison –*

sorry. Doing well. Chronic bronchitis but doing well. There: Evangeline Brewer summed up in a couple of scrawled lines, dashed off no doubt in a flurry of glorious pride. Oh, Evie. Always so full of energy. She could have used that energy at home helping make Ma's life easier, but she was full of the crusading spirit, and off she had gone on a jaunt to London to attend a women's rally and simply neglected to come home again.

It had hit Ma hard. Aunt Louise had muttered darkly about ungrateful girls flying the nest, while Gran's knitting needles had clicked ever more rapidly.

He had grown up in a house of women. Dad died when he and Evie were small, and thereafter Ma and Aunt Louise worked all the hours God sent. Gran kept house and earned a few bob from unravelling second-hand woollies and knitting them into new garments.

They lived carefully. Things would have been easier had Ma used Dad's money differently.

'That's Nathaniel's education money,' she insisted.

He wouldn't be a doctor now but for Ma's determination. The young Evie had resented it passionately.

'I'm Dad's child as much as you,' she used to flare.

Poor Ma, she was shocked speechless the first time Evie was arrested. Evie didn't get a sentence that first time, but she got a couple of days the second time, and longer the third time. That was when she sent the infamous postcard. *Chronic bronchitis but doing well.* Nathaniel could have crowned her for that. Ma had been eaten up by worry and shame.

Now here was another postcard.

Lost my job. Bolt-hole needed. Arrive tomorrow. Hope all well. E.

* * *

'Let me look at you, love. Eh, don't you look bonny – doesn't she, John? Doesn't she look bonny?'

Mary watched as Dadda smiled approvingly at Emma. Today was her first day at work. Gone was the pinafore in favour of a neat black dress with white collar and cuffs that marked her out as a shop girl in a better class of establishment. Her dark hair was plaited, as per the instructions of Mrs Price, the owner of the dressmaking business and the shop, who had said she might wear her hair up when she turned sixteen.

Dadda had arranged to go in late to the office in order to walk Emma to work on her first day and formally hand her over. How proud Dadda and Lilian were today of Emma. So was Mary, but there was a voice inside her muttering something ungracious about being proud of Emma simply for starting work when there was no pride in her achievements as a writer.

Her revised Happy Evenings article had been accepted by *Vera's Voice* and the deputy editor, L. Newbold (Mrs), had written that she would be interested to see another piece.

'Quick! Get something written,' said Angela.

She had used her idea about ways for women to increase their chances of better jobs. When she sent it in, submitting it to Mrs Newbold personally, she signed herself *Mary Maitland (Miss)*, though she still used her pen name on the article. When she received a letter by return, her heart sank: an instant rejection! But Mrs Newbold had written to say it was desirable to give F. Randall a first name. She suggested Fay – *quite a new name, and one which suits the modern tone of your work.*

Her gut reaction was to reach for a pen and insist upon Florence, but second thoughts stilled her hand. Fay had been chosen specially for her. Besides, using Florence would look like out-and-out defiance at home.

Not that Dadda was likely ever to know. Her writing successes since that first article – not just the piece in *Vera's Voice*, but an article about the sweated industries that was turned down by the *Manchester Evening News* but accepted by the *Stockport Echo and Cheshire Daily Echo* – had gone virtually unnoticed at home. As a matter of principle, she had informed her parents of each success, doing so when Emma wasn't present so she couldn't be accused of leading her astray; but Dadda had done nothing more than grunt and there was no knowing what Lilian thought.

Arriving at the agency, she unlocked the front door and the door at the top of the stairs. She generally arrived first, though she never said so at home, fearing a repeat of Lilian's cry of 'Dogsbody!'

She busied herself on the card index she was compiling. When the door opened, she looked up with a smile for her colleagues, and found herself bestowing a welcoming smile on a young man. A handsome young man: dark hair, dark eyes. He responded with a smile of his own and she toned down her own from friendly to professional.

'Good morning. May I help you?'

'Miss Kennett and her chum not here?'

He was nattily dressed, trouser creases and turn-ups sharp as knives, the band on his boater matching the gold silk of his tie. His tiepin caught the light and winked at her.

'Not at present, but they will be shortly. Is there anything I can do for you?'

'Now there's an offer I shan't refuse. A cup of tea would go down a treat.'

She had him pegged now. A friend. A well-to-do young gent with an interest in the lower orders. 'Are you Ophelia's brother?'

'Sorry to disappoint. What a lovely name: Ophelia. I bet you have a lovely name too.'

'Sorry to disappoint. My name's ordinary: Mary.'

'Splendid name. Traditional.'

She couldn't help smiling. 'Gallant of you.'

'Does my gallantry earn me a cup of tea?'

'Possibly. No sugar, though. You're tongue's sweet enough already.'

Josephine breezed in and was already saying, 'Angela, look who it is,' before Angela followed her in, swinging a satchel onto her desk and approaching the young man with hand outstretched. He raised it to his lips, making her laugh.

'As you see,' he said, 'I took you at your word. Here I am.'

'You're an early bird.' Josephine glanced at the clock. 'You've discovered our dark secret. We slope in late, knowing everything's taken care of.' She smiled at Mary.

The young man smiled at her too. 'Mary looked after me beautifully.'

Warmth crept across her cheeks. 'I was about to put the kettle on.' She bustled into the kitchen.

Josephine squeezed in after her. 'There's no reason why you should always do it.'

'I don't mind.'

Josephine glanced over her shoulder. 'Chum of Bobby's. We didn't know he was going to pop in so early or we'd have been here, but you obviously managed all right if you got as far as first names.'

'Oh. We didn't exactly – I mean, I don't know his name.'

She fussed over the tray. How could she have been so forward?

'He's Charlie Kimber. You know, the Kimbers of—'

'Ees House.' She stopped moving; her muscles were squishy. Charlie Kimber. The heir. And she had practically flirted with him. Oh, dear heaven.

'Kettle's boiling,' said Josephine.

'You go. I'll do this.'

When she returned to the office, she concentrated on the tea tray, determined not to give herself away by even the smallest clink of china. The others were seated on the sofas. She set down the tray.

'Shall I be mother?' she offered. Too brightly?

Charlie Kimber – or should she think of him as Mr Charlie Kimber? – was describing his recent trip to London to watch the Olympic Games, which had started some weeks ago and would carry on until October.

'I'd rather they'd been held in Rome, like they should have been.'

'It's such a fag when a volcano ruins your plans,' Josephine mocked. 'I'm always finding that.'

Mary listened with half an ear. She had to tell Charlie Kimber who she was. Imagine if he returned to Ees House and mentioned dropping in to see Kennett's sister and her friend and, oh yes, there was another colleague, a girl called Mary . . . and then at some juncture, she was revealed as Mary Maitland, poor relation. She couldn't let that happen.

Charlie looked at her. 'I didn't realise there were three of you here. Kennett said it was his sister and her friend.'

'It is,' she said quickly. 'I'm only the clerk.'

'Only?' said Angela. 'She's a wizard for efficiency. You should have seen us bumbling along before she came.'

'Not to mention she's a dab hand at writing,' Josephine added. 'See these?' She plucked some leaflets from the table. 'They're now highly readable, which they never used to be.'

'And she's been publ—'

Mary slopped her tea. It was all she could think of to do. Dadda would give her a roasting if word of her articles got back to the Kimbers. 'Butterfingers.'

They all leant forward to rescue the books and leaflets. Charlie's fingers brushed hers and she moved her hand away.

'I'll fetch a cloth.' Angela stood up.

Josephine held up a stack of leaflets. 'We don't want these getting spoilt. They're for our next meeting.'

'Oh yes, your meetings,' Charlie said. 'All right if I potter along?' Mary felt his eyes on her. 'Do you attend the meetings as well?'

She nodded, taking the cloth from Angela and mopping up. The door opened and a woman entered. Angela and Josephine excused themselves and went to her.

'Must be getting along.' Charlie downed the last of his drink. 'You make a splendid cup of tea.'

She loaded the tray, aware of him picking up his boater and following her up the room. She dumped the tray beside the sink and heard him say his goodbyes, then the door opened and shut.

She flew after him.

'Mr Kimber!'

He stopped on the stairs, looking up at her with a smile that crinkled his eyes. He started to retrace his steps, but she ran down to meet him, wanting to push him out into the street, wanting to push him all the way back to Ees House.

'Mr Kimber—'

'That's very formal. What do you call Kennett?'

'Bobby.'

'Well, that makes me Charlie if I'm to come to these meetings.'

'I'm Mary Maitland.'

'Pleased to meet you, Mary Maitland – oh. *Maitland*.'

There was nothing else to say. She ran upstairs, catching the glances Josephine and Angela shot her way before they turned back to the new client.

When the woman left, Angela asked, 'What was that about?'

She didn't pretend not to understand. 'My father and Sir Edward Kimber are cousins.' She ignored the raised eyebrows. 'I had to make sure Mr Charlie Kimber knows who I am.'

'You never said you're related to the Kimbers,' said Josephine.

'We don't trade on it.'

'Of course not,' said Angela. Then she exclaimed, 'I know who you are! Wasn't there a scandal years ago? A younger son ran away with a shopkeeper's daughter.'

'That was my grandmother.'

'I say, I do apologise. Rather tasteless to blurt it out like that.'

She lightened her tone. 'You can see why I needed Mr Kimber to know.'

That was the difficult bit over with. No, it wasn't. Now she had to go home and tell Dadda. Oh, crumbs.

But when she and Emma arrived at the gate, the front door was thrown open and Lilian came hurrying out.

'Now you're not to worry,' she said and burst into tears.

Imogen met Nathaniel at the front door, her brow wrinkled with concern. 'She's here. She's—well, she looks rather the worse for wear.'

'Bad journey?' He entered the front room, but the greeting died on his lips as shock clobbered him. 'Evie! What happened?' The doctor in him leapt to the fore. 'Let me see.'

She sprang up and dodged away.

'What happened?' He experienced a surge of horror and protectiveness. 'You look like you've had seven bells knocked out of you.' Suddenly she was his little sister and it was his job to look after her.

Evie touched her face, the left side of which was heavily bruised, the delicate skin stretched to snapping point to accommodate the angry purple and yellow swelling. She parted her lips, but no sound emerged. She shut her eyes, clearly forcing herself to swallow; he swallowed too, as if he could swallow for her.

She ran the tip of her tongue across her lips and said – or rather, croaked – 'Prison.'

Prison: that would be – what? – her fourth time? He recalled the weary *Not again* feeling he had experienced last time, but he had no such feeling now.

'They beat you?'

She shook her head.

'Then how? Was it accidental or on purpose?'

'Bit of both, I suppose.'

'Evie, open your mouth. Let me see.'

She clamped it shut.

'Have you lost a tooth?'

'Two, actually.'

'Your face is battered and you've lost teeth—'

'Could have been worse. Might have been the front ones.'

'How?'

She shrugged. 'They didn't mean to, but I fought back.'

'Fought back? For pity's sake, just tell me.'

'Forcible feeding.' Her eyes dulled. 'They force-fed me.'

The undamaged side of her face went white. He was just in time to catch her as she crumpled into a dead faint.

The hospital building was a colossal structure, with a grand frontage that made Ees House seem plain. How strange that they had made a workhouse look so ornate. That was what the place had been originally. There was talk of changing its name to Withington Hospital. Mary hoped it would be changed. There was something shameful about being in a place that still bore the old name.

People huddled outside the ward, waiting to be admitted. Mary had taken the precaution of bringing Lilian and Emma early, so Lilian perched one of the few wooden chairs. Mary and Emma had given up their seats to a pair of older women with tear-streaked faces and the faded look of the genteel poor.

'I'm sorry to be so weepy,' said Lilian. 'I should be the one looking after you girls.'

'It's the shock,' Mary soothed her.

'It was a shock for you, too, but you've stayed calm. You're a good girl, Mary. I'll be all right now. What about you, Emma? We mustn't weep all over Dadda.'

A bell rang and the ward door opened.

'Maximum of two per bed,' announced the nurse.

'You go first,' said Mary.

As they disappeared, she let her smile drop. Down-to-earth, reliable Lilian had fallen to bits when she heard of the accident. Poor Dadda had tumbled down the stairs at the town hall and broken his leg.

When Lilian and Emma came out, Mary went in. Dadda's face was pale, but he gave her a nod and a smile. She didn't waste her precious few minutes repeating the conversation he must already have had. Besides, small talk wouldn't settle her butterflies.

'I've been thinking, Dadda. With you off work, we'll have to tighten our belts.'

'Charming,' he said drily. 'What happened to "How are you?"'

'How are you?'

'Aching like billy-o, but I'll be better for a good night's sleep.'

'Good. Dadda, can we talk about money?'

He flapped a hand to silence her. 'Keep your voice down.'

'I'm sorry, Dadda, but we must discuss it. You won't get paid while you're off work. I've been thinking—'

'Well, stop. There's no call for you to worry. I've already told your mother. I have savings.'

'I want to help.'

'You and Emma already hand your keep to your mother. That's all you need do.'

'Please listen. I earn less at the agency than I did at the town hall.'

'It's a bit late to realise that.'

She bit back a sharp reply. 'What I realise is that I didn't think twice about taking the job. The lower salary didn't worry me because we're comfortably off, and that's thanks to you.' She held his gaze. 'Now it's my turn. I'll give Mother my writing money.'

'We'll live off our savings.'

'That'd be daft when we don't need to.'

'Calling me daft, are you?'

'Of course not.' She took a moment to ensure her face had a pleasant expression and her voice was quiet. 'It makes sense, when you think about it.'

'Not when I think about it.'

'Dadda, please. I know you don't approve of my writing, but I can help the family. I'm not suggesting I can support us, but I'll spend all my spare time writing and contribute as much as I can. Surely that's preferable to digging into your savings.'

How demeaning it was to beg for permission to do someone a favour. If he climbed off his high horse and agreed, he would be the one conferring the favour on her.

'I'll give it my consideration,' he said.

'Thank you, Dadda.'

Chapter Nine

Arriving at Mr Clough's house, Mary felt the blood coursing through her veins and imagined it carrying words round her body. There was a lot riding on this article. Although she had sold a few pieces, her last two had been rejected, which was a severe blow with the Maitland household hard up.

She had given a couple of friends her rejected work to look at.

'What am I doing wrong?'

Katharine Fordyce looked thoughtful. 'Your other articles had something extra. In the Happy Evenings one, you wrote about special friendships between the different ages. In these, there's nothing extra, if you understand me.'

After the meeting, Katharine took her aside.

'My uncle's an alderman. He knows a fellow who wants to be one and is getting involved in good works to help his cause.

Do you remember my mentioning a clinic? This Mr Clough is involved with that. I'll get Uncle Oswald to arrange an interview.'

So here she was at the home of Barnaby Clough. She was shown into an extravagantly furnished room that said more about money than good taste. Mr Clough was a portly gentleman with protruding eyes. Fat fingers enclosed her hand. She was glad of her glove.

'A lady journalist, eh? Couldn't believe my ears when Alderman Fordyce told me. Still, we must move with the times.'

'I hope my article will be published by the *Manchester Evening News*, though I write for other publications as well.'

'Spreading your favours.'

'Earning a living. I understand you hope to become an alderman.'

'I do what I can for the general benefit. Should the good citizens of our fair city see fit to reward me by . . . well, let's just say I'd be deeply honoured. I've given my support to various projects.' He described them while she took notes. 'But the trouble with this clinic is that it looks less and less likely to open. The Means Test Office has pulled out, as has Projects for the Ignorant Poor, leaving me with egg on my face.'

She kept her expression blank. It was all too easy to imagine golden yolk oozing from the corners of those fleshy lips.

'We can help one another,' said Mr Clough. 'I'll grant you this interview and you can highlight my unfortunate position. People think philanthropy a straightforward matter, that you bestow your money and watch others benefit, but there's the responsibility of choosing causes wisely, choosing viable projects.'

'And this clinic is no longer viable? Why not withdraw your support?'

'Would that it were so simple. I don't want to appear unreliable or . . .'

'Mean?'

'Uncharitable. Doctor Brewer would make certain that was how I appeared. He told me as much in this very room.'

'He didn't!'

'He did. Threatened to expose my lack of charity to the local committees. You may well look shocked. It shocked me deeply.' A smile spread across his podgy face. 'You could highlight the precarious position of the philanthropist who backs a project that turns out to be . . . unfortunate.'

This was exactly what she was looking for. *The Perils of Philanthropy. Local Philanthropist Learns the Hard Way*. But to give her article credibility, she must see the clinic for herself so she could describe its problems first-hand.

Charlie attended the next meeting. Mary tried to keep out of his way, but she couldn't help noticing how genial he was. He was happy to talk and join in, but he could listen too. She found him affable and easy to like – too easy. The poor relation should keep her distance.

But Charlie seemed determined to acknowledge her. She snatched a quiet moment to remind him of their relative positions, but he shrugged.

'I know your family is invited to Ees House every summer, so you can't claim there's no social connection.'

'Once a year, for form's sake, by the kindness of Sir Edward.'

'He's a decent old stick, Uncle Edward.'

'That says it all. To you, he is "Uncle" while to me, he's "Sir Edward".'

'That doesn't mean we can't be friends.'

'I think you'll find it does.'

But she felt a pang. She liked him. He had a way of paying attention to you that made you feel you were the most important person in the room.

At the end of the meeting, he said, 'I'll walk you home.'

'It wouldn't be appropriate. What would Sir Edward say?'

'Uncle Edward is above all else a gentleman. He'd expect me to show courtesy to the daughter of the cousin he holds in high regard.'

Warmth radiated through her. 'He holds Dadda in high regard?'

'Made a point of telling me so.'

After that, it felt churlish to hold out, but the moment they left the building, she regretted it and insisted they part at the corner of her road. What if they were seen? What would the neighbours think? What would her parents think?

Rhetorical questions: she knew precisely what everyone would think.

Nathaniel opened the clinic door for the lady journalist. She started to step inside, then jumped back as the floor poured away with a clicking, scuttling sound and dissolved into the scabby, peeling walls.

She turned on him, flushed with indignation. 'You knew that would happen.' She had caught at the rotten door frame to steady herself; he saw the moment when she realised the woodwork, like the walls, must be widely inhabited and snatched her hand away. 'You should have told me,' she accused.

'Didn't you tell Doctor Cottrell you wanted to experience the place for yourself? Well, now you've experienced the cockroaches. Consider yourself fortunate: we've already had the rat man in.' He motioned with his hand. 'After you – or would you prefer me to go first?'

'I'm not scared of a few creepy-crawlies.'

He followed her in. He had raised his eyebrows at the idea of a lady journalist when Alistair told him about her. He was surprised by how young she was – early twenties – but then, girls these days . . . girls these days, indeed! When had he started thinking like an old fogey? It must be Evie's influence. Poor girl. The forcible feeding had knocked her for six. He hadn't known her crowd was using hunger-strikes as a strategy or he would have gone to London and hauled her home, even if he had to chloroform her.

Had she learnt her lesson? Poor brat, she hadn't had it easy since arriving. As if her swollen face and missing teeth weren't bad enough, he had seen how gingerly she moved. Then, to cap it all, she had gone down with a severe gastric complaint and there was nothing he could prescribe to prevent the violent bouts of vomiting.

Imogen was looking after her as competently as she did everything. She was a good little woman. He couldn't imagine anyone calling Evie that – or this lady journalist either. What was her name? Maitland. She was a pretty girl. How come she hadn't found someone to marry her? He caught the dismay in her face as she took in the dingy corridor with its walls sopping wet in places and the telltale scrabbling behind the wainscot. He saw too that convulsive little movement of her throat as the rotten-egg stench of decay streamed into her nose and mouth.

'You'll be tasting that smell for hours,' he warned her.

'This place is squalid.'

'It is now, but come back when the work is done and see the

difference. Those rooms on the left will be waiting rooms, one for shawlies, one for hat-women; and this will be the office.' He opened a door on the right. 'Picture it. Desks and chairs, cupboards, a noticeboard, a hatch in the wall where people announce themselves.'

Miss Maitland stepped inside. 'Your imagination is conveniently skating over the work that needs doing.'

'I want you to see the place through my eyes.'

'How realistic is that view, Doctor Brewer?'

'What's unrealistic about having office furniture?'

'I refer to the repairs and refurbishment the building requires.'

'If you listen, you'll hear the workmen upstairs.'

'Who is to pay them?'

'Mr Clough, who owns the property, generously offered to have it made good.'

'But other supporters have dropped out, haven't they? The Means Test Department and Projects for the Ignorant Poor?'

'You're well informed, Miss Maitland.'

'A writer needs to be.'

'I didn't know the *Manchester Evening News* was aware those organisations had parted company with us.'

'Oh – well . . .'

He gave her a hard look. 'You are from the *Evening News* – aren't you?'

Dear heaven, she had been rumbled. What an idiot she had been to imagine she could get away with it. Mary forced herself to look Doctor Brewer in the eye. His serious features hardened into unswerving sternness.

'I never claimed to be from the paper. I simply said I hoped they would publish my article.'

'And when Doctor Cottrell misunderstood, you failed to correct him.'

'I have previously been published in the *Evening News*.'

'That's all right, then,' he answered drily. 'That cancels out the lie.'

'I didn't lie—'

'A lie of omission. Come, Miss Maitland, you knew exactly what you were doing. Don't deny it.'

'I wasn't about to.' Did he have to twist the knife? 'Yes, I misled Doctor Cottrell, but it was with the best intentions.' She stopped. The best intentions as far as her article was concerned, but Doctor Brewer wouldn't think so when she denounced him for being foolhardy with his patron's money. 'Thinking I was from the paper, Doctor Cottrell was happy for me to come here.'

'That's all right, then.'

'Is that your only put-down?' she retorted. 'You'll find sarcasm more effective if you use a variety of ways to express it.'

'You're doing yourself no favours by being rude.'

'So when you say it, it's sarcastic and no doubt witty, but when I say it, it's rude.'

She saw his eyes flicker. He wasn't used to people answering back. He said, 'Perhaps it's best if I show you out.'

That brought her to her senses. 'No, wait – please. I'm a good writer; and to be frank, my family needs the money. My father had an accident and he's off work.'

Doctor Brewer regarded her. She returned his gaze earnestly, but it was impossible to tell what he was thinking.

'Let's start afresh, shall we?' he suggested.

'As long as it doesn't involve a repeat performance by the

cockroaches,' she dared to joke and, to her relief, he responded in kind.

'You inveigled your way in and I caught you out with the wildlife, so we're quits. Feel free to ask questions as we go round.'

She took out her pencil, opened her notebook and stuffed her gloves in her pockets: so much easier to write without them. She scribbled:

rat man
c'roaches – floor got up & ran away (a good line: she must use it)
hat-wm & shawlies

As Doctor Brewer showed her round, he described the work the clinic would do.

'Doctor Cottrell and I will work some hours for no remuneration and we hope to encourage other colleagues to donate time too. Nursing staff will be employed, as will someone in the office.'

This was her moment. 'So there'll be paid staff. Who will pay them?'

'They'll be employed by the clinic.'

'Who will foot the bill?'

'Originally, PIP was going to.'

'But now they've dropped out because they don't regard the clinic as viable.'

'No, they dropped out because the means test people have reservations.'

'So the Means Test Office doesn't regard it as viable?'

'No, they stuck their noses in because we're going to offer medical treatment at a reduced rate.'

'So you think you know better than the established system?'

'In this case, yes.'

'Who will subsidise your generosity? Who will pay the nurses' wages? And why do you persist in having work done on this building when these questions have yet to be answered?'

'Who says they've yet to be answered?'

'I do, since you avoid answering them. No one can deny your good intentions—'

'Gracious of you.'

'—but you can't say where the money's coming from. Aren't you taking advantage of Mr Clough by steamrollering on with the building work when there'll be no money to fund your altruistic but, let's face it, wild ideas?'

'Wild ideas?' His eyes glinted, hazel deepening to amber.

All right, she had gone too far, but this wasn't the moment to admit it, not when she had him cornered.

'I should have shown you the door when I realised you'd tricked your way in.'

'Avoiding the question again.'

'Two things, Miss Maitland. First, you'd get more information if you adopted a less forceful manner, and second, I have questions of my own. How do you know about our difference of opinion with the Means Test Office? How do you know PIP pulled out? These things aren't generally known, and I don't imagine you're in Lady Kimber's confidence.'

A chill streamed through her. 'Lady Kimber?'

'Barney Clough sent you, didn't he? As a matter of courtesy, we told him what happened and now he has despatched his tame would-be journalist to visit the clinic as a preliminary to writing a damning piece about this project to prove – to quote you, and I imagine you're quoting him – "it isn't viable".'

Heat tingled up the back of her neck and across her face.

'Turn left onto that corridor, Miss Maitland, and you'll see the front door. Close it behind you.'

When Nathaniel pronounced Evie recovered, she immediately retorted, 'Thank you, O mighty medical man, but I could have worked that out for myself, since I haven't thrown up since yesterday.' After a moment, she added, 'I'm sorry. I don't mean to sound ungrateful. Imogen's an angel.'

He was pleased to have Imogen acknowledged. 'You can get up today, but don't get dressed.'

She didn't argue, which told him how fatigued she was, and no wonder. She hadn't had time to recover from the forcible feeding before succumbing to this bout of sickness. Her bruises had cleared up and the swelling had subsided, returning her face to normal – no, that wasn't right. Her face had hollowed, as if the swelling had reduced but then continued deflating.

Telling Imogen that Evie could come downstairs, he started giving instructions about suitable foods until he caught her patient smile.

'I know what to do,' she said mildly.

'Of course you do. She's in good hands. I've a busy few days ahead.'

'You always have a busy few days ahead.'

That was true. He had never been one for idleness. As well as his regular rounds and surgeries, he must devote more time to the clinic. The infestation of bugs had been seen to and the repairs and renovations were almost done. Now the walls needed plastering and whitewashing, and the gas supply needed reconnecting, as well as a hundred and one fiddly jobs like putting up shelves, oiling hinges and scouring the place from top to bottom and back again. Some jobs, such as fitting locks and sweeping the chimneys, needed specialist tradesmen, but others could be tackled by the unskilled and his idea was to offer work, supervised by an experienced foreman, to local men.

'Then the clinic will feel like it's theirs,' he had said at a meeting at the colonel's house, 'and I hope they'll be happy for their wives to attend our classes.'

He felt cheerful as he went about his business, but the smile dropped off his face when he arrived home to find a postcard from Barney Clough, requesting him to come to his house tomorrow evening to discuss an important matter.

He called on Alistair, who had received a similar summons.

'Surely he can't intend to threaten us with the ill-informed scribblings of that would-be reporter if we don't let him pull out?' said Nathaniel.

'I wish we could let him pull out,' said Alistair, 'preferably helped on his way by a kick in the pants.'

When they arrived at Clough's house, another man was present whom Clough introduced as his legal man, Mr Saunders.

'Pleased to meet you, Doctors,' said Saunders. 'Mr Clough has placed this matter in my hands. I have here papers that require you to have Mr Clough's property finished and ready for use as a clinic by five o'clock on Saturday. Failure to do so will engender Mr Clough's full and final separation from all matters appertaining to your proposed clinic, and any and all agreements previously made appertaining to the use of his property as the premises for said clinic will be nullified.'

Nathaniel glared at Clough. 'You can't do that. I was here in this room when you assured Judge Rawley—'

'Ah yes, the late Judge Rawley,' Saunders cut in. 'I wouldn't attempt to go down that avenue, gentlemen. There is a case to be made that my client made the agreement with the late judge and not with yourselves. Of course, that would be for a court to decide and, for the duration of the proceedings, all works and other matters appertaining to the property in question would cease.'

Nathaniel felt the angry thump of his heart. 'We can't get the work finished that quickly and you know it.'

'Mr Clough knows no such thing,' Saunders replied. 'Given that he is generously footing the bill for all works, it is reasonable that he should specify a cut-off date. Of course, if you wish to state here and now your inability to have the work completed, we can bring matters to an immediate conclusion.'

'Certainly not,' said Alistair. He turned to Clough. 'I appeal to you—'

Saunders interrupted. 'All communication should be directed through me.'

'Very well. Mr Clough has made it clear he wishes to abandon the commitment he made—'

'Come, sir, "abandon" is a strong word.'

'Feel free to substitute a suitably bland one. Mr Clough is in too deep. If he withdraws now, it'll set the project back months.'

'It'll set it back to the beginning,' said Nathaniel. It was a bleak prospect, not least because Clough's self-seeking generosity had provided larger premises than they had been looking for and their plans had expanded accordingly. It would hurt to scale things back.

'Since you've admitted you can't have the building finished and ready by the fixed date,' said Saunders, 'should I take it that you wish to bring the project to a close?'

'No!'

They walked home rather than catching an omnibus, as they needed to talk. They hadn't even got time to feel shocked.

Leaving Alistair at his gate, Nathaniel marched home, his mind whirling with lists and plans.

As soon as he walked in, Imogen appeared on the stairs.

'It's Evie.'

He ran upstairs. Evie was in bed, white-faced, her breathing shallow and rapid. How had this happened so quickly?

'Hurts,' she whispered, 'when I . . . breathe in.'

He felt her forehead. She was burning.

'Fetch my bag,' he told Imogen.

He took Evie's temperature and listened to her chest, having to break off while she coughed and gasped. Catching Imogen's eye, he indicated with a tilt of his chin that she should accompany him onto the landing.

Evie snatched at his fingers. 'No . . . tell me.' She ended on a splutter and a cough.

'Pneumonia,' said Nathaniel.

Hearing Charlie's voice at the door, Mary didn't look round from the sofa where she was waiting for the meeting to start. Then she heard another voice and she did look round: Eleanor. She turned away again. No doubt Eleanor would behave beautifully and acknowledge her, but she mustn't appear to hope for that acknowledgement. Instead she became terribly interested in what Ophelia and Angela were talking about. Then she pictured the toe-curling embarrassment of being on the receiving end of Eleanor's civility in front of everyone else and that brought her to her feet.

She made her way down the room, not surprised when Charlie broke open the little group that he, Eleanor and Josephine made.

'Mary, there you are. I'd like to introduce you.'

'Don't be a chump,' said Eleanor. 'We've met.'

'Of course! The annual jolly. Stupid of me.'

Eleanor turned to Mary with a smile. She was such a pretty girl – more than pretty – beautiful, with eyes the colour of forget-me-nots. The fitted bodice and narrow skirt of her pale-green princess-line dress showed her dainty figure. Her narrow-brimmed hat with its tiny fabric flowers was engagingly simple.

'I'm pleased to see you again,' Eleanor said.

'I hope you enjoy the meeting.'

'Thank you. I'm sure I will. The best families have a tradition of service to the community, but there's more to it these days than broth for the sick and good conduct medals for the orphans.'

Questions rose inside Mary. How do you see your role? Do you think the charity committees will change? But she didn't ask – couldn't. Polite as Eleanor was, she was also cool, as befitted their relationship. This was how rich and poor relations should address one another. Yet how disappointing it was, compared to Charlie's affability.

When Angela came to welcome Eleanor, Mary slipped into the kitchen, but when she emerged with a tray, she was relieved to have it spirited out of her hands by Ophelia. Now she wouldn't have to walk down the room looking like a servant – or was she being oversensitive? Meeting Charlie seemed to have changed the rules.

She was careful to sit away from both Kimbers, though she felt a twinge of annoyance. Was their presence going to spoil her enjoyment?

At the end, while people chatted before leaving, the mention of a clinic caught her attention and she realised Katharine and Eleanor were talking about – not just any clinic, but *the* clinic.

'Yes, I know where you mean,' said Eleanor. 'My mother chairs the Deserving Poor Committee, which has decided to back it. Mummy is keen on education and one of the things the clinic will do is hold classes.'

'That's the clinic my uncle's friend is interested in, isn't it?' Katharine asked Mary.

'Yes.' She felt fluttery. 'Lady Kimber is backing the project?' Doctor Brewer had mentioned Her Ladyship. Now she knew why. 'So the clinic is . . . viable?'

'What a strange question. Of course it is. My mother wouldn't waste committee funds on a project that wasn't worthwhile.'

As people started to leave, Charlie made a point of saying goodbye to her, but he didn't offer to walk her home. Watching him depart with Eleanor, she forced herself not to hang her head in humiliation. Was it her own fault? Had Charlie's affability made her lose sight of her place as poor relation?

Chapter Ten

Pain burst inside Helen Rawley's hip. Her breath caught in a sharp hiss, but she didn't flinch. She froze, letting her heart settle, but that was the only concession she permitted before trying again. This time she got to her feet.

'Bally rheumatics,' she said. It was part of the daily ritual of getting her stiff, old body moving. When she was a girl, her grandfather had kept a parrot. Every morning, when the shawl was lifted from its cage, it would declare in a fractious voice, 'Bally short night.' Every time Helen said 'Bally rheumatics', she remembered that parrot.

That was her now, a game old bird. At least, she hoped she was game. She would need to be with Greg in charge. Her eyes prickled. This was the second time she had been left to an unwilling male relative. It was humiliating.

Robert had called her a chattel. 'The old man left me all his goods and chattels, including Helen here.' He would wave the stem of his pipe in her direction, inviting his dinner companions to enjoy the joke, but beneath the chuckle lay something more, a suggestion of pleasure and power.

Now she had been left to Greg. Robert knew she and Greg had fallen out badly, though he hadn't known why. But it hadn't stopped him linking them inexorably.

'It's right and appropriate,' she imagined him saying. 'Now get on with it.'

Or, losing patience, he might have said, 'If you'd troubled to make yourself agreeable when you were young, you'd have a family of your own to take responsibility for you; but you didn't, so you haven't.'

There had been a touch of malice about Robert. But there was probably a touch of malice about her too, so she shouldn't complain.

She washed and began to dress. She was rising earlier these days to compensate for the extra time she needed now her hip had worsened. She could have ordered breakfast to be put back, but that would have constituted giving in, and she would never do that.

Her day-dress was hanging ready, another of those old black creations Edith had dug out of the attic. But what she wore on top didn't signify, as long as it was tidy and starched. Her undergarments were a different matter. It was her one indulgence, known only to herself and the washerwoman.

Lace whispered against her faded skin as she drew on a chemise of the finest nainsook. The corset's back-laces were already adjusted, so she had only to fasten the pearl buttons up the front, while the ruched ribbon decorating the suspenders brushed her withered thighs. Then came the stockings, pure silk with a flower embroidered on the ankle, and with them a new concern that had clouded her morning ritual for weeks. Her dashed hip was getting worse and bending down hurt like the devil. Was the time coming when she would need help to dress? The indignity! And her elegant underwear would no longer be her precious secret. Would she be forced to face up to what a silly old fool she was?

At the top of the stairs she paused to gird herself for the descent, but today she was able to walk down normally. Sometimes her hip obliged her to descend one step at a time, like a small child.

'Good morning, Edith. Has the post arrived?'

'Yes, madam. It's beside your plate.'

'Perhaps there'll be one from Mr Rawley.' Greg had gone swanning off without a word. Not that she wanted him back, but not knowing was unsettling.

There was one letter, a condolence message from someone she hadn't seen in years. After breakfast, she penned a reply and took it to the pillar box. Being busy was what kept her going. When she returned home, she donned the floppy old straw hat she kept for the garden and scoured the rose beds for plants in need of dead-heading. It didn't take long. That was the trouble. Jobs never took long when you kept on top of them the way she did. She took pride in efficiency but, goodness, there were times when it was hard fending off boredom.

She settled down with the housekeeping book and the weekly bills from the tradesmen. She was quick at arithmetic. Nevertheless, she always did her accounts twice. Had anyone asked, she would have claimed it was her duty to take care with the household money, but really she was spinning out the task to fill time.

The doorbell rang three times in quick succession.

'How rude!' she exclaimed, deciding this person didn't deserve to be shown into her morning room – and that was as far as she got before Greg marched in.

'Aunt Helen, Porter tells me the money has been sorted out. Last year's interest has been set aside to cover this year's bills—'

'Greg – wait – you've just this moment walked through the door.'

'Yes, yes, good morning, how are you, all that tosh. Porter tells me any money left at the end of this year will be ploughed back into the capital to swell the coffers.'

'I believe so. There should be ample to swell the coffers, as you so elegantly express it. Robert made wise investments—'

'That's what I thought. I want you to work out what's needed to keep the place ticking over for a year. I'll be back later.'

And he was gone. Just like that. Her mouth had dropped open – she snapped it shut.

Edith materialised in the doorway. 'Well, madam, it fair teks the wind out of your sails.'

'Please prepare Mr Rawley's room.'

'What should I tell Mrs Burley, madam?'

'That we may be one more at the table or we may not.'

'She won't like it, madam.'

'No, I don't imagine she will.'

Neither did Helen. How dared he behave in such a way?

That afternoon, Edith appeared, in a terrific flap. 'There's a man outside, walking round the house.'

'What sort of man?'

'He's in a suit, but he doesn't look like a gentleman. He's got a notebook and he's writing in it.'

'Come with me.'

'Do you think we should tek the poker in case we need to bash him?'

'Certainly not.'

If only she could put a strong swing in her step. They went round the side of the house and there was the man, looking up at the building. He stepped backwards, still looking, then scribbled something.

'What do you think you're doing?'

'You must be Miss Rawley.' He jiggled his notebook and pencil into one hand to free the other to raise his hat. 'How do you do? Name of Stevens.'

'I repeat, what are you doing?'

'Assessing the house, as per instructions. I'll be indoors presently.'

'You most certainly will not. Leave the premises this instant or I'll send for a policeman.'

'There's no call for that—'

'Edith, go to the gate and look for Constable Vincent. He should be passing this way on his beat any minute now.'

Stevens looked past her. 'Mr Rawley, thank heaven you've come, sir. This lady's been yelling blue murder.'

Greg sauntered up. 'So I heard. No need for reinforcements, Aunt Helen. Stevens is here at my request.'

'To do what?'

'To do as I've asked.'

His expression was genial, but she caught the challenge in his eye. If she said one more word, he would squash her flat.

Pressing her lips together, she returned to the house, Edith clucking beside her.

When Greg appeared, she rounded on him.

'I've been mistress of Jackson's House since before you were born and unless you have a wife I don't know about, I'm still mistress. What is that man doing?'

'Sizing up the place. He's a builder.'

'You're having work done?'

'On the contrary, I want him to make sure that nothing needs doing. Have you got the figures I asked for?'

'What figures?'

'The annual outgoings. Isn't that the kind of information the mistress of the house has at her fingertips? If Stevens says there's no need for repairs, I'll present your figures to Porter and get him to hand over as much of this year's money as you won't need.'

'I don't think—'

'Just get me those accounts. I'm seeing Porter shortly.'

She complied. Presently, Mr Stevens came inside to continue his inspection. He went into every room. She felt angry and horribly vulnerable.

When Greg and Mr Stevens had gone, she did something she had never done before. She knocked on the kitchen door and went in. Edith and Mrs Burley turned drawn faces to her and scrambled to their feet.

'Sit down, please. I was hoping for some tea.'

'Of course, madam,' said Mrs Burley. 'Edith will bring it through in a minute.'

'Actually, I thought I'd sit here and have it with you – if you don't mind. I think we could all do with some.'

There was a silence. She bit the inside of her cheek. Had she offended them?

Mrs Burley said, 'Indeed we could. Sit down, madam, dear. Edith and me'll join you in a jiffy . . . if you're sure.'

'I'm sure,' she said.

Having forced her way in to see Mr Porter by dint of sitting in his clerk's office and refusing to leave in spite of repeated assurances that he wasn't available, Helen stopped in the doorway. She had expected a traditional office in keeping with the great man's dignity. Instead, everything was modern, from the clean lines of the art nouveau chairs to the blue tiles in the fireplace surround and the electric light hanging from the ceiling. Standing on the desk was the house telephone and on a table by the window was a gramophone.

He caught her looking. 'I play music when I'm working, though not, of course, when clients are present. Please be seated. Regarding your visit, I must respectfully insist that you request an appointment in future.'

'And make me wait a week, I suppose? What if my query is urgent?'

'Is it urgent today?'

'First my nephew tries to get his hands on this year's excess funds by bringing in that builder chap—'

'I'm aware of that. I've explained to Mr Rawley that just because the house doesn't require repairs, that doesn't mean he may have the money. If this is the reason for your visit—'

'Kindly let me finish. I'm aware you sent him away with a flea in his ear. Having failed to get money that way, he's now decided to rent out Jackson's House and says I must either move out or stay as housekeeper.'

'Mr Rawley has no power to remove you from Jackson's House.'

'Can he put in tenants?'

Mr Porter frowned. 'There's nothing in the will to prevent it.'

'That's outrageous. And would I have to be their housekeeper?'

'Miss Rawley, please understand. My job is to carry out your late brother's instructions. I can provide clarification regarding the terms of the will, but I won't be drawn into family arguments.'

'Then what's to happen? My brother made no arrangements concerning this eventuality.'

'But he did. He nominated an intermediary. You should speak to Doctor Brewer.'

Mary couldn't tell whether she was more pleased or relieved when she received two letters of acceptance on the same day, one for a *Vera's Voice* article, written with Angela and Josephine's help, about sharing digs with a pal, the other a piece for *The Gentlewoman's World* about managing on a limited budget. By the same post, a lively article about the pleasures of the suburbs she had submitted to the *Manchester Evening News* was returned to her, but with a letter suggesting she try a magazine instead, which provided some consolation.

'I'll take out all the bits that make it specific to hereabouts and send it to *Vera's Voice*,' she told Ophelia.

As she topped and tailed her article, the clinic grumbled away at the back of her mind. When she tried to think up fresh ideas for articles, the clinic material crowded her thoughts. It was a good story, even without the controversy Mr Clough had tried to drum up.

More than anything, she wanted to continue helping her family. Every time she opened her notebook and saw the clinic notes, she felt guilty. She could write a compelling piece, but in all conscience, she couldn't do so without seeking permission.

She had already been to see Mr Clough to tell him she couldn't write the article the way he wanted.

'Why not?' His jowls quivered.

'I've received different information—'

'From Doctor Brewer, I suppose? You're a fool. I'll move up in the world and I could have helped you, invited you to report on official functions. Think on that the next time you're out in the rain, writing up a potato-growing competition.'

She expected an equally narky reception from Doctor Brewer, but so be it. Anyhow, it might not come to that. Last time she had approached Doctor Cottrell, having been furnished with his address by Mr Clough. If she went to him again, there might be no need to venture back inside the clinic.

On Friday evening, she hurried out, but when she reached Doctor Cottrell's, his landlady said he wasn't in.

'He's over at yon clinic. They both are, him and t'other doctor. Hardly sleeping these days, it seems, what with visiting the sick and fettling away at that place.'

Mary made her way there. To her surprise, a couple of scrawny lads were sanding down a wooden table in the street while an old chap with a bent back and knobbly knuckles painstakingly varnished another table. A man up a ladder painted a window frame and, in a splash of sunshine, a group of women sat in a circle on chairs and upturned boxes, hemming bandages.

The door stood open. She stepped inside, catching her breath at the change. Gone were the scabby walls and the gut-churning smell. The floor looked solid and secure – the staircase at the far end boasted a complete set of treads. Two men were hanging a door. A boy held on like grim death to a piece of wood lying across a saw-horse, keeping it steady while a man sawed it in two. The air smelt of wood and whitewash. To her right, a hatch had been set into the wall. Peering through, she saw a chair turned upside down and stacked on top of another. A woman scrubbed the shelves of a tall cupboard while another mopped the floor.

She moved from room to room, phrases and sentences blossoming inside her. A group of men stood back from a chimney breast, looking at it in a way that suggested they had done something remarkable. Among them, shirtsleeves rolled up, collar discarded, face streaked with grime, was Doctor Brewer.

'Thanks, chaps,' he said. 'That's it for today. I've put money behind the bar for everyone to have a couple of pints.'

'Cheers, boss,' and 'See you tomorrow,' said the men, jamming their caps on their heads.

He turned and saw her.

'Oh – it's you. Come to do more of Clough's dirty work?'

He walked past her. It was only when she stopped smiling that she realised that being here, seeing these people working so purposefully, had brought a smile to her face.

She hurried after him. 'I heard how worthwhile the clinic is from Mr Charlie Kimber and Miss Eleanor Kimber.'

He stopped. 'Did you hear that crash?'

She looked round. 'No.'

'Sounded to me like names being dropped. Now if you'll excuse me . . .'

'Wait – please. Let me tell you why I've come.'

'Other than to drop names?'

'What an annoying man you are.'

That got his attention. 'I beg your pardon?'

'I was going to apologise, but—oh, never mind. I want to write a different article, about how you took a derelict building and turned it into a clinic – and I'm so glad I decided to.' Her anxiety about money, the pressure of rushing from one article to the next, had vanished. Here, now, what she felt was the excitement of finding something that cried out to be written. 'All this: it's a transformation. I had no idea it would be like this.'

'You've your friend Mr Clough to thank for it.'

'He isn't my friend—'

'What now?' Doctor Brewer looked in the direction of voices and footsteps. His face brightened. 'Evening, Saunders. Forgive my not shaking hands. As you see . . .' He displayed filthy palms. 'Come to view our progress?'

'Indeed I have.'

This Mr Saunders looked out of place in his smart suit and hat, even though he was the one correctly dressed and Doctor Brewer – well, she had never seen a gentleman looking so casual before. Even when he dug the garden, Dadda looked smarter than this.

'You've made great strides,' said Mr Saunders. 'It's a pity you won't finish on time.'

'Come back tomorrow at five and see.'

'I will indeed return at five o'clock . . . tomorrow morning.'

'What? Five in the morning—'

'You cannot hold my client to blame if you neglected to determine which five o'clock on Saturday was the deadline.'

'That's preposterous.'

'No, Doctor.' Mr Saunders stepped closer. 'It's checkmate.'

Chapter Eleven

Scribbling furiously in her notebook, Mary followed the doctors as they marched round the building, listing jobs.

'I've sent to the pub for our blokes,' said Doctor Brewer, 'but they came here straight from their factory jobs and they're tired. Now we need them to work through the night.'

The men filed back in, looking weary and put out. There were grumbles as Doctor Cottrell explained they must keep working.

Mary seized the chance to pop outside. Over the road, women were chatting. Their clothes were drab, their faces deeply lined. They looked old, or had life wrenched their youth from them? One saw her, which made the others look too. Consciousness of her smart appearance made her skin prickle.

Another woman appeared and rounded up her children. Mary went to her.

'Excuse me. I need someone to run an errand to Chorlton. I'll pay a florin and the fare both ways.'

'Our Eddie could do that.'

She tore a page from her notebook. It was a good job Dadda's leg was in plaster or he would come steaming to Moss Side to drag her home. As it was, he would have to wait until tomorrow morning to play merry hell, by which time she suspected she would be too worn out to care.

Back inside, work had resumed, but the pace of work had slackened. Rounding a corner, she stopped short of bumping into Doctor Brewer.

'Time for you to leave, Miss Maitland.'

'No. I'm going to write about this. Where can I leave my things?'

'You aren't reporting on the local tennis trophy and I can't offer you a locker in the clubhouse. This is serious. If we don't get finished in the next few hours, we'll lose the building.'

He strode away, rolling his shoulders as if they ached and slowly rolling his neck too. His hair had a slight curl.

She left her things in the office cupboard, transferring her purse and house key to her pockets. She went to see what the men were doing – but it would be a tedious night if that was all she did. Besides, wouldn't mucking in add more flavour to her article?

She found the kitchen, where an assortment of used mugs and cups was piled higgledy-piggledy beside the vast sink. No washing-crystals, so a rinse would have to do. There were two kettles and a tea caddy, but only a drop of milk. The sugar bowl needed replenishing. She removed the spoon, found it encrusted with granules and chucked it in the sink.

It didn't take long to find a corner shop. She had brought

a jug for milk and she purchased a few ounces of sugar.

'Are those today's loaves?'

'Aye, Mam bakes 'em. She's a good baker, our Mam.'

'I'll need a pat of butter as well.'

She took her bounty back to the clinic. Soon she had a tray of tea and doorsteps, which ensured she was greeted with smiles as she did the rounds. Even Doctor Brewer gave her a nod, which pleased her, but then she felt annoyed: why should his approval matter?

When she returned the tray to the kitchen, she dumped it on the table. She wasn't going to spend the night chained to the sink. She went in search of Doctor Cottrell.

'Give me a job.'

Armed with a chair and a box of small glass shades, she went from one gas bracket to the next, setting the chair underneath before climbing up to fit a shade. When she reached the last room and commenced her task, Doctor Brewer walked in.

'You needn't check up on me.'

'I'm not. I'm switching the lights on. In case you hadn't noticed, it's dark outside.'

She positioned the final shade. When she turned to climb down, Doctor Brewer offered his hand. In all politeness, she had to accept. She placed her hand in his and her heart thumped. *Be-dum, be-dum, be-dum.* As she stepped down, she looked at him, startled, dazzled, aware of herself as she never had been before, aware of him too and how close he was, how close they were to one another.

He moved round the room, setting the lamps burning. She watched, a breathless, yearning feeling pumping through her. When he left, she hurried after him, her fingers and palm warm from his remembered touch.

Doctor Cottrell appeared, looking serious. 'We won't get finished.'

Doctor Brewer shut his eyes. Then he opened them and his jaw hardened. 'We need more men. We'll send our blokes to wake their friends. It's the only way.'

'Even that might not be enough.'

Inside an hour, the workforce had grown. Everyone was bog-eyed and there was a lot of grumbling. Mary put the kettles on again, taking round strong tea in batches, as there weren't enough mugs. Everyone else might be fighting fatigue, but she was wide awake, senses tingling, wanting to be useful, wanting Doctor Brewer to notice, wanting him to rely on her.

Feeling hopelessly self-conscious, she approached one or two of the men to ask for the doctors' first names. 'For my article,' she said. Was the truth plastered all over her face? But the men didn't know. Finally, she asked Doctor Cottrell.

'I'm Alistair, he's Nathaniel.'

Nathaniel! Doctor Nathaniel Brewer.

The night dragged on, feeling at once long and heavy, and far too fleeting. She swept up, producing clouds of grimy dust that settled on her clothes and skin. Some of her hair came loose and she batted it aside.

When she saw Doctor Brewer – Nathaniel – sitting on the stairs, just sitting there, elbows on knees and hands dangling, slumped forwards, head bowed, she went to sit beside him. Her heart overflowed at seeing him dejected.

'We aren't going to do it,' he said. 'The men are exhausted. Some have gone home.'

'Talk to them. Make them want to stay.'

'Want to?' He almost laughed. 'I'm so tired I can barely think. I don't blame them for wanting their beds.'

'Well, I suggest you don't say any of that.'

She got up and walked away. She ached to stay with him, but he should be alone to sort out his thoughts.

Soon word went round for everyone to assemble in one of the waiting rooms. Mary's skin tingled with anticipation as Nathaniel walked in and stood on a box at the front. The men fell silent as he looked round at them.

'I'm a cross-country runner. I'm a member of a club and we run competitively against other teams. When you're running, you have to pace yourself, but even so there comes a point when it's almost unbearably hard to continue. When that happens, I look round the field at my fellow runners. The sight of them reminds me that we're a team and I don't want to let them down. I remember the training we did, the work that went into preparing for this event, and I picture the sense of achievement that comes when all our runners have crossed the line. Win or lose, there's always camaraderie among the team members, because we know we've done our best.'

He took his time looking round at the exhausted men.

'I look round today – tonight – and I see a fine group of men whom I'd never have met if it hadn't been for this project. I'm thinking of the commitment and the darned hard graft that has got us this far. I'm thinking of the people in this community whose lives will be changed for the better when we've achieved what we set out to do, and I'm thinking of the pride we'll all feel at knowing we made that happen.'

Silence, then a smattering of applause. Men squared their shoulders and stood taller. Some of them spoke and instead of grumbling, they sounded alert and determined.

'Come on, lads, back to it,' one of them said and the room

emptied, the men who had slouched in a while ago pushing forward to return to work.

Mary dashed to find her notebook and wrote at top speed, her heart bursting with pride at being part of this remarkable night.

Later, she couldn't resist – be honest, didn't try to resist – seeking him out.

'One hour to go,' Nathaniel said. 'Saunders wants the place finished and ready by five and we're going to do it.'

She beamed at him, but he was already working again. She went in search of a job, but something niggled at her mind. Finished: that meant repairs and decorating, obviously. But what did 'ready' mean?

She raced back to Nathaniel, who was eyeing a spirit level.

'What does "ready" mean?'

'Just a minute.'

'No – now.' She pulled his arm. Beneath the creased cotton, his muscle was taut. 'The work will be finished, but what if the clinic needs to look ready too?'

He frowned. 'It will look ready with all the work done.'

'It'll look finished, but if Mr Clough doesn't want you to have this building, his man might claim it isn't ready if it's dirty and unfurnished.'

He stared at her. 'What time is it? We'll never—'

'Yes, we will. If we wake up the street, the women can clean and we can borrow furniture. We need tables and chairs, a few cupboards if we can get them. It doesn't have to be perfect, just clean and habitable.'

Soon the clinic was alive with people. Women marched in with mops and buckets. A stream of furniture followed, shabby and rickety, but that didn't matter. Someone brought a hatstand

and an old man came wheezing in with a clock under his arm.

'I'll put this on't shelf and no one's to touch it. This is th'only clock our road has.'

At quarter to five, there was a scramble to tidy up, then the helpers stood outside, with the doctors in the doorway. Mary eased her way through until she was near the front door.

A motor car turned into the road and came to a stop. Mr Saunders got out, as did another fellow, a working man, to judge by his clothes, carrying a cloth bag. He was followed by a police constable, who set his helmet on and straightened his tunic before accompanying them to the door.

Mr Saunders spoke clearly. 'I am the legal representative of the owner of this building. I'm here to determine whether the place is finished and ready. If it isn't, Mr Phelps here will change the locks. Constable Todd will deal with anyone who causes trouble.'

'Come right in, Saunders,' said Alistair. 'You might as well put your bag in the motor, Phelps. Your services won't be needed.'

'We'll see about that,' snapped Mr Saunders and marched inside, followed by the doctors.

A few minutes later, he stalked out and threw himself into the motor. It was only the fact that the starter-handle needed turning that prevented him from roaring away without his companions.

The crowd cheered as he drove away, then everyone was shaking hands and clapping one another's backs. The doctors pumped the hands of those nearest. Mary edged closer, but as she presented herself in front of Nathaniel, he turned away, his face clouded.

'I'd better—'

'Yes, go,' said Alistair. He caught Mary watching Nathaniel

slip away from her. 'His sister is poorly. His wife is caring for her.'

His wife.

She expected her heart to deliver an almighty clout. Instead it went utterly still.

'I was about to send for an ambulance,' said Imogen. 'I kept checking her fingernails and toenails to see if they'd gone blue, but none of the symptoms you told me to watch for has happened – yet look at her.'

Fear washed through Nathaniel. Evie's skin was colourless but damp, her rapid pulse weak and fluttery, her blood pressure so low it barely registered.

'She's in shock, but there's no reason why pneumonia would cause that.'

He checked her symptoms again. Then he straightened up and forced himself to think. Evie was in shock, therefore either she had pneumonia plus another complaint that had caused shock, or else the pneumonia wasn't pneumonia at all.

The instant he accepted that, an ice-cold feeling ran through him.

'She must go to hospital immediately.'

Poor Evie, poor brat. What a vile thing to happen. There was a strong possibility the forcible feeding had caused this – but now wasn't the moment to get hot under the collar.

He only hoped it wasn't too late.

Just hours ago, Mary had felt too thrilled to be tired. Now, it was being stunned by disappointment that held fatigue at bay, the glittering hope of attraction replaced by a resounding emptiness. He was married. If only she had known beforehand, so that – so that what? Would it have made any difference? It was the touch of his hand that had sparked the reaction in her.

Bloody married men. They should keep their hands to themselves.

A stinging sparkle edged her vision and she blinked away tears. She had accepted what she was sure must have been a sound ticking-off from Dadda, only it had gone over her head. And now, here she was in the office, where Angela and Josephine, having discovered why she looked tired, had insisted upon her writing her article.

'Then you must deliver it,' said Josephine. 'They'll snap it up. You won't catch the first edition, but it'll get into a later one.'

It was a good job she had written detailed notes, because her brain wasn't working. Her pencil had flown across the pages last night, flinging down every detail. Her heart had flown too. How jubilant she had felt when Nathaniel had inspired the men to return to work with proud hearts. He had made her feel proud too, not just because his words had stirred everyone, but because of the personal delight she took in his achievement – as if she were entitled to be proud of him. She had stood there, smiling her head off, as if – as if there was something between them.

A mug of tea appeared beside her. 'How's it going?' asked Josephine.

She just wanted to get the damn thing finished. 'Actually, I wrote so many notes that I can type it up without writing it long-hand first.'

'I'd better take this away, then, so you can concentrate.'

She pretended to remove the mug; Mary made a play of hanging onto it.

'That looks a good game. Can anyone join in?' It was Charlie, his handsome face breaking into its ready smile. 'If we're picking teams, I'll be on Mary's.'

Josephine shooed him away. 'She's working to a deadline.'

Mary pulled the typewriting machine closer and fed in two sheets with carbon paper between. Last night, in her keenness, she had scribbled the opening sentences and once she had typewritten these, the rest followed without difficulty. She dashed off a covering letter.

'All done?' came Charlie's voice. 'Your chariot awaits. I've got the motor. I'll run you into town.'

'There's no need.'

'Yes, there is. It's not often I get the chance to do something useful. Which one's yours?' Charlie went to the hatstand. 'This one.' He took Angela's cartwheel.

The others laughed, Mary planted a smile on her face. The sooner this article reached the newspaper office, the sooner she could put last night and Nathaniel Brewer and that idiotic attraction behind her.

Nathaniel arrived home to find Imogen waiting, her face drawn with fatigue.

'She's going to recover,' he said.

'Thank goodness.' She sank onto a seat. 'Was it what you suspected?' She shivered. 'It doesn't bear thinking about.'

'It's rare. I've never seen it before, just read about it.' And thank goodness he had or Evie would be dead now.

'Might it have been the forcible feeding?'

He felt a flame of anger. 'Presumably. They could have torn her gullet when they stuffed that tube down her throat – but then again, it might have been all that violent vomiting that tore it while she had the gastric upset. Either way, each time she vomited, some of it spilt through the hole into her chest cavity.' He scrubbed his face with his hands. 'Any messages?'

She gave him an envelope with his name written in a bold hand.

'Miss Rawley.' He knew her writing from when her brother had been ill. 'I wonder what she wants.'

She wanted to see him, the brevity of her message suggesting she expected him to drop everything. Somebody ought to tell her that a bit of 'please' and 'thank you' and 'would you kindly' went a long way towards getting people to do your bidding.

'You aren't her doctor,' said Imogen.

'Since I was in and out of Jackson's House so regularly, she probably feels I'm hers to command, and never mind that Slater is back on his feet now. I'll call on her, but it'll be for the last time.'

And he wouldn't go until he had fulfilled his other commitments.

It was late afternoon when he arrived at Jackson's House.

'Miss Rawley,' he said a few minutes later, 'I thought you sent for me in my professional capacity.'

'Were I indisposed, which I never am, I'd summon Doctor Slater.'

'Had I known the nature of your problem, I'd have referred you to Mr Porter.'

'A fat lot of good that would have done. He's the one who referred me to you. My brother named you as arbiter of disputes. Well, there's a dispute for you to sort out. My nephew intends putting tenants in and says I must leave or stay on as housekeeper. Housekeeper, I ask you! What are you going to do about it?'

'What does Mr Porter say?'

'Hang Mr Porter.'

'Has he given an opinion?'

'The will doesn't state that the house may not be rented out.'

'But aren't you entitled to live here for the rest of your life?'

'I can presumably do that as housekeeper.'

'I see,' he said.

'Is that the best you can do? My nephew wants to bully me into quitting my home. Mr Porter couldn't get me out of his office fast enough. And you don't seem eager to ride to the rescue.'

'I don't see what you expect me to do.'

'Speak to my nephew, of course.'

'If Mr Rawley won't listen to you, he's unlikely to listen to me.'

Helen Rawley's eyes blazed; Nathaniel imagined those eyes in a younger, stronger body. He knew what was coming next. She would blast him to kingdom come and in two minutes flat, he would be marching out of the front gate with his ears burning.

Instead, she crumpled and he was unmanned. The thin shoulders sagged, even her face sagged, and his heart turned to putty.

'Please, Doctor Brewer,' she said, so softly her words barely travelled. 'Won't you please help me?'

Chapter Twelve

Greg strode home across the meadows. Home? That was a laugh. Jackson's House would never be home. Helen was vexed with him, to put it mildly, though she couldn't deny his right to dump his portmanteaux in the hall and order that middle-aged frump with the ridiculous frilly cap to take them upstairs. Helen had tried to fob him off with his old room, but he hadn't stood for that.

'I'd prefer Uncle Robert's room.' His tone had been one of intent, not request. 'The master bedroom.'

'It's not ready, sir,' the frump said.

'Then make it ready.'

The master bedroom for the master of the house. Not that he had any desire to be its master. All he wanted was to sell up. It was tempting to fling that in Helen's face, but he had held his tongue. He knew the value of keeping information close to his chest. It hadn't occurred to her that his plan to put in tenants stemmed from being strapped for cash.

His uncle and aunt had never had any notion of his financial ups and downs. As far as they were concerned, he had used his inheritance from his father wisely enough to remain independent – and he had ensured they never had cause to doubt that opinion. He wasn't having old Robert questioning his suitability as heir to Jackson's House and the money bags. Indeed, the prospect of his inheritance had been such a sure thing that he had been able to borrow on the strength of it, which now left him well and truly up a gum tree.

It was a damn nuisance not being able to get his hands on the money that was certain to be left over from this year's interest. Still, he couldn't see there being any objections to his renting out the house – well, plenty of objections from Helen, but none based on the wording of the will. He was coming round to the idea of being a landlord. Not as satisfying, or as instantly lucrative, as selling, but it would provide a steady income and there was something to be said for that.

Letting himself in through the gate in the back hedge, he walked round to the front of the house. A carriage waited on the lane and his heart beat a little tattoo. He couldn't see from here if there was a coat-of-arms on the door. Helen was out for the afternoon, so it wasn't a friend of hers. If it was who he hoped it was, it most certainly wasn't a friend of hers. He grinned at the thought of her splutters of outrage when she returned to find the two of them together.

He rang the bell, a quick dash of a ring, wishing he had brought his key, but he hadn't bothered because he liked keeping

Helen's servants on their toes. Two old maids – in both senses, even if one did call herself 'Mrs'.

The eyesore in the frilled cap opened the door.

'Mr Rawley, you have a visitor.' But even as his heart bumped madly, she was already saying, 'He said he was a friend of yours. I knew you'd be back before long, so I let him wait. He was . . .'

'Insistent?' He thrust his hat and cane at the stupid female. Who was it? A London acquaintance, obviously.

'Ever so polite, sir, but yes, you could say he was insistent. I put him in the morning room.'

He opened the door – onto an empty room. No, not empty – there was that vile smell and a smoke ring was rising from the wing chair that stood with its back to the door.

'Please come in, Mr Rawley. Dear me, I sound like the master of the house. It's a handsome place you have here, if I may say so.'

He stalked into the room, indignation replacing shock. His hands twitched towards the chair, wanting to tip it over backwards, preferably delivering Mr Jonas a knockout blow in the process.

'Hardly polite to turn up uninvited,' he remarked.

'Surely not, between old friends such as ourselves.'

'I've told you before. You'll get your money.'

'Indeed I shall.'

'I had a go at getting cash from the estate, but the family lawyer won't play ball.' He kept his voice casual. 'I'm looking into putting tenants in.'

'So I gather.'

'How can you possibly know that?'

'I like to protect my interests. But I have to tell you, Mr Rawley, it won't do. I don't want repaying over a period of years.

It works to your benefit as well. The longer the debt lasts, the more the interest grows.' Mr Jonas waggled a finger at him. 'I know what you gentlemen are like. You take the loan readily enough, then you cut up rough over the interest, as if it's the greatest surprise of your life.'

'The rent on this place is the best deal you'll get from me.'

'What sort of manner is that for addressing an old acquaintance? Hardly courteous, if I may say so.'

He shrugged. 'Take it or leave it.'

A sharp silence was broken by the ringing of the doorbell.

'My, you are popular this afternoon,' said Mr Jonas.

There was a knock and the frump appeared. 'Doctor Brewer to see you, sir.'

'Who? Oh, him. What the hell—heck does he want? Get rid of him – what's your name?'

'Edith, sir.'

'Tell him to sling his hook, Edith.'

She pulled her lips into a tight little circle like a cat's rear end. 'I'll say you're engaged, sir,' she replied primly and departed.

'Brewer,' Mr Jonas murmured. 'Ah, yes, the man nominated by your late uncle to see fair play. Don't tell me he's locked horns with you over this renting business?'

'I've no idea.'

'No matter. I told you, renting the house won't cut it.'

'And I told you,' he replied, his voice loaded with mock patience, 'take it or leave it.'

'You're not listening to me, Mr Rawley. People don't, sometimes. Not that I let it worry me. They all listen in the end, and you will too. And now, my dear fellow, I must love you and leave you.'

Greg was glad to see the back of him. His facial muscles ached from maintaining an affable expression; his shoulders were rock hard with loathing. Aunt Helen didn't keep so much as a decanter of sherry in her morning room. He jangled the bell.

'Fetch the Scotch,' he ordered the frump – Edith. He must remember her name or he would call her 'Frump' to her face.

When she brought it, he sloshed a couple of fingers into the glass and knocked back a mouthful.

'Hey, come back!' he yelled after her. 'Is this what my uncle used to drink?'

'I don't believe he drank Scotch, sir. We never had it in the house before you came.'

'This isn't the single malt I told my aunt to get.'

'I think she may have ordered something less costly, sir.'

'Less costly? Well, here's what I think of less costly. Tip it down the drain.'

'But, sir—'

His look silenced her. Darting forward as though he were a wild animal, she grabbed the tray and made her escape.

'Bloody females,' he muttered.

No wonder there was due to be so much left in the coffers at the end of the year if Helen scrimped on the bills. Well, she could do whatever the hell she chose regarding everything else, but he wasn't compromising on anything involving grain or grape. In fact, he would go out this minute and rectify the situation. Slapping a couple of bottles of his favourite malt, and a few of claret and hock onto the Jackson's House account would be recompense for having to put up with Jonas – and for not seeing the person he had hoped to see. Any that he didn't drink while he was here, he would take with him when he moved on, which couldn't come soon enough.

He neither knew nor cared where the Jackson's House liquor came from. He made a beeline for the smartest place he could find.

'Jackson's House? Certainly, sir,' said the wine merchant. 'We'll be proud to have the Rawley account.'

Helen would lay an egg when the bill came.

It was early, but he went home and togged himself up before heading into town. The Rawley name had secured him guest membership at not Uncle Robert's club, which was for old fogeys, but at the club inhabited by the old fogeys' reprobate sons. An early meal was followed by a game of cards. Gambling wasn't allowed, but there were a couple of rooms upstairs where the doors were shut and blind eyes were turned, and in one of these he passed a few hours, with an agreeable outcome.

Returning to Jackson's House, he opened the gate and walked in, turning to shut it behind him. In that moment there was . . . something, and he didn't know whether he heard or sensed it, but before he could react, they were on him, two of them – three of them. His knees folded, he huffed a great gasp as his ribs took one kick, then another. He held onto his cane, managed to get both hands round it, tried to swing, tried to get one of the bastards, but it was wrenched from his grasp. His empty hands flailed in the air after it, trying to wrest it back.

It bloody hurt being bashed with that cane. It bloody hurt.

Nathaniel came awake to an insistent rat-tat-tatting of the knocker. He shoved aside the bedclothes and stumbled to the window, throwing up the sash to lean out.

'Stop your noise. I'm here.'

'Doctor Brewer, sir? It's Wally Brown from Hardy Farm. I've been sent to fetch you urgent.'

'Wait there.'

Imogen began to roll out of bed. He put his hand on her shoulder.

'Sleep. Doctor's orders. You were up all last night with Evie.'

'So were you.'

'All the more reason for one of us to get a good night tonight.'

He threw on his suit, not bothering with the waistcoat, and laced his boots. Downstairs, he snatched up his bag and clapped his trilby on. The boy had come in a cart. He stood by the pony's head, stroking its neck.

Wally eyed him doubtfully. 'You sure you're Doctor Brewer? Only you don't look like a proper doctor.'

'I look like one who's been hauled out of bed in the middle of the night.' He climbed up and the boy followed suit. 'What's happened?'

'Dunno, sir. I were just sent to fetch you.'

'You must have some idea. Who's ill?'

'I'm not here for the farm, sir. I'm here for next door – Jackson's House. Their Edith came haring round in a reet frap and woke the household with her hammering. Then missus sent me for you. That's all I know.'

An emergency at Jackson's House? Had Miss Rawley been taken ill? Edith, used to his attendance on her late master, would understandably have sent for him with never a thought for Doctor Slater.

Wally dropped him at Jackson's House, then peeled off towards Hardy Farm. Nathaniel strode up the path. The door opened before he got there. Edith appeared, swathed in a vast shawl over a long-sleeved, high-necked nightgown, wisps of hair escaping from a plait.

'Madam says to go straight up. The late master's room, sir.'

He ran upstairs. It gave him an odd feeling to approach the

same old door. As ever, he opened it softly. As ever, Helen Rawley stood beside the bed.

She turned, her faded eyebrows climbing in a clear expression of surprise and displeasure. 'Doctor Brewer,' she said in her driest voice, 'you look very . . . workmanlike.'

'If you'd have more confidence in a doctor who spends time on frock coats and gold studs in the middle of the night, I can give Doctor Slater a knock on my way home. What are the symptoms? Ah.'

'Indeed,' said Miss Rawley. 'Ah.' She looked grey all of a sudden, a sickly grey in contrast to the dove-grey of her dressing gown.

He looked at Mrs Burley, hovering on the far side of the bed. 'Take the bowl and cloths away, and bring fresh. Warm water, not hot.'

He scrutinised his patient's condition as he spoke. It didn't take a doctor to see Greg Rawley had received a sound beating. One eye was swollen shut, his nose and mouth were bloodied, his moustache encrusted. Bruises were forming on his knuckles.

'I need to get him undressed to see what other damage there is.'

'A lot, I fear,' said Miss Rawley, 'judging by the gasps and groans as we got him upstairs. He passed out at one point. How we didn't end up all rolling down into the hall, I can't imagine.'

'You'd have done better to lie him on a sofa.' He leant over Rawley. 'Can you hear me? Good. I'm going to cut your clothes away.'

Rawley slurred something unintelligible that Nathaniel was sure included a fruity curse, then he tried to push himself up, only to collapse back with a groan. Beneath the bruising, his face was colourless.

'What can I do?' Miss Rawley asked. Nathaniel remembered her backbone.

'Make yourself scarce while I examine him. I'll see you downstairs.'

Soon he was fingering the tender marks on Rawley's torso, feeling his way carefully over the ribcage.

'Someone had a go at making mincemeat of you. Who was it?'

'Just do your job.'

'I'll give you something to help you sleep. There's no permanent damage, but you'll be laid up for a while. Lucky for you, your aunt's a competent nurse.'

Rawley muttered something, but Nathaniel didn't trouble to decipher it. Going downstairs, he looked into the morning room, finding it empty.

'Through here, Doctor,' came Miss Rawley's voice from the kitchen door.

Mrs Burley and Edith were sitting at a big table in the middle of the flagged floor. They jumped up as their mistress ushered him in. Mrs Burley moved hastily to close the scullery door, as if the sink weren't fit to be seen, though if it was in the same scrubbed state as the rest of the kitchen, it certainly was.

Noting the three cups and saucers on the table, he said frankly to Miss Rawley, 'I'm surprised to find you supping tea here.'

'There are times when you find out who your friends are. And if it's good enough for me, I'm sure it's suitable for a doctor minus his frock coat.' She waved him into a chair. 'How is he?'

'He's received a sound beating, but there's nothing broken. What do you know about it?'

'Nothing. We discovered him in a heap on the doorstep after he managed to get that far and use his cane to knock.'

'I noticed he still had his hunter and his pocketbook, and a rather swish cigarette case fell out of his pocket, so that suggests it wasn't robbery.'

'That cane is worth a pretty penny, an' all,' Mrs Burley added.

'Should I send for the police?' said Miss Rawley.

'No point right now. He's out for the count. And something tells me he won't let you in the morning.' He drained his cup. 'I'll be on my way.'

'You two get to bed,' Miss Rawley ordered the servants. 'I'll see the doctor out.' She led the way to the hall. 'You'll come tomorrow morning?'

'Tomorrow afternoon.' Tomorrow morning was for Evie.

'A word before you go.' She went towards the study. 'The morning room is out of bounds at present. My nephew had a visitor who stank the place out with his cigarettes. How did you fare with him? I put up with Lady Harrington's company for two hours to give you ample time.'

'I didn't get through the front door. Edith said Rawley had a visitor, though I wondered if he said that to fob me off. I half thought I ought to barge in and confront him. Good job I didn't.'

'I wish you had. He needs to be told he can't rent out Jackson's House.'

'I think you have an exaggerated idea of what I might achieve.'

'You won't achieve anything if you don't speak to him.'

'Miss Rawley, I didn't ask to be put in your brother's will.'

'You should be flattered.'

'Frankly, I'm not. I'm a busy man and your quarrel—'

'This is my future we're talking about.'

'I appreciate that.'

'But you're a busy man and you don't give two hoots.'

'I didn't say that.'

'You didn't need to.'

'I'd better leave. We're both tired—'

'I'm not,' Miss Rawley retorted. 'I'm wide awake.'

'I don't propose to argue the point,' he said. 'I'll bid you goodnight.'

'Wait. There's . . . there's something you can do for me.'

She paused for such a long time that he grew impatient.

'Well, Miss Rawley?'

'I . . . I was hoping that . . . well, that we might be friends.'

Not for the first time in Helen Rawley's company, he felt stumped. 'Surely you've got friends. What about those people at the funeral?'

'My brother's acquaintances, not mine. The two dear friends I grew up with both died last year. That's the trouble with getting old. Everyone you know falls off the twig and before you know it, there's no one left. Well, I've decided I won't stand for it, so I'm asking you to be my friend. I admired the way you looked after my brother, not just the medical side, but how you dealt with him as a person, the way you talked to him, sensible and direct but compassionate too. You gave him confidence. He was terrified, you know, simply terrified of dying. But you helped him find dignity and strength and I'll be grateful to you for that for the rest of my days.'

'Miss Rawley, if this is a way of manipulating me into taking your side—'

'I'm an old woman. I've outlived my friends; I've outlived my brother. He and I didn't always get along, but my position was secure. Now it's not.'

'Porter said the will is watertight.'

'Security isn't derived simply from having a roof over one's head.' She made a fist and struck her chest. 'It's in here. It's a feeling. God knows, I hated my brother at times, but I never once felt vulnerable. Ever since the reading of the will, I've been apprehensive. First my nephew found that builder fellow, now he wants to rent out the place. The will may be watertight, but he feels no obligation.'

Nathaniel said gently, 'The best friend you could have is Mr Porter.'

'I don't need legal protection. I have that, in so far as it goes, from the will. I want a friend, a real friend, and . . . I've chosen you.'

'You've chosen me?' Did she think this was how friendships were formed?

'You're an excellent doctor and you have a social conscience.'

'Are you trying to prick that conscience?'

She sighed. She looked tired and tetchy. 'Go home, Doctor Brewer. It's clear my offer is unwelcome.'

Lady Kimber waited as the coachman approached the Maitlands' front door. Moments later, he returned to open the carriage door and she descended, her features arranged in a pleasant expression. Good manners at all times, even when you were steaming with rage. There they stood, her husband's relations, having tumbled through the front door, John Maitland on crutches, one trouser-leg taut over a plaster cast, the wife in plain garb suitable for household duties.

'Your Ladyship,' said John Maitland. 'This is an unexpected pleasure. May I invite you inside?'

'Thank you.'

Lilian Maitland made an awkward movement, as if uncertain whether to curtsey. Lady Kimber stopped in the hall. Crutches tapping, John Maitland squeezed round to guide her.

'This way, please.'

She swanned into the front room. It was bigger than she had expected. Pristine too. No newspaper hastily flung aside, no mending on the go. Kept for best and hardly used: that was the lower classes for you.

She seated herself.

'May I offer refreshment, Your Ladyship?' Lilian Maitland asked. 'Tea, perhaps, or I make rather good fruit cordial, if I do say so myself.'

'I'm sure your cordial is delicious.'

She did the almost-curtsey again, then dived into the sideboard to retrieve what was presumably the best glassware. John Maitland lowered himself into a chair. The jacket, which had hung open moments before, was now buttoned. When his wife returned with a tray, she was wearing a fresh blouse.

She poured and Lady Kimber took a sip.

'This is very good.'

'Thank you, Your Ladyship.'

'To what do we owe this honour?' John Maitland asked.

She set down her glass. 'I'm here on an unpleasant errand. It has been brought to my attention that your daughter has become friendly with my nephew.'

'I know they met at the agency where Mary works,' said John Maitland. 'As to being friendly, she knows her place.'

'And her place is not in Sir Edward's landaulet.' Seeing their baffled expressions, she said, 'She was seen in my husband's motor car with my nephew.'

Oh, the indignity of being asked by one of her committee ladies who the girl was! But worse was to come when she had asked Charlie. Mary Maitland, poor relation, granddaughter of that frightful creature who had ensnared Martin Kimber years ago.

'There must be a mistake,' said Lilian Maitland. 'Begging Your Ladyship's pardon.'

'There is no mistake. My nephew informs me he drove your daughter to the newspaper offices to deliver an article she had written.'

John Maitland looked profoundly uncomfortable, as well he might. 'It's true that she has been doing some writing.'

'I'm not interested in the writing, Mr Maitland.'

Actually, she had read the article in question with great interest since it concerned the clinic, and had found it well written and informative. It had another quality too, something compelling in the style that made you want to read on. It had been a shock to learn later from Charlie who F. Randall was.

'I'm here because of this undesirable friendship. It must be nipped in the bud.'

'She'll have to stop going to the meetings.'

'She'll have to do more than that, since my nephew has taken to dropping in at the agency during the day.'

John Maitland hesitated. 'Could he be asked to stay away?'

'Don't be absurd. He and my daughter will benefit from an association with the agency people and their interest in social reform. Ultimately, the local community will gain.'

'I'm sure Mary—'

'At the very least, she has overstepped the mark. At worst . . . well, it wouldn't be the first time someone in your family has set their sights on a grand alliance.'

Silence rolled round the room, heavy with old shame.

'Mary is a fine young woman,' said John Maitland. 'She would never—'

'You must send her away for a spell.'

'She has her job to consider.'

'She has her duty to consider – as have you. If you have nowhere to send her, I'll make the necessary arrangements.'

'You must understand, Your Ladyship, this is a lot to take in. I have to think about it, and I'll want to hear what Mary has to say.'

'Nothing she says can be of any consequence unless she sees fit to apologise.'

She came to her feet and John Maitland made a grab for his crutches. There was no point in remaining. She knew her next move.

Chapter Thirteen

Mary walked into the office to find Angela and Josephine, early for once, looking strained. They sat her down.

'We're terribly sorry. It's bad news,' said Josephine.

'Yesterday evening, the rent man called on us at home. He told us that if we continue to employ you, it'll jeopardise our tenancy. So we must ask you to leave.'

Mary stared in disbelief. Seeing her friends' distress, she fought to overcome her shock.

'At least I'm in the right place to find another job.'

But she saw the look that passed between them and a sick feeling uncoiled in her stomach.

'We've been told—' began Josephine. 'God, this is frightful. You can't have any job on our books.'

Suddenly Mary was weeping. 'I'm sorry. It's the shock.' She

mopped her face. 'I'm on a fortnight's notice, so there's time to get sorted.' Her forced cheerfulness disintegrated as she intercepted another look. 'Don't tell me. You want me out today.'

'We don't want it,' Angela cried, 'but we can't afford to lose this place. It's not every landlord who'd tolerate what we do.'

'Well,' she said, amazed by how calm she could sound, 'do I work out my final day or must I leave immediately?'

'Maybe she should go away,' said Lilian. 'I'd rather we organised it than Lady Kimber.'

'It doesn't matter what anyone organises,' said Mary. 'I'm not going. I'll stay and find another job.'

'How easy do you think that'll be?' asked Dadda. 'I must say, Mary, I never thought you'd bring disgrace on us.'

'I never imagined accepting a ride would bring such consequences.'

'Rubbish! You've lived your whole life surrounded by the consequences of what Granny did.'

Mary started applying for jobs in the *Evening News*. Angela and Josephine had written a dazzling reference and she still had Mr Treadgold's, which, though grudging, listed her qualities and experience. She spent long days beside Lilian, cooking, cleaning, shopping. Knuckling under at home was, in some obscure way, frightening. She was aware of submitting all the time and having no say. What if she failed to find another job? What if her life had snapped shut for ever?

Mixing bath salts and buffing up the fireplace tiles with velvet provided too much thinking time. Well, she must put it to good use. She compiled some household hints and submitted them to *Vera's Voice* and *The Gentlewoman's World*.

They wouldn't earn much, though. She needed to write articles.

What about one giving advice on writing job applications? It was worth a try. And an article based on her experience of changing from clerk to homebody. The words poured from the pen, rejuvenating her. She sent off the article to Mrs Newbold and was stunned to have it returned along with a brief letter informing her that it was *unlikely to appeal to our readership, which is made up largely of housewives.*

Her wonderful article – rejected. She hugged her hurt to herself. There was no one she could tell. She could have shared her disappointment at the agency, but not at home.

What was wrong with it? She had added an extra dimension by using her personal experience. Her agency friends would have appreciated it, she felt sure.

Unlikely to appeal to housewives.

Housewives wouldn't want to read about her frustration. If they shared it, they wouldn't like having it underlined – and if they loved their roles, they wouldn't think much of a girl who baulked at conforming. She had alienated her audience. Would Mrs Newbold give her another chance? She rewrote her article, this time assuming the voice of a middle-aged woman.

A young friend came to me for guidance recently. She is about to marry, but she has been an office worker for some years and is concerned about adapting to her forthcoming role as housewife and homemaker . . .

It proved surprisingly interesting to write in the voice of another person. Perhaps this was a way of developing her writing.

'Look at this,' Dadda said that evening, folding open the newspaper. 'Isn't this the clinic you wrote about? They're advertising for a clerk. They owe you a job after that article you wrote.'

'I'd rather not.' Her pulse was speeding.

'You aren't in a position to be picky. Show me the letter when you've written it.'

A strong feeling of disbelief clung to Mary all the way to the clinic. Her thoughts felt glued together. Should she mess up the interview, thereby guaranteeing never seeing Nathaniel again? But this was the only opportunity she had been offered and suppose she never got another? Her insides were churning one moment and stiff as a board the next. She steeled herself to walk inside. Along the corridor, a middle-aged woman, plainly dressed in a black skirt and white blouse, was showing a woman wearing a bottle-green costume into a room, closing the door behind her and coming back along the passage.

Mary perked up. She knew a lady-clerk when she saw one. The woman disappeared into the office. Mary presented herself at the hatch.

'Good morning.'

The woman fussed with papers at a desk. It took her a moment to look up. She was a creature of ample proportions with roses in her cheeks, but her manner was all business.

'I'm Mrs Winter and I run the office. Are you here for the interview? Name?' Her eyes went to a list.

'Mary Maitland.'

The gaze snapped up again. 'You were here the night all the work was done.'

'How do you know?'

'Someone mentioned the name.' Mrs Winter consulted her list. She picked up a pencil and crossed out *Miss Maitland*. 'Candidates are waiting in the second room along on the other side of the corridor.'

She hesitated, waiting for the 'I'll show you', but it didn't come, even though the woman in bottle-green had been escorted.

'Was there something else?' asked Mrs Winter.

She stepped away from the hatch. 'No, thank you.' Mrs Winter knew she had been here before, so maybe she thought she didn't need her hand held.

As she entered the room, three others glanced up and smiled politely. They were all older than she was and soberly dressed. Presently, the door opened and Alistair looked in. Mary stared at the floor, relieved it wasn't Nathaniel – and then absurdly disappointed.

'Miss Chambers?'

One of the women rose. A little later, the woman in bottle-green was summoned.

At last it was Mary's turn.

'It's good to see you again,' said Alistair, but she didn't respond – couldn't. There was a roaring in her ears, a treacherous bumping in her heart. Please don't let Nathaniel be present.

Alistair opened a door and she walked in – and there he was, seated behind a large table. He rose as she entered. He smiled but she couldn't meet his eyes.

Alistair waved her to a chair. 'Thank you for coming.'

There were two women at the table, one plainly dressed with serious features, against whose sallow skin a string of pearls failed to appear luminous, the other a lady whose fashionable hat sported an oversized taffeta bow. She had a bright, interested air and Mary spotted self-conscious importance in the tilt of her chin.

'Miss Beamish, the lady almoner from the infirmary, and Mrs Parker-Jennings from the Deserving Poor Committee,' Alistair introduced them. 'Perhaps you can clear up a mystery, Miss Maitland. We've read the article about the clinic, but—'

She smiled. 'It's my pen name.'

Miss Beamish leant forward. 'Tell us about your journalism.'

She was happy to comply. It wasn't often she got the chance to blow her own trumpet.

'So the post here could be any old job, as far as you're concerned. What you're really interested in is your writing.'

She had walked right into that one. 'I started writing because of my interest in social matters. The night the clinic was made ready showed me how important it is to the local community. I have ten years of clerical experience and I'd like to put my skills to good use in a place where people in need are assisted.'

'And of course you'd be able to use the knowledge you gained here to write more articles.'

You don't catch me twice. 'I'm aware of the importance of confidentiality. I wouldn't write anything inspired by the clinic without the consent of the doctors.'

'You don't have a job at present,' said Nathaniel.

'Unfortunately, the agency was unable to keep me on. I believe the reference supplied by Miss Lever and Miss Kennett shows how pleased they were with me.'

The interviewers, however, seemed more interested in Mr Treadgold's grudging praise.

'He says he felt let down when you left,' said Alistair.

'It's true he wanted me to stay.'

'But you elected not to.'

'I'd worked in the town hall since leaving school, so I'm no fly-by-night,' she replied, using the word that had been flung at her during her library interview. 'I would gladly have remained at the agency, had circumstances permitted. My intention is to remain a long time in whatever post I am fortunate enough to get.'

She felt taken aback by the unsympathetic line of questioning. You'd never have thought she was the one who had rumbled Mr Saunders' nasty little ruse or that she had written such a favourable article.

At last Alistair said, 'I'll take you to the office, Miss Maitland. Someone will come to the hatch with an enquiry and Miss Beamish and I will observe how you handle it.'

She did her best to suppress a fluttery feeling as she accompanied the others along the corridor. Alistair knocked on the office door.

'Here we are again, Mrs Winter.'

Mary offered Mrs Winter a smile, but she walked straight past and left the room.

'Have a seat at the desk, Miss Maitland,' said Alistair. 'Miss Beamish and I will stay over here.'

A figure appeared at the hatch and she jumped up. It was a young woman. With tired eyes and a lined face, she didn't look young, but with a baby on her hip and another evidently on the way, she must be.

Mary smiled. 'Good morning. Can I help you?'

'I hope so, miss. It's our Betty's girl. She's got a new position over Seymour Grove way and it's give her some reet fancy ideas. She says it's dirty to use the same bar of soap to wash the floor as to bath the baby. I gave her a slap for her cheek, but what if she's right?'

'She could have expressed herself more tactfully, but she's right. It isn't hygienic. You should have two bars of soap.'

'Oh aye, I'll wave my magic wand and conjure up some money. I came here for help, not to be told to do the impossible.' She started to back away.

'Wait – please. Why don't you cut your soap in half?'

'You must think it's a bloomin' big bar of soap.'

'But suppose you washed the floor and a bit of cinder got embedded in it and then the baby got scratched.' Mary held her breath.

The young woman's mouth set in a stubborn line, then softened. 'Aye, I'll do that. Thanks, miss.'

She left, but before Mary could turn to her audience, another woman appeared, this one a shawlie with a dowager's hump.

'Can you help me?'

She found Alistair by her side.

'Your services aren't required, Mrs Turpin. Don't worry, you'll still be paid.'

'Was my advice wrong?' asked Mary.

Alistair smiled. 'On the contrary. We'd have stopped you if you'd said the wrong thing. You see, Miss Maitland, that young woman wasn't acting. You just handled a real enquiry.'

'You can start by typewriting a letter. I understand you're a competent typewriter.' The look Mrs Winter gave Mary suggested that competent typewriting made her the lowest of the low.

'Yes, I am.' She would keep this pleasant expression on her face if it killed her.

'I'll be the judge of that. There's no room for slackers here.'

When Mary finished the letter, she read it through to ensure there were no mistakes.

'Let me see.' Without looking, Mrs Winter wafted a hand in the air.

Mary put the letter into it, feeling a flare of resentment. The last time she had been involved in any checking of work, it had been she who had examined Spotty Ronnie's early efforts. Her own work hadn't been looked over in years.

'It'll do.'

It'll do? It was faultless. She opened her mouth, then changed her mind. She wouldn't give Mrs Winter the satisfaction.

'Of course, you'll have to do it again,' said Mrs Winter. 'We need a copy for office records.'

'I've already made a carbon copy.'

'Oh. Well, attend to the rest of the letters and make sure you do copies of them all.' Mrs Winter spoke as if she had neglected to copy the first one.

Fine. She would take all snippy remarks on the chin. Her work was of the highest quality and sooner or later this disagreeable woman would be obliged to recognise it.

There was a tap at the door and Mary, sitting with her back to it, heard it open.

'Morning, Mrs Winter.'

Nathaniel! Her heart turned over.

'Good morning, Doctor Brewer. What can I do for you?'

'I've come to see how your new assistant's getting on. Would you mind if Miss Maitland went out later with Nurse Evans, so she can get a feel for what we do?'

'Of course, Doctor. After all, it's not as though she's ever been a nurse, so she won't have any real idea.'

Was that a dig? She didn't care. All she cared about was that the big bass drum inside her chest was inaudible to the others.

She heard the door shut behind Nathaniel. Had she made a hideous mistake in working here?

'Are those letters finished?'

'Not yet.'

'And yet you've stopped working. Goodness knows, my expectations were low, but I didn't think you'd fall behind this quickly.'

She had had enough. 'With all due—'

'Save the speech. Everyone knows you got this job because of the smarmy piece you wrote for the newspaper.'

'Excuse me.' A faded-looking woman had appeared.

Mrs Winter went to the hatch. 'Are you here to see the doctor? The waiting room is the second door on the left.' She turned round. 'You'll leave all queries to me. I can't risk your giving out the wrong information.'

'I helped a real patient in my interview.'

'A fluke. I won't risk the reputation of this office in your hands. The clinic has four nurses working shifts, and the doctors give a few hours a week, so the office is essential. Not only do I keep things running smoothly, I'm the only one here all the time.'

'I'm now here all the time too. I have ten years of office experience—'

'So you'll know all about putting the kettle on. Two sugars for me.'

'Better if just one of us goes,' said Nathaniel. 'More . . .'

'Friendly?' Alistair took the word out of his mouth.

'Less intimidating.'

That wasn't the right word either. Thaddeus Lennox was

unlikely to be intimidated. You didn't get to be a slum landlord and factory tyrant by being meek and accommodating.

'Toss for it.' Alistair produced a florin.

Nathaniel lost, so he asked Mrs Winter to organise an appointment.

On his next clinic day, he walked the few streets to the closest of Lennox's factories, a dingy place that reeked of grease and sweat. He had expected bulk and complacency, but Lennox cut a lithe figure. He was fleet of foot too, and darted from room to room, conducting their conversation over his shoulder.

Nathaniel stepped in front of him. 'Do you have an office? Somewhere we can talk undisturbed?'

'Very well.' His eyes said, *If I must.*

The office was a dumping ground for boxes and ledgers, and none too clean, but presumably that didn't matter if the man was on his feet the whole time.

Nathaniel came to the point. 'In a nutshell, sir, the housing you own is a disgrace. Your tenants, many of whom are also your employees, live in unsavoury conditions that could easily be remedied. Rot, woodworm, leaking roofs, problems with the gas supply.'

'That's quite a shopping list.'

'Think of it as an investment. Improved housing means better health, which means a more energetic workforce.'

Lennox barked out a laugh. 'I don't need workers glowing with health, Doctor. If they aren't up to scratch, they get sacked.'

'If they're unemployed, they can't pay your rent.'

'And then I evict them. There's always another family to move in and always a queue of men needing work.'

'Where's your sense of responsibility? Your tenants have to

chuck bricks downstairs to make the rats go away before they venture down in the morning.'

'My responsibility, sir, is to support my family. Why should I pander to my tenants?'

'It isn't pandering to provide decent living conditions.'

'If I did up my houses, they'd be worth a higher rent, but the tenants couldn't afford that, so they'd be evicted. Have you considered that? I'm making a living, not running a charity. I'll carry on doing what I do best and leave the do-gooding to you.'

'Good morning, sir. Can I help you?'

Sir! Mrs Winter never called anyone sir. Alistair and Nathaniel were 'Doctor' and the men who came through the clinic's doors weren't anything. Mary continued filing, knowing Mrs Winter would bite her head off if she turned to look.

'Good morning. You can help me by letting me speak to the young lady over there.'

Charlie! With delight warming her cheeks, she hurried to the hatch, only to find Mrs Winter hadn't stood aside for her.

'Gentlemen followers at work? You've surpassed yourself, Miss Maitland.'

'He isn't – I mean, this is my . . . my . . .' Was it overstepping the mark to claim kinship?

'Cousin,' Charlie supplied. 'Charlie Kimber. How do you do?'

'So it's a family reunion . . . Oh.' Mrs Winter's mouth shrank into a knot.

'I know it's not quite the done thing, my turning up here,' Charlie said with genial courtesy, 'but I couldn't wait to see my cousin again. Would you mind if I took her out at lunchtime?'

'What Miss Maitland does in her dinner hour is her business, as long as she doesn't bring the clinic into disrepute.'

'Perfect. What time should I call for her?'

How extraordinary to have a name that obliged people to do your bidding. Mary was grateful for Charlie's good manners. She would have curled up and died had he chucked his weight around.

When he escorted her outside at one o'clock, the motor was there, being guarded from the grubby mitts of the local children by a couple of scrawny lads. Charlie flipped them a coin.

'Cor – thanks, mister.'

They darted away, whooping for joy.

'I brought you some motoring togs.'

He took them from the back seat. Standing beside a fancy motor, being helped into a long coat, was even worse than parading out of the house to climb into the Kimber carriage on the day of the dreaded Sunday lunch. She didn't dare raise her eyes to the clinic windows.

Charlie opened the door for her. The front seats were glassed in, but the rear seats were open to the elements, with a large hood folded down over the back.

'Like a perambulator,' she said.

'Like a landau, actually. Hence the name "landaulet".'

'Is it yours?'

'Lord, no. It belongs to the governor. You're behaving as if you've never been in it before, but I drove you to the newspaper offices in it.'

Something twisted inside her. 'I had things on my mind that day. Where are we going?'

He took her to a pretty tea shop near Seymour Grove.

'They do simple meals at this time of day. I thought you'd be more comfortable here than somewhere smart.'

'If you think I'm not good enough . . .'

'I meant, because of being in your office clothes.'

'Oh. I'm sorry I snapped.'

'My fault. I can't tell you how pleased I was when the girls said you'd dropped them a line about your new job.' He grinned, his handsome features melting into boyishness. 'And to prove it, here I am. Why did you leave the agency? They were vague about it.'

'It was time to move on.'

'Nonsense. You loved that job and left it without having another lined up. What happened? We're friends, aren't we?'

She sat back to allow the waitress to place her vegetable soup and crusty roll in front of her, but her hope that the subject would fade away in the pause was in vain. She decided to own up.

'I was seen in the motor with you that time. Lady Kimber complained to my parents and suggested they send me away. I refused to go and next news, the Kimber rent man told Angela and Josephine to get rid of me or else.'

'That's—'

'—what happens when you don't do as the Kimbers tell you.'

'It's—'

'—life, for those of us who aren't Kimbers. Thanks for being indignant, but don't forget how you swanned into the clinic and bent Mrs Winter to your will. You were charming, but you knew she couldn't say no.'

Charlie raised his eyebrows. 'I think I've just been put in my place.'

She laughed. 'I think your place is a jolly comfortable one.'

'I like it when you laugh. Tell me about the new job. I want to dazzle everyone at the next meeting with tales of your success.'

'I wish I could come and dazzle them myself, but my father put his foot down. Apparently, being with you at the meetings gave me inappropriate ideas, which was how I ended up in the motor.'

'You mean, if I stopped going . . . ?'

'Goodness, don't say that. My father had the audacity to suggest it to Lady Kimber and the idea wasn't well received. Forget I spoke – please. You say you're my friend. Prove it by not dropping me in it at Ees House.'

'Tell me about your new job.'

'I'm surrounded by ideas for articles, but I can't write about clinic matters. Last week I wrote an amusing piece about Ozzie – our cat. Ozymandias, King of Kings.'

'Splendid name.'

'Splendid cat, and doesn't he know it. I'm also putting the finishing touches to something I've called *A Summer Walk* – you know, wild flowers, butterflies, the benefits of fresh air, with a few flower meanings thrown in.'

'I take it *Autumn*, *Winter* and *Spring Walks* will follow in due course?'

'I hope so. I'm going to suggest it.' She leant forward. 'Actually, I hope Mrs Newbold at *Vera's Voice* will suggest it. Wouldn't that be grand?'

'You still haven't told me about your new job.'

She had been brought up not to complain, but it all came pouring out.

'. . . I'm happy to muck in, but there are limits. It's galling being treated like the office junior.'

'Shall you look for something else?'

'No, I've got to stick at it. I've already left two jobs in the past few weeks.'

'You'll think of something. You've got initiative.'

'Initiative? Me?'

'Certainly. You were tired of the town hall, so you did something about it, and you worked wonders at the agency. You should hear the girls moaning and groaning about how things have slipped since you went. Then there's your writing. Don't underestimate yourself. You're . . . well, earlier you thought I'd implied you weren't good enough. Just so you know, Mary, I think you're more than good enough. I think you're top-hole.'

Chapter Fourteen

Lady Kimber sat at the walnut bureau in her morning room, reading the Deserving Poor Committee minutes. Behind her, the door opened. Marking her place with a fingertip, she turned as her husband walked in.

'Might I disturb you for a few minutes?'

'Of course.' She went to the silk-covered sofa, inviting him, with a motion of her hand, to join her.

'My dear, you must prepare yourself for a shock.'

Her chest tightened. 'Eleanor?' No, Eleanor was here in the house.

'Not Eleanor and not Charlie.' Sir Edward sat beside her. Well, not exactly. Close but not touching. 'I've heard Greg Rawley has taken a beating.'

She forced herself not to drop her gaze. 'What happened? Is he all right?'

'Nothing that won't mend.'

'Who did it?'

'Unknown, apparently.' He laid a hand over hers, an enquiring look in his dark eyes.

'I'm fine. Just a little shocked.' A little shocked? She was weak as a half-set jelly.

'Should I ring for tea?'

Greg would have headed straight for the brandy. 'No, thank you. Look at the time. You mustn't be late.'

He raised her hand to his lips. Greg would have turned her hand over and kissed her palm, her wrist. She shivered.

When Sir Edward left, she sat, composing herself. Presently, she went in search of Eleanor. The thought of her daughter calmed her thudding heart.

Things were progressing nicely. The first time Charlie had seen Eleanor, he had looked twice – literally. He had glanced round, then immediately swung his head back to gaze at her. Lady Kimber had made a mental note to ensure the moment was included in the father-of-the-bride's speech.

Having the young couple under the same roof made it natural to promote their friendship. Eleanor was enjoying her first taste of masculine company and Charlie was as vulnerable as the next fellow to a lovely face. There had been a minor hiccough when the Maitland wretch had thrust herself under his nose, but she had been dealt with.

Eleanor was in the blue sitting room with Olivia Rushworth, their heads close together over a magazine. Eleanor turned the page, but not before her mother had glimpsed a fashion plate of a white gown with masses of lace.

Oh yes, things were progressing very nicely.

* * *

Charlie's words had given Mary the kick she needed. Being stuck at home, then landing in Mrs Winter's clutches, had dragged her down. It was time she pulled herself back up. She formed an idea. Unfortunately, she would have to take it to Nathaniel. It was either that or wait two days for Alistair to be on duty and – little as she wanted to be closeted with Nathaniel, much as she wanted to be with him – she refused to wait.

He was due out on his rounds that afternoon, which meant he should arrive shortly before the end of her dinner hour. She ran upstairs to the doctors' office and knocked.

'Come in.'

Trying to ignore the racing pulse that continued to respond to this man, she walked in. He was standing behind the desk, reading some papers.

'If you can spare a minute, Doctor Brewer, I have an idea.'

He dropped the papers onto the desk, but didn't sit. 'Let's hear it.'

'It's about the baby clinic. At the moment, a mother brings her baby, queues to see the nurse, then goes home. What if we made tea so the mothers stayed and chatted?'

'We aren't here to run social gatherings.'

'Maybe we should be.' His eyes widened: did he think she was answering back? 'It would mean getting to know some of the women and possibly giving general advice in an informal way.'

'An interesting idea.' He smiled, making her breath hitch. 'But I shouldn't expect anything less from you, should I? I'll discuss it with Doctor Cottrell.'

Her feet took her downstairs at a run. He had paid her a compliment. It was wonderful. It was heartbreaking.

'You're late,' said Mrs Winter as she entered the office. 'Where have you been?'

'With Doctor Brewer.'

'I want the stationery cupboard reorganised, the top two shelves swapped round, then the bottom two. You'll have to take everything out. And give the shelves a good scrub while you're at it.'

'Scrub the shelves?'

'It's easy to see you've never been a nurse.'

While she was on her knees, half inside the cupboard, channelling her vexation into wielding the scrubbing brush and blinking against the pong of carbolic in the confined space, she heard Nathaniel's voice.

'Is that Miss Maitland cleaning the cupboard? That's a job for—never mind now. Miss Maitland, might I have a word?'

She sat on her heels. She supposed she should stand, but she felt flushed and grubby and put out. She wouldn't have risen for Sir Edward himself right now.

'Doctor Cottrell popped in to collect some figures, so we discussed your idea and agree it's worth a try.'

'What idea?' demanded Mrs Winter.

'Miss Maitland suggesting turning the baby clinic into a social occasion with a view to discussing good domestic practice. Will you release her once a week, please?'

'I assumed it would be one of the nurses,' said Mary.

'We can't spare one, and it would put Mrs Winter in an awkward position. You'd be happy to, presumably?' Did his gaze flick towards the cupboard?

'Of course.'

'Right-o.' With a nod, he departed.

Without looking at Mrs Winter, not wanting her undoubtedly disapproving expression to sour the moment, she stuck her head back in the cupboard. Charlie was right. All it had taken was a bit of initiative.

On her way back to the office from putting away the cleaning things, she saw Nathaniel coming out of the office, black bag in hand. He headed for the front door, off on his rounds.

The moment she walked in, Mrs Winter pounced.

'You couldn't wait to go running to Doctor Brewer, could you? How dare you complain about me?'

'I don't know what you mean.'

'Don't play the innocent. You suck up to the doctors with your idea, then complain about being given menial jobs.'

'I never said a word—'

'Then why would Doctor ask for cleaning jobs to be left to the scrubbing woman?'

'Maybe because I'm not employed to do the cleaning.'

'Don't get fresh with me, madam. You may be Doctor Brewer's blue-eyed girl, and you may be related to the Kimbers, but in this office, you're the junior and don't you forget it.'

Helen's heart leapt. The Kimber carriage! The thought of seeing Christina filled her with joy. Christina: Helen wouldn't dream of using her first name now. She wasn't a fearful woman, but the thought of the snub she would receive made her quake with horror.

Had she brought Eleanor? The coachman opened the door and let down the step. Here came Her Ladyship in gorgeous turquoise and – oh, please, please – no one behind her. Of course, she had been a silly old fool to hope and if the disappointment hurt, then it was her own stupid fault. Her hip chose that moment to administer a jagged-edged pain deep inside the joint. It seemed linked to the anguish in her heart. It took all her willpower to put one foot in front of the other without dragging. She got to the hall, feeling as though her bad leg would crumble to pieces, just as Lady Kimber swept inside.

'I wish to see Mr Rawley.'

'He's indisposed,' Helen said, before Edith could reply.

Lady Kimber gave her a cool look. 'Is he conscious? Then he'll see me.'

'I'd rather—'

Lady Kimber looked at Edith. 'Kindly announce me.'

'Yes,' came another voice. 'Kindly announce Her Ladyship.'

And there was Greg, blast his eyes, propped against the door frame, one hand thrust into the pocket of his striped silk dressing gown. Damn him, he managed to strike a debonair pose in spite of his injuries.

'This way.' He removed his hand with its bruised knuckles from his pocket and waved his visitor into the room.

Helen took a decisive step forwards. Over her rotting corpse would these two spend time together privately under this roof.

'Not you, old love,' said Greg.

The door swung shut in her face.

God, she was beautiful. Older, of course, but so what? With a thickened figure, too, but again, so what? A girlish figure might be smooth and eager and downright flexible, but a womanly figure was there to be worshipped. And by the stars, he was ready and willing to worship this one.

He ached to tell her so. He said, 'Have a seat.'

'I assume all those cushions are for your benefit.'

'To keep the invalid propped up.'

She sat, and did she take a moment to settle her skirts around her so as not to meet his eyes? He lowered himself onto the sofa, holding his breath against a hiss of pain.

She looked at him and his heart turned over. Her husband wouldn't have let her come if he had any inkling of what was going on in her cousin's head.

'What happened?' she asked. 'It's said you were attacked.'

He shrugged. His shoulder muscles twinged darkly. 'I was attacked.'

'What do the police say?'

'They haven't been invited to say anything.' He raised his hand to silence her, a swift gesture – too swift – and he fought not to wince as pain stabbed his strapped ribs. 'I'd rather talk about you . . . about us.'

'There is no us, and hasn't been for a long time, not since . . .'

'Not since Aunt Helen dragged you back here.'

The look she gave him took him by surprise. Such ice. Her eyes were no longer a hazy blue that he could have drowned in, but grey as smoke and, as everyone knew, where there was smoke, there was fire – and clearly, where there was fire, there was also ice.

'I was going to say not since you went abroad when I needed you most.'

'That was because—'

'I don't want to hear it. I don't want to be told you changed your mind or were bought off by my family.'

'I would never—'

'Neither do I want to be told you couldn't bear the separation and the only answer was to drown your sorrows in the finest

French wines. You abandoned me and they prevailed upon me to marry my first husband.' Was it his imagination or did a shudder ripple through her? 'We had our chance.'

'We had two chances.' Oh yes, they had had another chance. She had been this close – *this* close – to leaving Henry.

'No, we didn't. Not once I found out about your way of life.'

He leant forward, twangs of pain intertwining themselves with the anguish of his memories. Before he could speak, she forestalled him.

'I want to talk about Eleanor. I've come to warn you off. I saw the way you looked at her after the funeral.'

'Of course I looked at her. How could I not? She's lovely. God, it was like looking at you all those years ago.'

'You couldn't take your eyes off her.'

'Only to look at you.'

'I mean it, Greg. You're not to come near. You're handsome and charming, and I won't put her at risk. My husband knows nothing of you and me. He's never understood why I don't keep up the connection with Aunt Helen and he won't understand when I don't admit you to our circle. I want your word that you won't make it difficult for me. There can't be any contact between Jackson's House and Ees House.'

'I shan't be setting up shop here. Aside from the fact that I'd swallow my razor sooner than have old Helen as a bunk-mate, I'm in need of funds and I'm more likely to win what I need in London or Paris.'

'You're in debt. How bad is it?'

'I raised a considerable sum in anticipation of the old boy's death, happy in the belief that my inheritance would enable me to pay everything back as well as setting me up. Unfortunately,

I have to wait for Helen to die as well. I considered renting out this place, but it's been made clear to me,' and he indicated his injuries with a rueful tilt of his head, 'that that wouldn't pay off my commitments speedily enough.'

'Oh, Greg.'

It came out in a thread of anguish that made even the bruised ribs worthwhile. His heart sang and the blood throbbed in his veins. She had always had this effect on him, always had, always would. When she left, he would die another death, but he would willingly die a thousand deaths for these few minutes in her presence.

They looked at one another, the past aching between them.

'I must go.'

'Not yet.'

'I must.' She went to the door, readied herself, then flung it open. 'Just checking whether Aunt Helen had her ear glued to the keyhole.'

A roar of laughter ended in a deep groan as his ribs threatened to shatter. He pulled himself to his feet, straining to disguise the effort.

'I'll see you out.'

'There's no need. Ring the bell.'

'There's every need. It will infuriate Helen. Just because she didn't fall flat on her face into the room doesn't mean she isn't hovering nearby.'

He followed her across the hall, filling his eyes with her innate grace, her proud bearing. Pain be buggered, he stood inches taller, invigorated by her nearness, though the elusive whiff of her perfume was enough to make his knees buckle. They were made for each other. He had never doubted it, even though she had twice married someone else.

Then she was gone and he died another death.

* * *

Nathaniel glanced up as Alistair walked into his office at the clinic. 'I've just seen our Miss Maitland setting off in a rather spiffy motor,' said Alistair. 'I asked Mrs Winter and apparently the fellow in the driving seat is Mr Charlie Kimber.'

'Kimber?' Nathaniel's ears pricked up. 'As in – Kimber?'

'Mrs Winter says he's her cousin, though she made cousin sound like secret code for married lover.'

'I'm not sure I like the sound of a Kimber connection.'

'You just don't like being reminded of our reliance on Lady Kimber's committee. But it's not as though Miss Maitland tried to use the connection to get this job. Give her credit for that.' Alistair sat down, leaning his elbows on the desk. 'I saw Palmer last night. The PIP people have got back in touch. It seems the means test chap put their backs up by telling the world that PIP won't support any schemes the means test turns down, and they're prepared to give us another look.'

Nathaniel exhaled softly. 'PIP funding would lessen our dependence on the Lady Bountiful Committee.'

'They want to send a Duncan Swayne here next Tuesday. Can you be here? I don't like to put upon you when you've got your responsibilities at home. How's your sister getting on?'

'Doing well, all things considered. She's been through the mill, poor girl.'

'But?' Alistair prompted. 'I thought I detected a "but".'

'If you were expecting me to say "but she brought it on herself", I wouldn't dream of it. No one deserves to be forcibly fed or to have their gullet-lining torn. I just hope she'll step back from her cause now.'

'Some people find something they believe in and after that there's no stopping them.'

'I know. Votes for women has been Evie's crusade.'

'I'm sorry, old chap, did you think I was talking about your sister? I meant you. It must run in the family.'

Nathaniel watched Alistair get up and leave the room.

He and Evie – the same? What tripe.

Duncan Swayne was a hearty man, who looked like everyone's favourite uncle, but he had a keen mind. His questions were shrewd and his examination of the paperwork thorough.

'You're doing good work here, Doctor. I noticed in the diary you have a baby clinic this morning. Is it well attended?'

'Come and see for yourself. A member of staff started a new initiative only last week.'

Miss Maitland had no notion she was about to get an important visitor, but Nathaniel had no qualms about dropping Swayne on her. If he had learnt one thing about Mary Maitland, it was that she could be relied upon, and he had no doubt she had planned this get-together meticulously.

He opened the door and nodded his approval. This was better than having a line of women sitting on chairs in the passage. Now they sat round a table, drinking tea and chatting, rocking sleeping babies and jiggling waking ones. Small children were playing – good grief, was that a toy box? Miss Maitland circled the table, topping up the cups. He caught her eye and beckoned her with a tilt of his chin. She was a pretty girl and that light in her eyes said she was enjoying herself.

He performed the introductions.

Swayne frowned. 'I'm not sure you should keep these women from their domestic duties with tea and chit-chat.'

'It's not chit-chat,' said Miss Maitland. 'Well, some of it is, obviously, but it's useful things too. Mrs Shaw's linoleum is cracking, so I told her about putting ground-up cork in the glue to mend it, and these women can only afford cracked eggs, but they didn't know about using salt to prevent the white seeping out in the pan. I've promised to bring my mother's recipe for home-made soap flakes next time.'

'So you're educating them.'

'I wouldn't say that.'

'I would.' Swayne turned to Nathaniel as if Miss Maitland no longer existed. 'I'm impressed with what I've seen this morning, Doctor, and PIP would be happy to receive an application from your clinic, on the understanding, of course, that these education sessions cease immediately. I would remind you that I stands for Ignorant. So, which is it to be: funding, or education disguised as chit-chat?'

'You're worried about your advice sessions, aren't you?' said Charlie.

'It would be a shame if they stopped,' said Mary, 'but the clinic has to be funded.'

Was he about to place his hand over hers? They were in their tea shop, their special place. She had now spent several dinner hours with him, rather to her surprise. That first time, she had assumed it was a generous impulse on his part, possibly encouraged by Angela and Josephine, but he had turned up the next day as well. Since then he never dropped her off without making another arrangement.

'We'll have to fill your diary with lunch engagements in case your spirits need lifting,' said Charlie.

'I can't think of anyone who'd do a better job of cheering me up. You're fun to be with.'

'Not witty, not debonair, but fun.'

'Are you fishing for compliments?'

He laughed. 'It wouldn't do me any good if I were. It's one of the things I like about you. I don't have your automatic approval. You've opened my eyes about your family. Until now, all I knew about the Maitlands was how your grandmother hoodwinked Great-Uncle Martin.'

'She didn't force him to run off with her.'

Charlie grinned. 'She didn't throw him over her shoulder and make a dash for the horizon?'

'I'm serious.' But she smiled. She smiled a lot when she was with Charlie. 'It's not always easy being the poor relations. We have to be the last word in respectability, never doing anything that reflects badly on the Kimbers. My father would throw forty fits if he knew I was here with you.'

'Then why are you here?'

His eyes, in which she was accustomed to seeing warmth and humour, were earnest and questioning. She quivered inside.

'If I'm not your idea of a Maitland, you aren't mine of a Kimber. At the agency, you treated me the same as the others, and I appreciate the way you've encouraged me at the clinic.'

'So you're not here for my irresistible charm and good looks?'

'Don't tease.'

'If you were, I wouldn't mind, because that's why I'm here.'

It felt like standing on the edge of a cliff. 'For my good looks and charm?'

'You're beautiful, Mary. You're clever and determined,

but there's also something vulnerable about you. Put all that together and I find you utterly beguiling.'

The office door opened and Nathaniel walked in. Mary's cheeks flooded, as if he could tell what Charlie had said to her. She had felt fluttery ever since. Charlie liked her. He *liked* her. She liked him too – she had done from the start, but she had never considered him in *that* way. But if he liked her . . . and they got along so well . . .

'Afternoon, ladies. I've come to tell you that Doctor Cottrell and I have decided against applying for PIP funding. Your mothers' gatherings can continue, Miss Maitland.'

'I'm delighted to hear it, Doctor,' said Mrs Winter and Mary looked at her in surprise. 'Funding is important, but so is education, especially in a community like this. This is a chance to feed useful information into homes where it could make a difference.'

'Of course, if it doesn't make a difference, we'll think again,' said Nathaniel, 'so you've got your work cut out, Miss Maitland.'

'Yes, Doctor.' But she was too astonished by Mrs Winter's support to feel pleased.

When Nathaniel left, Mrs Winter returned to her work. Mary watched her. Were they supposed to pretend nothing had happened?

'Thank you for what you said. I had no idea you approved.'

'That's hardly surprising, is it?' Mrs Winter put down her pen. 'I owe you an apology. I didn't want you here, but now I can see you've taken a real interest and I respect that.' Her shoulders dropped and the words came tumbling out. 'I wanted my friend to get the job. As former nurses, we'd have such insight into the work. It's not easy losing your job when you marry.'

Ah yes, the woman in bottle-green being shepherded into the waiting room. 'You used to be a nurse?'

'A sister, but now I'm not allowed to do nursing at all – simply because I'm married. I'm not even allowed to give advice here, except about hygiene, and then only if someone specifically asks for it. Otherwise I could be reported. That's why you have to run the mothers' gatherings: so no one can accuse me of using my knowledge to help people.'

'That's ridiculous. It must be frustrating.'

'A word of advice.' Mrs Winter pinned her down with her gaze. 'Think carefully about your future. If you marry and have a family, that's all well and good. I didn't marry until my middle years. I lost my position and no children came along, so I lost out on both counts.'

'Are you saying marry young or never marry?'

'I'm saying you can't guarantee what you'll get. You can only be certain of what you have to give up. A sad truth, but bear it in mind.'

Eleanor looked enchanting in a flared skirt of dusty-rose, trimmed with dainty velvet bows above the hemline, and an ivory lawn blouse, its stand-up collar showing off her slender throat. Lady Kimber felt a swell of pride. Eleanor was her shining star.

'Bad news should be delivered with the minimum of fuss,' she said. 'Express a proper regret and make the changed circumstances clear. That's why I want you here: to see how it's done.'

'Did the doctors ask to see you, Mummy?'

'No, which is worrying. Either they know and they're postponing informing the Deserving Poor Committee, in which case they aren't fit to receive funding, or they don't know, in which case they ought to know and—'

'—they aren't fit to receive funding.'

There was a tap at the door and the frock-coated doctors were shown in. Lady Kimber introduced Eleanor.

'A pleasure to meet you, Miss Kimber,' said Doctor Cottrell.

'My daughter is learning the work of the Deserving Poor Committee.'

'The clinic is doing much-needed work,' said Eleanor, and Lady Kimber was gratified by the use of one of her own stock phrases. 'Tell me, how is Miss Maitland faring?'

Only years of self-control prevented Lady Kimber from showing her surprise.

'She's doing well,' said Doctor Brewer. 'We're pleased with her. If you'd tell us why you sent for us, Your Ladyship?'

Lady Kimber recalled his dislike of chit-chat and was glad of it. Mary Maitland! She would sort that out later.

'It has come to my attention that a significant number of breadwinners in your clinic's households will lose their jobs next week. You appear surprised. Were you unaware?'

'This is the first we've heard of it,' admitted Doctor Cottrell. 'Our work at the clinic is voluntary and we're not there every day.'

'Neither am I at your clinic and yet I know. Many of your breadwinners work for a man named Lennox. Mr Lennox is closing that particular factory next week. The Deserving Poor Committee requires the breadwinners of eight out of every ten households to be employed in order for the community to be considered deserving. Your community will drop below this figure and hence we can no longer fund you.'

'That will put us in danger of closing, just when we're starting to do some good.'

'You may apply again, should your community find its feet, provided you prove you can keep a more effective eye on matters.'

'With respect,' said Doctor Brewer, 'funding that comes and goes is unsuitable. We need funding we can rely on.'

Doctor Cottrell frowned at him. 'Might I ask Your Ladyship how you came by this news?'

'Mr Lennox apparently considered it his public duty to inform the Means Test Office and they, knowing the Deserving Poor Committee has an interest, informed me.'

'So, as of next week, these people will no longer be deserving.' Doctor Brewer's voice was tight with annoyance. 'What will that make them instead?'

She met his gaze without a flicker. 'The official term is "afflicted", though I dislike it. So old-fashioned. I believe our business is concluded, Doctors. Thank you for coming at short notice.'

When they departed, she discussed the meeting with Eleanor before approaching her principal concern.

'Am I correct in thinking Mary Maitland is employed at the clinic?'

'Yes, Mummy. She worked at the agency, but she lost her job – I don't know why, though the girls swear it was through no fault of her own – and now she's at the clinic. Charlie told me. He went to see her.'

'Really? Now, our next duty is to arrange for the clinic's funding to be withdrawn, and this is how we do it . . .'

She went through the motions, but inside she was seething. So the Maitland girl was still trying to sink her hooks into the heir, was she? The first thing to do was dispose of Charlie temporarily. That would be simple, thanks to Sir Edward's love of cricket. Then she would turn her attention to the social-climbing Miss Maitland. Removing her from the agency hadn't worked and her parents had declined to send her away. So Miss Maitland must be made to want to go, something that could only be achieved in a subtle way.

Lady Kimber felt a glimmer of anticipation. She excelled at subtlety.

Chapter Fifteen

The off-duty nurses, who should have been at home, were in the common room: something serious must have happened. Mary exchanged glances with Mrs Winter. This was no ordinary meeting.

'Thank you for coming,' said Alistair. 'Lennox's is closing next week and the men will lose their jobs, which means the community will no longer count as deserving poor and we'll lose our main source of income. Doctor Brewer and I will do all we can to find alternative funding before that happens.'

'In the meantime,' said Nathaniel, 'it's business as usual. In fact, the more we do, the better, as it increases our chances of being funded. Miss Maitland, a picnic for the mothers and babies has been suggested. I'll speak to you in the office later.'

She glowed. He saw her as instrumental in keeping the clinic afloat. She clasped her hands in her lap.

Later, when there was a polite knock on the office door, she turned with a smile and found him ushering in a visitor – a woman with mousy colouring and kind eyes, her clothes smart without being fussy.

'Miss Maitland, this is my wife. Imogen, this is Mary Maitland, who's going to help you organise the picnic.'

Imogen Brewer held out her hand. 'I'm pleased to meet you. Thank you for volunteering.'

Mary stared at the outstretched hand. What would Mrs Brewer think if she knew that when her husband had touched Mary's hand, attraction had stormed through her like a runaway dray horse? Her own hand felt trembly as she extended it.

'I'll leave you to talk,' said Nathaniel. 'Use the common room – if Mrs Winter can spare Miss Maitland, that is.'

Next thing she knew, Mary was in the common room with Nathaniel's wife. His *wife*. She had known he was married. She had known it, but it hadn't stopped her heart speeding up in his presence.

'It's good of you to offer to help me.' Imogen smiled, but there was a question in her eyes. 'You did volunteer, didn't you? Only you seem surprised.'

Her heart beat sluggishly, making it hard to smile. 'I'm happy to help.' How could she get out of this?

Imogen produced a small book from her bag. 'I've made some notes. Shall we go through them and see what you think?'

There was a sour taste in her mouth. If only there was a looking-glass on the wall, so she could check her expression as Imogen's ideas washed over her. Did she appear normal and pleasant, or did she look the way she felt, wild-eyed and ghastly?

'What do you think?' asked Imogen.

Here was her chance to escape. 'You don't need my help. You've thought of everything. Why don't you organise the picnic and I'll arrange a party for the older children?'

'Well – if you think so. Are you sure my husband didn't push you into this? I know how single-minded he can be.'

Her muscles loosened in humiliation. Now Imogen would go home and tell Nathaniel off for strong-arming her into helping with the blasted picnic, and he would think her a chump for ducking out of it. Let him. It didn't matter what he thought. She never wanted to see him again.

'I would gladly have helped, but you don't need it. There's a list of mothers in the office. Let me fetch it for you.'

She dived out of the room. At the top of the stairs, she grabbed the handrail. Her legs felt as crumbly as Lancashire cheese.

As she was leaving the office to return to the common room, Nurse Evans came through the front door. Mary could have kissed her.

'Mrs Brewer is organising a picnic for your mother and baby clinic. She's in the common room. Why not have a chat? Here's the attendance list.'

'Mrs Brewer, as in Doctor Brewer?'

Mrs Brewer, as in Mary Maitland is an idiot.

'Organised already?' asked Mrs Winter when Mary sank behind her desk.

'Change of plan. I'm organising a children's party.'

'You'll need to be quick about it. We don't know what the situation will be by the end of next week. I'll help. We'll need a sack of children's shoes, for starters. Being shod is a deserving poor requirement. We'll talk about it this afternoon.'

Mrs Winter went on her dinner hour and Mary sagged in her seat, feeling as if she had been twice through the mangle.

'I'm looking for a beautiful lady journalist in need of something to eat. Do you happen to know any?'

Charlie! Dear, uncomplicated Charlie. Her heart swelled with gratitude. She had never been more pleased to see anyone in her life.

The meeting with Duncan Swayne didn't last long.

'It's the wives who are being educated, not the men,' said Nathaniel. He spoke as if he meant it, but he knew it was a specious argument.

And so apparently did Swayne. 'Don't split hairs, Doctor.'

'What if we withdrew the advice session?' asked Alistair.

'Do as you please with it,' said Swayne. 'If you cancelled it, it would only be to attract PIP funding and we aren't that gullible. We're looking for projects that promote our views, not ones that chop and change according to the bank balance.'

'Are you coming to the meeting at the colonel's house?' said Alistair when Swayne had departed.

'Give my apologies. Say I'll be along later, after I've seen Barney Clough.'

Nathaniel wasn't one to drag his feet when something distasteful needed doing. Soon he was admitted to the Clough residence and entered the overfurnished sitting room.

'Brewer! M'dear fellow, come in, come in.'

Nathaniel was careful to maintain a neutral expression. Clough's evident intention to enjoy the interview didn't bode well.

'You remember my legal man, don't you?'

He acknowledged Mr Saunders. 'I'm here to discuss the clinic.' He gave details of their successes.

Clough cut him off. 'This is all very fine, but that isn't why you're here. You're looking for another handout. Your funding is about to be withdrawn and you need to find the money elsewhere.'

'I wasn't aware it was public knowledge.'

'Word gets round.'

'After everything you put into improving the building, you won't want to see the clinic facing closure.'

'Won't I? Can't wait, old chap. I'll get my building back.'

'What use is it to you?' Nathaniel hid his scorn. At least, he hoped he hid it. 'What will you do with it?'

Saunders cleared his throat.

'I'll do nothing with it,' said Clough. 'It can fall to rack and ruin. But I'll be free from you doctors.'

'What of your ambition to be an alderman? You have to support the clinic.'

'It won't be Mr Clough's fault if the clinic fails,' said Saunders. 'It'll be yours.'

'Exactly,' said Clough. 'I'll be the philanthropist who trusted the wrong men – and when I support other causes, I'll be the philanthropist who continued his good works in spite of being let down.'

'Face it, Brewer,' said Saunders. 'You were clever enough to get the clinic ready on time, but that's the extent of your cleverness. Give in gracefully, man, while you can still hold your head up.'

A vase of pinks stood in the middle of 'their' table in the tea shop. Charlie thanked the waitress with the easy-going charm that made Mary proud to be with him. He was the sort to notice every small attention. It was one of the reasons she felt so comfortable with him. What a relief to feel comfortable with Charlie after the skin-tingling angst of being in Nathaniel's presence.

She told him about the party she was organising with Mrs Winter's assistance. 'A couple of the nurses are going to give up their Saturday afternoon off to help. I've arranged to use the church hall a few streets away. It's pretty run-down, but that doesn't matter.'

'If there's a fee for hiring it, I hope you'll allow me to pay. I want to support this scheme of yours.'

'That's kind, but it's already paid for.' She lowered her voice, a smile twitching her lips. 'I'm paying by writing a couple of sermons.'

Charlie threw back his head and laughed. 'Perfect! That's just like you, Mary. You can turn your hand to anything. But you must let me contribute – I insist. How about I stump up for prizes for the party games? Please say yes. It'd give me pleasure.'

'That's just like you.' She was happy to return his compliment. 'You do someone a favour and make it feel like they're doing you the favour. And I accept gladly. But I'll have to be careful what prizes I get. These children have next to nothing and the smallest toy would represent riches – and not just to the child. We don't want to give the children things that would end up in the pawnshop.'

'Really? Things are as bad as that?'

'I know it probably sounds mean to you, but a marble would be a suitable prize. May I use your donation to purchase some games – a quoits set, skittles, things like that? They could then be left at the clinic for future activities.'

If there were any future activities. Surely the doctors would find alternative funding?

Saturday came round. To make the party even more of an occasion, Mary, for the price of an extra sermon, let some of the children into the church hall during the morning to make paper chains. Mrs Winter arrived with a sack of old shoes, borrowed from various poor boxes.

When the children arrived, wriggling with excitement, they shoved their feet into shoes, not caring about comfort, and had to be persuaded to try on a couple of pairs in search of a better fit. Then they were allowed into the hall. Mary's heart creaked at the sight of the paper chains, made from old newspapers, making the little ones gasp with joy. She wanted to hug each and every child to her.

The hall had chairs, a couple of wonky tables and, joy of joys, a piano that was nearly in tune. Nurse Kent bashed out lively accompaniment to musical chairs and musical statues, but frankly it was better to rely on their voices for oranges and lemons and the farmer's in his den. They enjoyed riotous games of blind man's bluff, pin the tail on the donkey and grandmother's footsteps, which Mary, seeing how many of the children were limping, used as an excuse for them to take off the shoes.

'You can't creep properly with shoes on.'

'Goodness me, look at those blisters,' said Nurse Kent in a jolly voice. 'I'll nip round to the clinic for some salve and then we'll have a competition for the biggest blister.'

Charlie's donation, as well as paying for the games and the bag of marbles, had run to the cost of a simple tea, which Mrs Winter had advised Mary to ask the corner shop to provide – so the children went home with their bellies full of paste sandwiches and jelly, which was the heartiest meal most of them had seen in ages, if ever.

'A cup of tea before we clear up?' suggested Mrs Winter, closing the door on the last of the children and leaning against it.

'I'll put the kettle on,' said Mary. It was the least she could do after the others had helped make the party such a success. She was tired, but it was a happy kind of tiredness, the gratification of a job well done.

The donation from Charlie had made such a difference. Thinking of him brought a glow to her cheeks. She liked him – she was starting to realise how much. Meeting Imogen Brewer had been horrible, but it had done her good. The attraction she had felt towards Nathaniel had been . . . well, like when you lose a tooth and your tongue can't resist probing the gap. The gap was well and truly plugged now, thanks to Imogen.

It wasn't the most elegant comparison. As a writer, she should be able to come up with something better. No, she shouldn't, because it didn't matter. She was well and truly over Nathaniel – Imogen was welcome to him. And just when she would otherwise have felt lonely and miserable, she had Charlie to make a fuss of her. Charlie would make anyone feel better.

Helen snipped a deadhead off a rose, bringing it close to her face to inhale the lingering scent, but she wasn't going to cower among her roses until Doctor Brewer left. She might have made an idiot of herself last time he was here, but that didn't mean she was going to avoid him. That wasn't her way.

'Thank you, Edith. I'll come indoors and when the doctor has seen Mr Rawley, would you ask him to join me in the morning room?'

What was she going to say? Small talk bored her and she didn't think Doctor Brewer had much time for it either. Trying to plan a conversational gambit had always been a sure way of wiping her imagination clean.

In the event, she did what she always did. She said the first thing that popped into her head.

'Good morning, Doctor. I'm surprised my nephew tolerated your presence for this long. I've found him a poor patient.'

'It's true he wasn't interested in being checked over; but I had an ulterior motive in calling. It's been preying on my mind that I ought to speak to Mr Rawley about your concerns regarding the future of Jackson's House.'

Her hand crept to her throat. 'Does he intend renting it out?'

'No, he doesn't.'

She blinked rapidly. 'Don't worry. I'm not going to embarrass either of us by crying. In any case, these aren't tears of weakness. They're tears of anger. I've lived in fear since my nephew announced his intention. If I were a man and thirty years younger, I swear I'd punch him on the nose.'

'I hope you don't expect me to do that for you.'

'You should smile more often. It suits you. You look stern most of the time.'

'There's always something to worry about.'

'Is there a problem at the clinic? I'd be interested to hear it. I lead a dull existence and I miss hearing about the projects my brother supported.'

She waited while Doctor Brewer looked at her thoughtfully. He was a good-looking man. Not breathtakingly handsome like Greg, but worth a second look, with his intelligent eyes and that smile that was worth waiting for.

'The clinic has a serious problem. Most of the local breadwinners will lose their jobs next week, which means they'll no longer count as deserving poor and most of our funding will go down the drain.'

'What about Mr Clough? My brother said he was rolling in money. Surely it's in his interests to tide you over?'

'He's eager to see the back of us. I went to a clinic committee meeting yesterday and there's a rumour that Lennox, the owner of the factory, wants our building.'

'For factory premises? So the community would lose its clinic but get back its jobs?'

'Apparently, he wants the building for a sweatshop. He'll fill it with women, who'll work every waking hour making artificial flowers and trimmings for clothes, and earn next to nothing for the privilege.'

She had never seen the point of offering sympathy. Practical help was of greater value. 'Have you tried the Withington Fund?'

'Never heard of it.'

'Not many people have. It was set up when the old workhouse became a hospital. There are all kinds of rules attached to it, but it could be worth a try.'

'I'll look into it.' He shook his head. 'It's a good thing Judge Rawley isn't here to see how quickly the clinic might fail – though, of course, had he been here, Barnaby Clough would be toeing the line.'

Oh, the temptation! How she longed to say, 'It was me all along. Whenever Robert showed an interest in a social project, it was because I nagged him into it. It suited him, of course – anything to throw his weight around. I can't do anything under my own name because I have no influence. My brother denigrated me in front of his associates, so they had no opinion of me, and, shunned by Lady Kimber, I have no place in the community. But make no mistake – in every way that matters, it was I who provided the support you needed.'

The devil of it was, she could never tell anyone. Not to protect Robert's reputation, but to protect her own, such as it was. Telling would make her appear petty. It might even make her seem a liar.

Better that people had no opinion of her at all than that they held her in contempt.

Mary couldn't wait to see Charlie again. They ate toad-in-the-hole and she told him about the party, thanking him again for stumping up for the prizes.

'Pleasure,' he said. 'You should write an article about it – the party, not the prizes.'

'I can't. It's connected to the clinic. What were you doing while I was busy with the party?'

'Aunt Christina's friend Mrs Rushworth held a bit of a garden party. Very jolly. There were a few young boy-cousins, so we got up a spot of cricket.'

'Sounds fun.'

'It was. Talking of cricket, the governor's going to watch W. G. Grace's last match and he's asked me to tag along. Can't miss the chance to see the great man mash Dorset into the ground.'

'How long will you be away?' She wished she could take the question back. Did she sound clingy?

'Don't know exactly, a few days. Will you miss me? I hope so. I hope you'll miss me very much.'

He squeezed her fingers under the table. Later, when he opened the door of the landaulet for her, he stole a kiss. Mary pressed closer, but he stepped away. They never had any privacy. They were always in the tea shop or in the motor, always on show, which was fine for friends but frustrating for a young couple on the brink of something more.

Were they on the brink? And if they were, shouldn't she pull back? What a mess she had made of her personal life. First a married man, now the Kimber heir. But she hadn't thrown herself at him, she honestly hadn't. They had things in common; they had met at the agency; they had been friends before the possibility of anything more had arisen. And it had arisen, hadn't it? Charlie had made that clear. It wasn't just her this time, like it had been with Nathaniel. This time, it was safe to have feelings, because Charlie shared them.

Anyway, she wasn't going to mope around in his absence. She had had a couple of articles sent back unwanted and she needed to get something accepted.

A letter was waiting for her at home. The envelope was typewritten. From Mrs Newbold, requesting *An Autumn Walk*, followed by the remaining seasons? Her heart quickened in anticipation. It would be the first time her work had been commissioned, a major milestone. Then she realised the envelope was too thick to contain a letter . . . It must be an article being returned unwanted.

No, it wasn't. Inside was another envelope, addressed to *Miss Fay Randall, c/o Vera's Voice*. She opened it and started to read. Her body filled with heat. She finished the letter and read it again to make sure.

It was the offer of an interview – for a job as a journalist.

'I'm bored to death,' said Evie. 'Come and talk to me. All Imogen does is clean the house and sew pinafores.'

'Show some respect,' said Nathaniel. 'You're lucky to have her caring for you.'

'I don't mean to be ratty, but I'm a rotten patient. I do appreciate her, truly.'

'Tell her, not me.'

Why did she do this? Why did she always put him in the position of being the sensible one . . . the spoilsport? But her boredom was a good thing. It showed she was recovering.

'I'm tired of resting. I'm sure I could have managed to go on Imogen's picnic.'

'She had enough to do without worrying whether you were about to collapse in a heap.'

Evie pulled a face, looking for all the world like the pigtailed little horror who had plagued him to death when they were children.

'I wish I could go with you this afternoon. God, listen to me. I sound like the worst kind of brat.' She put on a childish whine. 'I want to go on the picnic, I want to go to the meeting. But I *do*. I'm desperate to be up and about.'

'Save your energy for coming up with more ideas if this one doesn't get taken up.'

'Are you suggesting the Withington people won't snatch your hand off in their eagerness to fund my brilliant idea?'

'Your idea,' said Nathaniel, 'is a corker. And so are you.'

'Really? I thought I annoyed the hallelujah out of you.'

'Evangeline Brewer, you cause me more anxiety and frustration than everyone else put together, but it was pointed out to me recently that we share our crusading spirit. I'd be a hypocrite if that hadn't made me think again about you.'

Evie smiled and her face, still thin from her ordeal, brightened, restoring her old self. Nathaniel felt his lips twitch in response. He made sure to keep the smile on his face as Evie's smile widened into a cheeky grin, forcing himself to concentrate on her saucy expression, not the gap where two back teeth had been knocked out. If he could get his hands on the brutes—

'In that case,' she said, 'you won't mind if I go to Alexandra Park this afternoon. There's an event on where I wouldn't mind bashing a placard over someone's head.'

'Very funny. I may not be a hypocrite, but I'm still your big brother whose job is to protect you. Besides, you wouldn't get to the garden gate before your legs caved in.'

Inside the enormous building, with its echoing stairwells and the windows set high in the walls, Nathaniel and Alistair were shown to a spacious room with a long table down the centre. Two rows of chairs stood over to one side. Four of the seats were occupied by men with notebooks.

'Gentlemen of the press,' murmured the clerk who had shown them in. 'If you'll take your places on this side of the table, the members of the fund committee will join you shortly.'

Nathaniel nodded to the reporters. Would they write up a story of success or failure later on?

A door at the far end opened and the committee filed in, five smartly dressed, affluent-looking gentlemen in their fifties and sixties. They took their places, putting down papers in front of them. A sixth man came in carrying what looked like ledgers; he sat at the end of the table.

The man in the middle bestowed a brief smile on the room.

'Good afternoon, gentlemen. I am Alderman Fordyce, chairman of the committee.' He introduced his colleagues.

'And seated at the end is Mr Lockwood, clerk to the committee, who will answer any technical points that arise. We're here to discuss the proposal put forward by Doctors Brewer and Cottrell. Mr Lockwood?'

The clerk addressed the journalists. 'When the workhouse closed, a fund was established to provide assistance should a community be struck by events that, in former times, would have led to many of the people needing to enter the workhouse. In such a case, funds may be released to support a local project to assist the community for a limited time.'

'We have read your proposal with interest, Doctors,' said Alderman Fordyce. 'The floor is yours.'

'The community in question relies heavily for employment on a local factory, which is about to shut down,' said Alistair. 'We seek funding to employ these men to improve their local area. This will keep the community afloat while they seek employment elsewhere.'

'So, they'll be labouring on your project and also seeking work?' said Mr Shaw. 'We don't pay men to look for jobs.'

'Payment will be by the hour for work done on the project,' said Nathaniel.

'Very well. Continue.'

Alistair resumed. 'There is waste ground that can be turned into a playground by clearing the rubble, laying cinders, and building swings and a sandpit, and there are empty buildings that can be turned into a bathhouse and a wash house.'

'So you have a community of plumbers?' asked Shaw.

'No, sir. Certain work will have to be done by tradesmen and everything will be supervised by a foreman. It's in the costings.'

'When we set up the clinic,' Nathaniel added, 'the local men helped prepare the building, so we know they can do what we propose.'

'Furthermore,' said Alistair, 'the local school building is in a poor state and we plan to improve it.'

'An ambitious project, Doctors.'

'But achievable,' said Nathaniel.

'We should discuss the clinic,' said Mr Lightfoot. 'This situation with the factory closure means you'll lose your Deserving Poor Committee funding.'

'But if the Withington Fund supports our project,' said Alistair, 'the clinic will once again be eligible for that funding because the men will be employed.'

'We understand,' said Mr Richards, 'that there is a plan to open a new factory in place of the clinic.'

'Not a factory, sir – a sweatshop. The workers will be women and the pay will be pitiful.'

'We know what happens to women in these places,' said Nathaniel. 'Some go bald from carrying heavy boxes on their heads. Many ruin their eyesight struggling to do close work in poor light. Industrial injuries are common and working hours excessive.'

'Nevertheless, the women will have jobs, so the community won't be eligible for funding through us.'

'General philanthropy is not in our remit,' said Alderman Fordyce. 'Our sole interest is the workhouse question. Would these people in previous times have been sent to the workhouse? This new factory, however undesirable, means that they would not. You have made an interesting proposal – a compelling one, if I may say so – but it doesn't fulfil our terms.' He looked from side to side, gathering the glances of his fellow members. 'We must reject your proposal.'

It was all Nathaniel could do not to leap to his feet. There was a commotion as the door was thrown open. He felt a burst of irritation. Just when he needed to fight back! He looked round, ready to glare the intruder into silence.

In the doorway stood Helen Rawley.

Chapter Sixteen

As she talked with Mr Gladwin, Mary was aware of her interested smile, her outward poise, even as she battled against a whirl of emotions that threatened to drown all possibility of intelligent conversation. She had felt this way ever since she woke at some ridiculously early hour. By rights, she should be exhausted by now, but she felt exhilarated.

Mr Gladwin, the proprietor of *The Gentlewoman's World*, a silver-haired gentleman with a full set of whiskers, had offered her a position.

'I like the pieces you wrote for my periodical, Miss Randall – Maitland, I beg your pardon – and I made it my business to see what else you've written. I admire your writing and I'd like to employ you.'

It was wonderful, yet at the same time dreadfully upsetting. The offices of *The Gentlewoman's World* were in Sussex. Her parents would never agree. But she was over twenty-one and if she insisted . . . would she insist? The thought of going so far away was scary – but exciting, too. How would she feel in months – years – to come if she turned down this opportunity?

'Our readers are more genteel than those of *Vera's Voice*. They appreciate the finer things. We're planning a series of articles on England's country houses. As a spinster, you would be free to travel to various places to work on these.'

'That sounds interesting.' She kept her voice level when inside she was whooping for joy.

'Should you accept my offer, I'd ask a lady member of staff to find you suitable lodgings before you arrive.'

'Thank you. You've given me a lot to think about.'

'I appreciate this has taken you by surprise. Here's my card. Perhaps you would write to me by this time next week with your decision.'

As she left the Midland Hotel, she felt punch-drunk. The opportunity was dazzling, but it involved leaving home. Was she prepared to do that? She hadn't said a word to her parents about this interview and Mr Gladwin hadn't referred to her family. He had treated her as though it were her decision alone.

Climbing aboard the omnibus, she pictured railway journeys through the countryside, visiting wisteria-clad stately homes. What a way to earn her living!

She knew what Lilian would say: 'Given up on getting married, have you? A spinster travelling around – they'd never expect a married woman to do that. You might as well have "On the shelf" tattooed on your forehead.'

Something caught her eye through the window. The bus was passing Alexandra Park and a rally was in progress.

'It's them votes for women females,' a man's disapproving voice declared. 'See them placards? Daft buggers. I'd crown 'em with their flaming placards, that's what I'd do.'

She hadn't known a women's rally was planned, but what luck that she was here, her trusty notebook in her bag. She rose and moved down the aisle. She was going to take advantage of the moment. It was what journalists did.

Helen lurched into the committee room. Pain was eating her hip but she mustn't let it show. Were Messrs Clough and Saunders behind her? She couldn't look round to check. She might topple over. Reaching the table, she grasped the edge and leant against it, angling her body forwards, as though leaning towards the committee was part of the urgency, though really she needed the support. The doctors had come to their feet, the other men had half risen, clearly unsure whether to show courtesy to this madwoman.

Doctor Brewer grasped the back of his chair, ready to bring it to her. He knew, damn him. He could tell she was in pain. She must say her piece before his gallantry showed her up.

'Allow me to introduce myself.'

'If you'll permit me,' said Doctor Brewer. 'Miss Rawley, may I present Alderman Fordyce, who chairs this committee, and . . .' He rattled off some names. 'Mr Chairman, this is Miss Rawley, sister of the late Judge Rawley.' He waved a hand, indicating behind her. 'Mr Clough, Mr Saunders.'

She channelled all her strength into her voice. 'I must address the meeting.'

'You're too late, madam,' said Alderman Fordyce. 'The committee has made its decision. Funding is denied.'

'Then we'll withdraw, with our apologies,' came a voice from behind her – the smooth tones of that lawyer fellow, drat him.

She started to turn, but the movement caused the pain in her hip to erupt into a blaze. She shut her eyes, then forced them open. Show weakness? Never!

'May I offer you my seat, Miss Rawley?'

Doctor Brewer had positioned his chair for her. She made a point of bestowing a gracious nod before she sat, holding herself rigid on the way down so she couldn't crumple. As her hip was relieved of the burden of her meagre weight, there was a single moment of blessed relief before pain flared, storming into every corner, bringing a twist of nausea with it. It would subside in a minute.

She had evidently ruffled Alderman Fordyce's feathers.

'This meeting is concluded, madam.'

'Then reopen it.' She mustn't let the pain speak for her. 'I apologise for the intrusion, but it is imperative you hear me out. You said funding was denied. Why is that?'

'You can read about it in the newspapers,' said Mr Shaw.

'I'm sure Alderman Fordyce will indulge the sister of the High Court judge whose influence was instrumental in setting up the clinic.' Although she twitched the corners of her mouth into a suggestion of a polite smile, she didn't crinkle her eyes. It would be good to think she could appear intimidating, but they probably saw her as a worn-out busybody.

Alderman Fordyce's glance flicked across the room and, without turning her head, Helen looked that way, too. Ah, those men must be reporters. Good. They were paying rapt attention. They had probably been bored rigid before her arrival, poor devils.

Mr Lockwood cleared his throat. 'It would be inappropriate to award funds in this instance. The men of the community may be about to lose their jobs, but the women will be employed instead. Hence this community would not in former times have been reduced to workhouse status.'

'Besides,' added Mr Shaw, 'when the clinic closes, who would lead the proposed project? Communities of this sort need leadership and while no one doubts the benevolent intentions of the good doctors here, why would they interest themselves in the community once their clinic shuts its doors?'

'Good point,' said Mr Clough from behind Helen. She narrowed her eyes. He wasn't going to worm his way out that easily.

'We wouldn't leave these people to sink,' said Doctor Brewer.

Time to take control. 'That's a moot point,' she said, 'since it isn't going to happen. Alderman Fordyce, I have the honour of being accompanied by Mr Barnaby Clough.' Might as well lay it on with a trowel. 'It was through his generosity that the clinic, which is of such value to the people of these deprived streets, was founded. Mr Clough has an important announcement.'

The generous benefactor didn't speak. Helen glanced round. Mr Clough had gone an interesting shade of puce.

'Come, Mr Clough. This is no time for modesty.'

Mr Saunders stepped forward. 'If I might address the meeting on Mr Clough's behalf? It appears there has been a misunderstanding regarding the clinic's future. While it is true that Mr Clough was approached by a businessman who expressed an interest in taking over the clinic's premises, no formal or binding agreement was made between them. Indeed, Mr Clough would never jeopardise the future of the clinic in which he takes such an interest.'

'Mr Clough is to be commended for his philanthropy,' Helen threw in for good measure. 'My late brother, the High Court judge, often said so.'

'So the clinic is to stay open?' asked Alderman Fordyce.

'Through the generosity of Mr Clough.' She had thought it would hurt to butter up the odious Mr Clough. Instead she was having trouble keeping a straight face.

'So the clinic won't become a factory and the local men will be unemployed?'

'And Doctor Cottrell and I will remain at the clinic,' said Doctor Brewer, 'should there be any need for us to lead a local project.'

'Alderman Fordyce,' Helen said in honeyed tones, 'under the circumstances, will you reopen the hearing?'

Alexandra Park was heaving – women waving placards, plenty of men too. For a second, Mary's heart lifted at the thought of so much male support, then it hardened as she saw the men were strong-arming the women, trying to clear them out of the way, while the women – good for them! – were giving as good as they got.

She hurried through the gates, her ears ringing with the roar of the demonstration. Men! Votes for women demonstrations were peaceful – unless the male spectators decided otherwise. She paused to take in the scene, alarmed by the boisterousness. Women were being manhandled. She felt vulnerable, but she set her lips in a determined line.

'This is no place for you, miss.'

She turned to see a bobby. 'Shouldn't you do something? Look – three men against one woman. They're picking her up. It isn't decent.'

'They'd probably say it's votes for women that isn't decent.'

With one hand diving into her bag for her notebook, she stepped forward, only to have a strong hand clamped round her arm.

'I'd advise you to take a closer look.'

She tried to pull free, but the hand didn't let go. As she realised what she was looking at, her resistance melted away out of sheer astonishment.

The bobby released her. 'See?'

She had heard of these before: pretend riots. These women were men dressed up – hamming it up too, some tottering and squealing, with rouged cheeks and ridiculous hats, while others had entered into the spirit of the event by wielding their placards like giant fly-swatters.

'It's outrageous!'

'Hoity-toity. Important training, this is. It's a competition between the firemen and the tram drivers. They have to suggest possible injuries and how to deal with them. It all adds up to a fine old ding-dong.'

She wanted to wade in and drag the whole ignorant lot of them apart like the stupid little boys they were. A group was standing by the ornamental pond, observing the proceedings. Two had clipboards, another was consulting a notebook. One looked lofty and important, letting the others point things out to him. And one was Mr Treadgold.

She marched across.

'Mr Treadgold!'

'Good gracious – Miss Maitland!'

She said what Mr Treadgold used to say when he was displeased with one of his minions. 'What's the meaning of this?'

The gall of the man! He smiled as he surveyed the scene. 'I'm sure you don't need me to tell you this is a make-believe riot.'

'With make-believe women.'

'It is essential training. You never know when these abnormal females will cause a disturbance of the peace.'

'The only time a women's demonstration becomes a riot is when men turn it into one.'

Mr Treadgold looked down his nose at her. 'I shall, of course, report your insolence to your father.'

'Really? Then tell him this as well.'

Darting forward, she delivered a hefty shove that caught the pompous oaf off guard and sent him stumbling sideways. He cannoned into the important-looking man, who tripped and landed with a splash in the pond, followed a second later by Mr Treadgold, arms windmilling fruitlessly, who landed on top of him.

From nowhere, a photographer appeared.

A policeman, two policemen – three. Mary was pulled in all directions while being shouted at to stand still. The last thing she saw was Mr Treadgold puffed up like a bullfrog before she was marched away with her hat askew.

The police station didn't come as a surprise. Neither did the small, windowless room where she was asked questions, or the writing of the statement. What did surprise her, what made her heart leap into her mouth, was being informed that she would be detained overnight.

'But all I did was duck a town hall clerk.'

'A *senior* clerk,' the sergeant corrected, as if someone had insisted upon the distinction, as was undoubtedly the case. Thank you, Mr Treadgold. 'You'd probably be spending the night in your own bed if that was the extent of it, but not when you duck two in one go and the other is the deputy mayor.'

'My parents don't know where I am. Could you send them a message?'

'Think me and my men have nothing better to do?'

But her family must have been informed, because when she was led into the dock the next morning, her parents were sitting on the public seats – and there, too, was Granny, looking . . . surely not smug? Yet what other word would describe it?

'You've given your name as Maitland,' the magistrate said, 'but the court has received information that you are in fact a Kimber.'

Interest fizzed around the room. Granny preened.

'I'm not a Kimber.'

'You state for the record that you are not related to the Kimber family of Ees House, Chorlton-cum-Hardy?'

'Well, I am related to them, but—'

'Which means I cannot hear this case. No local magistrate can, since we're all acquainted with Sir Edward. You'll have to be shipped off at public expense to a court sufficiently far away that the old and respected name of Kimber is unknown.' He let her stew while he sorted his papers and capped his pen. 'It so happens a magistrate from Shropshire is visiting these parts. Arrangements are being made for him to hear this matter, assuming it fits in with his social engagements. Take her away.'

A hand grasped her arm. She was taken back down the same flight of steps she had walked up a while ago and deposited in the same tiny room. When would this Shropshire magistrate make himself available? The possibility that it might not be today made her press a hand to her heart.

She wanted her mother – both her mothers, her adored Mam who had been torn from her, and Lilian, kindly and capable, whom she had sensibly accepted into her family, only to realise, years later, that Lilian had crept into her heart. When this nightmare was over, when Dadda had stumped up the fine and they went home, all she wanted was to hurl herself into Lilian's arms and sob her heart out. Dadda could be as angry as he wanted, just so long as she could have some motherly comfort.

It was midday when she returned to court. The chamber was packed. Granny's mad idea of declaring her a Kimber had turned her into a peep show.

She confirmed her name and address, then she was asked her age and whether she was married.

'No, I'm not.'

'Louder, if you please.'

'I'm not married.'

'I can't say that surprises me,' the magistrate remarked.

Mr Treadgold appeared and Mary tried not to be dismayed as he was treated with the utmost courtesy as he described what had happened.

'Of course, it was not just myself, sir,' he ended. 'It was also' – and he dropped his voice impressively – 'the deputy mayor himself.'

'You say the defendant selected you as her target because you're known to her?'

'She worked in my department for a number of years.'

'It must have been a relief when she left.'

'At the time I felt let down by such ingratitude, but now . . .'

'Quite so. That'll be all, sir, other than to congratulate you on your part in organising the splendid training exercise that ended so unfortunately for yourself.' The magistrate glanced at the clerk. 'I believe there is a character witness?'

Angela was brought in. Mary could have cheered. Looking round, she saw Josephine in the public seating and the tightness in her chest relaxed as some of her burden lifted.

But the magistrate cut short Angela's statement.

'Your praise is of no interest. You're another such female as the defendant. I prefer to accept Mr Treadgold's testimony as to character.'

The clerk murmured something.

'Another character witness? Oh, very well.'

Alistair entered and took his place. When he had finished, the magistrate asked questions about the clinic.

'Will you continue to employ the defendant after this, Doctor?'

There was the tiniest of pauses, but a pause nonetheless.

'We would be reluctant to dispense with Miss Maitland's services.'

The magistrate delivered a level look in her direction.

'Let's hear from you, then, young woman. Why were you at Alexandra Park? The event wasn't advertised.'

'I was passing and I saw it.'

'And decided to join in?'

'I intended to write about it.'

'In your diary?'

'I write articles for newspapers and periodicals.'

'Do you indeed? An amusing hobby for a girl with a smattering of education.'

'It isn't a hobby. I take it seriously.'

'If you say so.'

'Others take me seriously, too. As a matter of fact—'

'As a matter of fact what?'

Cripes. This wasn't how she wanted to tell her parents. 'I was on my way home from – from an interview for a job as a journalist.'

She lifted her chin, ignoring the murmurs. The magistrate shook his head. She felt stung but kept her mouth shut as his expression altered, disapproval hardening into something sterner.

'It was your intention to write for profit about the training exercise?'

'To write an article, yes, but I didn't realise what was happening at first. I thought it was a proper rally.'

'And when you discovered it wasn't, did you start writing?'

'Well . . . no. I saw Mr Treadgold and went to speak to him.'

'To harangue him, you mean. I see it all now. Denied the opportunity to write in praise of women who should know better, you decided to make a headline of your own, thereby avenging yourself on your former superior and pandering to your silly views into the bargain. Disgraceful. Seven days without the option.'

It was stifling in the carriage, even with the windows down. Lady Kimber would have liked to fan her face with her hand, except that she wouldn't stoop to such unpolished behaviour. Never let it be said she conducted herself with anything less than perfect taste and refinement. A long time ago, she had thrown dignity, seemliness, good taste, the lot, to the four winds, and just look what that had done for her.

Strangely, on the surface it hadn't done her any harm. Here she was now with two prominent marriages to her credit. Underneath, though, it had ruined her – ruined her for other men. There were still moments when she was hot and willing, and it was Greg her body was ready for. Marital duties with Henry had left her as dry as a bone, with a raging soreness that had nearly torn her in two each time she visited the water closet.

Thank heaven for Eleanor, whose arrival had provided her heart with a reason to carry on beating. Eleanor made up for the childlessness of her second marriage, too. Of course, it was a disappointment not to have produced an heir, but that hadn't lasted, dashed aside by the glorious possibility of Eleanor's becoming the next Lady Kimber.

Disposing of Charlie had been easy. And if the Maitland girl took the bait, she would vanish before he returned. Writing to darling Pa, pouring out her concerns, had done the trick. Judge William Rawley had fingers in many pies and if he wanted the proprietor of *The Gentlewoman's World* to offer a job to a budding journalist, then offer a job he would.

She smiled her satisfaction; then she caught sight of the board outside a newsagent's and her smile turned to a death mask.

LADY KIMBER IMPRISONED.

No, not LADY KIMBER – she looked again. KIMBER LADY. That made no sense either.

She pulled the check-string and, when the coachman drew the vehicle to a halt, sent him to get a paper. There it was, on the front page. Following an incident yesterday afternoon involving the ducking of the deputy mayor and a town hall official, a young woman had been up before the bench this morning.

Not a Kimber lady. Not a lady of any description. How had the *Evening News* got hold of the Kimber connection? She must have flaunted it in open court, believing it would buy clemency.

The Maitland creature.

* * *

Mary couldn't eat, couldn't face it, though the other women at the long, scarred table fell upon the food.

'What are you in for?'

'I pushed the deputy mayor and a town hall official into a duck pond.' She hoped to raise a chuckle, but all she got was cold stares.

'Oh aye? Thought you was being clever, did you? Make me sick, your lot do. Some of us have committed real crimes. Not like you, arsing around, trying to shock.'

'Ain't you gonna eat that?' her neighbour demanded.

'No.' She tried for a rueful smile but couldn't pull it off.

Knowing grins went round. She felt baffled and uneasy.

'One of them, are you, chuck?'

'Aye, one o' them bloody fools.'

She wanted to ask, but missed the chance, because, with a loud, 'Give it 'ere, then,' her plate was grabbed and squabbled over.

She reached for her tea, but it was stewed to the point of having turned a strange orangey-brown and it tasted like . . . well, not like tea, anyway. She pushed it away, only to garner more looks.

'Earl Grey not to your taste?'

Under everyone's eyes, she deemed it wisest to draw her mug back again and take a sip, trying to keep her expression neutral, but apparently failing, as the collective shout of derisive laughter informed her.

'Aw, leave her be. Don't you pay no attention to them lot, love. Like a spot of water, would you?'

'Yes, please.'

'Give us your mug then.'

She pushed her mug across the table while the woman swilled down the last of her tea and set down her empty mug with a bang. Mary looked for the water jug. It took her a moment to hear the sniggers. She looked back at the woman and received a wide smile in return.

Locking eyes with her, the woman worked her mouth, then spat copiously into the empty mug, holding Mary's appalled gaze as she passed it to her neighbour, who also worked up a hefty spit and spewed it into the mug. Mary watched in horror as it was passed round and each woman gobbed into it. Dear heaven, would they force her to drink it?

'That'll do. Back to your cell, Maitland.'

With cries of 'You haven't drunk your water, chuck' and 'Aren't you thirsty no more?' ringing in her ears, she stumbled from the table.

Chapter Seventeen

'Wake up. We want you moved before morning bell.'

Mary struggled to her feet. Her situation came flooding back, sending through her a wave of dread so potent she staggered. Her sleep had been deep and thorny; she had lurched into wakefulness any number of times. Once, it was her bladder that woke her and she had been forced to use the bucket in the corner. When she again slept, the stench from the bucket had invaded her dreams.

There was a wardress beside her, hurrying her along, another in front setting a brisk pace along the landing with its bleak row of locked doors. A face appeared at a grille and a voice set up a cry of, 'She's going! She's going!'

Next moment, there was a ghostly face behind every grille and a clamour filled her ears. A sharp yank on her arm prevented her from cannoning into the wardress in front, who had stopped to unlock the door. Down a flight of steps. When the steps dog-legged, they peeled off onto a corridor – along there, up more steps, waiting for the door to be unlocked, then onto another corridor, a short one this time, its cell doors standing open.

'Inside.'

She had barely stepped in before she felt a swish of air behind her as the door banged shut, followed by the sharp rattle of the key.

Why had she been moved? It was a relief to be away from those women. She would take more care with her new companions – though did those open doors mean there weren't any?

The key turned and the door banged open.

'Water.' A wardress thrust a jug into her hands. 'I hope you're still drinking?'

'Why—?'

But the woman was gone. A chipped mug stood on a shelf. How long had it been there? She poured some water, swilling it round before emptying it into the inevitable bucket. Finally, she poured a drink, not without reservations, but she was too parched to hold back.

She was hungry too, with a wishy-washy sensation in her head. It couldn't be long until breakfast. The wishy-washy feeling invaded her empty stomach and she had to lie down. Gradually her stomach steadied.

She dozed. When she woke, her mouth was stale. The sound of the key in the lock brought her to her feet. There was a swinging sensation inside her head. Hunger.

The wardress was carrying another jug. 'More water.'

'I have plenty.'

'The governor wants to be sure you don't run out. It's important he can say that afterwards. Have you had a drink? Good.'

'Why wouldn't I drink?'

'Some of 'em don't. It just makes it worse.' She turned to leave.

Mary asked quickly, 'What time is it?' At the same moment, a bell clanged.

'Midday. That's the dinner bell. Not that you care, you and your hunger strike.'

'Me and . . . ?'

'The women told us how you wouldn't touch your food last night. That's why you're here. The governor likes to keep hunger strikers separate. Less fuss. The other women think you're barmy, you lot, and I for one don't blame 'em. I can't stand here gassing. I'll leave you to it.'

Hunger strike.

Her knees gave way and she sat down, landing heavily on the bunk. She must set the wardress straight the next time she brought water.

Weary hours passed before that happened. She stood the moment she heard the key.

'Please, there's been a mistake. I'm not on hunger strike.'

'Then what are you doing here?'

'There's been a mistake.'

'I don't see how.'

'Please – there has.'

'Oh.' The woman looked at the jug in her hands, then pushed it at her. 'Here, take this. I'll – well, I s'pose I'd best tell someone.'

'Thank you. And if I could have something . . .'

The door was already closed. She found herself speaking to musty air.

'. . . to eat?'

'The governor wants you, Maitland. Look sharp. No time for that,' the wardress added as she tried to smooth her appearance. 'Governor knows what prisoners look like. The posh 'uns are the exact same as the reg'lars.'

Wobblier on her feet now, or perhaps just wobblier in her head, she was aware of corridors and stairs, of doors being unlocked in front of them and locked again behind. She was brought into an office with a closed door on the far side. A man got up from behind a desk, crossed to the farther door, knocked and went in, shutting it behind him. The wardress stood ramrod-straight and silent. Mary endeavoured to do the same, but exhaustion vibrated inside her. It was all she could do not to tremble.

The door opened and they went in. There was a vast desk with a bewhiskered man seated behind it, looking stern. The man from the outer office stood at his shoulder, looking snooty. She didn't mind the sternness, but the snooty expression made her stand up straighter.

'Maitland, Governor,' the wardress said.

'So you've come to your senses. Good, good. Stupid females like you cause a deal of bother, silly pieces with unwomanly ideas, who think it's clever to get sent down for knocking off a policeman's helmet. Utter balderdash, as I said to the chief constable over dinner only last week. Much as it goes against nature to have married women working, you modern females present a compelling case to allow the employment of married women teachers. Your problem is you've been educated, if you can call it that, by embittered spinsters and look where it's got you. Votes for women – I don't know. I'd as soon give the vote to my dog. Sign that.'

There was a sheet of paper on the desk.

'What is it?'

'Don't waste my time. Sign it.'

Bending forward, she inhaled sharply against the swooshing sensation inside her head. There was a pencil beside the paper. She picked it up. There was a space at the bottom for her signature.

'For pity's sake, woman, what's the matter with you? Sign it. If you can't write, put an X.'

'I'm reading it.'

'There's nothing to read. It just says you won't go on hunger strike.'

'There's something about—'

'Yes, yes, you regret and renounce your unwomanly deeds and so on and so forth. Get it signed so I can send it to the *Evening News*.'

Mary stared. She couldn't believe what she had heard, yet when she listened to the words over again inside her head, they said the same thing.

'Give me strength,' the governor muttered. 'What's the matter with her?'

A sharp jab in the back made her swing round to glare at the wardress before she turned back to the governor.

'I won't sign. And you can consider me on hunger strike.'

The bruises had faded, from Greg's face at least. His body still bore marks, but, hidden beneath his clothes, they didn't matter.

What mattered was, could he move freely, with no hint of a wince to betray him? Not only that, but could he keep it up into the night? You had to be prepared to stay at the poker table for hours to accrue the sort of sum that would loosen Mr Jonas's hold.

Oh well, he would find out soon enough on the journey to London. He had sent a telegram giving instructions to have his rooms opened and the drinks cabinet restocked. What more did a fellow need? He didn't tell Helen he was going. He was sick to death of her. She had probably hoped to get on his good side by taking care of him, but it would take more than that. The only way for her to get on his good side would be by dropping dead.

Since the old bat didn't look like obliging, he must resume his old habits – and while that was an absolute bugger, part of him responded to the challenge. It felt like coming alive again.

The journey wasn't bad to start with, but by the time the train pulled into Euston, he was aching all over and there was a fire roaring below his ribs. Christ, if he looked as rough as he felt, he was done for. He climbed into the vehicle at the head of the taxi rank, pulling hard on a cigarette while the porter dealt with his luggage.

When he arrived at his rooms, he reached for the whisky decanter. The heat washed down his throat, simultaneously soothing and invigorating. He threw himself on the bed and slept.

It was evening when he woke. His body was stiff, but that never killed anyone. He drew a bath, letting the hot water do its healing. Later, clad in his dressing gown, he investigated the kitchen, where the woman who did for him had left a covered plate of cheddar and ham with pickles and tomatoes, and a generous helping of lemon pudding.

With the tang of lemon-laced custard still ringing on his tongue, he prepared for his night out, dressing as carefully as a warrior going into battle. Well, he was facing battle, wasn't he? He didn't play cards for the hell of it and neither did the men he played with. Do well, live well. Do badly and you might as well do everyone a favour and chuck yourself off the nearest bridge.

He was going to do well tonight. He felt lucky. No such thing as luck. But he still felt lucky.

After all, how hard could it be? She had already begun a hunger strike, albeit without meaning to, so she had a head start. If she held out for a couple of days, which meant only until the day after tomorrow, she would have struck her blow on behalf of women everywhere, honour would be satisfied, and she could resume eating without losing face.

Mary lay down for the rest of the day, lurching to her feet from time to time to pour some water, though moving made her feel woozy. Drinking water helped, but only up to a point. The day stretched interminably.

Through the long hours of the night, she dozed on and off. Her stomach burnt and her body ached.

The morning brought another jug of water. It was unexpectedly heavy, making her fingers fumble and clutch. How petty, filling it fuller to catch her out, but when she looked, it was no more full than before.

Later there was another jug. There was a message too.

'Thought you'd like to know your father's here to see you,' said the wardress, 'but your sort aren't allowed visitors.'

It was surprising how much it hurt. Even knowing Dadda

would have no truck with the hunger strike, she would have given anything to see him. Misery speared through her. Were the pains in her stomach hunger-pangs or homesickness? She eased her body onto the bed and curled up, wondering how in heaven's name she had ended up like this.

But she wouldn't give in. She had to hold out only until tomorrow. Afterwards she would tell Angela and Josephine about the hunger strike. They would organise a meeting and spread the word. When would Charlie return? Would he be proud? Horrified?

She slept, then woke again. She needed to use the bucket. That was the worst part, worse than the pains in her gut, worse than being muzzy-headed, worse than the slackness in her muscles or the trembling in her bones. The bucket had stood unemptied since her arrival in this cell – a punishment for the hunger strike? The only mercy was that it had a lid, though the stench that was going to spew out when she lifted it would set her guts heaving.

Needs must. She held her breath.

The door opened, but instead of a wardress, it was a man – a frock-coated doctor. Thank goodness she wasn't squatting over the bucket. Two wardresses came in behind.

'Sit,' the doctor commanded.

For an insane moment, she could think only of sitting on the bucket. One of the women pushed her onto the bunk.

'Top buttons,' said the doctor.

He made an impatient movement with his hand and the women stepped forward. One grabbed her shoulders while the other batted away her protesting hands, hands that were frighteningly weak, and pulled open her top buttons.

'Hold still,' rapped the doctor. He pressed the end of a stethoscope to her chest, a small, cold circle on her skin. He lifted her wrist and took her pulse. 'She'll do,' he decreed and the three of them left.

She pressed her fingers where the stethoscope had been. Were all inmates given this rudimentary check?

Later, the key turned and the door banged open. Were they trained to bang the doors? Was it done to make the inmates feel even more locked in?

People entered the cell, filling it, six of them, two doctors, four wardresses. Instinct told her to hide, to disappear. There was a wardress either side of her; they heaved her into a sitting position, propped her up, holding her fast as she struggled. The bunk sagged as a doctor knelt behind her. A muscular forearm fastened across her chest and throat, an elbow dug into one shoulder, a fist clamped round the other.

She tried to wriggle away, but more hands yanked her head back. The face of the man behind her was close beside her own; she caught a whiff of mulligatawny on his breath. She strained to pull her head away, but his hand was there, thumb and fingers digging into the flesh around her mouth. She fought to keep her mouth tight shut, but a jabbing sensation to either side of it parted her teeth and then he had her mouth wide open.

The other doctor bore down upon her. She saw a tube and a funnel, cloudy with filth. Next moment, the tube was inside her mouth, grazing her palate, butting her tongue. She whimpered as her tongue worked frantically to force the thing out. Her heart was pounding, her nose was running.

Her tongue lost the battle and the tube – her eyes popped open – ploughed into her throat. Her larynx flicked open, shut, open, then the doctor fiddled with the tube, muttered, 'That's it,' and pushed it straight inside her body.

Her mouth burnt. She started to choke, only she couldn't because her gullet was stuffed full. She arched her body, half in resistance, half in an instinctive attempt to accommodate the tube less painfully, but hands shoved her back, forced her back, all those people crowding against her, all those hands and arms containing her, controlling her.

Her breathing erupted through her nostrils in frantic little bursts of air and liquid snot. The animal inside her let loose a guttural moan of protest that reverberated from somewhere high in the back of her mouth, filling her ears and vibrating down her nostrils. The noise elongated, then faded to nothing as she lost the power to move.

The tube went on scraping its way down. Eyes frozen wide, she watched the dirty funnel jerking closer. Finally, the tube jabbed inside her belly, the sour-smelling funnel looming in front of her tear-spattered face.

A chunk of cork was pushed into her mouth and manipulated this way and that, prising her teeth further apart until she expected her jaw to crack. The doctor behind her at last let go, leaving the cork to hold her mouth agonisingly wide.

The jug came closer to the funnel. Her insides convulsed with panic. The jug tilted and some sort of slop glugged into the funnel. Stodgy semi-liquid edged down her throat towards her heaving stomach. Even before the first jugful arrived in her belly, another was poured.

When at last the jug was empty, the doctor waggled the funnel, helping the final portion on its way, then he pulled the tube out so fast that her eyes almost burst out of their sockets. The tube flew before her, coated with phlegm.

'Lie down now, lie down.' One of the wardresses laid her back.

'How's her pulse?'

'It'll do.'

'Give her a blanket.'

Her insides were raw. Her brain was stunned and spinning at the same time.

'Spit. Lots of spitting. It helps.'

There was no bowl. When she gathered sufficient strength to roll over, she hung off the edge of the bed and eased her battered, itching throat by spitting weakly onto the floor.

Chapter Eighteen

Mary tried to open her eyes. It took a couple of goes. Her lashes brushed her cheeks; a final flicker and they opened. Her head felt muzzy and she was covered in bruises – no, not covered. Filled with bruises. The aches and twinges were on the inside. She swallowed and had to shut her eyes against a shooting pain. Her gullet was a raw, itching line.

'You're awake.' A well-built woman with thick arms stood over her. 'This is the prison infirmary and I'm Sister Wardress. You've had an infection.'

Memory returned. The hours following the forcible feeding – hot, sweaty, breathless, tearful hours. Her stomach churned at the thought of the filthy funnel and tube. Were they the source of the infection? She breathed steadily through her nose, trying to settle her insides. She couldn't be sick. Her gullet would explode.

A hand slid beneath her head and the edge of a beaker grazed her cracked lips.

'You must drink.'

The water was cool. She imagined it soothing the prickling sensation. Instead it set it on fire. She spluttered and pushed the beaker away.

'Pull yourself together. A few sips, then you can rest.'

Afterwards she slumped back. Not for long, though. Sister Wardress and another wardress each grasped her beneath an armpit and hauled her into a lying-up position. Her head swam. When the queasiness subsided, she took in her surroundings, a long room with green-tiled walls and a row of beds, each with a chain dangling from the bedhead. The hairs lifted on her flesh. Would Sister Wardress clamp a chain round her wrist?

But Sister Wardress merely folded her arms.

'Governor is frightened to death of hunger strikers. They all are, all the prisons. They're under orders that no women campaigners must die incarcerated.'

She remembered conversations at agency meetings about hunger-striking campaigners, discussions laced by an accompanying worry about forcible feeding. Was it real, was it happening, was it a rumour? Yes, yes and no. She felt fierce and shaky at the same time. No, it bally well wasn't a rumour.

Dadda came to take her home. He helped her into the cab and she half collapsed onto the seat. It was frightening to be so weak and the look on Dadda's face didn't help. His eyes were anxious, but his jaw was set.

He said, 'We've been so worried,' and he said, 'How could you, Mary?' but she couldn't afterwards recall which he had said first. Which was uppermost in his mind?

At home, Lilian put her to bed. Sheer relief plunged her into sleep and she woke feeling stronger.

Dadda came to sit beside the bed.

'I've promised Mother not to take you to task . . . yet. But I will tell you you've lost your job. One of the doctors came round to explain that they can't afford adverse publicity, so they can't have you back.'

'Which doctor?'

'Does it matter? I tell you you've lost your job and all you care about is who delivered the news.' He pressed his lips together. 'That's not the only job you've lost. After your public announcement about your interview, I found the letter about it.'

'You searched my things?'

'I've written to Mr Gladwin to refuse the position. How could you think of leaving home?' He held up his hands as if in surrender. 'Now is not the time. Recovery first. When you're up to it, I'm sending you and Mother on holiday. Do you good.'

'There's no need.'

'There's every need. I'm your father.' He replaced the chair by the wall. 'I'm back at work now, but even if it had taken every last shilling of my savings, I'd have spent it to help you get better.'

Her heart swelled with love. She was sorry to have let him down, yet she couldn't regret anything she had done.

'Dadda, please will you go to the agency and tell them about the forcible feeding?'

'Certainly not.'

'Please. They need to know it's happening.'

'Well, if it stops another girl doing something stupid.'

It was a day or two before he went, by which time she was no longer bed-fast.

'They wanted to visit you,' he said, 'but I refused. I blame them for this and I told them so. You're not to see them again, do you hear?'

'They're my friends.'

'No, they're not. They're your former employers, who didn't even make good their promise of a lasting job, and who led you astray. Friends is the last thing they've been to you.'

'He isn't really angry, not with you, anyroad,' Lilian murmured later on. 'He's all shaken up because of you being in this state, that's all.'

But Mary knew he meant every word. She had gone from prison to the doghouse.

To Mary's amusement, Lilian, who buzzed about all the time at home, loved strolling. They were guests in a boarding house a few minutes from the promenade in Llandudno and they went for walks – strolls – each morning and afternoon, ambling up and down the prom and the pier, joining the crowd that watched when the steamer docked from the Isle of Man.

Dadda had provided ample spending money and Lilian, who was nothing if not sensible with the housekeeping, had blithely announced on their first day that they were jolly well going to spend the lot even if it meant they had to stop an extra week to do it.

This morning they had ambled along Invalids Walk and through Haulfre Gardens and now were returning, arm in arm, for one of Mrs Davis's ample dinners when Lilian stopped dead – stopped speaking, stopped walking.

'What's wrong?' asked Mary.

Charlie stood at the gate.

* * *

'No, you can't take her for a walk,' Lilian snapped. 'Her father would never forgive me.'

She was flustered but standing her ground. Mary's arm felt warm as Lilian clamped it to her side, as if expecting Charlie to drag her away.

'Then you'll have to come along.' He sounded breezy, but his rough-edged frown and intent gaze said he was as determined as Lilian. 'I haven't come here to be given a clip round the ear and sent home.'

'You shouldn't be here at all. Why are you here, anyroad? What's our Mary to you? You've not seen her since that time you spirited her off in your motor car.' Lilian's posture slumped slightly as she looked at Mary. 'Please don't say you've been seeing him on the sly. Oh, Mary, what have you done?'

Her heart pumped hard, refuelling her body with vigour. Charlie had come looking for her. He had come to find her. He cared about her. Mary's chest hitched. Tears weren't far away, but they were tears of relief and gratitude. Charlie cared; he *cared*. She felt herself emerging from the weighty shadow of disapproval. She wasn't alone any more.

'Mother, please, it's fine.'

'It's not fine,' said Lilian. 'I'm vexed at you, our Mary, for thinking it could be.'

'Don't speak to her like that,' said Charlie.

'I'll speak to her any way I choose. I'm her mother and I've her welfare at heart – which is more than you have, Charlie Kimber, or you'd leave her be.'

Charlie's genial features turned to stone. 'I think, Mrs Maitland, you've forgotten whom you're addressing.'

Mary died a thousand deaths. She felt Lilian's body stiffen, then the tiniest slackening, as if something inside her had crumpled.

'I believe you owe me an apology,' said Charlie.

'Oh, Charlie – no.' Mary made a move towards him, or tried to, but, crumpled or not, Lilian's restraining arm didn't budge.

'Nay, love, he's right,' said Lilian. 'I should apologise for being rude to my betters. I apologise, Mr Kimber. I shouldn't have spoken out – and doesn't that tell you something, Mary? You've got yourself tangled up with a lad your own mother can't speak her mind to.'

Panic snaked through her. She had no control over what was happening. She remembered all those people piling into her cell, grabbing hold of her. Her heart had thudded then, and it was thudding now.

'Are you all right?' asked Lilian. 'Let's get you indoors.'

She found herself being borne resolutely through the gate. Lilian snapped at Charlie over her shoulder.

'You'd best stop out here, *sir*. Mrs Davis won't want strangers in her house.'

Mary stopped dead. She faced Lilian.

'I want to speak to him.'

'No, you don't, lady. Your dad would throw a fit if he knew.'

'Well, he doesn't know and he needn't unless you tell him.'

'I'm not keeping your mucky secrets for you.'

'He's come all this way.'

'That doesn't mean you have to speak to him. He's in the wrong. Don't put yourself in the wrong an' all.'

'He's my friend. We saw a lot of one another while I was at the clinic.'

'My dear girl, oh, my lovely girl, it's all make-believe. Your heart will get broken and the longer you let it go on, the worse it'll be.'

'We're just friends.' But it wasn't true. He had used friendship to court her, but it was his staunch support, his belief in her, that had won her heart. Yes, her heart. If her feelings had been in any doubt, seeing Charlie today had swept them aside. He had defied every convention to find her.

'Oh aye? Listen, love. He's young and rich with nowt to do but enjoy himself. He goes to those meetings—'

'He goes because he cares. He takes his responsibilities as heir seriously.'

'He goes because it makes him feel dashing and modern, and he enjoys the young company and – yes, I will say it – he loves being with the girls. Why wouldn't he? But he's not like us. He's had everything handed to him on a plate and now, because he attends meetings, he thinks he's doing summat worthwhile.'

'It is worthwhile.'

'I'll tell you what he's doing. He's enjoying mixed company without any pesky old 'uns keeping an eye out.'

'You wanted me to attend meetings to meet someone suitable.'

'Aye, love,' Lilian answered. 'Suitable.'

There was a sharp silence.

'I'm going to see what he wants.'

Lilian gave her a look. 'And nothing I say will stop you? Then how about what he said? Demanding an apology from me like that. It was humiliating.'

'Mother, I'm sorry—'

'Blind, that's what you are. Blind.'

Mary took a step.

'No, you don't, not on your own. I'm coming with you and don't kid yourself I won't report every last word to Dadda, because I will.'

Charlie's face lit up as they approached. Mary didn't dare look at Lilian.

'Fifteen minutes, Mr Kimber,' Lilian said loudly, 'and then we must head back yon for us dinner. Our Mary wants bonnying up a bit. Powky as a stick, she is, poor lass.'

Mary willed Charlie not to rise to the bait. He indicated a bench along the road.

'Oh aye, tek the weight off us feet,' said Lilian. 'Oh, no you don't – I'll walk in't middle, and I'll sit in't middle an' all.'

To Mary's relief, Lilian clamped her lips together and said not another word. She plonked herself in the centre of the bench. Mary sank down on one side, Charlie sat on the other.

'When Uncle Edward and I came home from our trip, I went to the clinic and heard you no longer worked there,' he began, 'so I went to the agency, thinking they'd have helped you find another job, but they told me about the prison sentence. I couldn't believe my ears. They told me about the hunger strike.' Leaning forward, he looked across the implacable Lilian. 'You poor girl, what you've been through. I went to your house, but no one was in. Then I remembered Emma works at that shop near the agency, so I tried there. I threw the family name around until they let me speak to her. She didn't want to tell me where you were, but I made her.'

Lilian came back to life. 'You coerced her? She's just a child.'

'There was no coercion. She told me willingly enough . . .'

'Our Emma? Never!'

'. . . when I told her she could be a bridesmaid.'

The cards had been good to Greg. Not that he believed in luck. If good things happened, it was because you made them happen. Equally, if bad things befell you, it was your own fault for slipping up – either that or someone had it in for you and they had worked to bring you down, in which case it was still your fault, because you shouldn't have let your guard slip.

From that thought, it was an easy step to picturing Mr Jonas. Of all the moneylenders to be ensnared by, Jonas was the worst. He was ruthless. They all were, but other moneylenders didn't chop off the tip of your finger if you failed to pay up at the appointed hour.

He had met a fellow that had happened to. Barrington, his name was. They had met just the once, at a country house on the Continent. The lady of the house was the middle-aged English widow of a wealthy frog, who kept her house full of company. If you were the friend of a friend, that was all the introduction that was required. His hostess was like an overblown bloom, past her best but clinging to the remnants of her loveliness by buying popularity and paying a personable young chap to dance attendance in public and, so it was widely assumed, roger her senseless in private. Of course, payment wasn't supposed to enter into it, but everybody knew that was what it came down to. Those gold collar studs sported by Trevelyan were known to be a gift from Moira, as were the glossy new evening togs, not to mention the monogrammed cigar box, the monogrammed dram-flask, the monogrammed Meerschaum and – Greg recalled how he and some other fellows had pretended to throw up before laughing themselves silly – those coy cufflinks, one monogrammed *JT*, the other *MdeV*.

'That's nothing,' said Trevelyan. 'She's having my dick monogrammed next week.'

That remark had made Greg look at him with new eyes. Apparently, the lapdog wasn't as tame as dear Moira supposed. Perhaps it wasn't so easy after all, being a kept man. The other fellows might josh about the going rate for a gold cigarette case, and Greg's contributions to those conversations were as lewd as anyone's, but, by the stars, what a price to pay.

It was at Moira's country house that he and this Barrington chap had crossed paths in the wee small hours in a sitting room well away from the raucous partying that was another of the things that was apparently meant to make Moira appear youthful and vibrant. Greg, who had found all the company he wanted in a decanter of the finest French cognac, wasn't pleased when Barrington walked in, but since he was clearly in search of the same sort of company, they proceeded to drink themselves into oblivion, swapping the odd remark.

The subject of money came up – or the lack of it. They agreed that living the way they did could be a bugger when funds dried up.

'Things are pretty dry at present,' said Greg, 'or I wouldn't be here.'

'Me neither. Haven't had a decent win in ages. Looks like it'll be back to the moneylenders for me.' Barrington held up his left hand. 'I 'spect you've been wond'ring how this happened.'

'How what happened?' Greg peered. 'Oh, that.' The top joint of Barrington's little finger was missing. 'Born like it, were you?'

'Nah. A snake called Jonas did it. Sliced it off. Well, not him personally, but his people. Vicious people he's got. Know him, do you? If you don't, you're a jammy sod. If you do, take it from me: if he says to cough up by such a date, make damn sure you do. If you don't . . . chop, chop.'

He had never seen Barrington again, but a year or so later he heard he had blown his brains out. Had Jonas lurked somewhere behind Barrington's desperate decision?

Since quitting Jackson's House, he had done well at the card tables and paid Jonas a hundred or so, but how long would it keep him sweet? It had bloody well better be for a decent amount of time, because he wasn't sodding well wasting his skill on lining that bastard's pockets day in, day out.

As he adjusted his bow tie, he vowed Jonas wouldn't receive a penny more until he had relined his coffers with sufficient caboodle to keep him in comfort and firewater for the autumn.

That night, he lost. Badly.

'Whatever possessed you?' Lilian asked. She dumped the groceries on the kitchen table and glared at Mary in a mixture of vexation and despair. 'Do you know what the neighbours are saying?'

'I don't care,' Mary claimed bravely, though it shook her to see Lilian agitated.

'Well, you should. There was enough talk when I married your father, most of it started by Granny, I might add, about how I could have had the butcher but I fancied linking myself to the Kimbers. And you know what they'll say about you, don't you? Like grandmother, like granddaughter, that's what.'

Indeed, Granny was the only one in favour. It was Martin this and Martin that, as if it had been a match made in heaven, when everyone knew Martin Kimber had made a nitwit of himself by eloping with a pretty face.

'You're always on about needing summat to write about,' said Granny. 'What about how love conquers all?'

She felt like cringing, but Dadda or Lilian would be certain to pounce. Love conquers all: was that how Granny saw herself? It was a far cry from the way the rest of the world saw her and Grandfather Martin.

Was Mary alone in seeing equality between herself and Charlie? They had started as friends; they had interests in common. This was the twentieth century. The status of women was changing – and if it wasn't, it should be.

'Get your mother to invite me to tea,' said Charlie.

But, 'I couldn't possibly,' Lilian cried. 'Us inviting a Kimber – what sauce! It'd be social climbing.'

'It's his idea, not mine.'

You didn't keep the heir waiting. Mary was duly authorised to invite her intended for that Saturday.

Saturday morning saw Lilian separating eggs, whites for macaroons, yolks for maids of honour. The butcher's boy came whistling along with tomorrow's joint and a tongue for today's tea.

'That'll want careful boiling,' Mrs Bethell decreed in an ominous voice, 'else you'll never peel the skin off. I'll get off now and give our Frank his dinner and I'll be back later.'

She pulled her shawl around her and departed.

'She's coming back?' Mary asked with a sense of foreboding.

'Just to lend a hand.'

Emma arrived home from the shop. Dadda had written a letter, explaining that Mr Charlie Kimber was visiting and so Emma had been given special permission to be home for the occasion.

As four o'clock approached, Mary and Emma made sandwiches.

'Proper sandwiches, not butties,' said Lilian. 'Thin slices, no crusts.'

'Shouldn't Mrs B be doing this?' Emma whispered. 'I thought she was coming back to help.'

A shriek had them hurrying to the front room. Ozymandias, King of Kings was sprawled in ginger splendour on the best chair, untroubled by Lilian's horror.

'Emma, put him out – Mary, the upholstery brush—'

Mary took charge. 'Emma can finish the sandwiches. I'll sort this out.'

Mrs Bethell returned as they were disappearing upstairs to change. Not a word had been said, but they all reappeared decked out in their Sunday best. You developed certain instincts when you were a poor relation.

The clock on the mantelpiece pinged the hour and everyone sat up straighter, but nothing happened and Mary felt deflated. At one minute past, the knocker sounded, causing a feeling of anxious bustle to descend on the Maitlands' seldom-used front room. This was worse than going to Ees House. It ought to be easier to have Charlie here, but it wasn't.

But at the sight of his easy smile, Mary felt a wave of relief and pride. He was so genial, so likeable. He would put everyone at their ease. Her family would warm to him and the social gap between them wouldn't seem so wide afterwards.

'It's kind of you to invite me,' said Charlie.

'Our pleasure, I'm sure,' Lilian replied in self-consciously refined tones that made Mary curl her toes inside her shoes.

'How are things at the town hall, sir?' Charlie asked.

Mary sat by with Lilian and Emma, hands in laps. She caught Charlie's glance. Did he expect her to chip in with an opinion? That was what she would have done at the agency, but it wasn't how she behaved at home. At home, Dadda spoke and everyone listened.

She noticed Lilian's eyes flicking in the direction of the clock. The moment there was a gap in the conversation, Lilian shook the little ornamental brass bell and Mary stared in horrified fascination as the door opened and in hobbled Mrs Bethell, done up like a dog's dinner in a vast apron.

'Tea, if you please, Bethell,' said Lilian.

Mary felt an overwhelming desire to laugh. Then mortification streamed through her veins. Pity, too. Poor Lilian, trying to be genteel.

Mrs Bethell returned, bearing a huge tray, which got the better of her at the last moment and she plonked it down with a clatter of china.

'This looks splendid,' said Charlie. 'Your maid has done us proud.'

'I believe the girls made the sandwiches,' said Dadda, 'and Mrs Maitland is a dab hand at cakes.'

'Then I must try a bit of everything.'

Mary leapt in before Dadda, thickheaded male that he was, could commit the ultimate blunder of adding that their supposed maid was actually the daily char. 'Won't you tell us about the Olympic Games, Charlie?'

'The Olympics . . .' Charlie talked and the Maitlands listened politely like the poor relations they were.

Chapter Nineteen

No wonder Grandfather Martin and Granny had eloped. Being engaged to Charlie was surprisingly uncomfortable. Both families disapproved – apart from Granny, and her triumph was as hard to bear as the displeasure. The Kimbers wanted a long engagement, which meant Dadda and Lilian did too, and Mary, more than willing to prove their strength of feeling, would have agreed, only Charlie insisted upon marrying at once.

'We're sure it's what we want, so why wait?'

She found herself agreeing, not just because she was eager to marry him, but also because she couldn't leave the house without being stared at.

Lilian found it difficult too.

'All those years when you were an office girl, it got harder and harder for me to smile and say "Congratulations" to other women when their lasses got wed. I used to dream of you finding a young man. I wanted people to say "She's done well for herself" because you'd got a fellow who had a steady job with prospects. Now they're saying it, but you should see the looks on their faces.'

Mary gave up trying to find a suitable answer. The remarks were every bit as bothersome to her, only she couldn't say so for fear of being told she had brought it on herself.

Dadda arrived home from the office, white-faced and ruffled because a reporter had nabbed him outside the town hall and fired questions at him all the way to the tram stop.

'I hope you're proud of yourself, Mary,' he said stiffly.

Then, on Saturday afternoon, Miriam arrived.

'A reporter came to Candle Cottage. I tried to turn him away, but Mother made me invite him in. I wanted you to know it wasn't my doing.'

Everyone looked at Mary and she felt herself being lumped together with Granny.

'My grandmother has talked to a journalist,' she confessed to Charlie. 'I can't apologise enough.'

'Not your fault,' he said, but not before she had seen him flinch.

It would be a relief when the wedding was over. She caught her breath. What a wretched thought. Her life seemed crammed full of censure and she longed to break free and feel normal again.

The clinic.

Why not? She had never said her goodbyes.

'And I ought to apologise for bringing the place into disrepute,' she said in her mildest voice.

'You could do that by letter,' said Dadda.

'It would do her good to get out,' said Lilian. 'Heaven knows,

I'd like the chance to go somewhere away from the whispers.'

Mary tried to squeeze her hand, but Lilian withdrew it.

'Very well,' said Dadda. 'You may go tomorrow.'

'I thought I'd go on Friday.'

'You can't spend your wedding eve in a clinic in the slums.'

Well, no, put like that, she couldn't, but Friday would have suited her because Nathaniel wasn't there on Fridays. But so what if she saw him? He meant nothing to her.

As she walked through the shabby streets to the clinic, she marvelled at all that had happened since she last came this way. Coming back was refreshing.

Imogen Brewer was on the other side of the road, heading the mother and baby group. Some women carried their babies in their arms; a couple had baby-carriages fashioned from boxes on wheels. Most also had small children in tow.

She crossed over to greet them.

'We're on our way to the church hall to sing songs,' said Imogen. 'I believe the hall has a piano.'

'It could do with tuning.'

Imogen laughed. 'We'll manage.'

'Jimmy, come away from the lady,' said an exasperated voice.

Feeling a tug, Mary glanced down at a snotty infant clinging to her skirt. She kept her smile in place in spite of the sour smell.

'Sorry, miss.' Jimmy's mother, arms full of twins, pushed him away with her foot. 'He's into everything, this one.'

'That's all right, Mrs Whelan,' said Mary.

'We mustn't keep you,' said Imogen and led her followers on their way.

Mary headed for the clinic, feeling lighter of heart with every step. Inside, she presented herself at the hatch and was surprised by a whoosh of nostalgia. She wouldn't go out to work ever again. Goodness, she would miss it.

A couple of nurses were in the office with Mrs Winter. They all looked her way and her nostalgia was swept aside by the delight in their faces. They drew her inside and pushed her into a chair, at the centre of a cluster of exclamations.

'I hardly know what to say first,' said Mrs Winter. 'Congratulations, or you poor love, being put in prison.'

'Congratulations, definitely,' said Katie Evans. 'You bagged yourself a good 'un there, girl.'

Everyone laughed. These women had been accustomed to seeing Charlie collecting her from the clinic, so maybe the engagement felt like a natural progression to them. Did they know she wasn't the social-climbing sort?

Nurse Reilly returned from her rounds and joined the chattering group. Katie disappeared and came back with a tray of tea. Mary could have hugged them all for their warm welcome. In fact – why not? She did hug them.

'Sounds jolly in here.'

Nathaniel. Mary went cold with embarrassment but stepped forward.

'I'm sorry if I damaged the clinic's reputation.'

'You understand we couldn't have you back.'

'Of course.'

'But she's getting married now,' said Katie, 'so all's well.'

She felt embarrassed all over again, which was stupid, because no one had ever known of her feelings for Nathaniel. Would he show some reaction to the news?

'Congratulations. I'm off on my rounds, Mrs Winter.' He

turned away, then turned back. 'Miss Maitland, I hope your time in prison wasn't too . . . arduous.'

Oh, those serious hazel eyes. Times were when she would have sold her soul to have her gaze held by his.

'Thank you.'

He nodded and left.

'Let's hear about the dress,' demanded Nurse Reilly.

She felt her attention being pulled back to the others.

'It was made at *Constance and Clara*, where my sister works. It's ivory silk with a fitted bodice, and the skirt falls straight down at the front and flares at the back, and I'm wearing Mother's veil.'

That was a minor disappointment. She would have loved to wear Mam's, but Lilian had done so much for her.

A great boom sounded. Thunder? No, a rounder noise than that, more contained. The room quivered. Mary froze – they all did. Then they all reacted at once.

'What was it?'

'An explosion?'

'Come on. We must help.'

She joined the bustle rushing into the corridor. The front door banged open and a woman stumbled in. She was grey with poverty. No, she wasn't, she was coated in a thick layer of dust.

'Come quick! The Marshalls' house has blew up.'

'Blown up? How could it?'

'That damn gas supply—'

'You go ahead. I'll fetch medical supplies—'

'Where's Doctor Brewer?'

Mary ran outside. Tiny particles stung her eyes. A powerful rotten-egg smell poured into her nostrils, her mouth. Her gut uncoiled, faltering at the stench. She felt sick and light-headed, but the sight of a house, a whole house, missing from the row brought her senses sharply into focus. She ran towards rubble, bricks, sticks of furniture. Two women, crying, bent over another lying crumpled in the gutter.

'I'll see to her,' said Katie.

Mary moved on, darting between women frozen in shock, others swarming about grabbing at children. Part of her mind registered surprise at the number of women, then she caught sight of Imogen – the mother and baby group had been heading for home.

Hurrying across, she caught her foot on a clump of bricks and pitched forwards. Imogen's hands gripped her arms. Their faces were close. Imogen's hat was gone; her hair was matted with dust.

'Are the mothers and babies all right?' asked Mary.

'I think so. We'd just come round the corner. The line was straggling or lord knows what would have happened. The first few women were blown clear across the street and their babies flew through the air. Fortunately they're all crying, so they're alive, but they need checking over.'

'We should see if anyone's under the rubble.'

Mary felt a hand on her arm and swung about to see Mrs Winter.

'We should evacuate the street in case there's another explosion,' said Mrs Winter.

'You see to that. We're going to dig in the rubble.'

'It's not safe,' began Mrs Winter, but Mary gave her a push.

'We'll be careful.'

She and Imogen edged forwards. The odour of gas was more pungent with every step and she took the shallowest of breaths, but the gas must have been playing with her senses because she could hear squealing. She closed her ears to it, tried to listen for crying or groaning, the scrape of brick being clawed by a feeble hand.

'Here.' Imogen hurried towards fabric showing beneath a heap of bricks and floorboards.

Mary dropped down and put her mouth close to the heap.

'Can you hear me? We're going to dig you out.'

Piece by piece, they lifted the obstacles away. The bricks, fixed together in clumps, were heavy. Try as she might, Mary couldn't put them down carefully, each one tipping from her grasp at the last moment and smashing apart as it landed.

'Mind out. We'll do it.'

A man stepped in front of her. He didn't shove her aside, but he might as well have done. He seemed to want to stand precisely where she was. She stumbled backwards. Several men set to work removing the debris and looked like making short work of it. She watched, her heart twisting with anxiety for whoever was trapped beneath, but when she glimpsed Imogen also watching, it gave her a jolt.

'We must see if anyone else needs help.'

She looked at what remained of the Marshalls' house, but before she could start climbing over the rubble, a voice halted her – Nathaniel's.

'No, you don't. Make sure the mothers and babies are accounted for.'

'Here, Doctor,' a man called. 'We've nearly got Mrs Banks out.'

Nathaniel crouched, dumping his medical bag beside him. 'She's alive. Get the rest of this stuff off her. We'll need a stretcher. What the hell are those idiots doing? That building's unsafe. Look at that ruddy great crack down the wall.'

Mary turned. Out of the house beside the gap came a couple of lads carrying a table, followed by a little girl clutching an aspidistra.

'You check the mothers and babies,' Mary told Imogen. 'I'll see to this.'

Taking care where she put her feet, she hurried over.

'You can't go back in,' she said as the boys set down the table beside assorted possessions.

'Mam wants everything out.'

'The house isn't safe.'

The boy shrugged. She pushed ahead of him and entered the house, trying to call out, but dust crowded her mouth. Pressing her hanky against her lips, eyes smarting, she marched across the room to check the scullery. No sign. She hurried back to the stairs, dancing impatiently behind the boys, who were manhandling a squalid-looking armchair. The stairs creaked and shifted beneath her feet.

She found the mother in the upstairs front, moaning as she hurled bits and pieces into a patched and darned blanket on the bed. When Mary attempted to take her arm, she wrenched herself free, her dust-thickened features twisted with grief.

'I'm not going without me things.'

A deep shudder vibrated through Mary's body and the floor dropped by several inches. Her stomach whooped in fear. Was she about to die? The woman shrieked, then choked, but there was no time to let her recover. Mary shoved her at the door, stumbling behind her down the stairs into the street.

She ought to forbid the family to go back inside, but a fit of choking overtook her. She doubled over, coughing so hard her ribs almost cracked. When she recovered, the tears that had poured down her face had melded with the dust, leaving her with a mask that tightened her flesh, rendering her skull too big for her skin.

Over the road, Imogen hovered around the mothers. Going to them, Mary saw dazed expressions and smears of blood.

Imogen raised her voice. 'Everyone ready? Let's get the children away from here.'

As the group started to shuffle off, a woman darted out.

'Jimmy Whelan's missing—'

Mrs Whelan, a baby clutched within each arm, tried to break free. Mary stood in front of her and looked into panic-filled eyes.

'Take the babies to safety. I'll find Jimmy.'

The group absorbed Mrs Whelan. Mary grabbed a couple of onlookers.

'Jimmy Whelan's missing. He might have returned to the church hall. Go and see – Doctor Brewer's orders.'

She headed for the gap between the houses. A hand caught her arm. Imogen.

'I'll help. Mrs Winter's seeing to the mothers.'

Rubble shifted as they clambered over it. Mary waved her arms, snatching at balance, then lurched down the other side. Imogen thudded into her from behind and she staggered forwards, stopping dead as she took in what was before her. The explosion had caused more than a gap in the row – it had blown a massive hole in the floor, too, in the ground. Jagged edges of floorboards remained round the fringes.

And there was that squealing again. The adjacent walls creaking? Her gaze fixed on the hole. She didn't want to look, but didn't dare look away. A hand nudged hers and she curled her fingers through Imogen's. Together, they crept forward. Mary craned her neck to peer into the chasm from as far away as possible.

'Oh, dear heaven,' murmured Imogen.

The hole teemed with rats – hundreds of them, some as large as terriers. Beneath her dust-mask, Mary's expression tried to crumple in disgust but was locked in position. Sourness trickled down her throat.

Imogen nudged her. 'Over there.'

On the far side, Jimmy Whelan bobbed about at the edge of the crater. Losing his balance, he plonked down on the brink, but his wail was cut short when he saw the rats. They stepped forward instinctively as he leant over to stare.

Mary looked up as the wall gave a groan. Did it shift a fraction or was that her imagination?

'We'll go round the hole on different sides,' said Imogen. 'One of us will catch him.'

Moving as swiftly as the wreckage permitted, Mary started on her way.

'Oy! Come back,' yelled a man's voice. 'I'll fetch him.'

'We're lighter,' Imogen called. 'You'd fall through.'

A scraping sound was followed by a flurry of dust that spurted into the air from high up in the wall. Bits of plaster crunched as they landed. Mary stood still for a moment, then pressed on, her shoes filling with grit.

As she approached Jimmy, the floor wobbled and her stomach flipped. She stopped moving. So did the floor. She took a tentative step and the floorboard flew up like a see-saw. Imagining her leg being thrust down into the rats' nest, she hurled herself sideways, jarring arms and legs as she landed. Pulling herself up, she crept closer, testing every step before entrusting her weight to it, holding her breath as if that would make her lighter. She stopped a few feet away, glancing at Imogen, who nodded encouragement from beside the cracked wall.

'Jimmy,' Mary called. 'Jimmy, come to me.'

He turned, took one look at her, then threw back his head and wailed. She inched forwards, horribly aware of the rats in the hole beyond the child. Snatching him into her arms, she staggered back the way she had come. Jimmy didn't struggle – couldn't, given how tightly she was holding him – but, goodness, could he bellow.

Regaining firm ground, she stopped and turned. Imogen waved to her and smiled. There was a prolonged grinding sound followed by utter stillness. She wanted to yell at Imogen to run. Then the wall dropped, simply dropped. Mary hugged Jimmy, cradling his head into her neck and turning away from the great cloud of filth and the bits flying through the air. Something struck her sharply on the back and she landed hard on her knees. She doubled over, rocking Jimmy, rocking herself, knowing she would never dare stand up again, because that would mean looking across at the place where Imogen used to be.

Mary was dimly aware of Jimmy being prised from her arms. Her arm was held, she was led up and over, and through the piles of rubble. Her legs were rubbery and she stumbled any number of times, but with no sensation of falling, no sense of needing to be careful. Her head felt as if a gigantic bell had pealed right beside her and the clang had stupefied her mind.

She wriggled free from the kindly hands and gaped at the mound of debris where Imogen had been. Men lifted clumps of bricks and chunks of plaster, passing them to one another. Nathaniel dug furiously, like a dog. More hands – why did they all want to touch her? Mrs Winter, her mouth moving, saying something that she couldn't focus on. She turned her face away and looked again at the heap that used to be a wall. She couldn't tear her gaze away. It was impossible to believe it had happened. She had to watch to make it real.

Her skin was moist, her pulse skittish. There were so many noises she ought to be able to hear, but the only one in her ears was the sound of her own breathing, rapid, shallow. Arms went round her, holding her: Mrs Winter. Mrs Winter used to be her enemy, but now here she was, holding her, steadying her. Mrs Winter's arms disappeared for a moment, a coat went round her shoulders and Mrs Winter's arms slid back into place.

The digging went on. Mrs Winter forcibly lowered her onto a wooden chair. A chair from the house next door, rescued by that stupid woman and her children? The side of the house gaped open for all to see. The upstairs floor was broken apart and a bed had slipped into the crack. The blanket which the woman had been filling with her possessions flapped down. Stupid woman. As if possessions mattered.

The digging continued. Some of the men stood back, moved away. Arms were raised, beckoning; a couple of men looked round, gesturing, giving orders. Then everyone stilled as Nathaniel lay down, wriggling into the hole they had dug. Mary stopped breathing. Mrs Winter's arms tightened. Mary's hand fluttered and came to rest inside Mrs Winter's grasp.

Nathaniel backed out of the hole and came to his feet. He stood there without moving. Some of the men came closer, but he didn't respond. He turned and stomped away down the heap of rubble, his feet sinking in. He rounded the chasm and left the site.

Seated on the wooden chair within the clasp of Mrs Winter's arms, Mary tracked his progress. He walked into the road and stopped. He swayed and her body tilted forwards in sympathy. When he sank onto his knees, right there in the street, she shook herself free from Mrs Winter and tottered across to him. She sank down beside him and reached out, one human being to another, to draw him into the circle of her arms. Her forehead rested against the side of his head, against hair clogged with dirt. Her body tried to rock, instinctively seeking to give comfort, but Nathaniel didn't move.

Chapter Twenty

Standing before her cheval looking-glass, Lady Kimber studied her expression, cheekbones high and brittle, eyes a dangerous pearl-grey. Was this what she had come to? Wishing someone dead? If Mary Maitland had been under that wall when it collapsed, the Kimbers would have been saved from catastrophe and Doctor Brewer would still have a wife.

Her gaze swept over her reflection. Yes, it had occurred to her to trot out an old rag, but everyone knew her opinion of this wedding without the need for her to snub it with a gown that had been seen a dozen times before. Better – loftier, more worthy of her station – to have something new. Show the world what a true Lady Kimber looked like. That conscienceless chit would never look the part.

Unlike Eleanor, who would have been perfect. A hot pain tore through her heart, though Eleanor had taken it remarkably well.

'I shan't lie to you, Mummy,' she had confided. 'When Charlie first came, he was attentive and I was flattered. I said things to the Rushworth girls that I wish now I hadn't. They were every bit as excited as I was, especially Olivia. And yes, I did think of wedding bells. If this is difficult for me now, it's my own fault for being a chump.'

'This is one person's fault: the Maitland female. She's a social climber of the worst sort, like her grandmother before her. That boy will live to rue the day.'

They had done everything they could, she and Sir Edward, to talk Charlie out of this match, but he was having none of it.

'Cut off my allowance if you like. Throw me out of Ees House. But I have my mother's money, which is enough to get by on until I come into my father's.'

Her head had filled with most unladylike language at that.

'I want them to live here when they're married,' Sir Edward later decreed.

'But that girl—'

'That girl, my dear, will be the heir's wife. This isn't like when Uncle Martin ran off with his fancy piece. They could be set aside because Martin wasn't in the direct line, but we can't do that to Charlie.'

'I refuse to have that creature under this roof. Put them in Brookburn House if you must, but that's the most I will tolerate.'

'Very well, my dear. You're mistress of this house and if you wish to install them in the dower house, that's your prerogative, but if Mary lives here, you can control the comings and goings of visitors, whereas if she has Brookburn . . .'

'Dear heaven, the family will move in, lock, stock, and grandmother.'

She felt a twist of anguish and bitter impotence. Her life had been punctuated by heart-rending dilemmas. Remain a heartbroken spinster or settle for an older man. Throw everything to the winds and run off with Greg or cast him aside for ever and tolerate the dull despair of marriage with Henry. How desperately she had wanted to be with Greg, and how close she had come . . . but then she stumbled on the truth about his way of life and his financial situation, truths he had intended keeping from her until she had committed herself to his protection.

Thank heaven she had subsequently had Eleanor, whose birth had filled her life with joy and purpose . . . and whose marriage to Charlie was to have been her crowning achievement.

Eleanor and Charlie.

Charlie and Mary.

Here she stood now in her brand-new best to do honour, superficially at least, to the heir and his intended. The gown was perfect, a silk-satin in greeny-gold, its skirt boasting less of a flare. Styles were changing and who better to demonstrate this to the neighbourhood? Best of all was the hat, a colossal affair smothered in ostrich feathers. She knew precisely how she would appear in public – cool and remote – but the feathers would tremble with indignation with every move she made. The hat was a triumph.

It needed to be. The day promised to be excruciating.

She could almost wish Charlie had eloped when she saw the crowd outside St Clement's. The air smelt of lower-class eagerness.

She proceeded up the aisle on her husband's arm. Charlie sat at the front, beaming his head off, poor deluded idiot, though it was hard to have sympathy at this stage.

All her sympathy was with Eleanor, ethereally beautiful in silk of palest yellow. How well she was carrying herself through this private humiliation. But she evidently knew her own limits, because a few days ago she had asked a favour.

'The Rushworths are going to Switzerland. I didn't hint, Mummy, honestly, but Olivia wants me to go with them. You'll say yes, won't you?'

With a heavy heart, she had done just that. A heavy heart – and an angry one.

The organ sounded and the congregation rose. She fixed her eyes to the fore, though she delivered a sharp scrutiny when Mary reached the altar. Would the sight of her bring Charlie to his senses? Would he look from Mary to Eleanor and—?

Evidently not.

The service began. She could have sworn waves of complacent glee came her way from the bride's side of the church. They were making their vows now. Charlie went first, thus sealing his doom.

When her turn came, the Maitland girl's voice was quiet and trembly, as well it might be, considering the scale of her victory.

'. . . love, honour and cherish . . .'

Lady Kimber's head jerked up. Cherish! What sort of modern claptrap was that? And to hear it from the lips of a steerage-class upstart was appalling.

Charlie slipped his mother's ring onto Mary's finger. Poor Dulcie must be turning in her grave. Then it was over, except for signing the register. After that, the Maitland girl hooked her hand through Charlie's arm for him to escort her down the aisle.

It should be her beautiful daughter she was following out of church. That was what she had planned. Oh, Eleanor.

'Well, well, well,' Greg murmured, watching over the top of his brandy. 'I come to France and who's the first person I see? Dear old Moira, dear old desperate-for-it Moira. Where's the lapdog? Not trotting to heel?'

'Off the leash, old boy.'

'Surprised she permits it.'

'Off the leash permanently, I mean. Not sure which one tired of t'other. Either way, he won't be on his own for long: can't afford it. Watch out – here she comes.'

Greg gained his feet in a fluid movement, though his companion made a hash of it, but that was Batty Lombard for you. Drank less, but stumbled more, poor dolt.

Moira bustled over, smelling like an exotic hothouse bloom and dressed in hideous salmon-pink that put years on her, arms encased in long evening gloves, though that hadn't prevented her from wearing rings. She stretched out her hand, affording Greg an eyeful of jewellery before he raised her fingers to his lips. One of the rings was a socking great sapphire and he dropped his kiss on that, feeling more respect for the gleaming stone than he did for its owner.

'Greg, darling, what a treat to see you. You too, Batty.' Moira thrust her rings at Batty. 'I'm getting up a house party.'

'Aren't you always?' Greg remarked.

'Darling, too cruel. Can I help it if I like to be surrounded by friends? Lucky me, having the dibs to fund it.'

'Lucky for your friends too,' beamed Batty.

'Sweet of you, darling. Consider yourselves invited. Don't disappoint me.'

She moved on, leaving behind a fug of intensely sweet perfume.

'Will you go?' Greg asked as he and Batty resumed their seats.

'Cripes, yes. A few free dinners never go amiss. I'm not as handy with the cards as you. Will I see you there?'

'Probably not.' By which he meant definitely not, but he had an aversion to laying out his intentions for all to see.

He wasn't playing cards tonight, urgently as he needed to. Things hadn't been going well – deuced badly, in fact – and his funds had taken a clobbering. That was why he had given himself the night off, tomorrow night too. When you were known to be on a duff streak, carrying on playing made you look desperate. By stopping, he could make a joke of his bad luck, while holding up his head in public suggested he could afford his losses. Impressions were half the battle.

It was a bugger, though. He needed a decent win, preferably a run of wins, and soon. No other moneylender would give him the time of day now that Jonas had bought up his debts. If his luck didn't turn pretty smartish, he might be reduced to touching an acquaintance for money. His stomach clenched. He had never done that, had never sunk so low.

Looking round the room with its fine furnishings, two vast chandeliers twinkling above the expensively dressed ladies and gentlemen, liars and scoundrels every single one of them, he felt a burst of fury. Christ, he had had enough of play-acting for one night, and there was the whole bally charade to repeat tomorrow, worse luck. But he was done with it for today, that was certain.

The following night, he again sat out, waving aside offers to cut him in.

'Not tonight,' he joshed. 'Only fair to give others a chance.'

'Letting your virginity grow back as well, are you?'

He felt like throwing a punch in reply to that, but he forced himself to laugh along with the others. The group broke up, most heading for the card tables, while he was condemned to another night of looking affluent doing bugger all. Throwing himself into an armchair, he prepared to sit it out.

The exotic smell enveloped him before a pair of gloved hands covered his eyes from behind.

'Guess who?'

'Moira, my sweet.' He came to his feet. If the silly bitch knew how it infuriated him to be crept up on, she wouldn't pout like that.

'Darling,' she purred. 'How did you guess?'

The stench. 'The feather-light touch of your lovely hands.' He seized her gloved fingers and sized up tonight's rings. Maybe, when you lived as she did, luring in a succession of lapdogs, you had to put your goods in the shop window to entice the customers.

Moira sank into the chair opposite. He resumed his seat.

'Are you going to accept my invitation? I'll be in residence at least a fortnight, longer if everyone is having too good a time to leave. Do say you'll come.'

'I'm sorry, my dear. I must remain here.'

'Oh, darling, such a bore.'

'Business.'

'If by business, you mean cards, there'll be plenty at my place. I'll even invite some dud players for you to fleece. If you were to tear yourself away from here, I'd take it as . . . a personal favour.'

She rose and leant over him, affording him a close-up view of her ample bosom. It was the real thing, too – no modest monobosom for Moira. Her necklace hung away from her, the showy pendant – sapphire? or aquamarine masquerading as sapphire? – waiting to nestle once more in the top of the luscious cleavage.

'I can be generous, you know.'

The words were soft, for his ears alone, then she moved on, leaving him in no doubt that he had been offered first dibs on the goods in that particular shop.

The golden glow of October sunshine cast a mellow pool on the library floor. Mary had spent yesterday afternoon skimming her fingertips along the tooled spines, ignoring the sets of worthy volumes and lingering on Jerome K Jerome, Sir Arthur Conan Doyle and – delight of delights – ten or so Beatrix Potters.

'The library might become a favourite haunt of mine,' she had said to Charlie. Something quivered inside her. Excitement? Unease? 'Imagine Mary Maitland saying that about the library at Ees House.'

'You aren't Mary Maitland any more. You're Mrs Charlie Kimber.'

Mrs Charlie Kimber. The quiver this time was one of pure pleasure.

Now she was back in the library, this time with Charlie. Sir Edward had sent for them. He looked grave, but that was nothing to worry about. He always looked grave. Mary folded her hands in her lap and looked up at him. He was on his feet, hands behind his back.

'Now you're home from honeymoon, it's time for a talk. You've had your fun, you two. You formed a relationship on the sly—'

'I say.' Charlie sat up straighter.

Sir Edward raised a hand. 'Now it's time to take things seriously. I don't wish to give offence, Mary, but I must speak bluntly if we are to understand one another. My boy, you should be setting off on your Grand Tour and seeing a bit of the world.

Instead you've married young. In my book, marriage means responsibility, so you'll knuckle down and help run the estate. Mary, all eyes are upon you, but with your common sense and refinement, I'm confident you'll adapt once Her Ladyship takes you under her wing. Not only has this marriage reawakened unfortunate memories, but your own past is also a source of interest. You're the lower-class relation who was sent to prison, went on hunger strike, then saved a child's life and topped it all off by marrying the Kimber heir. It won't do. The two of you must lie low while everyone adjusts to the situation.'

While I show what I'm made of, you mean. Her momentary chill of doubt was replaced by resolve. If Imogen's death had taught her anything, it was to make the most of the good things. Her heart pitter-pattered. It might so easily have been she who had passed under that cracked wall. She felt as if she had been given a second chance. That it should coincide with the beginning of her new life as Mrs Charlie Kimber was a good thing, surely?

There was a lot to learn. Lady Kimber gave her a book on the social niceties and she read with wonderment about the correct way to draw on or peel off a pair of gloves. She wanted to laugh, only there was no one to share the joke.

Not even Charlie.

'Don't make light of it. We'll both be judged by what you do. Mustn't let the side down.'

'I wouldn't dream of it.'

Had he just put her in her place? Charlie? He had had nothing but admiration for her before. But he was right. It was up to her to show the world he had made a good choice.

She observed Lady Kimber, boggling at how she filled her

days. She was an energetic correspondent, though Mary had no idea to whom she wrote. She had daily conferences with her housekeeper and weekly meetings with the cook, to none of which Mary was invited.

And there were the calls.

'There will be the bridal visits to start with,' Lady Kimber informed her. 'Ladies will wish to pay their respects. After that you may accompany me on my calls. But first – dresses, and quickly. This sort of thing,' and a wave of her hand dismissed Mary's skirt and blouse, 'won't do.'

'I could have something made at *Constance and Clara*.'

'Where your sister works? Certainly not. We'll see what Mademoiselle Antoinette in St Ann's Square can do with you.'

Once she was appropriately decked out with a quantity of clothes she found embarrassing, she was put on display. Ladies visited and everyone was politeness itself, but she wondered what was said behind her back. Her spine stiffened. She would make these grand ladies respect her if it was the last thing she did.

She entertained great hopes of charity work. With years of clerical and administrative experience under her belt, plus the knowledge she had gleaned at agency meetings, she had plenty to offer, but when she put herself forward, Lady Kimber refused.

'You couldn't possibly attempt committee work. We can't have people saying how appropriate it is, because you come from a family of clerks or, worse, that someone who was employed at a slum clinic must know all about the poor.'

Her family would sympathise – or would they? Letters home were surprisingly tricky to write. When she described items from her new wardrobe, Lilian's reply asked why she hadn't gone to

Constance and Clara, and she could hardly say Lady Kimber had forbidden it. The last thing she wanted was a barrier between her and her family, so maybe it was time to visit.

But she was warned off.

'Best to put distance between you,' said Sir Edward. 'Things are different now.'

Charlie thought so too.

'But you came to our house for tea,' she protested.

'What matters now is getting your corners rubbed off and turning you into one of us. Then we can start living our lives properly.'

'Properly?'

'Getting out and about on our own, enjoying ourselves, instead of being confined to barracks. Best steer clear of your folks until then, eh? When they next see you, you'll be a fully-fledged Kimber and you'll all know where you stand.'

'I don't want to be above them.'

'That happened the moment you said "I do". Are you worried about not coming up to scratch?' He chuckled. 'If all else fails, you'll see them next summer.'

She went cold. 'The annual visit.'

'You wait. Aunt Christina will have you dreading it as much as she does.'

'She will not. And I don't appreciate your talking about my family this way.'

'We're your family now.'

She slipped her hand into his. 'I know, but it would mean so much to me if you . . .' Please let him take up the cue.

He pressed a kiss on her temple. 'I've nothing against your old man. Uncle Edward thinks highly of him and that's good enough for me. To be blunt, it's your grandmother who sours the milk. Wait until she pops her clogs and then we'll see, eh?'

'Our esteemed hostess has her eye on you,' said Mungo Waller, glancing up from his cards.

'As long as she keeps her hands off me.' Greg sounded casual, but inside he was seething. Bloody Waller, making a remark like that in public.

'You're older than her usual fodder. Likes 'em young and tender, does our Moira. But you're younger than she is, and that's what counts.'

That was it. No one got away with speaking to him like that. He opened his mouth to deliver a put-down so devastating that Waller would never again raise his thick head in public – *At least Moira enjoys men, which I've heard is more than can be said for Mrs Waller* – when another voice chipped in.

'I say, Waller, put a sock in it, won't you? Join the ladies if you want to gossip.'

Gruff as Algy Prescott sounded, Greg's sharp ears homed in on a note of anxiety. Algy was in trouble. The cards were against him and he was sinking.

Greg drew a satisfied breath. Mingled with the cigar smoke, he caught the reek of Algy's fear. He knew what would happen next. Instead of bailing out and cutting his losses, Algy would continue playing, telling himself he had nothing to lose. He was that sort. Greg didn't permit the tiniest facial muscle to flicker as he planned the kill. Algy had a wad of banknotes at his elbow, but if he was as desperate as Greg believed, that must be all he possessed. Soon it would belong to a certain Mr Rawley.

Quite right, too. The only reason he was attending this cursed house party was to skim as much money as possible off his fellow guests. His luck hadn't changed for the better in Paris and he had been tempted by Moira's promise of dud players. Easy money was what he needed, though the thought made his heart sink. There were those who adored Moira's house parties, but he wasn't among them. Too loud, too brash. Still, needs must.

He pushed up the bidding and watched others pull out. Algy couldn't afford to, poor bugger. He clung on to the bitter end, the scent of his blood vivid in Greg's nostrils, until his eyes went blank with shock as Greg scooped the pot amidst congratulations as the tension broke.

Later, he counted his winnings into the secret compartments in his portmanteaux. Others might send their luggage off to the box room, but not Greg. A couple more wins of this magnitude and he could pack his bags and hotfoot it to the railway station before you could say 'lapdog'.

Mungo was right. He was fed up of Moira's meaningful glances and her attempts to brush against him oh-so-accidentally.

He glanced at the time. Almost one in the morning. He had no desire to socialise, but success pumped through his veins. He needed a nightcap.

As he went downstairs, music and laughter floated from the ballroom – and was that a distant splash? Who had been chucked in the lily pond this time? Leaving the sounds of revelry behind, he entered the same secluded room where once he had shared a quiet though alarmingly informative interlude with that fellow Bassington – Barrington?

He helped himself to a drink and was about to open the cigarette box on the table when a voice offered, 'Have one of mine.'

How the devil had this fellow sneaked in? Or had he been here all along, in which case why hadn't Greg noticed? He eyed the man narrowly. He was tall, well built . . . well-muscled. His hair was thick and dark, slicked down with a quantity of oil that suggested curls. His moustache was thick and dark, too, and needed a trim.

'Thanks.' He helped himself from the proffered case. 'Greg Rawley.'

'Tom Varney.' He took one as well.

'Can't say I've seen you about, but then Moira does tend to fill the place to the rafters.'

'To put it mildly.'

Then it hit him – Christ almighty, that confounded smell. Turkish cigarettes: the smell of Jonas. His gaze flew to meet Varney's.

'You bagged a good scoop tonight,' said Varney. 'Mr Jonas will be gratified that you're working hard to settle your account.'

'Now see here—'

'Don't make trouble, Rawley. You know what happens to men who kick up – or maybe you don't – but believe me, it's not a good idea to find out.'

He weighed up his chances. Outright refusal? A punch-up? But Jonas made an evil enemy. Even so, it went against the grain to hand over his winnings.

'In case it helps you decide . . .' Varney produced a pistol with a mother-of-pearl handle, showing it for a moment before it vanished.

He shrugged. 'I'll fetch it.'

'I'll come with you. I know the mad ideas that flit across men's minds. We wouldn't want you climbing over the balcony and shinning down the ivy, would we?'

Greg uttered a growl deep in his throat but led the way upstairs. Even now, he had hopes. Varney hadn't mentioned the amount he had won, so maybe he didn't know. Removing the wad of banknotes from one portmanteau, he held it out.

Varney eyed it. 'And the rest.'

Bugger. Greg retrieved it. With calculated coolness, he peeled off some notes.

'I'll need this for my opening stake tomorrow.'

He watched, his face consciously blank, as Varney pocketed the rest and quitted the room.

Chapter Twenty-One

The trees in the parkland, recently a blaze of red and gold, were bare, but today's skies were an endless blue. A burst of well-being refreshed Mary as she set off for her walk, even though she couldn't leave the grounds. Barmy as it sounded, ladies didn't go beetling off whenever they felt like it, certainly not on foot, anyway, and especially not when they had a lower-class past to live down.

She gazed down the drive towards the gates. Ambling round the gardens wasn't her idea of a walk, particularly not on the sort of day that reminded you to make the most of being outside. This fine spell might not last. It was November, after all. Her new woollen jacket and skirt of royal blue and hyacinth pinstripes was designated a walking costume, and she was fed up of not putting it to its proper use. She headed to where the park was bordered by the Mersey and set off along the broad riverbank, filling her lungs with air that tasted crisper than Kimber air.

Could she interest Charlie in a daily walk? It would give them some time together, which they sorely needed. Sir Edward had meant it when he said they were to live quietly. Charlie spent his days with Sir Edward and the land agent, she spent hers tagging along behind Lady Kimber or else alone. As for a social life, yes, they went to the theatre or to concerts or dinners, but always in the company of the senior Kimbers.

Sir Edward was keeping Charlie's nose to the grindstone and Charlie's affability had lost some of its warmth.

'It'll be better once you're a fully-fledged Kimber,' he said.

She wished he would say more. She wished they could discuss it, could face up to it together – face up to it? That sounded as if they had a problem. And they didn't. Not a problem. Just something they needed to get through . . . together.

On a morning like this, anything felt possible. She walked to Jackson's Boat and back. It wasn't far, but she felt invigorated and serene.

Not for long.

'Aunt Christina tells me you went for a walk,' said Charlie.

They were tidying themselves before luncheon. It being inconceivable that she should wear her walking costume at the table, she had changed into a lilac day-dress with long sleeves beneath lacy oversleeves. Charlie's words, spoken through the open door from his dressing room, rang alarm bells. He might be unselfconscious where servants were concerned, but she wasn't.

She smiled at the maid. 'Thank you. I'll do my own hair.'

'Yes, Mrs Charles.' Was she fooled? Probably not.

Mary sat at the dressing table, then changed her mind. She wasn't going to have this conversation through the mirror. She swivelled, hooking her arm over the back of the chair.

'I went along the riverbank.'

'You shouldn't have gone alone. Not the done thing.'

'I only went to Jackson's Boat.'

'You should have asked.'

'Am I expected to ask every time I want to do something?'

Charlie walked in, pulling at his cuffs. 'It'd be preferable to showing me up.'

'If I made a mistake, I'm sorry. But you always liked it when I thought for myself. You admired my initiative.' And since when did taking advantage of a fine day constitute initiative?

'I did – I do. You're a clever girl and I appreciate that.'

'But?'

'No buts.'

He drew her to her feet. She laughed, warmth flowing through her.

'I like the sound of that,' she said. 'No buts.'

'Is it worth a kiss?'

She gazed into his dark eyes for a heart-stopping moment before her eyes fluttered shut, her lips parting beneath his, his kiss making her tingle all over. With a happy sigh, she snuggled close.

'No more walks alone?' He rubbed his cheek against her hair.

'Who saw me?'

'One of the gardeners, but anyone might have seen you along the riverbank, and it wouldn't have looked good. You should know that.'

'Come with me. Then we can go as far as we like.'

'Daily walks? That's hardly what the smart set is up to.'

'What would you like to do?'

'I want us to be a stylish young couple-about-town. I want to be out and about without hanging on the coat-tails of the olds. I'm doing my bit towards it by toeing the line, but it all comes down to you and how well you fit in, and toddling off on your own doesn't help.'

'I realise I have to conform, but surely today's walk wasn't that important?' She spoke in the moderate tone she used to use when she disagreed with Dadda. Surely she wasn't trying to placate Charlie?

'Of course it was important. Everything you do is important. You have to show you fit in. We can't have you popping up in the society columns for doing something singular.'

'Taking a walk down the riverbank can hardly be called singular.'

'Anything you do that is the smallest bit unconventional can work against you – which means against me too. I don't want to be for ever seen as the fellow who married the girl who was forcibly fed and the family doesn't want you pointed out as the wife who went to prison.'

'But those things happened.'

'And now they must be set aside. I want you to be seen as the girl who did splendidly for herself by marrying me. Isn't that how you want to be seen?'

Greg glanced at Algy, drinking himself quietly to death in the corner. What would Algy say, what would any of them say, if they knew Algy's worldly wealth had passed straight through his hands into Tom Varney's? Greg played cautiously to start with, aware of the relatively small amount he possessed. As the sum increased, he played a bolder game. Soon he was into his stride, senses sharp and ruthless. He ignored the general surprise when he dropped out. He had no intention of scooping another big haul, only to lose it to Tom ruddy Varney.

He strolled down the room, settling into an armchair for a drink and a smoke. It wasn't a surprise when Varney slipped into the chair opposite. Varney gazed at the fireplace until Greg wanted to drag him from his armchair and beat his brains out.

He threw back the last of his whisky, then came to his feet, heading for the French windows. He stepped onto the terrace. There was a nip in the night air.

Presently Varney joined him.

'I take it,' Greg remarked, 'you have your friend with the mother-of-pearl handle?'

'Never without it. You didn't perform so well tonight.'

'There isn't the same incentive when you're winning to line someone else's pockets.'

'It's money you owe fair and square.'

'I prefer to choose when I pay it back.'

'Not that this is paying back as such. This is interest.'

'What? All that money last night?'

'And tonight, Rawley. Hand it over . . . please,' he added, turning the word into an insult.

Once again, he debated. Not because he had a choice, but because he plain hated to do it. Keeping some for himself, he placed the bulk of it on the wall.

Varney made no move. 'All of it.'

'I kept some last night.'

'Mr Jonas said I should let you.' Varney paused to light a cigarette, striking the match against the stone balustrade. 'He also said you wouldn't put yourself out to win much the second night and I should take all of it.'

'That's ridiculous. He can't mean you to take everything. Things are tight at present.' How he hated explaining himself to this man.

'Mr Jonas understands that. He suggests you find employment. There's a suitable opening under this roof. I hear that as a mistress, Moira's very . . . accommodating.'

Varney ground out his cigarette beneath his heel, stuffed the winnings into his pocket and walked away into the night.

Mary was on her best behaviour, submitting to a lesson in flower-arranging, determined to do Charlie proud.

'Not bad,' said Lady Kimber. 'No natural taste, but that's a class thing.'

'Excuse me. Are you suggesting . . . ?'

'I'm suggesting nothing. I'm stating a fact. It's because of your origins that Charlie likes you. He's slumming. Had he been older and more worldly-wise, and had you been less ambitious, he'd have set you up as his mistress. That would have been bad enough, though preferable to this.'

She caught her breath. Lady Kimber had made the odd remark before, but never an outright attack.

'Charlie isn't slumming—'

'He's naive. He fell in with some lively fellows at Cambridge, who had modern sisters who smoked and attended rallies, and he lost his heart to the ideal. The meetings at the agency are part of it, part of the fantasy.'

She pounced. 'If that's so, why did you let Eleanor go?'

'I require them both to develop a sense of social responsibility and that means being informed. Unfortunately for Charlie, you were there to dangle the possibility of an illicit relationship in front of him. Crossing social boundaries is a dangerous thing. For two men, such as Sir Edward and your father, a relationship of sorts based on mutual respect is possible. But for a man and a woman of different stations . . .' Lady Kimber's eyes were like flint. 'One has to be on one's guard.'

'And Charlie wasn't.' She said it quickly, before her tormentor could.

Lady Kimber touched the flowers, rearranging them. 'He found it . . . titillating. And you made the most of your opportunity.'

'I'm not staying to listen to this.'

'Goodness, anyone would think I'd called you a social climber.'

It was odd how you could be steaming angry and bored to death at the same time. Welcome to life as a kept man. No wonder Trevelyan had buggered off. Or maybe he had broken the rules and Moira had chucked him out on his ear. Ah yes, the rules. Unspoken but crystal clear. Moira required a handsome, suave younger man to be her escort and to bed her, in return for which she paid for everything and provided costly gifts, though Greg hadn't been in tow long enough yet to merit one of those.

Perhaps the gifts were in proportion to the quality of the lovemaking. Ten shrieks of ecstasy – and Moira shrieked like a stuck pig; he would need earplugs at this rate – for a cigarette case, twenty for solid gold studs. Or perhaps he could bank the screams and save up for a motor.

Lapdog. Vile word. He preferred to think of himself as a kept man when he could bear to think of it at all. But that wasn't the expression others used, as he was all too well aware.

'Woof, woof,' someone had murmured behind his back at the casino and although he had spun round, ready to do battle, he had no idea who had spoken. It could have been any of them.

'Gregory, darling.' Here Moira was again, purring in his ear. He had told her not to use his full name, but she still did it. She had despatched the duds, replacing them with top-notch players who gambled on stakes higher than he could stump up at present.

He ground his teeth, hating to feel anyone had power over him. Moira – Jonas – what wouldn't he give to turn the tables? An idea appeared in his mind. They both thought they had him penniless and subservient.

Well, not for much longer.

Goodness alone knew why it was called the blue sitting room. The carpet was deep red, the walls a colour that made Mary think of mushrooms. Ornaments stood on shelves in arched alcoves while arched windows looked into the mass of leaves and statuary that filled the conservatory. In the centre of the room was a circular table, which was precisely the right size for spreading out the newspaper.

Reading the newspaper had become a necessity. Anxious for intellectual stimulation, she crammed articles, letters and opinions into her head.

Everyone else was out. It was Sir Edward's day for the bench, Lady Kimber had one of her committees and, as for Charlie, she wasn't sure where he was.

'Seeing some chums,' was all he had said.

When she had adopted the blue sitting room, an Indian summer had filled the conservatory with sunshine, pleasant golden light edged with green filtering through the interior windows. Now the December days were grey, the sunlight milky at best, and the room was sombre – or was it just her mood?

She still hadn't seen her family and she was worried about the snub if she didn't see them at Christmas. Lilian hadn't said a word in her letters, an omission that felt as glaringly obvious as an outright demand. Neither had the Kimbers said anything. It was up to her. She would approach Sir Edward and trust to his sense of family honour.

It was time to get ready for her walk. As she crossed the hall, the butler was answering the front door. He said, 'I'm sorry, Mrs Maitland. Mrs Charles is not at home.'

Lilian! A wave of joy propelled her towards the door. 'Yes, I am.'

The butler turned commanding eyes upon her. 'Her Ladyship's orders are explicit on this point.'

I bet they are. She stepped forwards, obliging Marley to make way. 'Mother, I'm so pleased— oh! Granny! It's you.' She froze.

Granny didn't. 'Answering the door yourself, our Mary? What sort of behaviour is that for a Kimber? Well? Aren't you going to ask me in?'

Mary met Marley's frosty eyes. She steeled herself. 'Come in, Granny. Oh – Aunt Miriam, I didn't see you at first.'

Granny swept in with Miriam creeping behind, looking like she might bolt out again at any moment.

Mary didn't dare meet Marley's eye. 'Could you send tea to the morning room, please?'

'The morning room, Mrs Charles? Her Ladyship's morning room?'

'Maybe the blue sitting room . . .'

'Fiddlesticks!' Granny exclaimed. 'Don't be so lily-livered, girl. It's not up to the servants to say what's what. That's your job.'

'Mother . . .' Miriam whispered, throwing Mary an anguished look.

Mary hesitated, but she was determined to do the right thing by her relatives. 'Tea in the morning room, if you please.' She led the way. 'Let me take your coats.'

'Certainly not,' Granny retorted. 'Ring the bell.'

'It's just us.' Mary strove for that breezy tone that was so beguiling coming from Charlie. 'Let's be cosy.'

'Here you are.' Miriam stuffed gloves in pockets and undid buttons.

Granny snorted but submitted. 'Well, that's charming, I must say,' she snapped, 'sitting yourself down and not offering us a seat. Where are your manners, girl?'

Mary flushed. 'I'm sorry. When lady-callers come, you aren't meant to offer them a seat. You sit and they follow your lead.'

'Really? I'll remember that for next time. Where does Her Ladyship sit? Then that's where I'll sit, being as I'm the senior Kimber present. There's no call to look at me like that, our Miriam. Once a Kimber, always a Kimber.'

The door opened and Mary knew it was too much to hope that Granny's devastating remark had gone unheard. Tea was brought in. Just that. Tea.

'No biscuits? No cake?' Granny demanded. 'What sort of cook do you keep, Mary?'

'She isn't my cook,' Mary said in a desperate attempt to appease the parlourmaid. 'Mrs Woods is Lady Kimber's cook and she is aware of what is appropriate.'

'Doesn't look like it.'

'Mr Marley said you asked just for tea, Mrs Charles,' the maid observed, deadpan.

'Oh aye, and since when did that mean just tea and not tea and cake, eh?' Granny challenged.

'Cake – anything – whatever Mrs Woods has,' Mary said. 'Please.'

'You don't say please to servants,' Granny said. 'Don't ask 'em, tell 'em. No wonder they run rings round you.'

'They don't. It was a misunderstanding.' Who in the servants' hall had had the simple but stunningly effective idea of taking her literally?

The cake-stand arrived, with an array of macaroons, ginger biscuits and slices of batch cake.

'Will Her Ladyship be joining us?' Granny enquired.

'Lady Kimber is out; so is Sir Edward.'

'And Charlie-boy?'

'Charlie is out too.'

'Leaving you all on your ownio.' Granny drained her cup. 'I want a good look round, especially upstairs.'

'What?' Mary's hand flew to her chest.

Miriam spluttered into her tea.

'Why not? All these years I've wanted to look round the ancestral home and never been allowed.'

'Mother, you can't expect Mary—'

'Why not? She lives here. She's entitled. And there's no one to stop us.'

'You think not?' And in walked Lady Kimber.

Another evening, another dinner, but with new cufflinks to provide variety. Greg had qualified for gifts early in December, starting with a fine pair of studs. Since then he had received a dram-flask and a morocco stationery case, both of them monogrammed, which had made him remember Trevelyan's crude joke. Today's cufflinks were inlaid with mother-of-pearl, so he had been spared the coy his and hers monogramming. Nothing would have induced him to wear the damn things had Moira attempted to inflict that abomination on him.

He slotted them through his cuffs, then stood in the doorway between the dressing room and Moira's bedroom. She was seated at her triple-mirrored dressing table. Her maid was pinning some God-awful feathers in her hair. She saw him through the mirror.

'Mr Rawley will see to my jewellery – won't you, darling?'

On the dressing table lay a velvet-lined box in which Moira's rubies glowed, a heavy necklace, drop-earrings, a bracelet and an aigrette for her hair. He settled the necklace into place against skin that was milky-smooth, thanks to devoted application of indecently expensive creams. The low wide scoop of Moira's neckline ended in tiny apologies for sleeves that barely clung to her shoulders. This was her favourite style and one that suited her, despite the middle-aged thickening of her arms. It made her look sophisticated but at the same time available for a roll in the hay.

Her gown was the colour of claret, a clever hue that brightened the rubies, as well as being kind to her hair. It was amazing what you found out about a woman by living with her. He knew about the arsenal of lotions and creams, he knew she half killed herself cramming her bunions into elegant shoes, and her hair colour came out of a bottle. Again, it was a clever colour, a faded chestnut that was infinitely more natural than a rich one would have been.

For a wonder, they weren't dining in. Moira's house guests, a mere half-dozen at present, were being entertained by the

Beavens, who lived a couple of miles away, before heading, along with the Beavens and their own house guests, into town for a night at the casino.

At dinner in the Beavens' opulent dining room, Greg had, on his left, an actress who had seen better days and, on his right, a radiant young bride, though whether that really was what she was, was open to debate. She was young and lovely all right, but was she a bride or was that radiance the glow resulting from a few nights between the sheets with a skilled lover? Under some people's roofs, you could guarantee the couples were married, but the Beavens weren't among those people any more than Moira was.

And then there was the girl's ring. The plain wedding band was a decent fit, but the engagement ring, a square-cut emerald surrounded by diamonds, kept slipping round her finger. If the supposed Mrs Ronald Hurstman had once been his affianced bride, wouldn't the ring have been altered?

At the end of the meal, the dishes were cleared away and finger bowls were produced. Finger bowls! Greg thought it quite possibly the most vulgar thing he had ever seen, but one glance at Moira's face assured him he would soon be seeing finger bowls under her roof.

He had more self-respect than to use his, but the lovely Louisa Hurstman had no such reservations. Engaged in conversation with the man on her other side, she dipped her fingers, waggled them and shook out the rolled-up cloth that had been provided, all without watching what she was doing.

Which meant she didn't see the emerald slide from her finger and land beside her bowl.

Taking his napkin from his lap, Greg dropped it on the table beside his place, covering Louisa's ring. He did nothing hasty. She might miss it.

But she didn't.

Amelia Beaven gathered the ladies' glances, rising to lead the way to the drawing room. Along with the other gentlemen, Greg stood politely, then sat again to smoke and pass the port. They weren't long about it. A couple of fellows were champing at the bit to get to the roulette table and commence losing what they couldn't afford to part with.

As the gentlemen came to their feet, Greg patted his pockets as if checking their contents. He took out one or two things, his cigarette case, his silver flip-topped matchbox, his pen, and put them on the table for a moment before replacing them, leaving the cigarette case behind.

Presently the party assembled in the hallway, with its mixture of Frenchified shabby sofas and Italianesque marble. The gentlemen helped the ladies into their wraps before donning their evening cloaks and top hats.

As the first step was made towards the door, Greg excused himself to no one in particular and returned to the dining room, where, in a single fluid movement, he scooped up his cigarette case from beside his napkin and Louisa's ring from underneath it, sliding both into an inner pocket.

Success.

Christ. Was this what he had come to?

Chapter Twenty-Two

There was magic in the air. It felt like the Christmas Eves of Eleanor's childhood when Lady Kimber had scattered soot around the fireplace in the hall and Sir Edward planted careful footprints while the servants looked on, smiling and chuckling. And, oh, that happy moment when the housekeeper said, 'It's such a pleasure, My Lady, to have a little one in the house.'

That was when she knew the servants regarded Eleanor as one of their own, a Kimber and not some interloper. Not like Mary. Lady Kimber had been scrupulous about treating the girl with civility, but she knew that the staff's willingness to give Mary the benefit of the doubt had been well and truly trounced the day Old Mother Maitland arrived on the doorstep.

Now Eleanor was expected and everyone was happy. Upon their return to England, the Rushworths had escorted her to her grandparents' home in Sussex and the three of them were arriving at Ees House today.

The moment the carriage appeared, Lady Kimber hurried into the hall.

'Darling! It's wonderful to see you.'

'And is it wonderful to see us too?' came her father's crusty voice.

Laughing, she passed Eleanor into Sir Edward's arms and drew her parents inside. With one hand linked through the age-softened tweed of Pa's trusty Inverness coat, and the other through that of Mama's sealskin coat, she watched the loving reunion of her husband and her daughter. A movement caught her eye: Charlie was coming downstairs with Mary. How vexing that Mary should intrude upon this family moment. Then Charlie bounded ahead of her to scoop Eleanor into his arms and swing her in a circle.

'Take Eleanor through, Charlie,' said Lady Kimber. 'We'll follow.'

No one else noticed Mary and they crossed the hall without a backwards glance, including, Lady Kimber noted, Mary's husband. With luck, that would provide the slap in the face the girl deserved and she would slink back upstairs.

Alas, that was too much to hope for. Once everyone was settled in the morning room, the door opened and Mary came in, smiling self-consciously.

'There you are, Mary,' said Sir Edward. 'Charlie, will you do the honours?'

Lady Kimber wasn't surprised when Pa got her on her own later and said frankly, 'So that's the social climber who stepped into Eleanor's shoes. Shame she didn't take up the job I wangled for her on that *Gentlewoman's World* periodical.'

'It would have been best for everyone, herself included.'

'Damn shame, pardon my French. Don't suppose there's any chance of the boy coming to his senses?'

'What do you mean? It's far too late for that.'

'I'm going to say to you what I used to say to clients when I was a barrister. Tell me everything, no matter how insignificant. I'll decide what's useful.'

She discovered the meaning of the saying about a shiver running down your spine. 'Do you think . . . ?'

'You never know. Go back to the beginning. I want to know every single thing.'

Mary thought she would never recover from the shame of Granny's visit. Lady Kimber's freezing politeness to Granny and Aunt Miriam, and afterwards her cool dismissal of the incident, made Granny's impudence appear even more brazen. It made it hard to ask about seeing her family, but she refused to let that put her off. When Sir Edward consented, her shoulders sagged. Then she felt vexed. It shouldn't be a relief to see her family. It should be an ordinary part of her life.

But when Charlie declined to accompany her, other feelings vanished in a gasp of astonishment.

'But you've been to our house before.'

'Our house? You mean their house.'

'Their house. You've been before.'

'A courtesy call on my fiancée's family.'

'And now you can go as their son-in-law.'

'It's one thing to call as a politeness, another altogether to call as family.'

'But you are family.'

'When your people come here for the annual visit, it's

hardly a loving reunion, is it? It's a well-bred duty, the head of the family making a gracious gesture towards his humble relatives.'

'*Humble?*'

'If I were to visit your family as your husband, it wouldn't be seen as an act of civility but as something personal, and that wouldn't be good form, Kimbers rubbing shoulders with Maitlands.'

'We can't have that,' she said sarcastically.

'Don't sulk. I don't think you appreciate the damage you did by allowing your grandmother to call.'

'What was I supposed to do? Turn her away?'

'Frankly, yes. Marley would have seen her off. You should have let him do his job.'

'Seen her off? You make him sound like a guard dog.'

'Can't you admit you're in the wrong?'

'I refuse to be ashamed of my family.'

'Maybe a spot of shame wouldn't be a bad thing.'

'Charlie!' She was mortified. 'My parents . . .'

'. . . are decent people who know their place, but the old lady is the giddy limit. It would have gone in your favour if only you'd apologised to my uncle and aunt. It would have shown you see things our way.'

'Have you been discussing me behind my back?'

'As a matter of fact, I defended you. I said you were in error, but it was because you missed your family.'

Sir Edward's consent didn't taste as sweet any more. 'Is that why Sir Edward gave me permission to call on them?'

'Yes. Aunt Christina disagreed, but he was prepared to give you the benefit of the doubt.'

It was offensive to receive the benefit of the doubt, but the possibility of letting down Sir Edward went against her entire upbringing. Her convictions wobbled. Should she apologise? But that would make her seem ashamed of Granny.

Well, she was ashamed of her. All the Maitlands were – only they didn't say so to outsiders. Besides, it would stick in her craw to apologise to Lady Kimber after she had called her a social climber to her face. Just think of the ammunition that would place in Her Ladyship's smooth hands.

'Give your parents my best wishes,' said Charlie.

She wanted to shove his best wishes down his throat.

'So you've found time for your family at last,' Lilian said bitterly. 'Two whole months. I never thought we'd have to wait two whole months.'

They all looked at Mary, not exactly accusingly, but expectantly, awaiting an explanation. How could she say she had been kept away to give the class difference time to grow? Or would they understand that? After all, here they were, in the seldom-used front room instead of the back room, where they lived and were cosy.

'I'm here now. That's what counts.'

'I'll put the kettle on,' said Lilian.

Mary stood. 'I'll help.'

'Suit yourself.'

Lilian filled the kettle in the scullery, then came back into the kitchen, banging the kettle down on the range. She rounded on Mary as if about to have a real go at her. Mary braced herself, but Lilian said, 'Eh, I'm sorry, love. I'm pleased to see you, really I am.'

'Are you sure?' She made a joke of it, but she was feeling her way carefully.

'Course I am. I'm like Ozzy. That dratted animal. Do you remember how, when we came back off holiday, he'd sit with his back to us, purring his head off but determined to punish us by not looking? That's how I feel, all out of sorts. I've wanted to see you for such a long time. Folk keep asking after you, in the butcher's, in the grocer's, but they don't say, "How's your Mary?" any more. They say, "Any news of young Mrs Kimber?" It makes me feel like an old family retainer instead of your mother.'

She didn't know what to say. Lilian held her gaze for a moment, then bustled about, setting the tray. Mary fetched the tea caddy.

'Where's Ozzy?' she asked. 'I should be covered in ginger hair by now.'

'He died,' Lilian said, warming the pot. 'He was quite old for a cat.'

'When? You never said.'

'A few weeks back. I'm not good with letters, love. What is there to say when you do the same things day in, day out? Then Ozzy died and I thought: there, that's a piece of news. Then I thought: What's it come to when a dead cat is a piece of news? So I never said.'

The tray was ready. Mary was about to pick it up, but Lilian got there first.

'You do the doors.'

'Shall we go in the back room?'

'Well, I don't know, love. I mean . . .'

'You take the tray in there and I'll ask Dadda.'

Dadda said, 'I suppose so, if you want to, and seeing as you've come on your own.'

'Good. That's settled,' she said quickly. Please don't let them ask why Charlie wasn't here.

Lilian tried to usher her into an armchair by the fire, but she insisted on having her old basketwork chair. Belatedly she realised this was probably now Emma's and she had unwittingly relegated Emma to the rush-seated chair.

'That's a lovely dress,' said Emma. 'Is it by Mademoiselle Antoinette?'

'I still think it's a shame you never used *Constance and Clara*,' said Lilian.

'Miss Clara said it would have been a good idea,' said Emma, 'less daunting, you being an ordinary person and not born to grand things.'

She couldn't help smiling at her little sister sounding like a woman of the world. 'Did Miss Constance say so too?'

Emma's eyes widened with hurt. 'There is no Miss Constance. Oh, Mary, you've forgotten.'

'No, I haven't,' she exclaimed. 'It slipped my mind, that's all,' but Emma didn't look convinced.

Lilian stood. 'Time for tea. You lend a hand, our Emma. Mary, you stop here and talk to Dadda.'

Mary watched from the corner of her eye as a spread appeared on the table. She couldn't possibly do justice to this meal and still have room for dinner this evening, but not for worlds would she say so.

'Make sure you leave room for Christmas cake,' said Lilian. 'We're cutting it early, as this is a special occasion.'

'Your mother makes the finest Christmas cake there is,' said Dadda.

'She certainly makes the booziest,' said Mary and suddenly they were all chuckling and smiling.

'I'm glad you're here,' said Dadda.

'Tell us about Granny's visit,' Emma urged.

'You know about that?'

'The whole of Chorlton knows,' Lilian said drily. 'She's most put out that she never got to have a snoop round upstairs.'

So she told the story. To her surprise, she was able to make it sound funny in a groan-worthy sort of way.

Dadda said, 'We'd never let you down like that,' and the atmosphere changed. She was back to being their important visitor.

There was a knock at the door.

'It'll be the carriage.' She couldn't meet their eyes.

In no time at all, she had her hat and coat and was ready to go.

'I've brought presents. I'll fetch them.'

The coachman held the carriage door open. 'Shall I take those for you, Mrs Charles?'

'No, thank you. I want to hand them over myself.' She hurried back.

Lilian handed her two small parcels in return. 'Here you are, one each.'

'Thank you.' They would be opened privately, not as part of the Kimbers' ritual. 'I'll see you at church on Christmas morning, won't I?'

'Not this year,' said Dadda. 'We've always attended the same service as the Kimbers, but it'd be strange showing that kind of deference to our daughter. You've done well for yourself and we respect that, but, well, there it is. Besides, we don't want the Kimbers thinking we're taking advantage.'

'Especially after what Granny did,' Lilian added.

'They know you'd never do anything like that,' cried Mary.

'Then how come you're here on your own?' asked Dadda. 'That's a message from the Kimbers, loud and clear. They don't want any presumption. Well, neither do I, and I'm offended that young Charlie Kimber thinks a snub is required to tell me so.'

'Dadda . . .'

'It's all right, love. Off you go.' He took her shoulders and bent his head to kiss her, but the wide brim of her new hat got in his way and he missed.

The coachman handed her in. She waved, then felt wretched because it seemed such a regal thing to do.

That was it, then. To her family, she was a Kimber. To the Kimbers, she was a Maitland.

And you. What do you think you are?

'Who's that with Moira?' Mungo Waller plonked himself down at the baize-covered card table where Greg was playing patience.

'Lady Dalrymple.'

'You said that without looking.'

He didn't need to look. The Dalrymple was Moira's latest acquisition.

'So that's the famous Dalrymple,' said Mungo. 'Or should I say, infamous?'

'You sound like a gossipy washerwoman.'

'M'dear fellow, don't you know the story?'

'Evidently not,' Greg lied.

'In the words of maiden aunts everywhere, Lady Dalrymple is no better than she should be.'

He quirked an eyebrow. 'At her age? I take my hat off to her.'

'I don't mean now. I don't know whether she has the opportunity these days. At least, I can't imagine . . .' Mungo frowned, then grimaced. Apparently, he could imagine and it wasn't a pretty picture. 'I mean years ago. Dalrymple, Lord or Sir or whatever he was, divorced her for adultery and she's been gadding about the Continent ever since, dripping with diamonds.'

Too soon to show an interest in the diamonds. 'If she's divorced,' said Greg, glancing up from his cards, 'is she still entitled to call herself Lady?'

'Don't know. Good point. Poor old Moira,' Mungo added obliquely. 'Makes you wonder about the diamonds too. She wouldn't have been allowed to walk off with the Dalrymple jewels.'

'She found herself a rich protector or two along the way, according to Moira.'

He bent his head over his cards. Getting Louisa Hurstman's ring had been a stroke of luck, but he was leaving nothing to chance in the Dalrymple matter. Moira's busybody chatter had told him all he needed to know about Lady Dalrymple's habits. In fact, he had understood better than Moira herself, so that when Her Ladyship had decamped from Moira's in favour of the equally snobbish and gullible Buffy and Amelia Beaven, he hadn't been surprised, though Moira was astonished. It amused him to see how they fought to entertain the ageing sponger.

No, it didn't: it disgusted him.

It was time for Moira and her hangers-on, together with the Beavens and their hangers-on, to descend on Paris for a few days and nights of restaurants, dancing and casinos. Greg looked on as, hoping to tempt Lady Dalrymple, Moira booked her the best room in the hotel she always used when she came to Paris, but she was outflanked by Amelia, who dangled a suite as bait.

The Beavens favoured a different hotel, which was perfect as far as Greg was concerned. When one or two of Lady Dalrymple's baubles vanished, who would suspect a man-about-town staying at another hotel half a mile distant?

Courtesy of Moira, he knew that Lady Dalrymple kept her jewels in a strongbox, its key in the bottom of whichever handbag she was carrying. First get the key. Tricky, that, as the Dalrymple kept her bag looped over her bony arm – except while she was dancing, when she would pass it into the keeping of another lady.

On their third night in Paris, she gave the bag to Moira.

Greg turned to Buffy Beaven. 'This tune is one of Moira's favourites. Ask her to dance, why don't you?'

Buffy lumbered to his feet and Greg took the bag from Moira so smoothly that she probably thought she had handed it to him. It was the work of a moment to find the key and press it into the small wedge of putty he had been carrying about with him.

Then he waited. The Beaven party was living it up in Paris for two days longer than Moira's lot. On Moira's last night, the two groups visited the casino together. He sauntered about, making sure he was seen here, there and everywhere, then slipped down the backstairs and cut through the dark streets to the Beavens' hotel.

Inside, he paused beside an arrangement of potted palms and dropped a stink-bomb into the soil. Ensconcing himself in an armchair, he picked up one of the hotel's newspapers and hid behind it. Sure enough, voices were raised in distaste. The night-receptionist came round the desk, speaking reassuringly, only to thrust his handkerchief to his nose as the pong hit him.

With attention focused elsewhere, Greg slid behind the desk, took the key to the second-floor suite and nudged his way through the service door. Upstairs, he let himself into the suite, standing in the silence, assessing its quality, ensuring he was alone. He had gambled that Lady Dalrymple's maid, who was even less of a spring chicken than her mistress, would be elsewhere, snatching forty winks, and he was right.

This was the sitting room. Through there must be the bedroom. He opened the door: yes.

The strongbox was beneath the dressing table. He lifted the stool aside, put his topper on it and knelt down. He didn't pull the box out but crouched to insert the key. Inside, padded trays were stacked on top of one another, each holding an array of jewels. The second tray down was empty: that must be what she was wearing tonight. There were four trays in all. He homed in on the bottom one. It wouldn't be looked at until tomorrow evening at the earliest.

There were earrings with stones so huge and heavy it was a wonder the Dalrymple earlobes weren't flapping on her shoulders; a bracelet; and a necklace. This was what he had come for. A necklace with stones that could be separated.

He bared his teeth in a smile.

'Jackpot.'

* * *

'Another February, another Snowdrop Ball,' Aline gushed. 'Which is this one? The twelfth? Thirteenth?'

'Fourteenth,' Lady Kimber took pleasure in telling her.

'Is it really? We all rely on it, you know, to give us something to look forward to after Christmas.'

'That's why I started it.'

It wasn't true. Her real intention had been to start a tradition, to be continued by future Lady Kimbers, with herself remembered with admiration as the one who had conceived the delightful idea. When her portrait was painted five years ago, she had, with perfectly judged spontaneity, had the charming idea that she should be represented holding a nosegay of snowdrops.

Eleanor looked adorable in ivory silk, embroidered around the swirling hem and diagonally from shoulder to slender waist with tiny beads that shimmered like dew as they caught the light. Lady Kimber had given Eleanor her own sapphires to wear, an elegant pendant and matching earrings, not too heavy, quite suitable for a young girl. Eleanor was having a wonderful time, as her radiant smile showed. Guests who hadn't seen her since her return from Switzerland were fussing her and she had entranced the whole room when she danced the first dance with her proud father.

Mary, on the other hand, looked pale and tense in silvery-grey, though the garnets Charlie had given her for Christmas – the dear boy had been quite open to the murmured suggestion that Mary would find rubies too showy – looked surprisingly good beside the fabric. This was Mary's first ball and even if Eleanor hadn't been present to outshine her, she would still have looked uncomfortable, smile too bright, eyes guarded.

Charlie's problem, no one else's. But he seemed to have forgotten her. He had stuck loyally by her side to start with, but as the son of the house, he had a duty to the guests, as indeed did Mary. Not that you would know it from watching her. She appeared shy of approaching people, as if fearing they wouldn't wish to speak to her, which just showed her middle-class roots. The upper classes placed civility above everything.

Charlie appeared at her side. 'Your Snowdrop Ball is a huge success. Congrats.'

'I'm gratified you're enjoying it.'

'I wish the same could be said for Mary.'

'I'm sure she's doing her best.'

'Absolutely. The last thing she wants is to let me down, but I fear this is rather overwhelming.' He smiled ruefully. 'So many grand people all in one go.'

'I fear she appears rather gauche.'

'I can't take my eyes off Eleanor. She's changed, hasn't she? More grown-up, more sure of herself.'

'She has developed confidence without compromising her natural grace and charm and with no loss of modesty. It's a class trait. That's why Mary has never quite . . . well, this is neither the time nor the place.'

Charlie said nothing, but he was thinking so furiously she could practically smell it. 'Mary isn't really cut out for all this, is she?'

She said nothing. He was trying to make her join him in running Mary down, but she knew Charlie. That would arouse his gallantry and put him on the social climber's side again.

'I made a mistake, didn't I, marrying her?' He blew out a breath. 'Still, I've made my bed, and all that.'

Having envisioned this moment any number of times, Lady Kimber expected to experience a great surge of triumph. What she actually felt was serenity.

She said, 'Not necessarily.'

'What do you mean?'

'We'll discuss it tomorrow in your uncle's presence. Now I must attend to my guests and you'll oblige me by doing the same.'

Greg forced himself to wait for any fuss concerning the Dalrymple diamonds to die down. He had stolen the jewels on Tuesday night and Moira's travelling circus had high-tailed it back to the country after breakfast on Wednesday. His heart had thudded throughout that meal. Every time someone entered the dining room, he looked to see if it was the police, but he wasn't afraid. On the contrary, he was elated. He felt truly alive for the first time since being forced into servitude.

After they had been back in the country a day or two, word reached them of Lady Dalrymple's loss, which hadn't been uncovered until Thursday. Better and better.

'If only she'd stayed with us,' Moira lamented. 'Our hotel had a safe.'

'I'm sure she'll bear that in mind next time.'

Now he just had to have the necklace dismantled, flog the stones and hey presto, he could kiss his debts goodbye.

He sent a servant to fetch the shoes he had left outside his door last night for polishing.

The next thing he knew, Moira burst in.

'You're packing,' she cried.

'Word gets round.'

'Why?'

'Had enough.'

'You can't go. You haven't had a good win in weeks and selling my gifts won't get you far.'

'Good thing I'm not relying on them, then.'

'You scoundrel!' Her eyes flashed.

He laughed. 'Scoundrel? You can do better than that.'

'Beast!'

'A bit better, but not much.'

She lashed out, then squealed as he caught her wrist.

'Let me go!'

She twisted this way and that, then stumbled as he took her at her word, her hands landing slap on the bed as she steadied herself. She splayed out her fingers and ran them enticingly across the counterpane, tilting her head and slanting him a sideways glance. Did she imagine herself kittenish?

'Save it for your next gigolo.'

She sprang up, flames of anger highlighting her cheeks. 'Lapdog!'

He hit her for that, not a hard blow, more of a sharp clip, but it was enough to send her sprawling onto the rug. She made a great performance of struggling to her feet, clutching her cheek. Silly bitch, didn't she realise he could have clouted her a great deal harder and loosened a few teeth, if not removed them?

'I hate you!' she flared.

'Then you won't mind my leaving, will you?'

She stamped her foot. 'Get out of my house!' She pointed a quivering finger towards the door.

He gave her his most winning smile. 'My pleasure.'

'*Oh!*' It was a yowl of frustrated rage. Some locks of hair had come adrift, revealing a trace of grey at her scalp. She thrust out her hands to push past him, but he sidestepped with the grace of a matador. With one final outraged pout, she rushed from the room.

Half an hour later, he ran down the front steps, light-headed with relief. He was free of Moira and soon he would be free of Mr Jonas.

Settling himself on the train, he grinned. Courtesy of the lovely Louisa's ring, which he had flogged in Paris, it was first class all the way.

Chapter Twenty-Three

The address of Mr Jonas's office in Charing Cross Road was on the paperwork for Greg's original loan. When he arrived, it turned out to be a bookshop. The air smelt of wooden floorboards and leather binding. Bookcases stretched almost to the ceiling, stocked with a pleasing mishmash of different-sized books, interspersed by the occasional uniform set. An elderly man sat at a desk, on the wall behind which was a framed print of a jolly painting of a plus-foured cyclist taking a tumble into the middle of a picnic, and beside it, a framed poster from the last century for Singer's Cycles, showing men and women calmly riding penny-farthings and those three-wheeled contraptions with two gigantic wheels behind and a tiny one in front.

'May I be of assistance?' the old boy enquired.

'I have this address for a Mr Jonas.'

'Up there.' The man indicated a staircase in the corner.

Something made Greg tread lightly so as not to make a noise. At the top was a door. He knocked and entered, finding a drab little room with a fireplace on one side, cabinets on the other and a desk in the middle. For one moment, Mr Jonas went down in his estimation, then he knew, he just knew, that Jonas never set foot here himself.

A young man sat at the desk. There was nothing obviously unpleasant about him, but Greg disliked him on sight. Perhaps it was those clever eyes.

'Greg Rawley to see Mr Jonas.'

'Certainly, sir. Let me make a note of your name. Mr Gregory Rawley of . . . ?' He looked up. His expression was bland, but it was impossible for those eyes to look innocent.

'Mr Jonas knows my address. I can also be contacted through my club. Wentworth's.'

'Mr Jonas will be in touch, sir.' The fellow looked at him, a professional half-smile fixed on his face.

Greg didn't ask questions, certain the fellow would take pleasure in not answering them. Nodding a brusque farewell, he departed. It was a breezy day in early March. He set off at a brisk walk, intending to have a glass of something stiff at his club. He felt unsettled. He hadn't necessarily expected to see Mr Jonas, but he had expected something more conventional. But then what was conventional about a man who did business by having the living daylights kicked out of you when he didn't care for your proposed method of repayment?

He received no word the next day at his rooms or at his club, but the following morning there was a message at Wentworth's. Could he be available at two o'clock?

When he returned at two, expecting to be taken elsewhere, he was shown upstairs to one of the private rooms.

'My dear Mr Rawley, thank you for favouring me with your company.'

He could do little more than gape. 'Are you a member?'

'No, but as you see, I have influence. Take a seat – or perhaps you should be offering me a seat, eh, since you're the bona fide member.'

Greg sat, throwing one leg across the other, but he didn't feel relaxed.

'You wished to meet with me,' said Mr Jonas. 'To what do I owe the pleasure?'

He felt better, in control. 'I'm pleased to inform you I'll shortly be in a position to repay my debt in full.'

'In full? That's a considerable sum, Mr Rawley.'

'Nevertheless. I'd be obliged if you could make a final reckoning of the interest.'

'I'll calculate it to the day, you may be sure. Which day shall we say?'

'In two days: Friday.'

Mr Jonas bowed his head. 'I look forward to it.'

And I'll look forward to never seeing you again, you snake.

But when he took the necklace to a jeweller down a side street near enough to Bond Street to have a veneer of respectability, he was informed the jewels were fake.

'Excellent fakes, sir, but fakes nonetheless.'

With a thumping heart, he tried elsewhere, only to receive the same assessment. Something dogged and horrified inside him made him try a third jeweller. This time he was beyond being shocked. He was sickened. Sickened and furious. Damn the

Dalrymple woman. What a fraud. Now he would have to extend his loan and doubtless Mr Jonas would use it as a reason to crank up the interest.

He thought with regret of the money from Louisa's ring. He had already made inroads into that. Now the rest would have to be sacrificed as part-payment. He scowled. The Louisa funds had been destined to keep him in comfort for some time. Perhaps he wouldn't hand over all of it, perhaps three-quarters or maybe half. It was only a matter of keeping Jonas sweet.

On Thursday evening, he ate the cottage pie the woman had left for him, adding HP sauce because she never made it savoury enough, then took his time over a glass of port that was the finest his wine merchant stocked, drinking a wry toast to the lovely Louisa, who had sprung for a case of it.

Afterwards he dressed to go out. He was buttoning his silk waistcoat when there was a knock at the door. When he opened it, his heart seemed to leap with surprise and sink in dismay at the same time.

He said the first words that popped into his head. 'It's Thursday.'

'It is indeed, Mr Rawley, and a very good evening to you. May I come in?'

He stood back and it was only as Mr Jonas passed him with his evening cloak rippling that Greg saw the muscle he had brought with him. He was immediately on his guard. He might have slammed the door in their faces, but that would have smacked of fear. There were two of them, both in evening clobber, and his jaw hardened at the sight of Tom Varney.

He was holding the door open like a bloody doorman. He

swung it shut, stalking past the henchmen to face Mr Jonas. He wanted to stand with his back to the men to exclude them, but he wasn't angry enough to lose his wits. He waved Mr Jonas into a seat and sat down.

'I've caught you getting ready to go out,' said Mr Jonas. 'I won't detain you.'

'I hope you don't imagine I intended to avoid our appointment.'

'I'm glad you've raised the subject, my dear Mr Rawley, because who can say what tomorrow might bring?'

'What are you talking about?'

'I'm aware of your disappointment. I refer, of course, to the diamonds, or should I say the fakes you've been attempting to sell. It made me wonder what might happen tomorrow.'

'I'd have honoured the appointment.'

'There.' Mr Jonas beamed at his companions. 'Didn't I say Mr Rawley is a gentleman? And here's proof. He was going to keep his appointment in spite of not having the wherewithal to repay his debt.'

'About that—' Greg began.

'I have at your request calculated the full amount owed as of tomorrow. Will you be in a position to repay me?'

'You know I won't.'

'Then shall we conduct our business this evening instead?'

He spread his hands. 'I can give you something on account.'

'Not good enough, Mr Rawley.'

'Not as good as repayment in full, but I can't manage that.'

'But it's what you agreed. You committed yourself.'

'Because at the time,' he replied, allowing his vexation to show, 'I thought I'd be in a position to close matters between us.'

'You selected the date yourself, as I recall. That in itself is a token of my esteem. Normally I'm the one who says, "You must repay me on such a date," but I permitted you to choose. And you've let me down.'

'I had every reason to believe those stones were the real thing.'

'And in that belief, you agreed to settle your account. The fact that your belief was mistaken is immaterial. A date was set and I require payment. It's a matter of reputation. I cannot permit settlement dates to be broken. It grieves me to have to do this, Mr Rawley, but you've brought it on yourself.'

Greg thought of Bassington, Barrington, whatever his name was, and was on his feet in a moment. He threw a couple of punches before they had his arms pinned behind him so viciously that he felt his right shoulder joint lift in its socket. Varney and his crony spun him round to face Jonas. Greg remembered the beating he had taken; he remembered being left to rot in purgatory with Moira; and he knew those punishments were nothing compared to what was coming next.

He fought as they hauled him to the dining table, slapping his hand palm down on the surface, grabbing his wrist to hold it there. He caught the flash of a blade. He yelled and struggled, stronger in that moment than he had ever been in his life, but still not strong enough. There was a horrible loosening in his bowels and he clenched every muscle in his body so as not to disgrace himself.

The blade slashed downwards. It tore through the thin flesh at the base of his little finger and bit into the bone. For a second he felt nothing, followed by an excruciating pain as the blade was wrenched out. He stared, blinked, stared.

The blade came down again. He distinctly felt it sever the bone and then—

Hyacinths – Mam's favourites, planted in her memory – filled the garden with sweetness. The rockery was awash with tiny alyssum flowers, as rich a yellow as egg yolk; and primulas contributed a mixture of pretty hues. It was April, but Mary felt like winter – when she felt anything at all. Other times, she felt nothing. She was numb.

'Annulment?' she had repeated blankly when they told her. 'You mean we were never married in the first place?'

'We believe there was a marriage,' Sir Edward had said. 'There are two kinds of marriage that can be annulled. If a marriage should never have happened in the first place because it has no legal standing, the annulment is retrospective to the date of the supposed marriage. The other annulment is not retrospective. The marriage is deemed to have existed until the annulment dissolves it. This is the category we believe your marriage falls into.'

'It is our belief,' said Lady Kimber, 'that you weren't stable at the time of the wedding. What woman in her right mind would love, honour and cherish when she should love, honour and obey?'

Mary stared at Charlie. He was on his feet, as was Sir Edward – but while Sir Edward stood before the fireplace, centre stage and exuding authority, Charlie skulked behind a chair.

'Charlie!' She jumped up and ran to him, horrified when he backed away.

'Best if you cut along now,' Sir Edward said, and Charlie bolted for the door.

She ran panic-stricken across the hall, with Charlie striding away from her. She grasped his arm, but he wrenched free and ran upstairs, leaving her clinging to the newel-post to stop herself sinking to the floor.

She felt as though she were in a dream, but in a corner of her mind, something fiery and compelling made her follow him – but when she burst into their bedroom, he wasn't there. She sat on the bed, then got up again. She wafted round, unable to be still.

Something was different, but she couldn't think what. She pushed open the door to Charlie's dressing room and saw his things had gone, which meant . . . which meant the servants had known of the collapse of her world before she had.

She flew downstairs, where Marley, with the dexterity of a conjurer, ushered her into the morning room, where Sir Edward and Lady Kimber were . . . but not Charlie.

'He'll be putting up at my club for the time being,' Sir Edward explained. 'Better that way.'

'Not for me!'

'Especially for you,' retorted Lady Kimber. 'We can't have the two of you under the same roof.'

'I know this is a shock,' said Sir Edward. 'The fact is, Charlie made a mistake and the sooner it's rectified, the better.'

'A mistake.' Mary's heart beat in slow, dull thuds. She couldn't think.

'His gallantry got the better of him. He was fond of you, more than fond, and was sneaking behind our backs, seeing you on the sly. Very exciting, I dare say. Then he went away and returned home to alarming tales of imprisonment and forcible feeding. It aroused his protective instincts, d'you see?

Poor lad. He's been through the mill one way and another, and now there's the annulment to face. He feels bad about everything.'

She stared. Poor lad? What about poor lass?

'Once the matter is settled,' said Sir Edward, 'you'll receive an allowance.'

'I don't want your money.'

'Don't say anything hasty.'

'Why? In case I appear unstable?' She stood. 'I want to see Charlie.'

'Better that you remain apart. More dignified. You'll thank me one day.'

'I will not!'

'You're right – you won't,' Lady Kimber concurred. 'You shan't get the chance. This puts an end to everything between the Kimbers and the Maitlands.'

Mary glared at her. 'You've wanted this all along. You're getting rid of me and my family in one fell swoop.'

'That's enough,' Sir Edward boomed in what must be his best courtroom voice. 'While you remain under my roof, you'll be treated with courtesy and I expect you to conduct yourself in an appropriate manner. You appear fond of the blue sitting room, so it'll be set aside for your use. Finally, I would remind you that Eleanor, my daughter, an unmarried girl, lives here. If you do or say anything to distress her, I'll personally escort you to your bedchamber and turn the key on you. Do you understand?'

That night, she barely slept. She was too shocked even to cry. The next morning, she had no intention of going to breakfast, but a maid appeared.

'Her Ladyship's compliments, and will you be coming down, Mrs Charles?'

She knew a command when she heard one and duly made her appearance. It was a bizarre experience. Clearly no one was going to refer to her situation. It was as if she had stepped into the wrong life.

Later, Eleanor slipped into the blue sitting room. 'Mummy swore me to silence, but I wanted to tell you I'm sorry. Truly.'

'Are you? Your parents aren't.'

'They want what's best for Charlie and so do I, but it's beastly that his mistake has hurt you.'

His mistake. That was how it would go down in Kimber history and, if Lady Kimber had anything to do with it, she would be remembered as a ruthless social climber.

She vowed to see Charlie. She wanted to go immediately but, hard as it was, she must wait until the day after tomorrow because that was Sir Edward's day for the bench as well as a committee morning for Lady Kimber and Eleanor.

Only as she was getting ready did she realise she possessed no money for her fare, since Kimber ladies wouldn't do anything so infra dig as carry a couple of bob with them, just in case. Fortunately, Charlie had chucked a handful of change from his pocket onto her dressing table the other day and she had scooped it into a drawer while laughingly telling him off for being messy. Oh, Charlie.

Soon she was on her way, but when she arrived, the doorman wouldn't admit her.

'This is a gentlemen's club, miss.'

'I must see my husband. It's urgent.'

'I'll see what I can do, madam.' He disappeared for a few

minutes. 'The porter says he'll see if he can locate your husband, seeing as it's an emergency.'

A request from a third party didn't seem sufficient. She rooted in her bag for a calling-card and a pencil. She wrote *Please* on the back.

'Mr Charlie Kimber. Thank you.'

Again she waited. Finally the door opened and out came . . . the porter. She fought against a spasm of pain and astonishment as he told her Mr Kimber wasn't on the premises. He must be lying, but what could she do?

Returning to Ees House, exhausted with distress, she hid herself away in the blue sitting room.

The door opened and in came Lady Kimber.

'So the social climber has made a desperate attempt to claw back her meal ticket.' In reply to Mary's blank stare, she gave a derisive laugh. 'You surely didn't imagine you could set foot outside these four walls unaccompanied.'

'I was followed?'

'Of course. Not that you'll be permitted to go out again.'

'Then why was I *permitted* to go today?'

'To frighten Charlie, of course. I knew you'd try to see him. If he were going to weaken, your hounding him in his place of refuge will have put paid to that. Perhaps I should thank you.'

She breathed hard. She absolutely would not cry in front of Lady Kimber.

'I want to see my family.'

'There will be no contact of any description, including letters.'

'They must be told.'

'Sir Edward will see to that once we have a court date.'

A court date. She had to brace herself before she could speak again.

'And in the meantime, I'm to remain here as your prisoner.'

'Don't be ridiculous. Anyone might think you . . . unstable. Face reality, girl. You worked jolly hard to get Charlie, but the game's over.'

'It wasn't a game.'

'No, it wasn't. You were in deadly earnest.'

Lady Kimber left the room, triumph in every step. Mary sank onto a chair, too battered to be angry. The Kimbers wanted this annulment and so it would happen, and all because she had flouted convention in her marriage vows – not to be different or clever or modern, but because it had felt right.

The matter duly went to court and Mary stood in the dock like a criminal while the judge, who was surely meant to be impartial, asked her how she could claim to have been sane when she made 'that preposterous vow'.

Now here she was, back in her old home, waiting for the annulment to be finalised. That wasn't the only thing she was waiting for. She was waiting for her mind to catch up with what had happened. She was waiting for it to be real.

She didn't know where Charlie was. He had gone away immediately after his court appearance. *A delayed Grand Tour*, it said in the newspaper. Everything had been reported, including her so-called instability. Her prison sentence had been dragged up, too, as had her so-called heroism the day Imogen died. Her parents had tried to keep the paper from her, but she wasn't having that.

She decided to revert to her maiden name.

'Is that wise?' asked Lilian.

'If you mean is it respectable, I don't see why not.'

'Sir Edward says you're entitled to call yourself Mrs Kimber,' said Dadda, 'as the marriage was legitimate until the annulment, but you're Mrs Mary Kimber, not Mrs Charles Kimber.'

She didn't want to be any kind of Kimber. 'I'm sure the Kimbers would prefer it if I didn't use their name.'

She knew this was the one argument they would fall in with. All except Granny.

'You fool!' she screeched. 'That's the mistake I made, giving up the family name. Stick with Kimber, girl. You're entitled. Tell her, our John.'

She was painfully aware that her ignominious return had placed the family under intolerable strain. Day after day she saw the pinched expression on Lilian's face when she came home from the shops. Emma had been removed from the drapery counter and set to work spring-cleaning the back of the shop.

'And when I've finished that, I'm to go next door to the dressmaking business and be a tidy-upper in the workroom.'

'They want to protect you from gossip,' Lilian soothed her.

'Be grateful they haven't asked you to leave,' Dadda added brusquely.

It wasn't like him to be sharp. Was he having his nose rubbed in it at the town hall?

'At least when I lost my Martin, it was because he died,' said Granny, 'not because my head was full of women-are-wonderful twaddle. What the hallelujah was you thinking of, girl? Cherish, indeed! You've let us all down.'

Lilian stepped in. 'Please, Mrs Maitland, things are bad enough. Please don't make them worse.'

'Worse?' Granny retorted. 'How could they possibly be worse?'

Mary's hand fluttered, an instinctive movement, but she had the presence of mind to stop it before it could reach her stomach. She knew precisely how much worse things could be.

The bugger of it was he could still feel it. He could flex and bend and wiggle it, but when he looked, it wasn't there. He had dreams in which both his hands were complete. Imagine one finger, one poxy little finger, taking over your mind to that extent. They had chopped off the entire finger, not just the top joint as they had with Barrington-Bassington. Greg had blacked out, only to come bursting back into a roaring red haze of consciousness as they cauterised the wound with a hot poker. He remembered the sizzle of blood, the stench of burning flesh, the slivers of skin sticking to the poker.

He had blacked out again and woken in his bed, only it hadn't been a proper awakening. It was the start of the nightmare time, a fog in which sleep or unconsciousness, whichever it was, had given way fitfully to confusion, pounding heartbeats and hot skin, only sometimes it had been cold skin, teeth-chatteringly cold, and sickness all through his body, sickness that invaded the murk of his dreams.

At last he woke properly, realised his body no longer rang with illness, and went back to sleep.

'Blood-poisoning,' the doctor said later. Evidently the woman who did for him had summoned the quack, who had called several times. 'Could have been a lot worse.'

He made a show of resting up, not because he needed to – in fact, his strength returned rapidly – but so he could regroup. He thought long and hard about Mr Jonas. He also decided what to do with his mutilated hand. He wasn't about to admit to what had happened.

He visited his tailor, who recommended a bespoke glove-maker, who in due course provided some left-handed gloves made from the sheerest Italian kid, each little finger cleverly padded to create the illusion of a full set of digits and each glove fitting like a second skin, so perfectly that he could wear ordinary gloves on top. Not until he was in possession of these gloves did he start going out, briefly dismissing the glove to his cronies with the mention of a burn.

'The glove keeps the dressing in place,' he said, studying his cards, and that was the end of that.

A letter came from Uncle Robert's solicitor. This was the sole address Porter had for him and was he currently in residence? Greg dashed off a line to say he was, wondering what it could be about. Since he couldn't get his hands on the money, or on the house to sell it, the only reason he could think of was that Helen had snuffed it. He felt a surge of excitement and was in good spirits that evening. When the cards fell his way, it felt like an omen. He laughed at himself for thinking such rot, but it felt good even so.

A waiter murmured that he had a visitor. His spirits froze. This could mean but one thing. Well, sod him, let him wait. He wouldn't bow out in the middle of a hand for anyone.

This time, the cards fell the wrong way and he was obliged to wave goodbye to twenty guineas of the Louisa money. Perhaps this was an omen, too – he dashed the notion aside.

Tom Varney, decked out in evening dress, waited in the foyer. 'This way, Rawley.'

He signalled for his things. Outside, a hackney carriage waited.

'Trollope's,' Varney directed the driver, following Greg into the vehicle.

He employed his best blank expression, refusing to be impressed. Trollope's was a club so exclusive it lent a new meaning to the word.

They were ushered upstairs to a carpeted landing of closed doors. Varney showed him to a door halfway along, knocked and let him into a private sitting room.

'Good evening, Mr Rawley. How good of you to come.'

Greg made a vague gesture that encompassed Trollope's and all it stood for. 'Very impressive.' He used a light tone, making a polite joke of it.

'Don't misunderstand. I'm not a member, though I'm flattered you think so.' Mr Jonas smiled. 'Who needs to be a member when one can gain access by . . . other means? My dear Mr Rawley, where are my manners? Have a seat – but before you do, since you're on your feet, would you mind?' He held up his glass. 'Help yourself too, of course.'

Greg's jaw hardened but he did as he was asked. When they both had drinks, he made a point of savouring his before glancing at his host.

'Forgive me,' said Mr Jonas, 'but I can't help noticing your glove. Most discreet. Far more gentlemanly, if I may say so, than flaunting the old war wound for all to see.'

'Why the whole finger? I met a chap once who had you to thank for parting him from just the top joint.'

Mr Jonas sighed. 'Evidently your misdemeanour was greater. You promised settlement and then reneged. So disappointing. Bad enough when I set the date, but worse if a gentleman does. I can be most accommodating, as you know, but I'm a stickler for dates.' He shrugged. 'It's a foible of mine.'

'Christ,' Greg muttered.

'I would remind you, Mr Rawley, that it was you who set the date. I'd gladly have carried on dealing with you, but now, alas . . .' Another shrug. 'Such a pity.' He took a sip of his port, closing his eyes. 'I require settlement in full.'

His heart didn't skip a beat. 'You know I can't. I thought those stones were real. They were going to set me up as well as you. As it is,' and now it was his turn to shrug, 'you'll have to wait the same as I will for my inheritance.'

'Ah, the inheritance. You borrowed a great deal in expectation of it. Settlement in full, Mr Rawley.'

'No can do.'

'You're a brave man – either that or a foolish one. Already you're so blasé about your war wound that you try to brush me aside.'

Greg's heart gave a thud. He thought of Porter's letter and the possibility of Helen's demise, but he remembered where speaking of the Dalrymple diamonds had got him and held his tongue.

'You can talk all you like, but I haven't got a bean.'

'Then perhaps it's time for the next war wound. That unpleasant little incident wasn't merely punishment, Mr Rawley, it was also a warning. You have until the end of September. You see, I've a spark of generosity left after all.'

For the next day or two, Greg waited impatiently for a reply from Porter. If he was right about its contents, all his troubles were over.

But Porter simply wrote to inform him that the first year's books had been balanced and closed. Did he wish to have a copy of the summary forwarded to him or would he favour Mr Porter with a visit? Mr Porter was at his service.

He ripped up the letter.

Helen was alive.

Well, not for much longer.

Chapter Twenty-Four

Helen plodded home from Southern Cemetery. It had seemed a vast distance when she was a child, but her father always insisted they walk. 'It's the least we can do,' he said, as if they were doing their departed relatives a favour. As she grew older and taller, it became less of a trek; and here she was now, elderly and plagued by her blessed hip, and it had gone back to being a devil of a journey, but that wasn't going to stop her. Once you gave in, that was the start of the slippery slope.

She turned into Hardy Lane, which was the final stretch – stretch being the operative word. She peered down the hedgerow-lined lane.

'Best foot forward,' she said, whereupon her hip delivered an almighty twinge that made her curtsey almost to the ground. She halted. But she got going again before the pain died away. She categorically would not let it dictate to her.

As she passed the cricket pitch and the line of cottages, she heard a horse clopping down the lane behind her. She turned to look, and if her interest stemmed from the opportunity to rest her leg, that was her business.

The carriage halted and the window was pulled down.

'Good afternoon.' It was Mr Porter. 'May I take you the rest of the way?'

'No, thank you.' The refusal was automatic, although her leg was screaming at her. Why did she find it so hard to accept help gracefully?

'It so happens I was on my way to see you.'

'We don't have an appointment.'

'I had to call on another client nearby and thought I'd take a chance. Just to keep you abreast of things, you know. I've heard from Mr Rawley.'

'Have you indeed?'

He apparently took that as assent, getting out to hand her in. To her horror, she experienced a swoony moment as she put her weight on her bad leg, but a sharp gasp brought her to rights. She sank gratefully onto the seat. Her bones felt like glass.

'What's this about my nephew?' Perhaps it would be more polite to wait until they were indoors before asking, but she had never been one to beat about the bush.

'He's entitled to see the annual accounts, so I wrote to him at his London address in case he should be in residence and not away travelling, which I understand occupies a considerable proportion of his time. I had a reply from him, and rather promptly, too – ah, here we are.'

He escorted her indoors and Edith brought tea.

'Mr Rawley wishes to go over the accounts in person, as he will be up here in a day or two,' said Mr Porter. 'I've offered him an appointment on Thursday afternoon.'

'Good of him to let me know,' Helen said, waspishly. 'I suppose he was going to descend on Jackson's House unannounced as usual.' She sighed. 'I shouldn't take it out on you.'

'Think nothing of it. When one deals with wills, one is often on the receiving end of other people's frustrations.'

After he departed, she couldn't stop thinking about Greg. She couldn't bear the thought of his returning. It was a long time since he left – vanished without a word, more like. When was that? Months back – last summer. Now it was June again, over a year since Robert died.

It had been a lonely year. She and Robert used to bicker, but at least he was company. It had been easier for him: he could go to his club. But since the deaths of her two lifelong friends before she lost Robert, she had been more or less friendless. Oh, she had acquaintances by the bucketful, and jolly irritating she found most of them, but no real friends.

She winced, remembering her abortive attempt to offer friendship to Doctor Brewer. What a fool he must have thought her.

'And you are a fool,' she said, 'not least because here you are talking to yourself.'

Besides, she did have friends. She had two staunch friends under this roof. Ever since the day Greg sent the builder round, she had counted Mrs Burley and Edith as friends. Sometimes she went to the kitchen, politely knocking before entering Mrs Burley's domain, to share a cup of tea. At such times, the three of them talked as frankly as women in the wash house. No liberties were taken, though Mrs Burley did make so bold as to call her 'madam, dear,' but only when her feathers were ruffled because of Greg.

Greg. All thoughts led back to him. One good thing: after her walk, she wouldn't lie awake worrying. She always slept like a log after her cemetery visits, apart from occasionally waking to a spasm of pain when her hip locked.

The worst bit was always getting out of bed the next morning. The fight to get moving turned her flesh cold and clammy; she was breathless when she gained her feet. She pressed her hand to her hip, trying to ease the savage discomfort. Her body rang with it, but presently it eased sufficiently for her to dress.

'Bally rheumatics,' she said and was horrified to hear the crack in her voice, so she said it again in her clearest voice.

She pulled herself up straight before she left the room. As she walked along the landing, she tried to crush her limp, refusing to hesitate at the top of the stairs, stepping forward—

With a violent swooshing sensation, she toppled and lurched forwards. Her head was flung back as her body plunged. Then her head snapped back into position and she saw the stairs rushing up to meet her. Her temple caught a glancing blow on the bannister, causing a frightful twang in her neck. Her teeth snapped together. She was still tumbling, at top speed and horribly slowly at the same time. She had the oddest feeling that while the rest of her was flying downwards, her feet had been left behind, caught on whatever had tripped her.

She flung out her hand, trying to rescue herself, but it got caught in the bannisters and there was a sickening crunch that flooded her arm with pain. She clunked her way down a couple more stairs, then came to a halt, stunned and winded.

'Oh, madam! Madam!'

The pain was excruciating, accompanied by a distant bewilderment that it wasn't in her hip. She tried to hang on but . . . but—

Pausing at the gate, Nathaniel looked at Jackson's House, wondering what sort of reception he would get. He hadn't been here since – was it really last summer? That was when he had been summoned in the dead of night after Greg Rawley received a battering. Imogen was alive then. His fingers wound tightly round the top bar of the gate.

Imogen.

She had occupied his thoughts far more since her death than she had during her lifetime, yet at the time, had anyone asked, he would have said he was a good husband. He knew she would have said so. She had run his house and cared for him, supporting him with her agreement in all things.

After her death, he had packed off Evie to finish her convalescence with Ma and Aunt Louise in Cheshire and appointed a daily cook-general to run his house and provide meals. Sometimes he stopped working for long enough to go home and eat them.

He strode to the door.

'Morning, Edith. Doctor Slater's unavailable, so I'm here. Miss Rawley, is it?'

'Madam fell downstairs. We've put her in the morning room.'

Miss Rawley was lying on the sofa, propped up by cushions – he could imagine her refusing to lie down properly. She looked ghastly, grey with pain. A pillow lay across her stomach, her right forearm nestling in it, swathed in a damp cloth.

'Well, Miss Rawley, I hear you've taken a tumble.'

'I did nothing of the kind. I tripped.'

'Madam, I swear there was nothing there.' Edith sounded agitated. 'I never leave things lying around, and certainly not on the floor, let alone at the top of the stairs.'

'There was something there.' Miss Rawley glared at Nathaniel. 'I didn't send for you.'

'Nevertheless, you've got me. Let's have a look, shall we?'

She gasped as he unwound the cold compress. The grey leached out of her face, leaving her hollow-eyed and deathly white. As he conducted his examination, she pressed her lips together and uttered not a sound. He had to hand it to her. She had real pluck. When he finished, she sank into the cushions, looking thin and frail.

'Rest now,' he said. 'I'll come back this evening. I'll leave you something to help you sleep.'

Even after some shut-eye, she was still pretty ropey when he returned that evening. The next morning, however, her doughty spirit was back in full force. She was wrapped up to her chin in a highly respectable housecoat and was again propped up by cushions, but her feet were on a footstool and there was a table by her side with a jug of cordial and, unless he was mistaken, the housekeeping books.

'Thank you for your attention yesterday,' she said formally, 'but Edith assures me she sent for Doctor Slater.'

'He had to attend a funeral.'

'I see, and is he otherwise engaged today?'

'No, and if you prefer, I can hand your case over to him, though I'd rather see it through myself.'

She thought about that. 'I'd prefer to keep you.'

'How's the wrist?'

'It aches a little.'

'Which I assume means it hurts like billy-o. I can give you something for that and if you want to get dressed afterwards, it should make it easier.'

Her jaw stiffened. Had he offended her by saying something too personal? She wriggled so she could sit up straighter and when she spoke, her voice was half confiding and half peeved.

'I can't dress without assistance. Last night I was obliged to let Edith help me, because it was either that or go to bed fully dressed.'

'And you declined her help this morning.'

'I've no wish to be lady's-maided by my housemaid. It isn't seemly.'

'You won't be able to manage unaided for some time.'

'It's other things too. Writing – I'm right-handed. All sorts of things.'

'It isn't nursing care you need, so I can't help you. Have you a friend you can call on, perhaps, or a relative? Someone who can live in?'

She brightened. She went from tired and vexed to animated in an instant.

'That's exactly it,' she declared.

'A friend?'

'Gracious me, no. My friends are dead and when they were alive, they were pretty decrepit. No, I wonder if the Kimbers could be prevailed upon . . .' The words drifted away, but her eyes were bright and busy.

'Didn't you tell me you and Lady Kimber . . . ?'

'Had a big falling out. Yes, yes, years ago. But in these circumstances . . . and if the request went to Sir Edward . . . I'll write directly—oh.'

She looked so crestfallen that he couldn't help smiling. 'I'll write and say you're in need of a companion-help and would rather rely on family.'

'Family,' Miss Rawley said with more satisfaction than the idea seemed to warrant. 'Yes, indeed, family.'

'So it's settled. You'll go as companion-help to this Miss Rawley. She's Lady Kimber's aunt, but they don't keep up the connection, so don't worry about that.'

Mary listened in silence. Dadda had spent the morning at Ees House, closeted with Sir Edward. She hid her indignation. It was tempting to refuse point-blank, but that would make life difficult for her family.

'Does Charlie know?' she asked.

'If you imagine he'll come rushing back to make an honest woman of you—'

'I don't need making an honest woman of,' she said tartly. 'The marriage was annulled in the middle of May, but before that it existed. I wish people would remember that.'

'Well, they won't. The popular view of annulment is that the marriage was never legal in the first place, more's the pity.'

'Does Charlie know?' Does Charlie know? Does Charlie know? It was humiliating and infuriating to be reduced to asking about her husband . . . her former husband.

'Sir Edward says he'll be told. What happens after that, I don't know. I don't think Sir Edward knows either. It depends whether it's a boy or a girl. If it's a boy, there'll be a devil of a legal question. At any rate, a boy might be taken by the Kimbers in case he ends up as heir.'

She swallowed. 'And if it's a girl?'

'Who knows? That wouldn't be such a calamity for the Kimbers. You might be expected to bring her up yourself.' Dadda cleared his throat.

A fist closed round her heart. 'What is it?'

'Probably better if Mother tells you.'

Later, Lilian said, 'It's to do with when the baby comes. It has to be born within so many days of the annulment.'

'I don't understand.'

'To prove it's Charlie's.'

'What? Of course it's Charlie's! What a monstrous suggestion. Did the Kimbers decide this?'

'It's the law.'

For one furious moment, she hoped the baby would be born on the wrong side of the time limit, and let the law and the Kimbers make of that what they pleased. But she would be damned for ever as a loose woman and an unmarried mother. Come to think of it, she would probably be regarded as an unmarried mother anyway, in spite of the wedding ring she had replaced on her finger and the Kimber name she had felt obliged to resume.

The baby was due in September or October. That was as precise as the doctor could be in the absence of helpful information from Mary. The trouble was that for her, it had never rained in Halifax regularly. She knew that for most girls, it rained in Halifax every month, but it never had for her. That was why it had taken her so long to realise her condition. There hadn't even been morning sickness to give her a prod. She hadn't put on weight, either. Quite the reverse: the shock and distress of the annulment had made the pounds fall off.

'You'll probably expand all of a sudden,' said Lilian. 'Some women do. They don't show for ages, then all at once they look like they're ready to drop an elephant. We need to get you off to Miss Rawley before that happens.'

She pressed her lips together. For now, her condition was a secret. Her parents knew, as did Sir Edward and Lady Kimber, but no one else – well, presumably this Miss Rawley knew. Emma didn't. Mary was under orders not to succumb in front of Emma to a violent craving she had developed for these new sweets called wine gums, in case it made her curious.

'It's more likely she'll notice I'm wearing your clothes,' she told Lilian. Her own were too tight.

But Lilian's sensible skirts and blouses were so similar to Mary's old clothes that Emma didn't notice the difference, merely asking, 'Aren't you going to wear your lovely new things any more?'

'Would you like some of them? It never felt right, having so many.'

'Oh, could I?' Emma's face lit up.

She had to smile. 'There'll be lots of turning-up. I'm taller than you.'

Neither did Emma question the business of sending her away.

'This Miss Rawley needs help, and it'll benefit all of you if I'm away for a spell,' Mary told her. 'You know, let things die down.'

How amazing that she could make it sound so reasonable, so normal, when she was being shunted elsewhere while everyone else licked their wounds.

Anyway, she might like being at Jackson's House. If this Miss Rawley was enemies with Lady Kimber, she couldn't be all bad. And if they didn't get along, she could use her Kimber allowance to set herself up in a cottage and settle down to write. She hadn't written any articles since before her marriage. Had *Vera's Voice* and the rest forgotten about Fay Randall by now?

Jackson's House was a tidy distance away, but travelling at a clip through the cool morning, it was no time at all before the cab turned into Hardy Lane. How countrified this part of Chorlton was, compared to the leafy roads of red-brick houses near the rec, where the Maitlands lived.

The front door was opened by a middle-aged woman in a frilly cap and apron.

'Good morning,' said Mary. 'I'm Miss Rawley's companion-help.'

'If you'd like to follow me upstairs . . .'

Soon she was in a pleasant room with a flowery china set on the washstand and cut-glass trinket dishes on the dressing table. An oil lamp stood beside the bed.

'Downstairs is lit by gas,' said the maid, 'but it's oil and candles up here.'

'Roses – how lovely.'

'It was Mrs Burley's idea.'

'Mrs Burley?'

'The cook. She thought – we both thought – you'd like them.'

'Thank you. I do.' Odd that the servants, not their mistress, had made the gesture.

'I'll leave you to settle in, miss.'

She put her things away. Wasn't Miss Rawley going to send for her? She went downstairs. The back of the hall must lead to the kitchen. She knocked and went in, her fingers brushing the green baize. A solidly built woman was chopping vegetables while the maid cleaned the household brushes in soapy water.

'You must be Mrs Burley. Thank you for the roses.' She turned to the maid. 'I'm sorry, I don't know your name.'

'Edith, miss.'

'Edith. And I'm Mary Kimber.'

'Kimber, is it?' said Mrs Burley. 'Only we've been wondering, being as we know how you're placed, not being wed any more.'

'I wanted to go back to Maitland, but . . . well, I assume you're aware of my condition. I want the same name as my child.'

'We'll take good care of you while you await your happy event, Mrs Kimber,' said Mrs Burley.

'I was hoping you'd call me Mary.'

'Nay, we couldn't do that.'

'Why not? I work here, same as you.'

She gazed at them, willing them to accept her on her terms. Never again would she allow herself to be set above those who did the work.

'Well, I don't know,' said Mrs Burley. 'After all, you were sent by Sir Edward himself. He wouldn't want us hobnobbing.'

'At home, my mother works alongside our daily, and that's how I want to be. It's how I was brought up.'

'Mary it is, then, but only when you're in here.'

'On the other side of that door,' said Edith, 'you're Miss Mary.'

'Mrs Mary,' the cook corrected her. 'It's only polite, given your situation.'

A bell jangled in the middle of a row of bells on the wall above a rack of labelled spare keys.

'That's the morning room,' said Edith. 'I'll show you.'

Mary followed her into the hall. Edith opened a door and she walked into a comfortable room with windows open onto the side and back gardens, but the pleasure and relief she had started to feel in the kitchen died an abrupt death when she saw the fixed, angry look on the face of the elderly lady sitting bolt upright, one arm in a sling.

'I hope you haven't unpacked. As far as I'm concerned, you can turn round and go straight back where you came from.'

Announcing himself to the clerk, Greg heard the swell of orchestral music. The clerk disappeared into Porter's sanctum and the music stopped mid-phrase. The clerk reappeared, holding the door open.

Greg walked in. 'I'd forgotten about that,' he said, nodding at the gramophone.

'Good afternoon, Mr Rawley. Harrison will bring the accounts through and we can get down to business.'

A few days ago, Greg had expected his business up here to involve burying Helen and putting the house up for sale, but when he received no word, he was forced to conclude she must simply have been injured in the fall. He waited for Porter to tell him so. He sat there through all the bloody accounts, remembering the many reasons he had hated his old job, itching to hear how bad Helen's condition was, but Porter made no mention of her.

Finally he asked, 'How's my aunt?'

'You don't know? Are you not residing at Jackson's House during your sojourn in Manchester?'

Residing? Sojourn? Pompous bastard.

'I came here straight from the train.'

'Then you won't know.'

'Not if you don't tell me.'

'I regret to inform you that Miss Rawley recently met with an accident. A fall. She has broken her wrist.'

'Is that all?'

'All?'

'I mean – no other injuries? Poor old girl.'

'A few bumps and bruises, as you'd expect, but I gather she's making a good recovery.'

Bloody hell. Bloody, bloody hell. If it hadn't killed her, that fall should at least have knocked her into the middle of next week, rendering her deeply unconscious and available for having a pillow pressed over her face. She must have rubber bones.

After all the trouble he had gone to as well, travelling to Manchester overnight and biding his time until he could sneak into Jackson's House, choosing a warm day when the windows were open. Helen had been outside fiddling with the roses. He had climbed into her morning room and crept across the hall to the study. The windows here were shut. Silently, he opened a sash, letting it down again to rest on a sliver of wood slender enough to make the window appear closed, but strong enough to hold it in position. He then left the house the way he had come.

He had returned that night, entering through the study window. He fastened a wire across the top of the stairs three inches from the floor, then waited in the master bedroom, watching through a crack as Helen took her tumble. He heard the frump in the frilly apron come screeching onto the stairs and then down again, presumably to fetch reinforcements from the kitchen.

A few seconds was all it took to remove the wire and sprint downstairs past Helen's limp body. Next moment he was out of the house via the study window.

Now he had the whole thing to do over again.

Except it couldn't be a fall next time.

Chapter Twenty-Five

Thanking Edith as she admitted him to the morning room to await Miss Rawley, Nathaniel realised the room was occupied.

'Pardon me. I hope I'm not—what are you doing here?'

'Doctor Brewer.' Mary Maitland – no, wait, she was married now – looked flustered. 'It must have slipped Miss Rawley's mind to mention you were expected.'

Of course: she was Mrs Kimber now. But weren't the Kimbers estranged from Miss Rawley? Then her words slipped into place or perhaps not so much the words as a certain tightness in her voice.

'Are you Miss Rawley's companion-help?'

'Yes.' And evidently that was all she was prepared to say. 'Won't you sit down? I haven't seen you since . . . since the explosion. I'm so sorry about Mrs Brewer.'

It still happened sometimes, someone offering condolences. Usually it discomforted him, but not this time.

'Thank you for your letter. It was most kind.'

It had been, too. Of all the letters he had received, hers had shown transparent compassion and sorrow. She had written movingly of Imogen's bravery.

'I see you two have met.'

Nathaniel glanced round. 'I'm pleased to see you up and about, Miss Rawley.'

'Did you expect me to wilt on the sofa because I've temporarily lost the use of my arm? Would you excuse us, Mrs Kimber?'

The moment she rose to leave, he saw the bulge in the front of her dress. He glanced away.

'You know that person?' Miss Rawley demanded as the door closed.

'That sounds scathing.'

'It's meant to. Do I take it I have you to thank for her presence here?'

'You wanted me to write to Sir Edward on your behalf.'

'But I didn't want you to suggest a friend of yours for the post.'

'She isn't my friend.'

'Then you won't mind informing Sir Edward of her unsuitability.'

'I'm not your secretary, Miss Rawley. I did you a favour by writing. If you don't like the outcome, sort it out yourself.'

'How do you know Mrs Kimber?'

'She worked at the clinic last year. I knew her before that, actually. She's a writer, a journalist – well, I don't suppose she is any more. I don't suppose she needs to write now she's married.'

Not for the money, no. But hadn't her writing been prompted by something more than money? He had read some of her articles and been impressed. They weren't the work of a money-driven hack.

'The marriage was annulled,' said Miss Rawley. 'You look blank. Don't you read the paper?'

'Of course I do.'

'Then I don't see how you can have missed it.'

'I'm not interested in tittle-tattle. The marriage was annulled, you say? But she's . . .' He hadn't been mistaken, surely?

'Precisely, and I'm to keep her here until after the child is born.'

'You won't require help that long.'

'Sir Edward's orders. He's assisted me by providing a companion-help and I'm to assist the Kimbers by providing a hidey-hole for the cast-off wife while everyone holds their breath waiting to see if it's a boy or a girl.'

'What difference does that make? No, don't tell me. I'm not interested in gossip. If you'll place this cushion across your lap, I'll undo the sling. Wiggle your fingers. How does that feel?' Presently he reapplied the sling. 'Your wrist is making a good recovery.'

'Good as in swift?'

'Good as in uncomplicated. Older bones take longer to knit.'

'I did trip over something, you know. There! That look on your face, that's the look everyone gets. You don't believe me.'

'The mind can play tricks.'

'Yours might, Doctor, but mine would never do anything so absurd. When I say I fell over something, that is precisely what happened.'

'Edith has taken your insistence personally. She feels you're blaming her.'

'If she left something lying about, she should say so.'

He felt sorry for Edith. He felt sympathy for Mary Kimber too, having to care for Miss Rawley in this mood. As if she didn't have enough on her plate with a failed marriage and a baby on the way. What sort of man discarded his pregnant wife?

Nothing to do with me.

But he kept thinking about it.

Hearing a man's voice in the hall, Helen looked up. She wasn't expecting Doctor Brewer, though she would be glad to see him. They were getting along better now. Did he think so too? When she first knew him, he had tried to deflect her bluntness with polite reserve, but now he gave as good as he got. She had always been a great one for arguing. She liked to think it was because she came from a legal family, but no one else had ever thought so.

Greg walked in.

'How do, Aunt Helen. Porter tells me you've been in the wars.'

'As you see.' She indicated the sling. 'Your room is ready.'

'Do you keep it ready at all times, just in case? How touching.'

'Mr Porter informed me of your appointment. Naturally, I assumed you'd stay here. This is Mrs Mary Kimber. Mrs Kimber – my nephew, Mr Rawley.'

'Kimber?' He looked at her with interest. 'How do you do?'

They shook hands. Greg's left hand was encased in a close-fitting glove.

Before Helen could comment, he said, 'It holds a dressing in place.' He turned to the Mary girl. 'It's kind of you to visit my aunt.'

'I'm not visiting. I'm the companion-help.'

Drat her, did she have to say that? Helen hated Greg's knowing the extent of her infirmity. She hated everything about having Mary Kimber here, starting with the simple fact that she wasn't Eleanor. With the annulment fresh in the neighbourhood's minds, what better moment for Sir Edward to spirit his beloved child away? Instead she had been fobbed off with the discarded wife.

'Not that I'm in need of assistance,' she said sharply.

'Porter says you fell.'

'I tripped over something – not that anyone believes me, including,' she added, 'people who weren't here and know nothing about it.'

'Edith swears there was nothing to trip over,' Mary said quietly.

Helen was annoyed with her for answering back, though she would have despised her if she hadn't. She eyed Greg. 'I suppose it's too much to hope you'll say how long you're staying.'

'Not at all. I'll trespass on your hospitality just the one night.'

'No longer?'

'Sorry to disappoint.'

That galled her too. She hated Mary for witnessing Greg's lack of respect. Fortunately, he evidently had no more desire for her company than she had for his. He went out, not returning till late. The next morning, he departed after breakfast.

'Is there anything you'd like me to do?' asked Mary.

Helen gestured, dismissing the offer. There were times when she had no option but to accept help, but that didn't mean she must appreciate it, even if Mary was a big improvement on Edith, who was a silly old fusspot.

'Then I'll go for a walk,' said Mary.

'Fine.'

It suited her to get rid of the girl. It was high time she made peace with Edith.

She knocked before entering the kitchen.

'May I come in?'

'Of course, madam,' said Mrs Burley. 'Would you like to sit down?'

'Only if you'll both join me.' The look they exchanged didn't escape her notice. 'I've come to say I don't blame you, Edith, for my accident.'

'I promise you, madam, there was nothing on the landing.'

'Then let's put it behind us,' Helen said, adding with a glance at her sling, 'in so far as this plague-y thing can be forgotten.'

'Thank you, madam.' Edith's voice rang with relief.

Helen felt relieved too. Not that she was backing down about having tripped, but from now on she must keep that to herself. It would be unbearable to alienate these two.

'Now, if you'd kindly put the kettle on, Mrs Burley.'

Soon the three of them were enjoying cups of tea, discussing, of all things, these newfangled rolls of toilet paper and whether they should be introduced into Jackson's House. When they had drunk the pot dry, Helen returned to her morning room. She didn't want Mary finding her being chummy in the kitchen.

Presently the girl appeared.

'No, I don't require your services,' Helen said before she could offer. 'Isn't there a letter you can write?'

'My parents would like to hear from me, but I needn't

write this minute. Is Doctor Brewer calling to see you today?'

'No. This is his prison morning.'

'Prison?'

'He does forcible feeding. Doctor Slater told me.'

Mary's face blanched. 'Excuse me. I think I will write my letter after all.'

When the door shut behind her, Helen felt a twinge of something unexpected. Guilt. What had made her say such a cruel thing? The truth was she admired these women who were prepared to go to such lengths to achieve their aims. It made her wish she were fifty years younger.

Yet, she had deliberately hurt Mary. Had she done it because she herself had lived with pain for so long? At times, loneliness was an ache inside her chest. People would be astonished if they knew how she yearned for closeness, for intimacy . . . for a friend. Yet there was something in her, something spiky and out of kilter, that made her push others away, punishing them and punishing herself because they weren't the people she so badly wanted them to be – because they weren't Christina or Eleanor.

Mary couldn't believe it of him. She couldn't believe it of herself either. Had she really once been attracted to a man who force-fed women? She swallowed hard, disgusted at herself as well as him. She had thought better of Doctor Nathaniel Brewer – yet why had she? Because she had liked him? No, he had battled and overcome all those obstacles to set up the clinic and that had made him seem a decent man with a conscience. She had admired and respected that. But how could the same man overpower and forcibly feed women?

And what was Miss Rawley's opinion? That sly look on her

face when she mentioned the force-feeding showed she knew exactly what she was saying. Had Sir Edward told her of Mary's experience? Maybe she had seen it in the newspaper.

Thank goodness for Mrs Burley and Edith, who were kindness itself. When Mary laughingly admitted to her craving for wine gums, dear Mrs Burley added them to the housekeeping list. She and Edith never asked prying questions, simply drawing her into their natter. She treasured these interludes, but were they enough to make Jackson's House bearable?

Miss Rawley detested her, that was clear. At first she had been taken aback by the hostility, then she had tried to let it wash over her. What did an old lady's carping matter? But it did, especially when she was feeling ropey, like today.

'You all right, love?' Mrs Burley laid a meaty hand on her arm.

'I feel a trifle odd. Nothing to worry about.'

She had been feeling off-colour since she woke up. It was part of her condition, nothing more. It was the strangest feeling, having something growing inside her. She touched her bulge. Lilian was right: she had filled out, as if coming here had given her body permission to display.

That night she helped Miss Rawley to retire as usual, marvelling at the old lady's exquisite undergarments, though ever since a tentative compliment had earned her a sharp put-down, she had concealed her admiration beneath lowered eyelids.

She was more than ready for her own bed, but when she undressed, she turned cold at finding spots of blood staining her underwear. Pulling her nightgown over her head, she jumped into bed. She lay on her side, drawing her knees up, trying to calm herself, but sleep proved elusive.

She rose early, her throat clogging as she checked her

nightdress. Sure enough, there were the stains she had dreaded finding. She dressed and went to assist Miss Rawley, then she went downstairs to Mrs Burley, clutching her nightgown.

Mrs Burley took one look. 'Back to bed with you.'

Next thing she knew, Doctor Brewer appeared. She didn't want him near her, didn't want him taking her pulse or asking intimate questions. His fingers were gentle on her wrist, but his was the hand of a force-feeder.

'I hear you're spotting. You must stay put until this scare is over.'

'If I'm to have bed rest, might I go home?'

Just until this scare was behind her. But after that . . . She imagined a little place of her own and her heart gave a leap of pleasure. But what about her allowance? Some of it was paid to Miss Rawley for her bed and board. Would Sir Edward pay her the full amount if she left here? Or would he stop paying altogether to make her come back?

'You're not going anywhere for a couple of days,' said Nathaniel, 'but after that you may.' He put his stethoscope in his black bag. 'Let your mother take care of you.'

'And my baby is safe? Good. That's all that matters.'

'Would you like me to inform the Kimbers?'

A whoop of shock made her insides stand to attention. 'It's nothing to do with them.'

'If you say so.'

She wavered. 'If there's nothing seriously wrong, they don't need to know.' Would they wish it was serious? 'Anyway, Charlie isn't here to be told. He's away on a tour of Europe.'

'I wouldn't go off gadding if I had a child on the way. I'd be at my wife's side.'

'I'm not his wife any more.'

'I shouldn't have said that. It's just something I feel strongly about.'

'Pressure was put on him and . . . here I am.'

'Is that what he told you? That he was forced into it?'

'We never discussed it.'

He stared. 'Your husband never talked to you about getting rid of you?'

'It wasn't like that.'

'It sounds exactly like that. Being under pressure doesn't mean you have to cave in. Either Charlie Kimber was pressed into separating from you, in which case he's a poor excuse for a man, or he chose to throw you overboard but allowed you to believe it wasn't his fault, in which he's still a poor excuse for a man. Whichever it was, you deserve better.'

The unexpected support pierced the layer of self-protection she had wound around herself. Warmth gushed through her, so sweet it hurt. But she mustn't be vulnerable. And certainly not in front of this man.

Force-feeder.

'What do you mean, she's going home?' Helen glared at Doctor Brewer. What had he organised behind her back? They thought they were God's gift, these doctors. 'She has duties.'

'Whatever happens, you can forget her duties for the next few days.'

She wouldn't have to go back to being fussed over by Edith, would she? Mary's help was infinitely more palatable, compassionate but not soppy, efficient but never cold. But Helen had alienated her. Belatedly, she realised she liked her young companion, admired her spirit. Was it too late to rectify matters?

For the next couple of days, she submitted to Edith's ministrations. She saw Mary once a day, a stiffly polite visit. She didn't want to be stiff and polite, but after the way she had treated the girl, she didn't know how else to be. Then she was ashamed of herself: she had paid Greg more attention when he was incapacitated.

The day Mary got up, Helen went to the kitchen, in need of company. To her surprise, she found Mary drinking tea with Mrs Burley and Edith. The three of them looked up, startled.

Mary stood. 'I was saying goodbye.' She left the kitchen.

Helen asked stiffly, 'Is there more in the pot?'

'No, but I can brew a fresh one,' Mrs Burley offered.

'It doesn't take a whole pot of tea to say goodbye. Am I right in assuming Mrs Kimber is a regular visitor to your kitchen?'

Mrs Burley met her eye squarely. 'Mrs Mary often pops in.'

'We like to see her,' Edith added stoutly.

'She's a good lass. There's no side to her.'

'Well,' said Helen. Her servants clearly thought the world of Mary while she, stupid old wretch that she was, had been busy resenting her for not being Eleanor.

Feeling for the sliver of wood holding the window open, Greg raised the sash. Just like last time. Picking up the canister, he leant into the study, placing it on a cupboard before hoisting himself inside. He shut the window and stood listening in the darkness. Just like last time.

Just like bloody last time. This was why he had been obliged to stay here overnight after Helen snapped her wrist instead of her neck. He had had to doctor the window again. Now here he was – again

– and this time Helen's death was going to be a lot more agonising.

He cracked open the study door and moved to the stairs, pausing at the top before approaching Helen's door. There was no light underneath. Grasping the knob, he turned it smoothly, opening the door a fraction. He could hear her breathing. He slid inside and pushed the door to.

He stood there a while. He was good at waiting. You had to be if you wanted to be any good at cards. When he was sure he hadn't disturbed her sleep, he set down the canister and removed the torch from his pocket, checking that the film of fabric was in place to dull the beam before he switched it on, noting how the furniture was positioned.

He unscrewed the lid of the canister, releasing a whiff of paraffin. Taking exquisite care, he moved about the room, stopping here and there to let oil trickle out. Three ha'pence a pint resulting in a sizeable inheritance wasn't a bad investment. Helen shifted and mumbled and he stood like a statue, waiting for her to settle before he resumed his task. When the canister was empty, he lifted the lamp from Helen's bedside and laid it on the floor. Let it take the blame.

He withdrew to the door. As he opened it, his wrist brushed the key. Yes? No? Yes: he slid it from the lock before striking a match and dropping it. Stepping backwards onto the landing, he turned the key and pocketed it.

Mary's mind was crammed full. She couldn't stop thinking about the baby, trying to imagine handing over a son. Would she be allowed to see him? Would he grow up believing the social climber story? What if it was a girl? Would her allowance be expected to provide for them both?

She threw aside the bedclothes. A warm drink might soothe her into sleep. Pulling her dressing gown around her, she tied the cord above her bump, slid her feet into her slippers and padded from her room. Could she smell something? She started down the stairs. The smell was still there. Smoke!

She scuttled down a few more stairs before realising the smell was getting fainter. As she turned back, there was the loud crack of glass exploding. She gasped. She hurtled upstairs, tripping and barking her shin.

'Fire! Fire!'

Her voice wasn't anything like loud enough. Making a split-second decision, she raced up the attic stairs, barging through the first door she came to.

'Get up! Get up!' She tried to pull Mrs Burley from the bed.

'What is it? What's happening?'

'Fire! Wake Edith and get out. I'll fetch Miss Rawley.'

She darted out again, heading for Miss Rawley's room. The smell was getting stronger. Had she made a terrible mistake by going to the attic first? She grabbed the door, but it wouldn't open. She shoved hard, then banged her fist on it.

'Miss Rawley! Miss Rawley!'

Drat the woman, she had locked herself in for the night. There were spare keys in the kitchen. As she hurried downstairs, Mrs Burley and Edith were ahead of her. They rushed for the front door as she ran to the kitchen and then back to Miss Rawley's room. With a shaking hand, she thrust the key into the lock, knowing she must push Miss Rawley's key out the other side. To her surprise, the spare slid in.

She threw open the door – and faced a stinking wall of heat, smoke and flame. Her heart went cold with panic. Gulping a breath, she plunged in and floundered across the room, eyes streaming, lungs bursting. Crashing into the foot of the bed, she threw out her hands, scrabbling to find Miss Rawley's prone figure. The old lady wasn't moving. Mary felt her way up her body, shaking her.

As she reached Miss Rawley's shoulders, there was an explosion inside her chest and she gasped in a mouthful of rancid air, coughing it up again immediately. Her head was buzzing, her chest tight and getting tighter, her throat red-raw, the backs of her eyes at melting point. She yanked the bedclothes aside and heaved Miss Rawley's arm. The old lady flopped to the floor.

Mary's anguished sob turned into a choking fit. Bending, she grasped Miss Rawley beneath her scrawny armpits and staggered backwards towards the door, her feet scrabbling for purchase. Her flesh felt as though it was peeling off in the heat. Her eyes were clogged with smoke.

At last she bumped into something – a piece of furniture. Not daring to let go of Miss Rawley, she felt behind with one foot, trying to make sense of where she was. She kicked and the thing behind her moved – the door! Choking, head spinning, she made one final effort and heaved her burden onto the landing.

Coughing her guts up, she felt her body trying to crumple, but she mustn't stop, not yet. Lugging Miss Rawley further, she let go of her and stumbled round her prostrate form, heat searing her flesh as she pulled the door shut.

She had the oddest feeling she was still dragging Miss Rawley, because there was a dull pulling sensation deep in her abdomen. A sticky warmth appeared between her legs.

Sick and dizzy, beyond making even the smallest effort, she felt her body fold as the floor came up to meet her.

Helen sighed as she woke, eyelids fluttering. She started to swallow, then halted on a gasp. Her gullet was like sandpaper. Her eyes flew open. She was sore all over. Her wrist was throbbing, as if the fracture had only just happened.

'There, there, madam dear,' came Mrs Burley's voice.

Her eyes smarted. The inside of her mouth was raw, coated with a nasty taste. When she tried to speak, a gurgle rasped against her throat.

'Hush,' said Mrs Burley. 'You're safe now. I'll fetch Doctor Brewer.'

Helen lifted her good hand to stop her, but she was as weak as a kitten.

'I won't leave you. I'll just go to the door and call.'

She was in a strange bedroom, a plain room with whitewashed walls instead of wallpaper. What had happened?

Mrs Burley called to someone, then returned.

Helen managed to whisper, 'Water . . .'

She heard it being poured. Mrs Burley cupped a hand behind her head to raise it and a glass touched her mouth. Her lips were cracked, each crack a tiny line of exquisite pain. The water mingled with the horrid taste in her mouth, taking it down her throat.

Doctor Brewer appeared. He looked tired, no jacket, sleeves rolled up. 'When you're up to it, you can berate me for tending you without a frock coat, but until you get your voice back, you'll have to tolerate it.' He smiled and something inside her melted. He smiled only when he meant it.

'What happened?'

'A fire. Don't worry. Everybody got out.'

'Don't . . . remember.'

'That's because you slept through it. Smoke inhalation. Mrs Kimber pulled you to safety. How do you feel? Headache? Groggy? Those will pass. Try to rest now.'

'Want . . . to get up.'

'Mrs Burley, sit on her if she moves.' He patted her good hand and left.

'Where . . . ?'

'Hardy Farm. While Mrs Mary was getting you out, Edith and I ran here for help. They brought buckets and we used water and earth, then someone had the idea of taking up a carpet to smother the flames. Then the fire brigade arrived. One of the farm lads went on his bicycle to find the bobby on the beat and he organised the fire engine.'

And she had been unaware of any of it.

The next day, she felt stronger, though no one would let her climb out of bed without Doctor Brewer's say so.

'Anyone would think you were King Solomon,' she grumbled at him.

'If that's your inimitable way of politely asking to go home, yes, you may.'

'Fetch some clothes,' she ordered Edith.

'Unnecessary,' said Doctor Brewer. 'You can have a dressing gown and, if you insist, a coat. You'll be going straight to bed in Jackson's House.'

'You're enjoying this, aren't you?'

'One of the perks of the job is bossing old ladies about.'

Wobblier on her feet than she was prepared for, Helen hoped

no one would notice. Edith fetched her dressing gown and Helen sent her back for a hat. Then she descended the stairs, offered heartfelt, if croaky, thanks to her hosts and tottered home, supported by Doctor Brewer's arm.

'What happened?' She stared in dismay at the front hedge.

'The firemen chopped down part of it to allow the engine through.'

'My flower beds,' she mourned.

'I suppose we should be glad you care about something,' Doctor Brewer said with asperity. 'You've displayed more concern for your garden than you have for Mrs Kimber.'

'You said everyone was safe.'

'Mrs Kimber saved your life, and at considerable risk to her own. When you publicly shamed Barney Clough into doing the decent thing, you earned my gratitude and my friendship, but after witnessing your cavalier attitude to Mrs Kimber, I wonder what your friendship is worth.'

Shame tingled in her cheeks. She had seen Mrs Burley and Edith with her own eyes, but she ought to have asked after Mary.

She started to speak, but he cut her off.

'Help Miss Rawley to bed, Edith.'

He stalked away, displeasure radiating from the set of his shoulders.

Edith opened the door and Helen recoiled. The house reeked. They went upstairs, the smell growing stronger. Helen turned towards her room.

Edith protested. 'You're in the master bedroom. Your room . . .'

'I want to see.'

She opened the door. The stench rolled out to envelop her as she stared into the blackened room, taking in the charred furniture, the dollops of earth and the mound of carpet. She looked at her precious flower album, made by her mother when she was a girl, lying on the chest at the foot of her bed, its singed pages warped and swollen by water.

She clutched the door frame.

'I had no idea. Mary – Mrs Kimber – is she all right?'

'Yes, madam. Let's get you to bed.'

She submitted. Soon the door was pushed open and Doctor Brewer came in, carrying Mary in his arms. Edith pulled back the bedding and he set Mary down beside Helen, standing back to let Edith tuck her in.

He eyed Helen. 'I expect there are things you wish to say to Mrs Kimber. We'll leave you to it.' Allowing Edith to precede him from the room, he looked back. 'You might start by asking why I insisted on carrying her here.'

The door shut.

'I assume he means you were injured.' Helen was appalled by how cold she sounded. She didn't mean to be cold. It was shame that held her rigid.

'There was danger of losing the baby.'

'It would have got you out of a difficult situation if you had.'

'I'm sure the Kimbers will think so. My parents probably will too. I'm sorry everyone else finds my baby such an inconvenience, but I love it.'

'Love it? It's not even born.'

'Not born, no, but it's here, it's real.'

Helen retreated from the subject, frightened, as she sometimes was, by the distant yearning of childlessness. 'I ought to thank you.'

'Ought to?'

'Want to. It didn't hit me until I saw my bedroom. It was brave of you to enter a burning room. I'm deeply grateful.'

'I didn't think about it. I might not have been so brave if I had.'

'Yes, you would. You're that kind of person. You do what's right. The way I've treated you has been shabby and utterly undeserved. The truth is, I wanted them to send Eleanor.'

'Send their daughter as companion-help? They'd never do that.'

That roused her obstinacy. 'I thought they would, me being family, and – well, I hoped they'd want to get her away from the annulment unpleasantness.'

'The annulment unpleasantness: that's one way of putting it.'

'You know what I mean. I'm not the sort to dress things up in fancy words.'

'Why did you want Eleanor? I know you and Lady Kimber don't keep up the connection.'

'She doesn't, you mean. If it were down to me . . . but there's nothing I can do. She took great offence at something I did a long time ago. For years I've hoped she'd forgive me, but she never has. I thought, now Eleanor's grown up, she might wonder about me, might want to know me. Maybe she does. Maybe she's been forbidden. While you lived at Ees House, what was said about me?'

'I never heard of you until I was told about coming here.'

Helen quashed the gasp before it could give her away. Christina and Eleanor were never far from her thoughts. She had assumed . . . well, it proved what a muttonhead she was.

'I regret the way I've treated you and I don't want you to leave.

I promised Sir Edward you could stay until the baby is born, but if you'd like to stay beyond that, you'll be welcome. If you can stand an old trout like me, I'd enjoy your company. I know there's a question as to what will happen to the baby, but as far as I'm concerned, it'll be welcome here.'

Mary sat bolt upright and glared at her. 'First you wanted Eleanor. Now you want my baby. Do you propose using my child as bait?'

'That never occurred to me, I swear—'

The door opened and Edith and Mrs Burley entered, carrying trays. Helen pressed her lips together to stop herself telling them to clear out. She was making a right old hash of this.

'It's all invalid food,' said Mrs Burley, 'so it'll slip easily down your poor throats.'

She and Edith pulled up chairs while Helen and Mary ate a cucumber mousse followed by syllabub and the four of them talked about the damage the fire had done.

'We'll help you back to your own bed when you're finished,' Edith told Mary, but afterwards Mary dozed off.

'Leave her be,' said Helen. 'Bring me a book and I promise not to disturb her.'

While Mary slept, Helen tried to read, but there was too much to think about. She would write to Cousin William. Mary was sorely in need of legal advice and who better to provide it than a judge?

There was a tap on the door and Doctor Brewer entered.

'How are you?'

'Good as new. When can I get up?'

'Tomorrow.'

'And Mary?'

'Mary, is it? When did she cease to be Mrs Kimber?'

'When I came to my senses. I've been vile to her, poor girl, but that's going to change. I want us to be friends, and no, I'm not going to demand her friendship like I did with you. I'm going to earn it. What are you looking at?'

'You.' His eyes were warm. 'I'll leave you to rest.' Pausing at the door, he looked back. 'I'll see you tomorrow . . . dear Miss Rawley.'

Chapter Twenty-Six

It was disconcerting to wake in the master bedroom. Had she slept beside Miss Rawley all night? She was alone in bed now. Mary rolled out, stepping from a wool rug onto cool, polished floorboards. On the landing, the smell of smoke hit the back of her throat and she recoiled, holding her breath as she hurried to her own room to dress.

As she opened the door to go downstairs, she came face to face with Miss Rawley, hand raised, about to knock.

'I was going to offer you breakfast in bed. Perhaps we should wait until Doctor Brewer . . .'

'Did you wait for his permission?' Mary demanded.

'I suppose not. You'll be breakfasting in solitary splendour, I'm afraid. I've already eaten and I want to set to work.'

Mary looked at her sling. 'Doing what?'

'You'll see.'

'Word will get round about the fire. I must let my parents know I'm safe.'

'Leave that to me.'

She would pack her things before they arrived, then she could go home with them and leave this disagreeable old lady to her own devices – except that she wasn't being disagreeable this morning. Had she meant what she said last night?

Mary had a light breakfast.

'Madam says you're to sit outside in the shade,' said Edith when she came to clear away.

Madam could take a running jump. Emerging from the dining room, Mary found a couple of men manoeuvring a chaise longue downstairs. Miss Rawley hovered at the foot of the staircase.

'Mind the bannister rail. There's enough damage without that being knocked for six. There you are, Mary – may I call you Mary? This chaise longue is for you. It's been in the attic for donkey's years and needs a good walloping with the carpet-beater, but aside from that it's none the worse. These helpful fellows from the farm are going to pop it outside, so you can put your feet up and get out of this horrid smoky atmosphere.'

With the men smiling at her, having manhandled the dratted thing all the way down from the attic, she hadn't the heart to refuse. She spent the next half-hour propped up against cushions in the shade before muffled thuds drew her inside to investigate. She stood in the study doorway.

One man piled leather-bound volumes into boxes while Edith polished the empty bookcases. A lanky lad stood on a chair, taking down the maroon curtains while other men clustered round an enormous desk, preparing to move it.

Miss Rawley was directing operations. Seeing Mary, she abandoned the troops.

'You're a writer, aren't you? Here's a subject: how ruddy grim it is to live your life beholden to men. Pardon my language, but honestly, no other vocabulary will do. I've spent most of my life under my brother's patronising thumb. Look at this room: a testament to his importance.'

'What are you doing?'

'What I should have done when he died: dismantling the lot. But I didn't because . . . well, it never occurred to me. Why would it? The house and everything in it had gone from my father to my brother to my nephew. What say did I ever have? I've run this household since I was seventeen, but I never had a say. Well, I'm having it now. Today Judge Rawley's stuffy old sanctum sanctorum becomes a sitting room for Miss Rawley and her distant relation by marriage – that's you.'

A smile tugged at Mary's lips. 'What will Mr Rawley say?'

'I don't imagine he'll care or even notice.'

'What will you do with the judge's things?'

'If I had my way, I'd build a bonfire. As it is, it's all headed for the attic. There's a couple of small tables and a wall mirror stored up there that can come down, and the china cabinet from the morning room can move across – oh, and your chaise longue, of course.'

'Miss Rawley, I'm not staying—'

'Mary – oh, Mary!'

Her parents appeared at the open front door. Mary rushed into Lilian's open arms. Some of her strain seeped away as they clung together. A warm hand squeezed her shoulder and she gave Dadda a watery smile.

Sniffing and patting away tears with her fingers, she gently pulled free. 'Miss Rawley, these are my parents. Thank you for sending for them.'

'This isn't my doing. I was going to do it after this.' Miss Rawley waved a hand at the soon-to-be sitting room. 'But I should have done it straight away.'

Yes, you should. Mary's jaw tightened as the others shook hands.

'My morning room is at your disposal,' said Miss Rawley.

'We'll go outside, if you don't mind,' said Mary. She led her parents out to the chaise longue. 'Miss Rawley had it placed here so I can put my feet up.'

'I'm glad you're being looked after,' said Dadda.

She sat, drawing Lilian beside her and keeping hold of her hand, while her father seated himself in one of the garden chairs.

'I'm sorry you heard of the fire from gossip. I'd have sent word myself if I'd known Miss Rawley was going to take her time.'

'She should have acted sooner,' agreed Dadda. 'It's the least you deserve after saving her life.'

'How do you know about that?'

'We heard nothing from gossip,' said Lilian. 'Doctor Brewer came round. He told us what you did, and he said the baby is safe even though you recently lost blood.'

'He had no business saying that.'

'Don't be silly, love. Your father's entitled to be told since you don't have a husband.'

'Jolly decent of him,' said Dadda, then came to his feet.

'Please don't get up, Mr Maitland,' said Miss Rawley. 'May I join you?'

'Mary's coming home with us,' said Lilian, 'and if the Kimbers don't like it, they can lump it.'

'We're sorry if this lets you down,' said Dadda, 'but we must put our daughter first.'

Something inside Mary crumpled with gratitude.

'I was hoping she'd stay with me,' said Miss Rawley, 'though not here, in a smoky house with workmen traipsing in and out. My cook has two widowed sisters in Southport, who take in paying guests. Apparently, they're marvels in the kitchen and demons at whist. Mary wouldn't be expected to look after me, as my sling is due to come off any day now. In our absence, Doctor Brewer will watch over the repairs and redecoration.'

'Is he a friend of yours?' asked Dadda.

Miss Rawley lifted her chin. 'Indeed he is.' She looked at Mary. 'Will you join me for a few weeks by the sea?'

'I'm sorry, Miss Rawley,' said Dadda. 'It's out of the question. Mary's coming home with us.'

Seated on a bench on the pier, Mary shut her eyes beneath the brim of her straw hat and let the breeze play on her face. Here in Southport, the pier went on for ever. She wished this pleasant sojourn could too.

'Is being here a form of pretence?' she asked. 'A way of hiding from what lies ahead?'

'So what if it is?' said Miss Rawley. 'If being here is doing you good, try not to dwell on the rest. It is doing you good, isn't it?'

Mary couldn't help smiling. It had done her good in ways of which Miss Rawley knew nothing. If there was one thing Mrs Paxton and Mrs Ford liked better than a paying guest, it was a p.g. who was expecting a happy event. There had been various conversations from which she had emerged considerably better informed.

'I'm glad you came,' said Miss Rawley. 'Doctor Brewer said you'd be going home – and then your parents were so insistent—'

'Exactly. They didn't ask. They told me. I may be not married any more, but that doesn't make me the obedient daughter.'

'So you came with me to spite them?'

'I came because, if I hadn't, I'd always have wondered.'

'About what?'

'You. You were so unpleasant to me at first and I couldn't wait to escape. But that morning when you sorted out the old study, and you were so cranky, it struck me how remarkable you are. How many elderly ladies who survived a fire would emerge from the experience hissing and spitting like a cat?'

'Is there a compliment lurking in there somewhere?'

'Cranky old ladies don't deserve compliments.'

'But young, brave ones do. I wish I'd had half your courage when I was young. My life has been spent keeping house and bickering with my brother. Well, that's going to change. Sir Edward told me about you, so I know about the agency. Will you think me an old fool if I say I want to be involved? You'd be surprised how much I know from my brother's charitable causes.'

'I haven't been there for a long time.'

'We could go together.'

'I'm supposed to live in quiet seclusion.'

'Best not ruffle Kimber feathers, eh? I'm afraid you're going to spend a good many years walking the Kimber tightrope. Will you listen to a piece of advice from an old woman who hasn't done much more than keep house and bicker with her brother?'

She nodded, curiosity piqued.

'Suppose you weren't expecting your happy event. Suppose it was just you and your Kimber pension. What would you do?'

She pictured it. 'I would have found somewhere of my own.'

'And done what? Grow prize chrysanthemums? Dabble in watercolours?'

'Write.'

'That's what I hoped you'd say. It's what you should do now. Carve out a life for yourself beyond what the Kimbers require. Be true to the girl you were before your marriage. Don't let her vanish.'

Why had she stopped writing? Obviously, wanting to conform as a member of the Kimber family, she had stopped – obviously? Had she been so ready to give it up? Mad as it now seemed, she had done it willingly, wanting to show herself capable of taking her place as a Kimber.

Miss Rawley was right. She needed to reclaim herself. Yes, there were constraints on her life, placed there by the fact of her carrying a Kimber child, but within those constraints, and in spite of them, she must be true to herself. It would be good for the baby too, to have a mother with a brain and an independent spirit.

The words poured out of her, an article about Southport and another about the delights of seaside holidays in general.

Looking up from her work, she caught Miss Rawley watching.

'This one's finished. Would you like to read it?'

'I'd love to.'

Mary glanced at her as she read, wanting her to like it. She had never had family approval of her writing. Family? Miss Rawley wasn't family. But they lived under the same roof and spent most of their time together, which was what families did.

'You have an engaging style,' said Miss Rawley. 'Which periodical will you send it to?'

'The trouble is, it ought to be typewritten.'

'I'll get you a typewriting machine.'

She rented one from a secretarial school and Mary derived a ridiculous amount of pleasure from typewriting the piece, which she duly submitted to *Vera's Voice*.

When it was accepted, she laughed with delight to see Miss Rawley as excited as she was. The best bit was the kind letter from Mrs Newbold, saying how pleased she was to have received work from 'Fay Randall' once more.

'. . . *and I hope to hear from you again soon.* I haven't written for such a long time. I'd forgotten how much I enjoy it.' She sobered. 'I'd never have written again if I'd stayed married to Charlie.' Should she say it? 'And that would have been fine, if being married to him had been enough.'

'Wasn't it?'

'I don't know. If I'm honest, I was fed up to the back teeth much of the time. I couldn't see my friends, I couldn't join committees. And Charlie was different. He wanted us to be the dashing young couple-about-town, but it wasn't allowed. I tried to do everything that was required, but it wasn't the real me. I think if we'd stayed married, I'd have ended up regretting it. Don't misunderstand. I was appalled when the Kimbers announced the annulment, but if that hadn't happened . . . sooner or later, I'd have had to face it.'

'Face what?'

'The truth. Our marriage was a mistake. It's just that Charlie realised it before I did . . . though I'm sure he had help.' She stopped: could she admit it? 'When you asked why I came here, there was another reason that I didn't tell you. It was because I felt so grateful.'

'To me?'

'To my parents. When they said they'd take me home and they didn't care what the Kimbers thought, I was overwhelmed with gratitude. They never offered me that kind of support when I was waiting for the annulment or when I was engaged to Charlie or when I started writing. It meant so much to feel they were on my side. But then I remembered the last time I felt gratitude like that was when Charlie proposed.'

'You married him out of gratitude?'

'You have to understand what it was like. I'd been in prison, I'd lost my job, I was in everyone's black books and Charlie rushed to the rescue. I already loved him and now here he was, enveloping me in approval. It made me love him even more.'

'If you loved him, does it matter if gratitude came into it?'

'I honestly don't know.'

'I'm sorry. I'm a nosy old bat. I should mind my own business.'

'I haven't talked about it before.'

'Then I'm even sorrier.'

'Don't be. I'm not.' She paused, weighing her words. 'We aren't family, you and I, but we've been thrown together and it's ended up being the right thing. Thank you.'

'Oh, my dear. You can't imagine what that means to me.'

Miss Rawley stood up. She went to the window and looked out.

'Do you think you could do something to please a nosy old bat?'

'If I can.'

'Do you think . . . do you think you might call me Aunt Helen?'

'My dear Mr Rawley, always a pleasure. How are you? I would say what a delightful surprise, but of course the surprise is all on your side and I wouldn't presume to describe your feelings upon seeing me.'

A fruity chuckle escaped Mr Jonas. Greg thrust aside his surprise, which wasn't in the slightest bit delightful, and gritted his teeth. God, as if things weren't bad enough.

Just when he had thought all was well, after he had set the fire at Jackson's House, that bloody telegram had arrived. The message, which was signed Brewer (and who the hell was that? Ah yes, that doctor), had read FIRE AT JACKSON'S HOUSE STOP NOBODY HURT STOP.

He had written to Porter, requesting details, which Mr Porter duly supplied, including Helen's intention of convalescing in Southport for some weeks. Some weeks? Some bloody weeks? That was no damn use to him unless he fancied tipping her off the end of the pier in full view of the companion.

The end of August was approaching. He needed Helen back in Jackson's House to prove that third time was indeed lucky. Or in her case, unlucky.

Now, tonight, Mr Jonas had taken him by surprise. Greg had come to Wentworth's and was heading for the card rooms, when a waiter said, 'Mr Rawley, sir, you're invited into the back room.'

But when he walked in, expecting to find his usual cronies, there was Mr Jonas.

'Have a seat, Mr Rawley. I've been hearing about your esteemed aunt. She's been remarkably fortunate recently, or should I say remarkably unfortunate. First a fall, then a fire, both of which she survived – and each survival prevented you from coming into your inheritance. Such a blow, considering your financial position. Not that one wishes any harm on your dear aunt, naturally.'

'Naturally.'

'Nevertheless, time marches on, as they say. September will soon be upon us.'

'I have until the end of September.'

'My dear Mr Rawley, of course you do.' Jonas was at his most solicitous, damn him. 'I'm simply concerned on your behalf. There'll be no extension to the deadline, you appreciate that? Excellent. Then our business is concluded. I would suggest we enjoy a drink together, but you appear a trifle out of sorts. Do feel free to go and find a card game. That is, after all, why you're here, isn't it? To drum up a little cash?'

She was coming home today. It was ridiculous how much he was looking forward to it. Nathaniel had visited Jackson's House every day while the workmen were in. Since then, he had popped in a couple of times a week to keep an eye on the place, or so he would have sworn, though the truth was he was drawn like a lovesick schoolboy to where Mary lived, even though she wasn't there.

Mary.

She was in his mind constantly, which was mad, because her circumstances were complicated, to say the least. The last thing she needed was an admirer.

It hadn't been this way with Imogen.

Imogen.

Everything had been straightforward with her. She was

the girl from up the road and their mothers had nursed fond hopes, which in due course he and Imogen had fulfilled. She had devoted herself to being the perfect wife, looking after his home and his person, cooking his meals and doing charitable works that supported his interests. She never argued or complained, even when he worked long into the night. She had gone along with everything without question.

Without question.

Mary asked questions. Look at how determinedly she had tackled him when she believed the clinic was doomed to failure. She questioned everything – and thank goodness she did. Without her unease over the words 'finished and ready', the clinic would never have opened. That cleverness formed part of what made her a good writer, along with a confident style that was highly readable.

But there was more to her writing than that. She had written to help support her family. She was the type to muck in. That night at the clinic, she could simply have gone home and written her article, but instead she had rolled up her sleeves and helped. And just think of the guts it had taken to rescue Miss Rawley from that burning room.

Not that he hadn't appreciated Imogen. First and foremost she was a housewife, and an excellent one. How many times had he acknowledged her as a good little woman? And he had been content with that. It hadn't occurred to him that a wife might be any different, that marriage might be any different.

Imogen had agreed with everything he said.

Mary wouldn't agree with everything.

Imagine having the support of a girl like that.

* * *

Mary was hot and achy by the time the cab pulled up by the gate. The damaged hedge had been replaced by fresh planting, which looked odd beside the mature privet. The front door opened and Mrs Burley and Edith spilt out to welcome them.

Helen went straight upstairs to inspect her bedroom.

Mary followed. 'May I come in, Aunt Helen?'

'Of course. They've done a splendid job, haven't they? Though I'm not sure about this wallpaper.'

The previous wallpaper had been dark and formal. The new paper was green and cream with a pattern of roses. 'It's pretty.'

'Presumably Doctor Brewer's idea of how a lady's room should be. Like his taste, do you?'

Much of the old furniture was gone, including the bed. A chair from downstairs, a hanging-cupboard from the master bedroom, the marble-topped washstand from a guest bedroom and other pieces from around the house had been employed to fill the gaps.

Sensing the depth of Helen's silence, Mary said, 'It's sobering to remember how much damage was done. Maybe things would have happened faster that night if I hadn't had to fetch the spare key.'

'What do you mean? I never lock my door. The key lives in the lock, but I never turn it.'

'The door was locked. It opened the moment I used the spare.'

'You shouldn't have been able to put in a key from the outside if there was already one on the inside.'

'I assumed my key pushed yours to the floor.'

'Maybe it did, but the door wasn't locked in the first place.'

Mary looked at the lock. It was empty.

Edith appeared. 'Would you like tea, madam?'

'Where's the key?' Helen asked.

'I'm sure I don't know, madam. Before the fire, there were two, one in the door and the spare downstairs. Now there's just one.'

'The other must have been removed by accident when the room was cleared,' said Helen.

But that didn't explain why the door had been locked.

Mary sat on a bench on the riverbank, watching the Mersey slide by, just as she had each day since they returned home last week. The river looked peaceful and sedate, but Dadda always said it had a powerful current, or maybe he had said that to stop her going too close to the edge. That was how she felt now. Close to the edge. What was going to happen when her child was born?

She consulted the watch pinned to her dress. Hoisting herself up, she trundled along the path, branching off at Jackson's Boat onto the path that led to the back gate of Jackson's House.

Helen was sitting at the garden table with Nathaniel, who had been a regular visitor since their return. Something had changed between him and Helen. Before the fire, they had been acquaintances, doctor and patient, but afterwards they were friends. Yes, Helen was lonely, but was she so desperate for companionship that she would befriend a man who forcibly fed women prisoners? How could something so disgraceful not repel her?

'There you are,' Helen called.

'You look deep in discussion.'

'Deep in disagreement, you mean.' Nathaniel rose to hold a chair for her.

'I'll pour some cordial,' said Helen, 'and then you can have the casting vote.'

She laughed. 'I'm not sure I want it.'

'We're talking about Mr Balfour's opposition to the idea of the black people in South Africa having equal rights. He says it would undermine white civilisation. What do you say?'

'Goodness, and here I was thinking you were discussing whether to bring the tramlines further into Chorlton.'

'I won't let you joke your way out of it,' said Helen. 'Tell us your opinion.'

She was about to come down on the side of white civilisation, then she thought further. 'If you say you can't vote because you're black, that's like saying you can't vote because you're female, and I believe in votes for women, so I have to disagree with Mr Balfour.'

Nathaniel laughed. 'My words exactly.' He told Helen, 'You'd never have asked if you'd thought she'd share my opinion.'

Helen wagged a finger at her. 'As my companion, you're meant to agree with me at all times.'

'You'd soon show me the door if I did.'

'Probably.' Helen sighed. 'It's odd, isn't it? My brother and I disagreed all the time and it was hell, but I can disagree with either of you and there's no ill-feeling.'

'It's called being friends,' Nathaniel said lightly.

'It's called,' Helen said, removing her straw hat and using it to fan her face, 'being too hot.' She pushed herself to her feet. 'I'm going in. You two stay here and finish the cordial.'

'You don't have to stay if you don't wish to,' Nathaniel said to Mary.

About to murmur something polite and stay put, she rebelled. 'If you don't mind.' She started to heave herself to her feet.

His face fell. 'I'd rather you stayed.'

Impossible to walk away now. She sank back down.

'I've been hoping to talk to you on your own,' he began.

Anger sprang from nowhere. 'What makes you think I want to talk to you? I know what you do at the prison. How could you imagine that I'd want anything to do with you? Forcible feeding is brutal and I despise you.'

'Let me explain—'

'Mary, there you are.'

Her head swung round; her heart pitter-pattered. 'Dadda, Sir Edward. This is Doctor Brewer,' she said as Nathaniel came to his feet.

'Brewer? Ah yes,' said Sir Edward. 'You wrote to me after Miss Rawley's accident.'

The men shook hands, then Nathaniel took his leave.

'Does Miss Rawley know you're here?' asked Mary. 'I'll fetch her.'

'No need. We'll pay our respects before we go,' said Sir Edward. 'You're the one we've come to see. I'm aware, and have informed your father, of the enquiries that have been made. We're deeply dismayed that you've gone behind our backs.'

'What enquiries?'

'Don't pretend not to know,' said Dadda. 'You've embarrassed me.'

'It gives me no pleasure to come here to reprimand you,' said Sir Edward, 'but your actions give me no choice. You've done yourself a grave disservice by seeking legal advice.'

'But—'

He held up his hand. 'I'm a reasonable man. While I sympathise with your predicament, I must place the good of the family above all else. If you have a son, he might be the heir. This is a question I am looking into at present. Even if he isn't, I have to consider the most appropriate upbringing for him.'

'Appropriate?' She peeled the words from a dry mouth.

'Is it appropriate that a male Kimber be brought up in an ordinary household?'

She looked squarely at her father. 'You're a Kimber in all but name. Did it harm you to grow up in an ordinary household?'

Sir Edward sighed. 'It would grieve me to separate a child from its mother, but it would be unfair on any child, boy or girl, to grow up as the offspring of an unmarried mother.'

'But I was married—'

'And now you're unmarried. We must consider the good of the child.'

She forced her voice to remain steady. 'What does Charlie say?'

'That isn't your concern.' Sir Edward rose. 'Come, Maitland. We'd best pay our respects to Miss Rawley and be on our way.'

He strode away. Dadda stopped beside Mary, dropping a hand on her shoulder, an awkward gesture, and she wasn't sure what it meant. Not that it mattered. She felt betrayed.

Presently, Helen came to sit with her. 'What was that about? I don't imagine it was good news.'

After she managed to explain without breaking down, she realised Helen had sunk back in her seat. Her flesh seemed shrivelled, her face suddenly thin.

'My dear, it's my fault. I wrote to Cousin William – Lady Kimber's father. We haven't been in touch in years, not since . . . Anyway, I wrote and explained your situation – oh, it was a frightful liberty, I see that now, but I wanted his help, you see, his advice. It never occurred to me that . . . The thing is, it transpires it was he who advised the Kimbers about the possibility of annulment.'

'So when you asked him about me . . .'

'He informed the Kimbers. I'll write to Sir Edward and say you had no knowledge of it.'

'It won't make any odds.'

'I don't know about that.' Helen sat up straight. The light was back in her eyes. 'Cousin William was no help, so now we try Mr Porter.'

Chapter Twenty-Seven

Mary held her breath as Mr Porter cleared his throat.

'You appreciate, ladies, this is a separate issue to matters relating to the will of Miss Rawley's late brother?'

'Of course,' Helen replied with asperity.

'What I mean to say is, matters appertaining to the will are – ahem – paid for by the estate, whereas this matter . . .'

'I can pay,' Helen said immediately. 'I have my own money.'

Mary turned to her. 'I couldn't let you.'

'Fiddlesticks. You'll look into the matter, Mr Porter?'

'Indeed, Miss Rawley.'

Travelling home in the cab, Mary said, 'It's most generous of you.'

'Did you see Mr Porter's eyebrows shoot up when I said I had my own money?'

'Didn't he know?'

'No one did until today. The fact is, I never had a bean. My father's will didn't leave me a shred of independence and neither did my brother's.'

'Then it's a good thing you have something of your own. Did your mother leave it to you?'

'Goodness, no. She had some money before she married, but that went straight to my father. I was twenty-three when Father passed on and everything went to Robert. Time went on and there I was, thirty years old with a lifetime before me as Robert's housekeeper and I couldn't bear it, so I started filching coppers from the housekeeping, a few ha'pence here, a tanner there. You'd be surprised how it mounted up. I aimed for five shillings a month, which made three pounds a year. I called it my running-away money and, in a strange way, it helped me to stay. The point is, my dear, all those five bobs piled up. At the end of twenty years, I had sixty pounds and after forty years, a hundred and twenty.'

'Forty years!'

'I'll take that as a compliment to my youthful looks. I was seventy-one when my brother died and I had to give up fiddling the books because of their being open to scrutiny by Mr Porter. But I amassed quite a haul before that and never spent any of it. I thought there was bound to be a good reason one day, and here it is.'

'This is so kind of you.'

'You're the kind one. If I'd been you, I'd have called me all the names under the sun for writing to Cousin William. I'm an interfering old bag. Speaking of which, I have a surprise for you. Your friends from the agency are coming for tea. I hope you're pleased, because Mrs Burley has baked a special cake and it'd be criminal to waste it.'

Mary kissed her cheek. 'Thank you. That's perfect.'

She hadn't seen Angela and Josephine for such a long time, but the three of them fitted back together as if there hadn't been any gap at all. She asked after Ophelia, Katharine and the rest, drawing Helen into the conversation too, though after Edith cleared away the tea things, Helen withdrew.

Mary smiled at her friends. 'I can't think why I didn't put my foot down when I was at Ees House and insist upon visiting you. Well, I can. I was determined to be a good Kimber wife. That's one mistake I shan't make again: try to mould myself to someone else's expectations. What matters now is bringing up my child – that, and writing. No husband needed.' She looked straight at them, as if her heart weren't beating in fear. What would happen to her baby?

'Good for you,' said Angela. 'That doctor Miss Rawley mentioned, who oversaw the redecorating after the fire, is he the same Doctor Brewer from the clinic?'

'Yes,' Mary said crisply.

'Have I said something wrong?'

'He and I don't see eye to eye.' Her throat tightened. 'He does forcible feeding, so you can imagine what I think of him.'

Angela and Josephine looked at one another.

Josephine said, 'There's someone you should meet.'

The grandfather clock boasted a large face, which included each individual minute delineated by a black dash, which meant that when Madeline Bambrook came in, her late arrival could be recorded to the minute. Lady Kimber was a great believer in interrupting committee business to note a late arrival. It made others vow to be punctual.

This morning's meeting, at the Claremont Hotel, was of the Lord George Committee, as they jokingly referred to themselves because so many elderly folk were grateful to 'Lord George' for their pensions. Really they were the Five Shillings Education Committee, a body new this year following Mr Lloyd George's introduction of the Old Age Pension. Their work was to provide funds for educating needy old people in the best use of their pensions.

'First item: the pint of porter,' she said. 'We have, in conjunction with the Lady Almoner's office at the infirmary, drawn up a five-shilling budget, including burial insurance and coal, two ounces of tea, two pounds of potatoes, both at a penny, and a pound of mutton for sixpence. Do we include a pint of porter in our recommended budget?'

'Certainly not,' declared Thomasina Fitzpatrick, consulting her copy. 'It's cheaper to buy six pints of milk.'

'I agree,' said Aline. 'I don't see why our stocks and shares should be taxed more heavily than middle-class salaries just to enable the impoverished elderly to swill beer.'

'The increased taxes are a burden to us all,' the Honourable Vanessa Seymour agreed, 'but I don't see the harm in a weekly pint of porter.'

'As long as it is weekly,' said Marjorie Fairbrother. 'What if one pint leads to another?'

'It's our duty to educate these people out of that way of thinking,' Lady Kimber reminded her. 'That's why we're funding two lady almoners to work in the poorest communities.'

'Perhaps we should ask them what they think,' Eleanor suggested.

There was a rumble of disagreement.

'We tell them what to do. It's not their place to tell us.'

'We do indeed require the lady almoners to do our bidding,' said Lady Kimber, 'but they were selected because they're decent, sensible women and their opinions may be of interest.'

The door opened. Everyone else looked round, but Lady Kimber looked at the clock.

'Good morning, Miss Bambrook. So pleased you could attend. Ten-seventeen, Madam Secretary.' She consulted the agenda. 'That concludes the first item. Second item: the fund-raising ball at Ees House.'

She permitted a private sigh. The trouble with hosting a charity event was that one inevitably had to receive new money among the guests. As if they could buy their way into the top drawer.

As the Lord George ladies discussed the ball, the door opened. The hotel manager slipped in, waiting for her to acknowledge him.

'Pardon the interruption, Your Ladyship. I have a gentleman in the hotel who would like to be heard by your committee.'

'This is highly irregular.'

'I understand he wishes to offer his assistance to your cause, Your Ladyship.'

'Very well. Show him in.'

A man entered – a man, not a gentleman. Were he to exchange those smart clothes for corduroys and a neckerchief, he would look . . . brutish.

'My master asks that you excuse the interruption. He's aware of your intention to hold a charity ball and wishes to offer the ballroom and facilities of the Claremont at his own expense.'

A ripple of gratified surprise passed round the table.

'This is most generous,' said Lady Kimber. 'To whom are we indebted?'

'My master wishes his contribution to be anonymous. He has heard of your committee and wishes to support your good work.'

With a bow, the man withdrew.

'Well!' several ladies said.

'Kindly make a note, Madam Secretary,' said Lady Kimber. 'An anonymous benefactor to foot the Claremont's bill for accommodating the ball.'

And Ees House not to be sullied by upstarts. She didn't mind how many nouveau riche attended now. They could be as nouveau as they liked, as long as they were disgustingly riche.

'My brother doesn't know I'm here,' said Evangeline Brewer, 'though I'll tell him this evening. I won't keep a secret from him.'

'I wouldn't expect you to,' Mary answered coolly.

So this was Nathaniel's sister. She didn't look like him. His hair was dark, hers fair, his eyes hazel, hers brown. It was as though their colouring had got confused, mixing dark with fair.

'I'm staying with him at present. I was at my mother's before, but she lives in a village and I needed to get back into circulation. I've been attending meetings at the agency and they've found me a job. I feared I'd never work again.'

'Because of your health? I know you were ill last year. It's fortunate you were at your brother's at the time.'

'You don't know how true that is. But for him, I'd be dead.'

'You were that ill?'

Evangeline nodded. 'My sister-in-law nursed me – far more patiently than I deserved.'

Of course: Imogen. 'I'm sorry. I should have offered my condolences.'

'Thank you. Angela and Josephine said you worked at the clinic. Did you know Imogen?'

'Not really, but . . . but I was there when she lost her life. She was so brave.'

'So were you, evidently.'

'Lucky. I was lucky.'

'It still shocks me to think of it. If I'd died, there would have been some warning, but with Imogen . . .'

Mary searched for the right words. 'At least you were there to support Doctor Brewer afterwards.'

'Not for long. After the funeral, he sent me home with Ma and Aunt Louise. He said I needed to convalesce, but really he wanted to be alone. He has a daily cook-general now, but it's hardly the same as having a wife who devoted her existence to his well-being. I couldn't devote myself like that to being a wife, but Imogen lived, thought and breathed it. I couldn't subjugate myself like that.'

'Same here,' said Mary. An uncomfortable idea wriggled through her mind. Hadn't she suppressed parts of herself when she tried to be a Kimber?

Edith came in with a tray. Mary poured tea and offered petticoat tails. They were fresh and buttery.

'Miss Brewer, I've enjoyed meeting you, but I don't understand why you've come, except that Angela and Josephine swore it was a good idea.'

'It wasn't because of my illness that I wasn't expected to work again. It was because of my radical past. I went to London, joined the women's movement, had a couple of stints in prison – you know the form. My last boss chucked me out, said I was a disgrace to his firm.'

'But Angela and Josephine found you a position. Locally?'

'Through a contact in London. I'm going back there. Nathaniel blew his stack when I told him. He made me swear a great big swear never to do anything to get arrested again.' Evangeline shrugged. 'I'll be honest. Those days are over. Oh, I'll be there at the rallies, waving my banner, but I'll stick within the law from now on.' Evangeline looked as if she was bracing herself to continue. 'They force-fed me, you know.'

Mary stiffened. 'No, I didn't know.' Her pulse fluttered like a trapped bird.

'You know I was ill. Well . . .' Evangeline stopped. 'Heavens, I didn't think it would be so difficult to talk about it.'

Something in Mary reached out to her. 'I understand.'

Evangeline's brown eyes gleamed with tears. 'I know you do. They told me at the agency. When I was ill, I spent a few days heaving my guts up and some of the vomit leaked into my chest cavity through a tear in my gullet. I was – well, I didn't have long to live when Nathaniel realised what was wrong.'

Her heart twisted. She reached across and touched Evangeline's hand. 'You poor love.'

'It was the feeding tube that did the damage. Nathaniel says we can't be sure, but I know it was and no one can tell me different.'

The hand beneath Mary's flipped round and Evangeline grasped her hand tightly.

'That's why Nathaniel does the forcible feeding. It's not that he's heartless or he wants to keep women in their place. He does it so it's done as safely as possible. And if you must know, it was my idea.'

'Yours,' Mary breathed.

'Your friends wanted you to know, and if it stops you thinking wrong things about my brother, I want you to know too.'

Hearing the door open, Mary glanced up from her book and saw Nathaniel. The book trembled in her hands. She didn't have to dislike him any more.

'Aunt Helen's outside.'

'Checking the dahlias for earwigs. Edith told me.'

'Before you go to her, might I have a word?'

'More than one, if you like. It's you I was hoping to see. May I?'

She waved him into a seat. There was a short silence, then they spoke together.

'Your sister—'

'My sister—'

They broke off and looked at one another. She was the first to look away.

'I apologise for thinking badly of you. The thought of you force-feeding . . .'

'You weren't to know. It seems I didn't need to bring the peace offering after all.' He fished in his jacket pocket. 'Wine gums. Mrs Burley told me.'

He smiled, not a full smile that took her cordiality for granted, but a half-smile that assumed nothing. It made him look . . . boyish. She felt a frisson of surprise. She had thought him serious to the point of severity.

'Thank you. I'll extend my own olive branch by offering you one – but not a red one.'

As she reached to take the bag, her fingertips brushed his hand and her pulse wobbled. For one fleeting second, her heart leapt for joy before she clamped down on the feeling. She wasn't going to make that mistake again.

She rose. It took a hearty shove to bring her to her feet these days. 'Shall we see what Aunt Helen's up to?'

'I came to see you.'

'And we've sorted out the misunderstanding,' she said lightly, 'so let's go outside.'

She wasn't going to make that mistake again.

Too late.

It was on the tip of Helen's tongue to announce that the letter was from Mr Porter, but she thought better of it. She must be learning discretion in her old age. Usually she opened her correspondence at the breakfast table, an old habit designed to goad Robert, who had believed that while it was acceptable for a gentleman to do so, it wasn't good manners in a lady, who should no doubt focus her attention on her lord and master's teacup, ready to spring into action the instant it needed topping up.

Well, Robert could take his cup and shove it where the sun didn't shine – she stopped mid-thought. For a moment, she had felt all riled up, just like she used to when he got her fuming. Life was far pleasanter now. She hoped with all her heart Mary would stay here after the baby arrived.

Waiting until she was alone to read Mr Porter's letter, she muttered beneath her breath, calling him everything under the sun for not committing his information to paper. Then she dashed off a postcard, asking him to call at his earliest convenience. Should she tell Mary now or wait until nearer the time? No point worrying her.

And no point in treating her like a child either. Mary wouldn't thank her for it.

When she told her, the girl paled for a second but soon rallied.

'Good,' she said. 'Let's hope he's found something useful.'

Mr Porter's earliest convenience turned out to be the following afternoon.

Helen brushed aside the formalities. 'Please come directly to the point.'

'I've found some examples of legal precedent, dating from the last century. That is to say, they might or might not be accepted as legal precedent.'

'Kindly dispense with riddles.'

'The instances I've uncovered relate to the children of . . . divorced couples,' Mr Porter said, with a note of distaste.

Vowing to crown him if he sneered like that regarding annulment, Helen asked, 'What did you find?'

'Examples of divorced ladies who were permitted to keep their children until they attained the age of seven.'

'Seven,' Mary said in a tight voice.

'I stress that these ladies were divorced. I can find no precedent involving annulment. Moreover, they were ladies of rank, who married wealthy, titled men.'

'Naturally,' Helen said tartly. 'Mere mortals can't afford divorce.'

'This is the only precedent that could be of use to you.'

'I don't possess the wherewithal to go to court,' Mary began.

'You're welcome to every penny I've got,' Helen declared. 'You know that.'

'Bless you, but the Kimbers have stacks more money – and influence. Influence is everything.'

'No court will look kindly upon an unmarried mother,' Mr Porter cautioned, 'and that's how you'll be viewed. Then there's the question of what the Kimbers can offer the child. The provision they could make would be superior to what you can offer.'

'Mrs Kimber is welcome here for as long as she likes,' said Helen.

'This is a good address,' Mr Porter conceded, 'but Jackson's House isn't your property and hence her residency cannot be guaranteed.'

Helen's old heart creaked in anguish as Mary pushed herself to her feet.

'Excuse me. I . . . I need to think about this.'

She lumbered from the room, distress lending additional clumsiness to her pregnant waddle. From behind, Helen could see how thin her shoulders were, how narrow her back.

'I'm pleased Mrs Kimber has departed,' Mr Porter said. 'I couldn't have said this in front of her, but there is one thing that might help her case, though it doesn't apply to her, of course.'

'You're talking in riddles again.' Infuriating man!

'If she remarried respectably, it could go in her favour, but as I say, it doesn't apply. Nevertheless, I considered it my duty to pass on the information. Miss Rawley? Did you hear what I said?'

Helen was planning her next move.

Whenever Nathaniel dropped in, Mary contrived either not to be alone with him or to avoid him entirely, cursing the way her heart beat faster when he was near. She didn't want this. Not again. It introduced a troubling new idea. Had she married Charlie on the rebound? She didn't want it to be so, because that would make her marriage even more of a mistake. Yet once the thought was in her head, she couldn't dislodge it.

And it had happened again, the attraction that had taken her by surprise last year, turning that night at the clinic from exhausting to exhilarating. She was ashamed to feel this pull towards Nathaniel. Her life with Charlie had ended so recently. She was carrying his child, for heaven's sake. It wasn't decent to have feelings for someone else. All she could do was ensure she wasn't alone with him. She would stick to Helen's side and, if necessary, escape by feigning fatigue.

She came downstairs after a nap one afternoon to find Helen closeted with Nathaniel in the morning room. She felt a flush of consciousness, but she was safe with Helen here. Then Helen excused herself, murmuring something Mary didn't catch because her ears were ringing with panic.

She started to make her excuses, but Nathaniel interrupted.

'Mrs Kimber – Mary – I have a proposition for you. Well, not so much a proposition as a proposal. Miss Rawley took the liberty of explaining Mr Porter's findings to me, including a suggestion he made in your absence. It is his belief that, were you suitably married, it could go in your favour. So it seemed to me that it would help you if – well, it would help you with your child – so the fact is, I'd be glad to marry you.'

Chapter Twenty-Eight

Nathaniel kicked himself all the way home. How could he have been so crass as to make his proposal sound like a business arrangement? He should have thrown his heart at her feet and sworn to love her for ever. Only . . . how could he have said that to someone who until recently hadn't even seen him as a friend, let alone a suitor?

'I'd be glad to marry you,' he had said.

Not, 'All I want is to marry you so I can love you for the rest of your life and treat your child as my own.' Not that, oh no. Not the truth. Just, 'I'd be glad to marry you.'

She had stared, then looked away. He had felt a ridiculous urge to touch her hair. It was the colour of evening primroses. He longed for encouragement, a glance, a smile. When she smiled, which she didn't do often enough, her face assumed a glow of loveliness. He ached to ease her burden and give her reason to smile with joy.

At last she asked, 'Why would you . . . ?'

And he had said – damn him – he had said, 'We're friends, I hope.'

Not 'I love you. My heart beats for the time I spend with you' but 'We're friends'. Ha!

She had said yes. After a long interval, she had said yes – to his delight, and his despair. To her, he was a friend offering her a chance to keep her child. He didn't want to be accepted on those terms, yet those were the terms he had offered.

Actually, she hadn't said yes. She had said, 'If you're sure you mean it.'

Sure? He had never been more sure of anything in his life, but had he said so? Had he permitted her to glimpse his feelings? No, he hadn't. Dolt.

'I'm enormously grateful to you for this,' she had said, 'but I'm not accepting your offer simply out of gratitude.'

His heart flipped. This was it! She had feelings for him too.

'I feel more than gratitude. I feel trust. There is no greater act of trust than to put someone in the place of a parent to your child. I trust you to be a good father.'

He had to look away. What must she have thought? She had just offered him the greatest act of trust she could imagine; she had just given him permission to be a parent to her child; and he couldn't meet her eyes.

He swung round, ready to march back to Jackson's House, but he had to get back for surgery. There was always tomorrow – no, there wasn't, because he and Alistair were travelling to Sheffield to meet with doctors who wanted to establish a clinic for the poor.

It wasn't a brief visit either, as they were visiting the proposed premises and meeting sponsors.

When he got back, he would tell her the truth.

He barely slept that night for thinking about it.

The Sheffield visit, which for reasons that now escaped him he had been looking forward to, was interminable. He itched to get home, couldn't wait to see her again.

At long last he walked through the gate and up the path, elated and frightened to death, heart thumping. The door opened before he got there. It felt like an omen, an invitation to walk in and speak of his love. His face split into a daft grin.

Miss Rawley herself had opened the door.

'I must speak to Mary. It's important.'

'Charlie Kimber's here.'

Lady Kimber surveyed the Claremont Hotel's superbly appointed ballroom. The Lord George's anonymous benefactor had let it be known he expected no expense to be spared and she intended to take him at his word.

'A red carpet beneath an awning at the front steps, arrangements of flowers in the foyer. We'll have to choose a colour scheme. Perhaps a string quartet in the foyer as well.'

'And that's before guests reach the ballroom,' said Olivia Rushworth with a giggle. Eleanor had been taught at an early age not to giggle.

'Have you had any ideas?' Lady Kimber asked the girls.

'We wondered about hanging garlands from the balcony,' said Eleanor.

Instead of having its own ceiling, the ballroom was open to the dining room above, which overlooked it all the way round. It was the hotel's signature feature and worth exploiting. A magnificent chandelier, incorporating thousands of twinkling crystals, hung high above all the way down to the level of the dining room's balcony.

After the preliminary decisions had been made, Eleanor went home with the Rushworths. Lady Kimber kissed her and returned to Ees House.

As she stood in the hall, shedding her outdoor garments, Marley informed her she had a visitor.

'I let him stay, Your Ladyship, because he said he was your cousin.' Something must have shown in her face because Marley asked, 'Should I inform him it is not convenient?'

'I'll see him.'

What was he doing here? How had he dared?

Dismissing Marley, she marched to her morning room in full sail, imagining herself throwing open the door, but when she got there, she opened it softly. Greg was on his feet, facing the other way, examining a painting. The sight of his familiar figure caused something inside her to crumple. Thank goodness he didn't see. She drew herself up before closing the door.

When he turned, she was ready, weakness set aside. He was as handsome as ever in that don't-care, dangerous way, but was there something a touch jaded about his looks? Surely not. Not Greg, delicious, handsome Greg.

They had no need of formal greeting. She merely sat and indicated a seat, an invitation he chose to ignore, instead waving a hand to encompass Ees House and all it represented.

'I couldn't have given you this.'

'I did it for Eleanor and have never regretted it. Why are you here? It's inappropriate that you should say such a thing to me under my husband's roof.'

'I did a lot more than say inappropriate things under your other husband's roof.'

She felt a flush of anger; but there was remembered desire, too, as those secret moments rushed back into sharp perspective. The costly Phantom bustle – only the best for Mrs Henry Davenport – that folded neatly beneath her as she was pushed onto the sofa, the seductive rustle of her overskirts as the cascades of silk were thrust out of his way, allowing him access to the tiny buttons in the crotch of her broderie anglaise-trimmed combinations. How she had squirmed beneath him, struggling to thrust herself up to meet him, her heart pounding, and always, always that knife-edge awareness of the danger close by. If a visitor should call . . . if the maid should enter . . .

'Why are you here?'

'Money.'

'Money.' Oh, the shock and distress when she had discovered his way of life. And the dull, sick feeling that had followed. That was what she felt now.

'Debt, actually.' How could he sound so blasé? 'Glad you didn't take a chance on me? You must feel that all this,' he waved a hand, 'is justified.'

'How severe are these debts?'

'Debt – singular, but it's a whopper and I need to meet it by the end of the month.'

'How much?'

'Call it a thousand.'

'*How* much?'

'Guineas.'

'A thousand guineas.' The breath fled from her body.

'Guineas sound so much more sophisticated than pounds.'

'Don't make light of it. It's appalling. However did you get in so deep?'

'Oh, you know, run of bad luck.'

'Don't!'

'Don't what?'

'Sound so off-offhand, sound as if it's normal.'

'Don't look so frightened. I don't live like this all the time.'

'Just some of the time.'

'Scorn doesn't suit you.'

Anger speared through her. 'Don't presume to criticise my reaction. This debt is—'

'Appalling. So you said. The question is, will you help me? I mean it, Christina. I'm in it up to my wretched neck. I'll pay it back with interest, I swear. You know I wouldn't lie to you.'

She laughed. 'No, though you might conveniently omit to tell the truth, such as – oh, I don't know – maybe about your chosen way of life, which you were going to seduce me into without mentioning it.'

'You're never going to let me forget that, are you?'

'I don't want to talk about it. You've come here to ask for money, a phenomenal amount of money.'

'To be repaid. It'd be a tall order, I don't deny, but you know I'd pay it back.'

She did too. In spite of that devastating discovery about Greg's mode of living that had broken her heart for the second time, she believed him. She trusted him. She always had.

But that wasn't the point. 'Where do you imagine I could get my hands on money like that?'

'Eleanor. I know old Henry left a small fortune in trust and you're the trustee.'

'You want me to plunder Eleanor's money?'

'I want you to borrow from it. I don't suppose she's due to receive it until she is twenty-one at the earliest. That's ample time for me to repay it.'

'Twenty-five or upon marriage.'

'So what do you say?'

'I say no. Of course I say no. How did you ever imagine I'd say anything different?'

'For old times' sake, perhaps.'

'Greg, whatever existed between us—'

'It's still there. Deny it if you can. I'll know if you're lying.'

'I'm not going to hand over my daughter's money to you.'

Even had she wanted to, she couldn't. She wasn't the sole trustee. She shared the position with Henry's solicitor, which was the perfect excuse, yet she wouldn't demean herself by using it. That was how it would feel. Demeaning. She wanted Greg to know the truth, which was that she wasn't tempted to hand over Eleanor's trust fund. She wanted him to know she was strong.

'If not for old times' sake, how about the other reason?'

'What other reason?'

'Because Eleanor is my daughter.'

She almost raised her hand to her throat. Almost. She managed not to. 'That's absurd.'

'It's the truth. That time you came to Jackson's House to warn me off her, this was the real reason, wasn't it? Deny it if you can. I'll know if you're lying.'

'Eleanor is Henry's daughter.'

'She has my colouring.'

'As do I. We share the Rawley looks.' She rose. 'And now, if you've finished insulting me, it's best if you leave.'

Pain flashed across his face. 'I'd never insult you. I couldn't, because you're perfect. In my eyes, you're perfect.'

She made to ring the bell.

'No need,' he said. 'I can see myself out.'

'Not in this house. In this house, everything is done exactly as it should be.'

She pulled the bell. They looked at one another.

He asked, 'Do you regret it? Do you regret us?'

'We had some good times.'

'The best.'

His voice was light, but there was darkness in his eyes. In his face, she saw the naked longing he didn't trouble to disguise. The door opened. She glanced at Marley and when she looked back at Greg, his expression was a polite mask.

And then he was gone.

Christina couldn't bear it. She could hardly breathe.

Lady Kimber sent for the housekeeper to discuss next week's menus.

Charlie had caught the sun on his travels. His skin was lightly tanned. It suited him. But then, what wouldn't suit him? The dark Kimber looks lent themselves to anything. Mary had imagined this meeting so many times, yet now she couldn't think what to say. They sat in the morning room, with sunshine streaming through the window, neither of them uttering a word.

'A baby,' he said at last. 'This changes things. I've been told to ask when it's due.'

She stiffened. 'The time limit.'

'It has to be born on or before—'

'Stop! I know there's a date, but I don't want to hear it. The idea that you would come here and say such a thing – insinuate such a thing—'

'I'm insinuating nothing. This date is part of the process.'

'I don't care which side of the blessed date my baby is born: it's yours.'

Charlie held up his hands. 'I never doubted it. No one's casting aspersions.'

She made an effort to smooth her feathers. 'How long have you known about the baby?'

'Not long. The governor wrote to me *post restante* in Naples, asking me to come home. I arrived to be greeted by . . . this news.'

'Rather a shock.'

'With bells on. It's not what anyone expected.'

'Why shouldn't there be a baby? It's not as though we were leading separate lives.'

'How are you? You look well – more than well. I know people call mothers-to-be blooming, but I never understood what it meant until now.'

'I don't feel blooming. Mostly I feel worried.'

'I've been advised not to discuss the future.'

'By whom?' Lady Kimber, bound to be.

'The family solicitor, for one.'

'No one can tell us not to discuss our child. I shall live respectably and be the best person I can possibly be, for the sake of my baby.' She wanted to make a compelling speech, to sway him to her side, but old sorrows clogged her throat. 'You and I both know what it is to lose a mother. I loved Mam so much. I want to be to my child everything she was to me. Don't you think I'll make a good mother?'

'Of course, but—'

'I don't want to hear the "but". I live every moment with that "but" and I'll do everything I can to overcome it.'

Such as remarry. She almost laughed. *Telling Your Former Husband You Have Lined Up His Unborn Child's Stepfather*: how about that for an article?

'This is *our* child, Charlie. I know there are legal ramifications, but whatever is proposed, your agreement will be needed.' Her voice caught on a spike of emotion. 'Think hard before you say yes to anything – please.'

'For what it's worth, I'm sure you'll make a top-hole mother.' He scrubbed his face with his hands, then came to his feet, turning from her and going to the window. His shoulders rose and fell on a huge sigh before he swung round. 'The baby . . . it didn't become real until now, until I saw you. It's . . . overwhelming. I'm going to be a father.'

Dear heaven, was he about to say he wanted to bring it up? Her heartbeat raced and her hand flew to her throat. She forced it back to her lap. She mustn't let him see her panic, mustn't put the idea into his head if he hadn't thought it.

'Charlie, what brought you here? You've been content to stay away all this time.'

'It's not as though I could have dropped in. I'm here today because coming is the decent thing to do. It wouldn't have been gentlemanly to stay away.'

'Same old you. You always did have a gallant streak.' Memories crowded her. For a moment, it was more than she could bear. 'But you weren't gallant about the annulment.'

'Now look here—'

'No, you look, Charlie!' Soft with nostalgia a moment ago,

now she shook with fury. 'I didn't stand a chance. I never had an inkling until you all ganged up on me.'

'You make it sound like a conspiracy.'

'Wasn't it? I'm sure Lady Kimber schemed against me.'

He gave a click of impatience. 'This is how I remember it: you on one side, my family on the other, and me as piggy-in-the-middle. God, it was a strain.'

'Was the annulment on the cards for some time?'

'No, it wasn't. Look, there's nothing to be gained by rehashing old events.'

'Yes, there is,' she cried. 'We never talked about it. I never saw you again, apart from across the courtroom, from that day to this. If a sense of decency has brought you here, then do the decent thing and tell me what happened. All I know came from Sir Edward and Her Ladyship. You let them spirit you away while they did your dirty work. You talk about being a gentleman. Well, that wasn't gentlemanly.'

'No, it wasn't. You're right.' But he lifted his chin. 'I married you with the best intentions. You have to believe that. I'd never met anyone like you. The day we met, our fingers brushed and your touch was like a bolt of lightning up my arm. I looked at you, wondering if you'd felt it too. Until then I thought I was interested in Eleanor, but once I'd met you . . .' His voice trailed off. 'You were remarkable, a real peach. You grasped life with both hands. And, yes, I suppose part of it was the lure of the unattainable.'

Slumming it. Lady Kimber's voice in her head.

'When you disappeared from the agency, I realised how important you were. No one knew where you'd gone and there was a huge gap in my life. Then I heard about the clinic and dashed round there. I loved taking you out and feeling I had you to myself. It was an exhilarating time, first love, forbidden fruit, all rolled into one.'

'And after I came out of prison, you came riding to the rescue.'

'I wanted to look after you for ever.'

'What went wrong? I know you found it hard, not having the social life you wanted.'

'Well, that didn't help, but . . .'

'But what?'

'Did you think that was why I agreed to the annulment? Do you think I'm that shallow?'

'How should I know your reasons? You never told me.'

'I know, I know. I let the olds do the nasty stuff.'

'Was it because I didn't measure up?'

'You? Not measure up? That's a good one. I never met anyone more capable of succeeding in whatever she took on.'

'Then why?'

'If you insist on knowing . . .' Just when she thought he wasn't going to continue, he said, 'It was because you saved that child's life.'

'Because I . . . ?' Her voice came out as a squeak; she cleared her throat.

'You're right, I was bored rigid and it was deuced uncomfortable having you under scrutiny from everyone from Uncle Edward down to the kitchen cat. But I'd have weathered all that if . . . What I mean to say is, I never sought a way out. But when it was suggested . . . well . . .'

'What was wrong with my saving that little boy's life?'

Charlie looked straight at her. His dark eyes were full of sorrow, but there was a glint of something else too, something she couldn't fathom. Perhaps it was best if she didn't fathom it.

'I thought I'd rescued you. You want the truth – well, there it is. I thought I'd rescued you – you, this wonderful, beautiful, clever, determined girl, full of ideas and pluck. When you were laid low – you'd been in prison, you'd been force-fed, you'd lost your job, you'd brought shame on the family – I rescued you. I did, me, Charlie Kimber. When I proposed and you accepted, I grew into a bigger, better person – I felt myself grow. You needed me and I was so proud. This remarkable, spirited, talented girl needed me. Then, practically on the eve of our wedding, you saved that child's life and became a heroine. And it made me realise I hadn't rescued you at all. You didn't need rescuing. You were perfectly capable of rescuing yourself.'

The moment the front door closed, Helen bolted from the kitchen, Mrs Burley and Edith hot on her heels. They clustered in the hall, looking first at the morning-room door, then at one another.

'Should we go in?' asked Mrs Burley.

'She might want a few minutes alone,' said Helen.

'Or she might be crying her eyes out,' said Edith.

The door opened and Mary appeared, looking . . . Helen wasn't sure how she looked. Or rather, she could see perfectly well how she looked – serious and calm – but she couldn't tell how she felt. There was a smile on her face, but her eyes were guarded.

'Don't tell me you've all had your ears plastered to the door.'

'Certainly not,' said Helen. 'We've been in the kitchen.'

'Fretting ourselves silly over you,' Edith added.

'Come in and I'll tell you about it – all of you.'

'Eh, love, we don't want to pry,' said Mrs Burley.

'Speak for yourself,' said Helen.

She followed Mary in, wanting to sit close to her and offer the comfort of proximity, but Mary chose the wing-back chair. Edith and Mrs Burley stood on the rug.

'Why did he come?' asked Helen.

'Why did he wait so long, more like?' asked Mrs Burley.

'Is he going to make an honest woman of you?' Edith glared round. 'Don't pretend we weren't wondering.'

'We talked about the child but didn't reach any conclusions. He'd been warned against making promises. In any case, it didn't seem wise to discuss it deeply. I didn't want him getting ideas about bringing it up himself.'

Her voice was steady, but her hands fisted, turning her knuckles white. Glancing at Mrs Burley and Edith, Helen tilted her chin towards the door.

'Shall I fetch tea?' said Edith and they disappeared.

'Charlie Kimber wasn't the only visitor this afternoon,' said Helen. 'Greg's back, though technically he isn't a visitor, of course. I don't know why he's here or for how long. I just hope he leaves soon, blast his eyes. And he wasn't the only one to turn up. Nathaniel came too. I told him to come back later.' No response. 'I've decided to call him Nathaniel since he's marrying my honorary niece. Mind you, I haven't tried it out on him yet.'

She narrowed her eyes. Mary fiddled with her wedding ring, which wasn't like her. She wasn't a fidget.

For once in her life, Helen thought before she spoke. 'Charlie's visit must have been unsettling, especially coming out of the blue.'

Mary pressed her lips together, eyes lowered. Then she slipped off her wedding ring and held it out. 'May I give this to you for safe keeping? It doesn't feel right to wear it any more.'

Helen's old heart gave a creak of unease. 'You don't have to be brave with me, you know, if you're upset. When Nathaniel comes, should I put him off?'

'Don't do that. I need to see him.'

'Good. That's good.'

'I have to tell him I can't marry him.'

Chapter Twenty-Nine

Nathaniel closed his fingers over the little box in his pocket. Would she like it? It had seemed so appropriate when he saw it in the jeweller's window, but maybe she would prefer something conventional – a locket, perhaps – or something set with precious stones. Had Charlie Kimber showered her with expensive baubles? And what had he been doing at Jackson's House? Kimber should jolly well leave her alone, but it wasn't that simple. It would never be that simple.

What was it going to be like, being married to a girl who, through her child, would be for ever linked to the Kimbers? One thing was certain. He was going to make it as straightforward for her as he could.

He strode through the gate at Jackson's House, head held high. He was going to tell the girl he loved how he felt.

When Edith let him in, he was about to head for the morning room when Mary's voice called him back.

'I'm in here.'

She was standing in the doorway to the old study, one hand on the door frame. He couldn't restrain a smile, didn't try to. Her lilac gown suited her fairness, the elbow-length sleeves ending in a froth of lace that stopped three or four inches above slender wrists, a pretty style, but also a practical one for a girl who was adept at using a typewriting machine.

She went into the room, using the careful walk of advanced pregnancy. How slender her back was. Please don't let her require forceps. His heart did a little flip. The child she carried was his stepchild. His. Being part of its life from its first cry would make it more than a stepchild. In every sense that mattered, it would be his own.

He entered the room. Judge Rawley would be appalled if he could see it without his precious legal tomes and the acres of oak he called a desk. Even the dark curtains had been banished, replaced by pale stripes with a shimmer of silver.

Mary sat in a chintzy armchair. How much better if she had sat on the sofa, so he could sit beside her and take her hand at the crucial moment.

'Mary—'

'Let me speak first. I have something to say.'

He felt a frisson of unease. Had she patched things up with Kimber?

'First of all, I should say how grateful I am for your offer of marriage—'

'Don't tell me Kimber has changed his mind about the annulment.'

'Heavens, no.'

'Has he talked you out of marrying me?'

'He doesn't know about our . . . arrangement. If you'll let me explain. I've realised that our marrying would be a mistake—'

'Mr Porter said marriage would go in your favour.'

'Believe me, all I want is to keep my baby safe, but I can't do it this way—don't interrupt.' She drew a ragged breath, but then straightened her shoulders. 'I've already had one husband ride to the rescue and I refuse to let it happen again.'

Was that all she intended to say? And was he supposed to accept it – without question? He waited to let the clatter in his chest settle down. It didn't. But maybe his silence was a good thing, because she continued.

'Charlie proposed on a wave of gallantry, because things were bad for me, and I accepted on a wave of gratitude, because . . . because things were bad for me. And now here I am again in the same situation, and I won't have it.'

'Not even to protect your child?'

'Don't you dare say that! I'd do anything for my child. But I will not sacrifice my self-respect. I'll stand on my own two feet, and one day I'll explain the importance of that to my child. And yes, I know this puts me in a more vulnerable position, but that doesn't stop it being the right thing.'

'Oh, Mary.' He was across the room before he knew it, kneeling in front of her. He caught her hands in his, rubbing the pads of his thumbs into her palms. 'Don't pull away. Please don't pull away. Listen. It may have been gallantry and gratitude with you and Kimber, but it isn't like that for us. I wasn't gallant. As a matter of fact, I was idiotic. I was a fool to propose the way I did, but I didn't dare tell you the truth for fear of making your situation more complicated. But I'm telling you now. I love you, Mary; I want you to be my wife. That isn't gallantry, it's plain love. Please don't pull away.'

'I need to.' Her hands fluttered and a hanky appeared. She dabbed her eyes. 'I can't help it.'

Damn and blast. His love wasn't a reason for her to change her mind, not if she valued her independence so highly. He had to see it from her side.

'It isn't gratitude on your part. Have you forgotten giving me your trust? With my love and your trust, don't you think we could do well together? You've already done me the honour of allowing me to be your child's stepfather. Will you also do me the honour of accepting the offer of marriage I make to you out of love?'

A tear clung to her lashes, but there were no tears in her sparkling eyes. Her mouth sighed into a smile and his heart turned over.

'I can do better than that. I can accept – oh, Nathaniel, I accept out of love.' Leaning forward, she rested her forehead against his. 'I love you too.'

He made little nudging movements with his forehead, with his nose, until he captured her lips and could kiss her, a short, full, breathless kiss that they broke away from to look at one another.

'I had no idea,' he said.

When he moved to kiss her, she withdrew a fraction. 'I have to make sure.'

'Of what?'

'I'm not like Imogen. Your sister told me how she devoted her life to your care. I won't be like that. I'll be a good wife and mother, but I'm other things as well. I have my writing, as well as wanting to take an active interest in social reform.'

'Nothing was more important to Imogen than caring for her husband and her home. At the time, that suited me, but it isn't what I want now. I want you to be my friend and work partner as well as my wife. And I definitely want you to continue writing. In fact . . .'

Taking the box from his pocket, he glanced at her expression, catching the anticipation in her eyes, the way her top teeth grazed her lip. He held the box towards her but didn't open it.

'I feel now I should have had the courage to buy you a ring, but I saw this and thought you might like it.'

He tilted the lid.

'A quill pen brooch.' She laughed. 'It's perfect. Better than an engagement band. Let me put it on and then we'll go and tell Aunt Helen.'

'I don't need a new hat,' said Mary.

'Yes, you do, because if you don't, I can't. I want the full works – a hat the size of a cartwheel, smothered in flowers, like your friend Miss Lever favours. I've never had a new hat.'

'What, never?'

'My brother wouldn't have shelled out for one, not with all those trunks in the attic. I've always worn my mother's things. The hours I've spent hacking away at those flared sleeves with the false undersleeves, and I never did succeed in turning one of those frightful old cloaky-coaty things into a proper coat.'

Mary hesitated, then ventured, 'But you wear such beautiful things underneath.'

'Robert never gave me money of my own, but asking him to foot the bill for undergarments was one of the joys of my life. The mere whisper of *unmentionables* practically gave him palpitations. He never questioned what I spent – too embarrassing – so I started splashing out.'

Mary laughed. 'You're a wicked old woman.'

'A wicked old woman who has never had a new hat, and I know where I want to get it too.'

It was surprising how much fun it was to go to town. The cabby dropped them on Market Street outside Ingleby's and Helen headed straight for the millinery, where an assistant seated them before gleaming mirrors.

'I'd like to see the biggest hats you've got, with the most flowers on them,' said Helen.

'That fashion is on the wane, madam.'

'Then I'd best nab one while I can.'

'I don't want a gigantic hat,' said Mary, when the assistant left them. 'I've already got a gigantic belly.'

'Nonsense. A trim little thing like you could never be gigantic.'

The assistant reappeared with a couple of hats. 'Is it for a special occasion?'

'A wedding,' said Helen. 'I'm bridesmaid.'

The woman scuttled away in confusion.

'Don't you dare tell her I'm the bride,' Mary warned, 'or she'll faint clean away.'

She helped Helen select her cartwheel, then for herself chose a blue hat with an asymmetric brim, which was rather dashing.

Helen insisted on new gloves, choosing a lacy pair for her.

'Far too fancy,' Mary condemned them.

'Fancy is good for the bride. Your ring will show through.

And the cream leather for me. A frightful indulgence, but never mind. I have all those years of not being a bridesmaid to make up for. What else do we need?'

'I don't need anything.'

'I included you merely for form's sake. What I meant was, what else does the bridesmaid need?'

'Bridesmaids don't need anything else, especially the incorrigible ones, but the bride needs to sit down.' She stretched her spine as discreetly as she could.

'There are chairs inside the front door. We'll take the weight off our feet while the doorman finds us a cab.'

'Are you sure you don't want them to deliver everything?'

'I'm going to take my hat straight home and wear it round the house.'

Soon they were in a cab, their purchases in a pile beside Helen.

'My dear, tell me to mind my own business—'

'Would it do any good?'

'Very amusing. I'm more touched than I can say at your generosity in including me in your wedding plans, honoured as well. But I can't help thinking about your mother.'

Mary had been thinking about her, too. 'Is it cowardly to want to present everyone with a fait accompli? Possibly. Probably. But my father would tell the Kimbers, and I can't have that.'

'Are you sure he'd tell? I've met him only once, of course, but he and your mother were so concerned about you. It's obvious how much they love you.'

'And I love them, but I still don't want Dadda to tell the Kimbers. And I'm sure he would, because of the way he came to Jackson's House with Sir Edward to give me a wigging. If he hadn't done that . . . but he did. I know how mean I sound, but this wedding is so important. I couldn't bear anything to spoil it.'

Mary woke early. Her wedding day, less than a year after that other wedding day. Who would have thought? She breathed in sharply, like an animal sniffing the air, but in her case it was happiness she sensed.

There was a knock and Helen popped her head in.

'Slip on your dressing gown and come with me. We'll breakfast in my room. We don't want to face Greg over our boiled egg and soldiers.' The breath she huffed was less a sigh than an expression of annoyance. 'Of all the times for him to make one of his unwelcome appearances. But we won't let it spoil today. With luck and a prevailing wind, we won't even see him.'

When Edith came to clear away, Helen enquired as to his movements.

'Mr Rawley had a letter,' said Edith. 'Well, it was in an envelope, but it didn't feel like a letter. It was something small and harder than paper – like a calling-card.'

Helen and Mary helped one another to dress.

'Those new buttons we put on your jacket make all the difference,' said Mary.

'You've taken more trouble over my appearance than your own.'

'Well, if you will insist on being bridesmaid.' She gave the old lady a kiss. 'Time to go.'

Mrs Burley and Edith presented them with matching posies. Nathaniel had offered to collect them, but Helen insisted he mustn't see the bride, so they were taking a cab. Edith held the flowers while they climbed in.

Nathaniel and Alistair were outside the registry office, ready to help them descend. As she gave her hand to Nathaniel, a feeling of rightness, of completeness, enveloped Mary. They were ushered into a room that looked more like an office than a place to celebrate a special occasion, but she didn't care. Being here with Nathaniel and her beloved Aunt Helen made this place special.

Helen held her flowers during the ceremony. She repeated what she was required to say, the blood whooshing in her ears. She unintentionally held up proceedings by not having her left hand bared. She met Nathaniel's eyes, his gaze steady and reassuring. As he took her hand and gently pushed the ring onto her finger, she experienced again that sense of completeness.

'If you'll sign here,' said the registrar.

Mary Margaret Kimber, née Maitland. Previous marriage annulled.

'Congratulations, Mrs Brewer.'

Mary Brewer. Yes.

'I think you're meant to kiss the bride,' Alistair told Nathaniel.

Her eyes fluttered closed as he bent his head to hers. He dropped a kiss on her mouth. It was unbearably sweet, a promise for the future.

'My turn,' said Helen. 'Everyone has to kiss the bridesmaid.'

They all laughed. Amidst good wishes, they left the building.

Alistair had booked a table at the Claremont Hotel. As they went up the steps, Mary looked round, admiring the gracious surroundings.

The first person she saw was Lady Kimber.

'Christ,' Greg muttered. 'What's she doing here?'

He halted, just managing to avoid slamming into Helen's little group. Double-quick, he stepped behind a pillar. He recognised the companion-help and that bloody Brewer johnny who was supposed to be Robert's voice of reason from beyond the grave. As they headed upstairs to the dining room, Greg dismissed them. He had an appointment. By the morning post, he had received a Claremont Hotel card with a time written on the reverse. Should he announce his arrival at the desk?

Tom Varney materialised. 'Mr Jonas is expecting you.'

Varney led him upstairs. The landing at the top was all plush carpet and dark wood. Palms stood in vast pots either side of the double doors to the dining room. Greg followed him in.

Mr Jonas welcomed him as if they were dear friends. Greg's missing finger twitched and flexed. There was a coat stand close by. He hung up his hat and threw his outer gloves on the table.

A waiter hovered.

'Your best single malt.'

'And another glass of this delicious cordial,' said Mr Jonas. 'It's a little early for me. I like to keep a clear head.'

Greg glanced into the ballroom. Their table was right beside the drop. There was a gaggle of females down there. He was about to look away when he saw Christina and Eleanor. God, Christina was beautiful; she outshone every woman in the place. And Eleanor was enchanting, with a smile to take your breath away. He wrenched his gaze from them. He mustn't let Jonas catch him looking, couldn't have their beauty and immeasurable importance sullied by being looked at by bloody Jonas.

'Here we are in September. Such a delightful time of the year. I wonder what your dear aunt thinks of it.'

'She seems to be enjoying it.' He nodded towards Helen's table.

'So that's the famous Miss Helen Rawley. How sad to think her life is near its end. When the tragedy happens, will her companions look back on this outing and wonder at it? That's what people do, I believe. They say, "We had no idea when we enjoyed our roast duck with cider sauce . . . or our pork-and-rabbit pudding . . . that we would never see her again." So sad.'

'If you say so.'

'I suppose for you it will be cause for rejoicing.'

'And for you.'

'I never rejoice at receiving what is my due.'

The waiter approached. Greg hadn't even glanced at the menu.

'Will you permit me to order for us both?' Mr Jonas enquired.

While he did so, Greg looked over the balcony, ensuring his gaze was elsewhere when the waiter disappeared.

'She is lovely, is she not?' said Mr Jonas. 'Please don't feel you have to look away on my account.'

'Who?' It was worth a try.

'Now, now, no games, if you please.'

'Who is lovely?'

'I might ask you the same question. The mother or the daughter?'

'I'd prefer not to talk about them – either of them.'

'But of course. I wouldn't dream of taking a lady's name in vain, especially not in front of a gentleman with such a close interest.'

'You sent for me. I've come. Now what?'

'My dear Mr Rawley, so brusque, so abrupt. I'd hoped you would take pleasure in the surroundings.'

'Very swish. Now what?'

'Now we share a meal and discuss your plans for the autumn and winter. Such a dismal time to be in this country, don't you agree?'

'I haven't thought that far ahead.'

'But surely your immediate plans are in place, which should leave you free to decide what to do, where to go, when you've fulfilled your commitments. I take it you have plans in place, Mr Rawley? It would go deeply against your interests to let me down a second time.'

'What will you do? Help yourself to another finger? I've plenty left.'

Mr Jonas looked down into the ballroom. 'The dear ladies, so busy organising their grand charity ball.' He feigned surprise. 'Didn't you know? Your friend and cousin, Lady Kimber herself, she didn't confide in you when you visited her the other day?'

'You bastard, you've been following me.'

'No unparliamentary language, if you please, and I've done nothing of the kind. I have people to do these things on my behalf.'

The curried apple soup arrived. Greg ignored it, but Mr Jonas took a sip, closing his eyes.

'Do try yours, Mr Rawley.'

'No appetite.'

'Perhaps you're distracted by the ladies. So fortunate for them, having a rich sponsor to fund their use of the ballroom and dining gallery for their charity ball.'

'You?'

'Modesty forbids me to say another word. Are you sure you won't try the soup?'

'No, I ruddy well won't.' He pushed back his chair. 'You'll get your money.'

'I'm sure I will, because if I don't, it won't be you who pays the price this time.'

His insides turned to ice. Around him, all sound whooshed away. There was no one else present. Just the two of them, looking at one another.

Mr Jonas allowed his eyes to stray to the ballroom. 'She has a look of you about her.'

The ice churned. 'We're cousins.'

'Not the mother. The daughter. She has a look of you.'

'Her mother was born a Rawley.'

Mr Jonas looked at him. 'And her father? Was he also born a Rawley?'

The ice was so cold, it became red-hot. He had threatened Eleanor. This slimy, silver-tongued reptile had threatened Eleanor. Eleanor. His beautiful daughter. She was his daughter, wasn't she?

'You bastard.' His voice was soft, light, conversational.

'It's a matter of business, my dear Mr Rawley.'

'Then let me show you how I do business.'

Grasping the table, he heaved it over sideways. Crystal and china crashed. He grabbed the loathsome money-shark by his expensive lapels and dragged him to his feet before backhanding him across the face, the crunch of Jonas's neck bones reverberating up his arm. Jonas kicked and struggled, but he held tighter, his grip turning to iron as resolve pumped through his bloodstream, pouring down his arms into his hands. How had he ever believed himself to be in this scum's power?

He felt something sharp in his side, as if he had a stitch. Then the sensation was gone. He yanked Jonas so hard that he left the floor, plonking him on his feet hard enough that his ankles would be pulverised if there was any justice. Hauling Jonas closer to get good purchase, he delivered a sharp uppercut that had the blackguard spitting teeth and blood and saliva.

But something in the face of Mr sodding Jonas cut through his triumph. Looking down, he saw the blade in Jonas's fingers. The bastard had a flick knife.

He stabbed me.

That was what the sensation had been, the keen pain of a knife sliding in and out, slick as you like. He pressed his hand to his side and it came away red. There was a roaring in his ears. Shock? Blood? No – other people – bloody do-gooders trying to break up the commotion. Well, he wasn't going to hang about for that. He bent Jonas backwards over the balcony.

How do you like that, you piece of shit?

The moneylender's arms flailed, his eyes huge and rolling. Someone grabbed at Greg from behind. He felt another of those smooth dark sensations, this time in the back of his waist – Varney? He gasped, his grip slackening, and that was all Jonas needed. He grabbed at the balcony rail, but that wasn't going to stop Greg. Nothing was going to stop him. Jonas clung like a bulldog, but Greg mashed the hands on the rail, forcing the fingers to let go. Then, with a final up-and-over shove, he cast the viper to his doom.

There was a shrill scream. It might have been Jonas, it might have been a female about to collapse with the vapours.

There were strong arms behind him, pulling him – no, pushing him, bloody hell, pushing him, trying to push him after Jonas. Varney, it had to be. Greg jammed his hands against the rail, pushing back with all his might. Then – come one, come all and join the party – there was another set of hands. Two against one, he thought, before realising that he wasn't the one who was outnumbered.

Varney was heaved away from him so violently that Greg staggered backwards after him. Half turning as he stumbled, he saw Robert's bloody mouthpiece and another bloke tangled up with Varney. A blade flashed. Even as he braced himself for its bite, he saw Varney's target wasn't himself but Robert's lackey. There was a spurt of blood.

For a moment, or possibly for a long time, Greg stood there, then, to his surprise, he crumpled. His knees gave way, simple as that. Down he went. Robert's poodle had gone down too. There was a flurry and then the companion-help female sank down beside the good doctor.

Was he really wasting his time on those insignificant buggers? With chill pouring through him, he made a massive effort and flipped over to press his face between the balusters on the balcony rail so that his final sight would be—

Chapter Thirty

There was some sort of kerfuffle. A frown flickered across Mary's brow, but she banished it. Nothing could spoil today. Nothing. She leant forward, involving herself in the conversation.

An almighty crash – china, crystal. As her head swung round, she was aware of other heads, other bodies, doing the same.

'Greg!' Helen exclaimed. 'What's he doing?'

There was a shout. Mary's heart bumped. She didn't have a clear line of sight.

'He's going to tip him over,' someone said.

Nathaniel was on his feet. Tearing her eyes from what she couldn't see properly, Mary darted out a hand to grasp his.

He detached himself. 'Stay here.'

And he was gone. He had no business having such a reassuring voice when he was about to plough into a disturbance. As Alistair followed, Mary lurched to her feet. Helen's hand appeared on her arm, but she kept moving.

Others were on their feet now, some rooted to the spot, hesitating, vacillating, others scurrying for safety, men with protective arms around their womenfolk. She pushed her way through, fighting against the current to reach the centre of the chaos. Greg Rawley – another man – Nathaniel – Alistair. The stranger had Mr Rawley clamped against the rail. People in her way – she couldn't see – the way cleared. Nathaniel and Alistair heaved the man away and all three staggered backwards, locked together. Alistair and the stranger righted themselves, but not Nathaniel. He kept stumbling backwards, then stopped. And then – and then he fell, just dropped where he stood. Mary's bones turned to wax.

She plunged forward, sinking beside him, her skirts ballooning around her. Blood glistened on his fingers. Lifting his hand away, she pulled at jacket buttons, revealing a darkened patch that chilled her to her core. More buttons to fumble with. His shirt front – don't faint, don't faint – red and soggy to one side beneath his ribs. On her knees, flailing around, she grabbed at a linen napkin – two, three, that was all she could reach – and pressed them down hard against the wound. Was the flesh supposed to give like that on such a lean man?

Her insides creased as she shared his pain. Then a dark shudder and a gasp made her realise the pain was her own. She fought to ride it out, perspiration blooming over her flesh. She held her breath, head swimming, until the air burst from her in a groan and the pain subsided.

Alistair hunkered beside her. 'Let me see. Here! You, fellow! Lend a hand. Bunch up a tablecloth and take over from this lady.

Waiter! Fetch towels from the housekeeper, and quick about it.' He shot Mary a brief look. 'Well done. You did the right thing. Oh, you're back in the land of the living, are you, Brewer?'

Mary had been squeezed out of the way by Alistair and the man he had press-ganged into helping and she had felt light-headed enough from the tail-end of her pain to let it happen, but now she thrust her way between them. Nathaniel's eyes opened; he managed a grim smile. His hand moved and she clasped it.

'Not the best way to celebrate a wedding,' he whispered.

'Stay put,' ordered Alistair. 'There's an ambulance on its way. I must see to the fellow who took a header over the rail.'

He rose, issued a few instructions to staff and disappeared.

'Keep still,' said Mary. 'Don't try—' Her words cut off as the pain returned. 'It's all right. I'm all right.' She locked a bright smile in place, trying to look natural.

'Are you having pains?'

'No, I'm just worried about you.'

Alistair reappeared, crouching beside Nathaniel, capturing his wrist. Mary leant away, squeezing every muscle she possessed to try to contain the pain. Perspiration sprouted on her forehead.

'Good job you got injured,' said Alistair, 'or the ambulance men would have nothing to do. That other man is dead.'

'Mary's having pains.' Nathaniel's voice hitched and his face went grey. 'Get her home.'

'I'm staying with you.'

But she was surrounded by voices telling her otherwise – Alistair, Helen. She tried to refuse. She couldn't bear to be separated from Nathaniel.

He caught her hand. 'Even if you never listen to me again,

listen now. You need to be at home. Knowing you're there, being properly cared for, will help me.'

All she could do was agree.

'False start,' the midwife proclaimed. 'It was the excitement that sparked it off.'

Excitement? Mary pictured Nathaniel lying there with blood pouring out of him. 'When can I get up?'

'Tomorrow. It's evening now. Sleep would be the best thing.'

The moment Mrs Salisbury left, Helen, Edith and Mrs Burley came swarming in, clamouring to fuss and soothe her. Her chest was tight with anxiety.

The doorbell rang.

'That'll be Alistair,' Helen said. 'I told him to come any time, day or night.'

'Bring him up,' said Mary. 'If you don't, I'll come down.'

Edith scuttled away, returning a minute later with Alistair.

'I hear the baby changed its mind. How are you feeling?'

'Never mind me. How's Nathaniel?'

'They've patched him up. He'll be home in a few days, though he'll need to take things easy.'

'He'll come here, of course,' said Helen. 'We'll take care of him.'

'When can I see him?' Mary asked.

'We'll see.'

'What does that mean?'

'It means it's time for you to rest.'

After a long night, she rose early. Helen tried to shoo her back to bed, but she was determined.

'You can't visit now,' said Helen. 'They won't let you in.'

'Then I'll wait outside. I have to be there.'

'Now you're being silly – Alistair, tell her she's being silly,' Helen said as Edith showed Alistair in, looking splendid in his frock coat.

'I've come from the hospital, hence the togs. Doesn't do any harm to look the part. He's not awake yet, but he's had a good night.'

'I'm going,' Mary declared.

'Steady on. I had to pull strings to get in.'

'Then you can pull them for me too.'

'Let's see what we can do, shall we? Don't give me the evil eye, Miss Rawley. I'll take care of her. In fact, you can come along and do that job yourself.'

'Do you think your doctor friends will bend the rules for me?' asked Mary.

Alistair laughed. 'It's Matron we've got to get past.'

Matron turned out to be a no-nonsense-looking woman. Drawing her aside, Alistair spoke in confidential tones. She glanced at Mary and Helen, but it was impossible to tell what she was thinking. Mary squeezed Helen's fingers, then let her breath out in a rush as Matron led them to Nathaniel's bedside.

He was lying still, with not so much as a wrinkle in the pristine bedding. His skin was colourless, which made his hair look darker. Alistair positioned a wooden chair for her and Mary moved it closer to the bed. She wanted to hold Nathaniel's hand, but his arms were trapped beneath sheets that were crisply tucked in.

'You must leave before Doctor comes on his rounds in an hour,' said Matron. 'I'll send a porter to escort you.'

She walked away and Alistair went too.

Mary touched Nathaniel's cheek, willing strength and love to pour through her fingertips.

'He looks peaceful,' said Helen.

'Aunt Helen! That's what everyone says about dead people.'

He appeared to be sleeping well. They sat quietly, exchanging the occasional remark. Mary's back began to ache. She rolled her shoulders, failing to ease the discomfort. Rising, she took a few steps, but, aware of glances from the sister at the table at the end of the ward, she sat again lest she be told to leave.

Nathaniel murmured and stirred. Mary leant forward, saying his name.

He was smiling as he opened his eyes. 'You're here.'

'Couldn't keep her away,' said Helen. 'How are you?'

'Sore, but mainly happy to see my wife.' He frowned. 'What about . . . ?'

'False alarm,' Mary whispered.

'Then I'll have to wait a little longer to be a father.'

It was raining as Helen stepped from the carriage at Southern Cemetery. It had rained the day of Robert's funeral, too, though that rain had been relentless and miserable. Greg was going to be buried in summer drizzle. The grass would smell wonderful afterwards.

What a mess he had made of his life. He had been in and out of debt for years, living on his wits, getting money from gambling – and his family had had no idea. They thought he had made wise investments. A gurgle of laughter escaped her. She cleared her throat, trying to cover the gaffe. Not that there were many people to witness it. This was a private funeral.

That man Jonas sounded a nasty piece of work. Evidently Greg had been in hock to him to the tune of a thousand guineas. Just thinking of it made Helen's heart beat faster. Greg had never deserved Jackson's House.

A wretched fear sliced deeper with each thought. Greg had left a colossal debt and it must be repaid – but how? His major asset was Jackson's House. Could it be sold from under her, in spite of Robert's will?

She had tried questioning Mr Porter to no avail.

'I cannot reveal the contents of Mr Greg Rawley's will.'

'He made a will?'

'Not long before he died. Does that surprise you?'

'Considering he died with more debt than you could shake a stick at, I suppose it does.'

'Ah, but considering what we now know of his way of life, he might just as easily have died as rich as Crœsus.'

Mr Porter was here at the graveside. Sir Edward was present, representing the Rawleys. He had offered to represent her too. The mighty Sir Edward Kimber had called at Jackson's House and delicately suggested she needn't attend the funeral.

'I'll represent my wife and her parents,' he explained. 'I'll be glad to represent you also.'

'I'll represent myself, thank you.'

So here she was, though she wasn't entirely sure why she had come. Certainly not to pay her respects. Greg had long been her least favourite person. In acknowledgement of family? All said and done, he was Arthur's son, her nephew. But not a nephew to be proud of.

'Is it wrong to be glad he's dead?' she had asked Mary. 'Just think what would have happened had he lived. The trial, the publicity. They'd have hanged him. He killed that man before dozens of witnesses.'

As it was, there was just one man left to face justice and he would hang for Greg's murder. He had stabbed Nathaniel too. Helen closed her eyes. Nathaniel had been spared. Losing him would have been unendurable.

'Are you sure you wouldn't like me to come with you?' Mary had offered.

'Bless you, there's no need. It's not as though it's going to be a big occasion.'

She wasn't even sure it was right to call it a funeral, with no hymns, no service, just a burial. What a way to go. At least he was having a few prayers at the graveside. They had been granted permission to hold the sparse ceremony at the early hour of eight o'clock, so as to evade prying eyes and reporters.

Eight o'clock – that was when they hanged people, wasn't it?

Never had it been more important to be Lady Kimber. Never had it been more important to hold herself erect, to be cool and dignified and beautifully turned-out, not merely in her dress but in her demeanour, her complexion, the delicate telltale skin around her eyes. The carriage halted. The door was opened, the step pulled down. Sir Edward got out, turning to offer a hand to steady her descent, her husband bringing her to visit her cousin's final resting place. What could be more respectable?

She had brought flowers. Not a sombre wreath, but a glorious bouquet, roses and African daisies, golden and apricot and burnt orange, all in a frothy cloud of gypsophila, and at the centre a single crimson-tasselled stem of love-lies-bleeding. The coachman would have carried the flowers, but she gathered them within the circle of her arm, giving her other hand to her husband, laying her fingers within the safety of his elbow.

She felt distanced from the situation as they approached the mound of earth covering the fresh grave. She placed her flowers on top, then stood beside her husband.

She didn't ask for a moment alone.

'A waste of a life,' Sir Edward observed, though whether he meant a life frittered or a life cut short wasn't clear. 'Are you ready, my dear?'

'Certainly. What time is the solicitor due?'

'Half past three.'

Greg's solicitor had applied to Sir Edward for an appointment. Her heart delivered a thump. Had Greg made her his heir? Not that there would be anything to leave once the debt had been settled, but had he named her? It wouldn't arouse comment if he had. With no wife and children, no brothers or sisters in the picture, no one would think twice at his naming his cousin.

Except Helen.

Lady Kimber was in the library with Sir Edward when Mr Porter was shown in. Looking up to acknowledge him, she drew a sharp breath as Aunt Helen preceded him into the room.

'Forgive me if I appear surprised, Mr Porter, but I wasn't aware you were bringing anyone with you.'

'I beg your pardon if I failed to make myself clear, but since this is the reading of the will, it is desirable that all interested parties are present.'

Her husband ushered Helen to a seat. She looked a scarecrow in a mauve dress daubed with black velvet bows and an unfortunate black ruffle circling the hem.

'Will Miss Kimber be joining us?' asked Mr Porter.

'Eleanor is spending the day with friends.' And a good thing, too, with Helen rolling up.

'No matter. She is, I believe, under twenty-one and therefore under paternal jurisdiction.' Mr Porter opened his leather document case and removed some sheets that had been folded lengthwise. 'I have here the last will and testament of Gregory Arthur Rawley. It's a simple document. Mr Rawley left everything when he died to Eleanor Kimber, née Davenport.'

'Eleanor!' Lady Kimber exclaimed. Was that an echo? No, Helen too had cried Eleanor's name.

'As I understand it,' said Sir Edward, 'Rawley left a debt of hefty proportions.'

'I fear so, and it must be repaid from his estate to the estate of Mr Ezekiel Jonas.'

'Must Jackson's House be sold?' Helen burst out.

'This is nothing to do with you,' Lady Kimber snapped.

'Mr Rawley's will cannot overturn that of your late brother, Miss Rawley,' said Mr Porter. 'You are entitled to remain in Jackson's House, which now belongs to Miss Kimber.' He addressed Sir Edward. 'Neither may the debt be paid from the money Judge Rawley left to Mr Rawley, because that is tied up in accordance with his wish to provide a home for his sister.'

'Where does that leave us?' asked Lady Kimber.

'Sir Edward will wish to consult his family solicitor, naturally, but as I see it, there are two options. You may take the view that since the estate of Mr Rawley cannot pay the debt during the – forgive me – during the lifetime of Miss Rawley, that the estate of Mr Ezekiel Jonas must wait for settlement. In this case, Mr Jonas's representatives would presumably require interest to be added year on year.'

'And the second option?' Sir Edward asked.

'To repay the debt yourself. If you consider the debt now to be your daughter's, that would be appropriate. A woman's debts are for her husband to repay or, in this case, her father.'

'So, my dear, it seems I may be going to pay Rawley's debt after all.' Sir Edward gave her a wry smile. To Mr Porter he explained, 'Rawley sought financial assistance from my wife shortly before his death.'

Lady Kimber found Helen looking straight at her. She gave her back look for look. Helen was the one to glance away.

'There's no call for a swift decision,' Mr Porter said. He handed Sir Edward the will. 'Here also is a copy of Judge Rawley's will, so you can see the arrangements he made.'

'How good of you to come, Mr Porter,' said Lady Kimber. 'I assume you'll escort Miss Rawley home?' Just in case anyone was thinking how pleasant it would be if Helen stayed. 'Well!' she exclaimed the moment they had gone.

'Indeed. Fancy our girl being an heiress. She already was one, of course, because of the Davenport money. Now Rawley's made her an heiress twice over.'

'Heiress to Uncle Robert's estate, but also to a vast debt.'

'We shan't dwell on that, I think. I'm sure he had no intention of encumbering her.'

'I'm sure he didn't.' It was a moment before she was able to say, 'Thank you for recognising that.'

'I will pay the debt on Eleanor's behalf. I simply want what's best for our daughter.'

'Of course you do.' She gave him her hand. 'Of course you do.'

'Please don't leave yet,' said Mary. 'Won't you stay a little longer? Aunt Helen will be sorry to miss you.'

'You call her Aunt Helen?' asked Eleanor.

'We've become friends.'

Eleanor had come to Jackson's House. 'To pay my respects,' she had said, 'and . . . well – to have a look, since it's mine now.'

Of all times for Helen to be out. She would kick herself when she got home.

Mary had shown Eleanor round downstairs and introduced Mrs Burley and Edith, but Eleanor had baulked at going upstairs.

'It would feel so nosy.'

Mary guessed she was dying to get upstairs, but an unexpected flash of vexation prevented her from overcoming Eleanor's scruples. She showed her the garden instead.

'I thought I might meet your new husband.'

'He's out. You may know he's involved in the clinic where I used to work. There's a meeting he wanted to attend, so another doctor has taken him and will bring him back. He'll be exhausted, but at least that'll make him rest. Nothing else does.'

'Rotten patient, is he?'

'The worst.'

Suddenly they were smiling at one another. Mary felt them hovering on the brink of intimacy, but Eleanor pulled back.

'I must go.'

'Will you come again? It'd mean a lot to Aunt Helen.'

'One in the eye for my mother, you mean?'

'Not at all.'

'I don't know why Mummy and Great-Aunt Helen are daggers drawn, but I'm not going to fan the flames. Mummy didn't mind my coming today, because it's a visit of courtesy, but she wouldn't want it to be a regular thing.'

'And you're going to let her keep you away?'

'You would say that. I imagine you didn't pay much heed to

your parents or you'd never have married Charlie. Tell me, did you tell your parents in advance that you were marrying Doctor Brewer or did you make them wait to find out, the way you made the head of the family wait?'

Minutes after Eleanor departed, Helen came hurrying in, panting, hauling her bad leg behind her. She seemed to believe no one was aware of it. She would be appalled to learn that Mary, Edith and Mrs Burley discussed it regularly behind her back.

'A coach passed me in the lane. I saw the coat-of-arms.'

'It was Eleanor.'

Helen groaned. 'And I missed her. I must write immediately.'

'I don't think she'll come again. Today was a mixture of curiosity and civility.'

'I'll still write. It's the correct thing to do. Am I a silly old fool?'

Mary smiled. 'When did that stop you?'

'Have you seen this in the paper?' asked Nathaniel.

Mary looked up from the work basket she was tidying, its contents on the table in front of her. 'I haven't seen the paper today. I've been busy dusting.'

'The nesting instinct.'

'The what?'

'When the baby's due, a mother often starts cleaning and tidying.'

'Rubbish!' she said, instantly followed by, 'Really?' She fell silent. What would happen after her baby arrived? 'What's in the paper that's so interesting?'

'It's about forcible feeding. It's been officially admitted in the House of Commons that it takes place.'

'That's splendid – well, it isn't, but you know what I mean. They'll have to stop doing it now, won't they? They can't continue if it's public knowledge.'

'I'm not so sure. They might let it continue, using the excuse that it's the woman's fault. If she hunger-strikes, she knows what will happen. Let's hope I'm wrong.'

'What's this?' Helen came in. 'A man admitting he could be wrong? Have I ever mentioned how different you are from Robert? Take my advice, Mary, hang onto this one.'

'I'll consider it.'

'Thank you for the resounding vote of confidence,' laughed Nathaniel. 'If you'll excuse me, I have medical papers to look over.'

'Leave that work basket,' said Helen. 'I want to ask you about Greg. I can't stop thinking about him killing that man. Such a desperate act. It's made me wonder about how I tripped on the stairs and how my bedroom door was locked the night of the fire. Edith swore blind there was nothing on the floor, but I know I tripped over something. As for the door being locked . . .'

'It was.' Mary was as sure now as she had been at the time.

'Not because I locked it. But someone did, just as someone left something for me to trip over.'

'And you think . . . ?'

'I don't know. It's hard to believe. There was no love lost between us, and I don't want to believe him capable of such acts, but he had a lot to gain from my death.'

Mary's heart reached out to her friend. 'We'll never know.'

'But we'll always wonder.'

'What are you doing here? Do you imagine that because Eleanor called at Jackson's House, that entitles you to return the visit?'

Helen looked at Lady Kimber, remembering the beautiful, vivacious girl who had come to Jackson's House that fateful summer. After years of Robert's patronising company, how wonderful it had been to have her in the house. She had – oh, shame on her – she had pretended Christina was her daughter, a fantasy that had given her such joy.

She had welcomed Greg too, some young company for Christina.

But that was a long time ago.

'I wasn't sure I'd be admitted.'

'Of course you were admitted. I wanted to make your position clear.'

'You've certainly done that.'

'Good. I trust it won't be necessary to leave instructions that in future you aren't to be admitted.'

'If that's my cue to leave, I'm sorry to disappoint you. I didn't come here to presume on Eleanor's good nature. I've come to blackmail you.'

'I beg your pardon?'

'I suggest you hear me out, so we can get it over with quickly.'

'This is outrageous—'

'For years I've longed for your forgiveness and dreamt of being allowed to know Eleanor. But I finally accept that it won't happen. You detest me.'

'You flatter yourself. I don't think of you from one day to another – one year to another.'

'That's worse. All these years, I've felt so injured. But there comes a point where you can't go on feeling like that. I'm worn out with it. I have other people to love now, so I can put the past where it belongs: behind me. You can't hurt me, but you can hurt the people I love and I'm not having that.'

'What nonsense is this?'

'I'm talking about Mary.'

'Oh, her.'

'Yes, her. Charlie's inconvenient former wife, who has added to the inconvenience by expecting a happy event – and believe me, I intend to see that it is happy. I expect you know by now that she has married again. My solicitor uncovered some examples of legal precedent that could help her keep her child until it reaches the age of seven. He believes that having a respectable husband will increase her chances.'

'So she married this crusading doctor to keep the child.'

'They love one another.'

'Off with the old love and on with the new.'

'I prefer to think how lucky she is to have a second chance with a hard-working, honourable man.'

'Spare me the admiration society.'

'We believe this marriage could strengthen Mary's position.'

'You're taking the Kimbers to court? I've heard everything now.'

'Go to court? Whatever gave you that idea? No, my dear, there'll be no need, because you're going to persuade Sir Edward that if Mary has a girl, she'll be allowed to keep her for ever. If it's a boy, I concede that that's a different matter; but she must keep him at least until he's seven and thereafter he must stay with her regularly.'

'I'll do nothing of the kind.'

She pretended to misunderstand. 'If you think Sir Edward too tough a nut to crack, work on Charlie. If he puts his foot down, no one can gainsay him.'

'I repeat. I'll do—'

'—precisely as I say. If you don't, I'll ruin you. I'll make your sordid affair and attempted elopement public knowledge.'

'You wouldn't!'

'There's one way to find out.'

'That was years ago.'

'And since then, you've risen considerably in the world, which means you have more to lose. I'll leave you to mull it over. Don't worry about letting me know your decision. I'll know by what happens after the baby arrives. I rather think Mary will get good news . . . don't you? Now, if you'll excuse me, I'm on my way to visit my new friends at the agency.'

In the grip of a pain so intense she couldn't speak, Mary gazed imploringly at Mrs Salisbury.

'You're doing well,' the midwife assured her. 'Now push hard as you can. One last try or it's going to be forceps.'

Feeling as though her body were splitting in two, she made one final effort, fighting against the agony and exhaustion of the past gruelling sixteen hours. She knew how long it was because she could see the clock. She had kept herself going by promising herself that by two o'clock . . . three o'clock . . . four o'clock, it would be over. Now it was gone six in the morning and here she still was, her nightdress clinging to her body and her back ready to snap in half.

Gulping in a huge, ragged breath, she held it for a moment as she pushed and strained, before it came whooshing out, all mixed up with a sobbing groan. The pain reached a fresh pinnacle of intensity. Was she going to pass out?

She heard a fresh note in the midwife's voice. 'One more good push.'

She made a final gasping effort and felt something enormous

force its way out of her. She lay there, panting and sniffling, her pounding heart settling to a more moderate hammering.

A slap and a cry.

'You have a beautiful baby girl.'

When Mrs Salisbury placed the infant in her arms, Mary took one look at the little face and felt herself consumed by love. Everything became worth it – her Kimber marriage, the annulment, everything – because it had brought her this adorable, perfect child.

'You'll need some stitches. I'll clean you up first.'

The stitches stung like mad, but her tears were those of happiness. She was dimly aware of Mrs Salisbury bustling about but was too absorbed in these first moments with her child to take much notice.

'There now,' said Mrs Salisbury. 'Time to fetch Father.'

She wrenched her gaze away from the baby. 'Thank you. Thank you.'

'Pleasure. You were lucky you didn't get the forceps with those skinny hips. It's meant to get easier, the more you have, but you'll always have bother, I'm afraid. Still, it's worth it when you get a bonny chick like this one.'

The moment she opened the door, Nathaniel came in, brushing past her in his eagerness.

'It's a girl,' said Mary.

He leant over, his face soft with loving amazement. She ought to give him her daughter to hold, but she couldn't bear to let go, not even for a moment, not yet.

'Aunt Helen, Edith and Mrs Burley are going to spoil her rotten,' he said. 'They're going to spoil you rotten too, and quite right. You deserve it.'

'Do they want to come and see her?'

'Champing at the bit, but I wanted a minute first.'

'Go and tell them her name.'

'I didn't think you'd chosen.'

'I hadn't, not until now. The moment I saw her, I knew. I just knew.' She dropped a kiss on her daughter's forehead. 'Hope,' she said. 'Her name is Hope.'

Acknowledgements

I should like to express my gratitude to:

Elizabeth Hawksley, for her feedback on two drafts of *The Poor Relation*. Her sometimes stinging but always insightful comments led to my producing a much better book.

Melanie Catley, for encouragement and support during the writing of *The Poor Relation* and also for introducing me to the dilemma-risk-decision principle.

Annette Yates and Jacquie Campbell, who were by my side during the writing of early drafts of *The Deserter's Daughter* and *The Sewing Room Girl* as well as this book.

Jen Gilroy, for unwavering support.

ALSO BY SUSANNA BAVIN

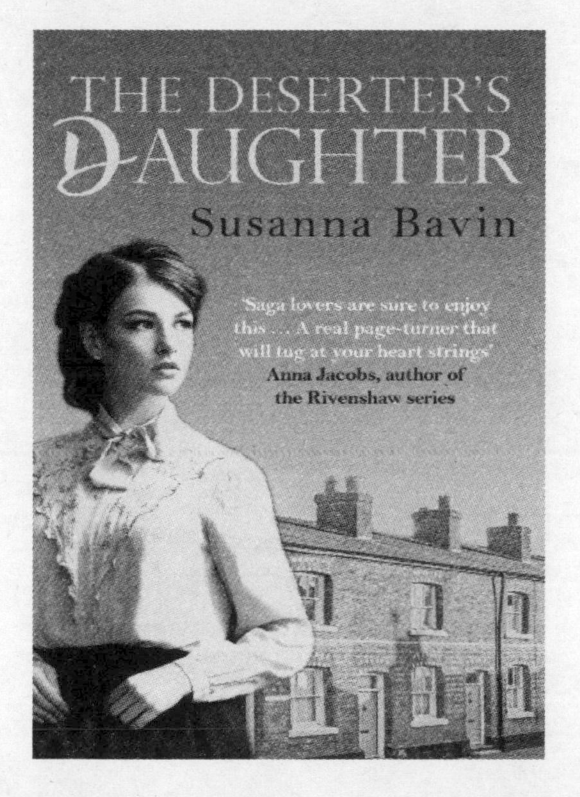

1920, Manchester. Carrie Jenkins is trying on her wedding dress, eagerly anticipating becoming Mrs Billy Shipton. But all too soon she is reeling from the news that her beloved father was shot for desertion during the Great War. When Carrie is jilted and she and her family are ostracised by the close-knit community, her plans and hopes for the future are in disarray.

Desperate to overcome her pain and humiliation, Carrie puts her faith in a man who is not to be trusted, and she will face danger and heartache before she can find the happiness she deserves.

After losing everything she holds dear in the Great War, Nell believes that marrying Stan Hibbert will help to recapture the loving family feeling she has lost. Five years on, she is just another penny-pinching, back-street housewife. When she discovers Stan is leading a double-life, she runs away to make a fresh start elsewhere.

Nell forges a new life for herself and her children in Manchester, working in a garment factory as a talented machinist. Her neighbours and colleagues believe she is a respectable widow – even her children think their father is dead – but when the past comes back to haunt her, Nell is faced with a court trial and will have to answer for her actions.

1892. When her beloved father dies, Juliet and her mother, the difficult but vulnerable Agnes, are left to fend for themselves. When Agnes lands a job as a seamstress for a titled family, things appear to be looking up. But just as the pair begin to find their feet, Juliet finds herself defenceless and alonc.

Without her mother to protect her, Juliet becomes the victim of a traumatic incident and is left to face an impossible dilemma. She flees to Manchester seeking support from her estranged family but comes up against her formidable grandmother, who is determined to bend Juliet to her will.

Susanna Bavin has variously been a librarian, an infant school teacher, a carer and a cook. She lives in Llandudno in North Wales with her husband and two rescue cats, but her writing is inspired by her Mancunian roots.

susannabavin.co.uk
@SusannaBavin